PAUL STIDOLPH

Paul Stidolph

FORESTS IN THE SAHARA

authorHOUSE®

AuthorHouse™ UK
1663 Liberty Drive
Bloomington, IN 47403 USA
www.authorhouse.co.uk
Phone: 0800.197.4150

Published by AuthorHouse 09/28/2017

ISBN: 978-1-5462-8235-8 (sc)
ISBN: 978-1-5462-8236-5 (hc)
ISBN: 978-1-5462-8234-1 (e)

Contents

To Adrienne, Doug and Greg, my loving and adventurous family.

When I started to write this story, all I knew was that an attempt had been made to take ice from Antarctica to Africa. The project, itself, was successful, but nothing had come of it, for some reason. I knew nothing about the people involved, the background to the voyage, or the adventures that took place. I hope, very much, that the demanding task of revealing these matters has translated into a rewarding, easy read. It is a novel, not a reference book, but it is based on the professional skill and dedicated work of others. In particular, I would like to thank Dr Susanne Bauer for her advice about moringa trees and seeds, as she was the first to identify the means by which they purify water, and for other areas of advice as well. I thank Dr Erich Stahel, who for many years has been closely involved in schemes to bring fresh water to villages in East Africa. I thank Norma Curtis, novelist, and Dr Ardré Marshall, lecturer in English, who were my literary guides. I also thank Ian Taylor and Oliver East for their professional guidance about shipping. I wish to mention, too, the influence of a brother and sister during my university days, whom I knew as Jeffrey and Susan Moeller. They introduced me to Thoreau's *Walden* and inspired me by their own adventurous example. To these, and many others, I extend my sincere thanks.

Part 1

THE SEEDS TAKE ROOT

Chapter 1

THE PAST THAT LIES AHEAD

Thursday, 8 October 2009: Holborn, Central London

Anna flicked a wisp of her auburn hair from her face. She was in her mid-twenties and ready to celebrate – not in a coffee shop.

She raised her cup. "To those forests in the Sahara that you are going to plant," she proclaimed.

She smiled at Jeffrey fondly, as they sat at their narrow, round table, nudged by the coming and going of customers in the café. She was excited enough for both of them, but he looked exhausted.

"To forests in the Sahara," he echoed, raising his cup. "One step at a time, but today is one hell of a step."

Anna had become the girlfriend of a man, again, but this time she had no regrets. Only thirty minutes ago, he had bought an oil tanker (a really big oil tanker), signing the purchase agreement on behalf of the Warlock consortium, and together they would travel to an iceberg in Antarctica, and she would stand on that iceberg, and they would take ice – and trees – to Africa.

"What are you going to call your ship?" she asked. "Do you know?"

"The *Moringa*," he replied, looking around at the decor.

"Could I suggest something else?" she ventured. "Something more exciting, perhaps?" Her Scandinavian accent made the question soft and inviting, with the hint of new ideas.

"Sorry, no," he said, glancing at her with a provocative smile.

"All right. Be like that," she replied, looking away. These were early days. She would change him.

"I'm not being obstinate," he said, sounding contrite. "It's just that I have had this ship in mind for so long. I know its name."

He looked at her for forgiveness, but she wasn't letting him off the hook that quickly.

"I spoke to my mother about you last night," she continued. "I told her what we would be doing today." Her right hand played idly with the wooden stirrer, testing its breaking point.

"Was she impressed?" he asked, looking at her expectantly.

Anna continued to show interest in the stirrer, not him. "She said I should be very careful about you, especially about falling in love. She said men like you sometimes win Nobel Prizes but often get shot dead." She licked the coffee-end of the stirrer suggestively as she let him absorb the comment, knowing she had his full attention.

Jeffrey grimaced. "So what did you say?"

Anna gave him a sideways look and then stopped teasing him; she turned joyously back to him. "I told her that unfortunately, her warning had come too late and that I was already madly in love with you; that you are the most exciting man ever to come into my life. I said that with me at your side, you will be one of the Nobel Prize winners."

"What makes you think that I couldn't do it alone?" he asked, with an edge of hurt in his voice.

"Because you never are alone, Jeffrey, not for long. Everyone knows that. And as I told her, if you misbehave with me, as you seem to have done with other women, I will be the one to shoot you dead."

"I'm too young to die," he joked but did not feel entirely sure about that.

"You'll be forty next year. That's not too young." She seemed to mean it.

He held her gaze. "You're not a hot-blooded Italian."

"No," she replied. "I am a cold, calculating Norwegian. I would take very careful aim."

She passed her hand through her dark locks and tossed them to expose a tantalising glimpse of her neck. Then she changed the subject.

"Why did you upset Mr Brage like that?" she asked, referring to one of the shipping team, coincidentally Norwegian, who had been paying her particular attention.

"I didn't like his attitude," he replied. "He was flirting with you, and he knew it."

"Sweetheart, I have more practice handling flirtatious men than you do. Let me look after myself in future." Her tone told Jeffrey that this was an order, not a recommendation.

"It made me jealous," he countered.

"Jealous, of Mr Brage?" She laughed and caressed Jeffrey's face; her look was soft and inviting. "Jeffrey, honestly"—she shook her head in disbelief—"nobody could replace you in my life."

Jeffrey softened to her touch and gently took hold of her hand. "He'll never get the chance, anyway. That's the last we'll see of him."

He kissed her wrist before she withdrew it.

She was silent a moment, as she finished her coffee. "That was good," she remarked, indicating that she was ready to move on.

"Yes, well, time to be going," he said. "If we go straight to Liverpool Street, we should be able to get a train within the hour."

"Well then, you have a choice, don't you?" Anna replied, as she put her coat back on.

"A choice?" he asked, puzzled. "What choice?"

"I also feel like spending some money. So I am going to book into a lovely hotel, go shopping, have a luxurious bath, possibly a massage, a glass of champagne, a delicious dinner, then stretch myself between the sheets. I will catch an early train in the morning." She glanced at him, dismissively. "You can come with me if you like, but you probably want to catch your train."

"Well, give me a moment to think about it," he replied, taken off guard by the offer, but she just kept slowly drifting away; she gave a little wave and turned to walk out of the door.

Jeffrey was at her side as she opened the door. "London isn't cheap," he said weakly.

Nor am I, my darling, she thought with satisfaction.

They were back in Cambridge just before eleven o'clock the following day. Jeffrey was already feeling guilty at having overslept after a night of wickedness and missing the early train. When he arrived in the office, his scientific assistant gave him a hard copy of an email that had come through the previous afternoon. A man from his past wanted a meeting.

"Does the name Tyro Mukasa mean anything to you?" she asked, clearly intrigued by her boss's sudden change of mood as he read the email.

"The only Tyro Mukasa I knew was a game ranger, walking round with a spear in the middle of Uganda," Jeffrey replied, with disdain embellished by a dismissive flick of his left hand, while his right kept firm hold of the message; his eyes didn't waiver.

Lucy was surprised by his rudeness. "Well, that's who it is, then," she said bluntly, with a look that conveyed her disapproval.

"Then why is he here? I haven't seen him in years," Jeffrey railed, asking himself the question before regaining his self-control. "Do me a favour and arrange the meeting; I don't mind when. Now I must have some time to myself."

Whatever it was he meant to do, it did not get done. He kept ruminating on why Tyro Mukasa would make a journey to Cambridge. He didn't contact Anna that evening – or the next one, either. She, too, was silent.

Chapter 2

TYRO

Tyro was impressed. He was impressed that his younger brother, Arthur, had ever been to this university; he was impressed by the beauty of the colleges spread along the small river; he was impressed with himself for being there that day. He had never been to university. Arthur, the academic light of the family, had flourished and then been murdered, while he, with basic schooling, had acquired wealth he could never have imagined. He was impressed by what he saw about him, but he was not in awe of it. His education was different; that was all. He was fluent in four languages. He could shoot anything in range of his rifle, fly a helicopter at treetop height, and pilot an airship across nations; that was his job. In lands beset by poaching and civil war, his small airline would get you and your contraband to safety, and he had become rich in the process. Above all else, he had learnt survival in a dangerous world. He finished his afternoon walk, returned to his hotel, collected a document folder from his room, and went to the committee room he had hired, where he poured himself some tea and waited. At four thirty precisely, Jeffrey Harvey walked in.

Tyro did not get up. He stayed seated, his elbows and forearms resting on the table as he occupied the armchair. Jeffrey looked him steadily in the eye, noting the expensive suit that Tyro was wearing, gave a half-smile of recognition, and went to sit at the other end.

"So what do we do?" Jeffrey asked. "Sit looking at each other in silence for half an hour?"

"You think yourself very clever, don't you?" Tyro replied, disregarding Jeffrey's question.

"Well, I don't boast about it, but actually I am."

"Clever enough to get away with murder," Tyro muttered, reflectively.
Jeffrey gave him a disdainful smirk. "Oh, not that again."

Tyro also smiled. "It was just a figure of speech. Don't excite yourself, Jeff."

"It's Professor Harvey, now," Jeffrey corrected him, but Tyro was
unimpressed.

"You were Jeff Harvey when Arthur knew you."

"You were always Tyro." Once again, Jeffrey managed to bring disdain
into his voice. "Tyro, the ranger, like his dad before him."

"And you were the bright boys of the university, always going off on
field trips to inspect each other's – let's just say, to inspect each other," Tyro
replied with equal disdain.

"It always satisfied you to find us on that one occasion, didn't it?"
Jeffrey said, reaching into his pocket for his mobile phone.

"I'm only sorry that I didn't go looking for you on the last occasion. I could
have saved my brother while there was still time," Tyro responded. "Don't
switch your phone off on my account. You might get an important call."

"So I might," Jeffrey said, trying to be annoying. "Tell you what," he
added condescendingly, "I'll just put it on vibrate." He concentrated on
his phone.

Tyro sat back at ease. "There's some tea there if you want it," he said,
indicating the tea things with a nod of his head.

"No thanks," Jeffrey said. "Let's get down to business. What is the
purpose of your visit here?" His mind was working furiously to equate
his memories of a half-educated ranger with this smart executive
confronting him.

Tyro was silent a while, contemplating the question. Slowly, he reached
out to the folder on the table beside him. "Jeff," he began, but Jeffrey
interrupted him.

"To you, I am Professor Harvey," Jeffrey repeated firmly. 'Address me
as anything else, and this meeting is over."

"I don't think so. *That* is the purpose of my business," Tyro responded
menacingly. He kept his hand on the folder as he spoke but neither looked
at it or opened it.

"If you had something to say to me, you could have said it in an email.
You knew where I was. You didn't have to travel all the way from Uganda

to voice all this nonsense." Jeff tried to hide the unease he was beginning to feel.

It was Tyro's turn to smirk. "I am rich, Jeff," he said, "much richer than you. I have my own jet. It was no effort to come here, I assure you. I am making money at the same time as watching you die of shame. Do you know what I have got here?" He tapped the dossier again with is right hand.

Jeffrey chose to be silent, not wanting to risk more scorn.

So Tyro tried another question.

"Do you know why you were never charged with my brother's murder?"

"Because it was such a ridiculous notion. Because you were the only person to even think it," Jeffrey replied heatedly, using bravado to hide his concern.

"Ridiculous?" Tyro pounced on the word. "I saw Arthur's body. I saw the injuries. I saw where you had broken his arm, struck his thigh and his back. You weren't protecting him. You were killing him. He was trying to escape. He ran to the boat, but you had put a hole in it, and the crocodiles got him. So I ask you again, do you know why you were never charged with his murder?"

Jeffrey sat silently, but Tyro, too, was silent, staring him down, until Jeffrey capitulated and sullenly replied, "I can't think."

In his moment of triumph, Tyro seemed to relax. He smiled, and his voice became gentle. "Because I couldn't think of a reason why. I could not give a reason – not to the police, not to the coroner, not to anyone. You were often alone together for your unspeakable acts. That would explain why someone else might want to kill him, but not why you would do it. There never was a reason."

There was silence. Jeffrey shrugged, and a look of relief came over his face. "You mean that's it? That's what all this has been about? Your final harangue? Your final attempt to discredit me? What's in that dossier you've been playing with, anyway? Is it a bunch of newspaper cuttings or something?"

Tyro, his hands lightly clasped and resting on the table in front of him, glanced down at the folder and smiled. "That?" he asked quietly. "That's the proof I've always needed. That's the reason why you killed Arthur."

He opened the file and started to turn the pages as if reading it, raising his eyebrows in mock surprise.

"You better get used to being Jeff Harvey again, Jeff. Nobody's going to be calling you Professor after this. I am telling you. This is Arthur's work, and you stole it."

You are screwed, Jeffrey, mate, the voice in Jeffrey's head said, echoing the sentiments of Tyro's words. Years of planning were at risk from a threat he had never imagined. The vengeful Tyro had become wealthy enough to follow him beyond Uganda, and Arthur's scientific work had been found. Either of those matters would have been a blow; together, they were a thunderbolt.

"I've made a mistake. I admit that," Jeffrey said casually, his cool manner being his only protection.

"You've made a big mistake," Tyro replied, with emphasis on the "big." "You killed my brother, and you're going to pay for it. You have no idea who you're messing with."

That last comment surprised Jeffrey, but he let it pass. "My mistake was in thinking that Tyro Mukasa was just a stupid thug who was content as a game-ranger with a bit of poaching on the side. I should never have underestimated your hatred."

"That's right," Tyro agreed. "It's a hatred so powerful it burns." He sat back with a satisfied smile and continued, "You know, Jeff, I made a mistake too. I was so disgusted by your friendship with Arthur, your safaris into the bush together to study each other's specimens"—he raised a hand to keep Jeffrey from interrupting him—"that I couldn't think beyond it when he died. I admired my brother and despised him at the same time. You, I just despised."

"You couldn't be farther from the truth," Jeffrey replied.

"I know, Jeff. I know that, now." Tyro opened his eyes wide, in a mocking gesture of how his eyes had been opened by the revelations. "I know because of this." He waved the portfolio. "When I got it, I sent it to Makerere University to see if it was known to them. They sent it back to me, saying they already had a copy of your research on moringa trees – *your* research. I have a copy of your paper. So I looked at your paper, with your name on it, and I looked at Arthur's paper, with his name on it. Whole sections are the same." Tyro began stabbing his finger, menacingly, at Jeffrey. "You killed Arthur. You killed one of your own students, your own lover, so you could steal his work."

Jeffrey stood up and shook himself; he took a few steps, took a deep breath, and then sat down again.

"Where did you find it?" he asked, perplexed at his own lack of thoroughness in removing all traces of Arthur's work.

Despite his manner, Tyro had been unsure whether he really possessed something to hurt Jeffrey. The way Jeffrey had reacted told him that he did.

"Doesn't matter how I got it. Let's say, a mutual friend found it. You have no idea who you're messing with, Jeff." There was that expression again. Tyro was, certainly, much more than the man he had been.

Jeffrey paused. "May I see it?" he asked.

"Don't you remember what you wrote?" Tyro taunted him. "Is that the trouble, Jeff? Do you want to remind yourself?"

He hurled the dossier the length of the table. Jeffrey picked it up and flicked through the pages.

Tyro had not expected Jeffrey to be so honest. He had expected more denials or another attempt to hide from his past behaviour. He watched the man he had despised for so long, as he read the evidence that threatened to be his downfall. In his moment of triumph, Tyro felt this hatred softening. Hatred is unreasoning, but as he watched this earnest, disciplined man studying the papers, he started to reason with himself. He had never seen Jeff as a violent man before Arthur died. In fact, he and Arthur were the two gentlest men he had ever met, always talking together about things he never understood. But he had come here to discredit Jeff, to "kill" him, and he had the weapon to do it, more powerful and more satisfying than the rifle that he might have used in former times. There could be no doubt, now, that Jeff had stolen Arthur's work. That was clear. The arrogance was still there too. It would be good to see him ruined.

While they were sitting quietly in this fashion, Jeffrey's mobile vibrated on the table. It was a text from Anna. He welcomed the distraction. "Excuse me," he said, putting down the dossier and picking up the phone. However, the message did nothing to ease his tension.

"Maggie found out about us. She has moved out. Need you badly. Phone."

"Shit," he muttered in exasperation.

"World falling apart, Jeff?" Tyro asked, taunting him.

Jeffrey stood up briskly. "Yep, Tyro," he said as if he were no longer interested in the dossier or its portent. "My world is falling apart. Years of hard work, years of hoping to do something worthwhile with my life, years of trying to make some sense of Arthur's death; it's all just teetering on the edge of nothingness. I didn't steal Arthur's work. Not really. We had worked together. I tried to stop others from stealing it. I didn't kill him. I admit that I lied and hid key facts for my own interests; I disregarded you. Who else knows about this?"

"I have my contacts with the university," Tyro said. "Everyone will know, soon enough. I have also prepared a statement that I intend to send to the Ugandan police in Kampala."

"Yep, that should do it." Jeffrey said bitterly. "Dishonour; dismissal; extradition for murder. That should do for me," he replied, listing the fates awaiting him. Now if you'll excuse me, I have to go and sort out a domestic crisis." With that, he left the room.

Tyro stayed behind, long after Jeffrey had left, thinking over his parting words. He sat, looking at this hands, contemplating how ruthless the urge for vengeance can be.

Jeffrey's entrance was not at all what Anna had expected. Her cool, impressive hero was gone. As she opened the door, he pushed past her in a highly agitated state. Her expectations of a sympathetic caress were trampled underfoot by this insensitive entry. He walked briskly down the hall and went into the living room, the kitchen, the bathroom, and then he poked his head into each bedroom. She stood, bemused, at the open front door, still trying to grasp what was going on, and her softness gave way to indignation.

"Jeffrey!"

"I just needed to check that nobody else is here," he called back.

"Maggie's gone. I told you. You're supposed to be here to comfort me. Remember?"

He came back to her, closed the front door for her, and looked at her.

"Anna, how long have we been going out?"

"About six weeks. Why?" She looked totally bemused.

"How can you say you love me after only six weeks? You don't know a thing about me. Why should I give a damn that your flatmate has moved out?"

"Look, just go and sit down," she said. "I'll bring both of us a glass of wine. If I didn't need it before, I do now."

He seemed out of control, his thoughts jumping around in a way she couldn't follow.

"I'm finished," he said, following her to the fridge.

She spun round, clutching a wine bottle. "What *are* you on about?" she asked crossly. "In fact, what are you on? Period." She pushed past him back into the living room, and he followed her so closely that she couldn't reach out to pick up a glass from its shelf. "Jeffrey! You're not a fucking lap-dog. Get out of the way."

He tried to step aside, tripped over his own foot, and fell without dignity onto the sofa. While he sorted himself out, she took the glass over to the table, poured out a quick splash of wine, and took a gulp. The wine, followed by a deep breath, restored her equanimity, and she turned to look at Jeffrey, registering the state of him.

"It looks like we're both in a mess," she commented. "Here; have this." She handed the glass of wine to him.

"What about you?" he asked, taking the glass all the same.

She came to sit beside him. "We'll share," she said gently. "Same glass. Same bottle."

Their hands touched on the narrow strip of cushion between their bodies, and they sat silently a moment, stroking each other's fingers, avoiding each other's gaze.

"Normally, there'd be two glasses and one bottle, but in this case, one glass and two bottles would probably be more appropriate," he murmured.

She tried to smile, but it was a weak effort. "I've got to tell you something," she said bluntly. "Something I should have told you weeks ago."

He squeezed her hand. "Then we're both in the same boat," he said.

"I'm serious," she replied.

"Me too," he replied. "I haven't dared hold you or kiss you since I came in. You're probably going to kick me out in about two minutes from now." Anna looked him straight in the eyes with her intense gaze, and it penetrated his self-absorption that he was expected to listen. "So tell me," he said.

"Maggie isn't, wasn't, just my flatmate," she replied. "It's not been a full-blooded relationship exactly, but it's not been entirely platonic, either." She paused to let this sink in. "Maggie knows what she wants; I'm the

13

one who's been dragging my feet." Anna paused again. "She's sweet, she's intelligent, she's witty, she's gorgeous. She's been my guardian angel, but I just haven't been able to give her the commitment she wanted. Perhaps it's to do with my upbringing; I don't know. Anyway, what we had was a sort of happy compromise that we could both tolerate, until, suddenly, there you were."

He was silent a moment, as he thought about her confession. "Actually, if I'm honest, I'd already guessed," he admitted calmly. "It seemed odd to me, before, when you told me neither of you had any sort of a relationship. It suited me to believe you. Is it over?"

Anna leaned forward, adopting a strangely masculine pose, elbows on her knees, hands clasped between them: an influence of her army life. "It seems to be," she said, sighing. Then she remembered what he had said. "Anyway, what's your confession?"

"By the end of the week, it will be all over the university that I've been accused of a killing ten years ago. He was a PhD student, and his brother has accused me of murdering him to steal his research work."

"Oh," she said, sitting back. "Did you murder him?"

"No. We were close friends, but he died violently, and I took his work in order to stop it falling into other hands. I'm going to have trouble defending myself."

They sat in silence, considering each other's confession. It was Anna who broke the silence: "Would you just give me two minutes and then come through to my bedroom and fuck me really hard? Please?" She stroked his face, got up, and went out of the door without waiting for his reply, adding, "And bring the wine with you."

Within a few nervous seconds of touching each other's naked bodies, they were lost in their own world, in which all their guilt and remorse fuelled an ardent flame and energised invention.

"Lesbians don't do this," he teased her at one point, gasping as he did so.

"This one does," she replied, accompanying her remark with a surge of pelvic thrusts, pulling his neck forcefully to shower small kisses on his face.

She played him to exhaustion, caressing and contorting him, alternately, until he gave up any attempt to control her antics and prayed that his orgasm might come before a heart attack, his prayer being answered in ejaculating pulsations inside her, each one of which she announced with a triumphant grunt.

When their lovemaking was over, Anna stretched herself alongside Jeffrey's body, her back to his chest, their legs entwined, feeling snug and secure in his arms. "So how many other women have you had in your arms, like I am now?" she asked, as the peace between them extended into the drowsiness before sleep. Her free hand squeezed between their bodies to stroke his groin. There was no threat in her voice.

"I don't know," he mumbled sleepily. "They don't signify."

She coaxed him. "Twenty? Thirty?"

"Forty-three," he replied in exhaustion, as this dreamy, boastful number drifted into his head from nowhere to halt the conversation. "Carrie was forty-three. So you'd be forty-four."

"I like that," she said, after a moment's thought. "Forty-four. It's a nice number. Memorable."

"Anna, sweetheart, you're unforgettable anyway. You're stunning, and you seem to run on nuclear energy. Why concern yourself with my past love life? It's over. It's behind us."

"No, my sweet, that's where you're wrong," she corrected him. "The past doesn't lie behind you. It lies ahead of you. You never know when it's going to spring out of nowhere and bite you. I should know." She paused enigmatically and then continued with simple candour: "You have a reputation; that's why I want to know. When I walk into a crowded room, I don't want any other woman there knowing more about you than I do."

After that, they went silent, and soon, both of them sank into a deep sleep.

Anna woke first and prised herself free from Jeffrey, who grunted but remained motionless. He was awake but felt powerless to sit up. It was blissful in the warm bed with the soft pillow and the scent of Anna's body. She put on a tee-shirt and jeans, left the room, and came back a few minutes later with two mugs of tea, which she put on the bedside cabinet, then sat on the bed and started to pinch Jeffrey's earlobe.

"Oh, don't torture me, please don't torture me," he pleaded. Then as her pinch tightened, he said, "Ouch, that actually hurt," and his head, at last, came off the pillow, and he looked at her. She was neat, beautiful, and smiling, and she immediately changed the pinch to a caress and kissed him on the forehead.

"Good morning, handsome," she teased him. "It's seven forty-five, and I think it is time you were stirring, as you have a rather full day ahead of you, I suspect."

"Oh Christ," he murmured as his mind started functioning, and he dropped his head back on the pillow. "I think I'll miss today and wake up tomorrow."

"Come on," she replied firmly, pulling the quilt down to his waist. "Get this inside you. If you don't take it in five seconds, I start pinching, again, and I am very good at pinching."

"I'll have the tea," he said, hastily pulling himself into a sitting position.

She passed him his mug and picked up her own, and they sat together on the bed.

"I don't suppose the papers will have anything about me just yet," he said, finding comfort in exaggerating his predicament. "However, I better be ready for a load of phone calls."

Anna had her hands wrapped round her mug. It was cold in the room, although with the curtains half-drawn back, the sunlight was ample.

"Jeffrey, you haven't told me any of the details about the trouble you're in. I think I've earned the right to know, don't you?"

"There isn't time now. I'll tell you this evening. But what about you and Maggie?"

Anna grimaced. "When you and I came back from London, she was here. She was supposed to be in Florence, and I thought I would have the place to myself. You see, I hadn't told her about you."

"So what happened?" he asked, fully awake and focused on the conversation.

"Well, it took about thirty seconds for her to work out that I had slept with you. I never wanted to hurt her. I wanted to break the news to her at the right moment, in the right way, whatever that was. Now I think about it, perhaps the way it happened was the best."

"What made you decide you wanted me, six weeks ago?" he asked.

"Nothing," she said, smiling triumphantly. "It happened four months ago at Bethany Hamilton's thirtieth birthday party." He looked puzzled. "You can't have forgotten it, surely?" she prompted him. "You balanced a glass on your head, even though Carrie told you not to."

"No, of course I haven't forgotten. I just wasn't aware that I had made such an impression. Carrie and I were still together at that party. Beverley was her friend more than mine."

"You arrived together, but you weren't really together. Anyone could see that. There were whispers all through the party that the two of you were unhappy."

"She refused to fly anywhere. I tried to be understanding, but I couldn't live like that," he said, defensively. "It was tearing us apart."

"Don't worry about it," Anna said dismissively. "It was obvious that she didn't understand you. I knew, then, that I wanted you."

Jeffrey thought about that assertion as he took a sip of his tea. "So I was hunted, was I? Even with my reputation, as you described it last night."

"The excitement of who you are is part of your attraction," she admitted, with a shy smile. "That, your looks, and the part of you that wants to do something good for the world, just like I do."

He paused. "You realise, don't you, that we didn't meet by chance at that party? I'd met Maggie a couple of times at the Polar Institute, and we'd talked about the voyage. She said that she knew a young army reservist – you – who would be ideal as one of the team to be on the iceberg."

"She never told me that," Anna said, laughing at this revelation. "So I was hunted too. I wish I'd known."

"She didn't want to put pressure on you. So we agreed to meet at Bethany's party, and she would persuade you to come. I didn't know there was anything going on between you. You just seemed everything I was looking for."

"You didn't show it at the time," Anna commented. "And I went home, desperate to find a way to meet you again."

"Am I the first man in your life?" he asked, forgetting, now, all the other matters that lay ahead of him throughout the day.

She glanced away for a moment, struck by an unpleasant memory, and reached for his hand, like a little girl seeking reassurance. Her voice was full of emotion as she spoke. "The first man in my life was – is – my father. He treated my mother so badly that I promised myself I would never let it happen to me. I was her support, even as a child. I refused to be like her. I was the one who persuaded her to divorce him. He destroyed her spirit. He was killing her. He was the great professor who everyone applauded, without seeing what he was doing to her, physically and mentally. In the end, it was him against me."

"Did you have any brothers or sisters?"

"No."

"Who won?"

"My mother is happy now, so I like to think I did," she said, shrugging. "I hate brutality, all of it, but men can be so brutal, even if they don't mean to be, and I've learnt to play the game." Then she looked at him, shook her head, and laughed apologetically, as she dismissed those thoughts and focused once more on him. Her hand squeezed his in a loving gesture. "Isn't it funny? I feel so incredibly safe with you, and yet you're facing a murder charge. Have you really killed someone?"

"No, but I may have trouble proving it," he replied.

"Don't you have time to talk about it?" she coaxed him. "Perhaps I can help. Who knows?"

"Lucy will be furious if I'm late," he muttered. "I promised to go through my appointments calendar this morning. She's been on at me for days."

"Who's more important, Lucy or me?" Anna asked, in a tone that left room for only one answer.

"I'm going through to the bathroom," he said, without bothering to reply, "and when I come back, I will give you the full story. You better make yourself comfortable. This could take some time."

While in the bathroom, he had the chance to think over what he would tell her and what he could leave out. When he came back she had taken off her clothes and was sitting in the bed, her breasts above the duvet, her back propped with pillows, and his pillow ready beside her.

"Come and lean on me," she said. "We all need someone to lean on, sometimes."

He stood, naked, looking at her for a moment. "You're not even thirty yet, are you?" he asked.

"Not even close, thank you," she chided him, light-heartedly.

"Then you shouldn't be my counsellor, I should be yours."

"Time isn't passing us, my love," she replied. "We pass through time – some of us more quickly than others." It was such a curiously profound observation that he raised his eyebrows in surprise, but she was not abashed.

"The years on a calendar aren't nearly as important as what has happened in those years," she told him.

When she said that, he looked at her again and saw the fine lines about her eyes and mouth that were easy to miss at first glance. He decided not to tease her.

"I don't care what's happening to me," he said. "I wouldn't swap places with any man in the world, right now." And with that, he climbed into bed beside her.

"And I wouldn't swap places with any woman," she replied, as he slid under the covers and put his arm around her. "Now, tell all," she coaxed him.

Jeffrey told the story of the final minutes of Arthur's life, in a boat, on a lake, in Uganda. When he had finished, the two of them sat in silence for a while, until it was broken by Anna.

"What a tragedy," she said quietly. "But I still don't understand how Tyro Mukasa comes into the picture and why he's here."

"Tyro thinks I killed Arthur. He went to see Arthur's body in the hospital and noticed the marks where I had caught Arthur with the paddle. He didn't accept the elephant story, and he said his brother was too experienced to risk getting caught by a crocodile. He claimed I had tried to kill Arthur with the paddle. He claimed Arthur had run into the jaws of the croc when trying to escape me, and it had simply finished the job for me."

"How could he say that? What would have been your motive?"

"That's just it. He couldn't come up with a motive. Everyone knew how well Arthur and I had been getting on. Nobody believed Tyro. They saw it for what it was: the misplaced anger of a grieving brother. I was never in trouble with the police or anything like that. Actually, people were very kind."

"But all this happened years ago. Why is he here now?" Anna asked.

"He found a paper written by Arthur. I never knew Arthur had submitted it," Jeffrey muttered. "I published the same data in my seminal article about moringas, which made my name. It underpins my whole reputation."

"I can see that you're worried."

"Tyro now thinks he has found the motive that would make me kill. He's accused me of stealing Arthur's work and killing him to do so."

"Have you googled him?"

"Who?"

"Tyro whatever."

Jeffrey had not even thought of it. Still naked, they both jumped out of bed and sat together, side by side on the same chair, as Anna entered the name on her laptop. There were several men with the name Mukasa, but only one recorded as Tyro Mukasa, Chief Executive of Jinja Air Cargo (JAC). Next, Anna clicked on a link to JAC, Uganda.

Jinja Air Cargo was written above an aerial panoramic photograph of the JAC fleet: two light aircraft, a heavy-duty helicopter, an Airbus A 320, and tethered beside the airbus, a light-blue airship. Anna became aware of the intense interest Jeffrey was showing in the photograph.

"If I wasn't so scared of him, I'd put him in touch with Gary. He looks as if he could provide just the air support we need for the Antarctic," Jeffrey mused.

"Forget it, my love. Stay away from Tyro," Anna advised him calmly. Her mother's warning that men like Jeffrey often get shot dead was uppermost in her mind.

Chapter 3

REVELATIONS

Vicarage Farm was just that: an eighteenth-century vicarage with its elegant long windows and neat limestone walls, French windows leading into the garden from the drawing room, and high ceilings and heavy oak doors. The Emmerson family had bought it after the First World War, and in 2009, it was into the fourth generation of their possession, at the centre of an estate of many hundred hectares owned by David and Jacqueline Emmerson.

Thursday the eleventh of November was full of autumnal colour, with blue sky and grey-white, scudding clouds. Howard and Dot, Jacqueline's parents, along with Jacqueline and David, and Lucy and Tom, their children, left the lunch table full of good food and banter.

Lucy took her grandmother's arm and gave it an affectionate squeeze. "It's a real treat to have you here, Grandma Dot," she said.

"Lucy, my love, it's a real treat to be here, I can tell you. It makes me feel years younger being with you and Tom, instead of having to put up with my decrepit old husband all the time."

"I might remind you that this decrepit old husband has brought you morning tea in bed for the past forty years," Howard interjected from the comfort of the sofa, where he had begun to scan the newspaper, "and you'd better be nice to him if you want your tea tomorrow."

"I didn't realise you could still hear that far," Dot replied tersely, "and anyway, it's forty-four years, otherwise Jacqueline would have been born out of wedlock."

Howard glanced up with a look of mild surprise. "Jackie? I thought she was only about thirty. That's all she looks these days."

"Daddy, you old charmer," Jacqueline responded delightedly, bending down to kiss his cheek.

"Oh, for heaven's sake, don't encourage him, Jacqueline," her mother continued. "He's just flirting – always has done."

"I would hardly flirt with my own daughter," Howard replied with mock indignation. "Tom, come to my rescue. Don't you think your mother looks about thirty?"

Tom's momentary hesitation caused them all to laugh, and while the banter continued, Jacqueline went to the study to search for her husband.

"Davy, do you want a cup of tea before you go?" she asked; she had seen how serious he had become. All his light-heartedness at lunch seemed to have gone. She went over and gave him a hug. "You've time for a cup of tea. I'll bring it to you in here," she said.

"I don't want to seem antisocial," he replied. "It's not often we have your parents and the kids at the same time."

"They won't mind. We all know that you have an important meeting this afternoon. It was lovely that we could all have lunch together. I'll be back in a moment."

She disappeared, and he could tell that she had said something to the others because the sound of their voices suddenly dropped. She came back carrying two cups of tea.

"Here you are, my love," she said, passing him his cup.

There had never been anyone else for either of them, ever since their sixth-form days. At moments like this, they just bonded as a team. They were made for marriage. They had enjoyed their first furtive sexual experiences with each other within weeks of meeting, while their parents were still innocently expressing satisfaction at how well they seemed to be getting on, much to the amusement of their various brothers and sisters. So as not to cause concern to either family, they had avoided talk of marriage throughout their student years. Jacqueline had chosen nursing as a career, so that they would have some money to start life together, which allowed David to continue his studies. Within weeks of him getting his first degree, they announced their engagement. It was against his parents' wishes. Her parents paid for the wedding, but his parents refused to give them financial support, yet somehow (David never knew how), Jacqueline provided the money for them both, and though they had never been poorer, they thrived during his postgraduate years at Cambridge.

"Now tell me why you're looking so concerned," she prompted him.

"It's the Moringa project," he said, as if that explained everything. "It was just a bizarre idea that took root. After years of failing to make something of myself in some mainstream walk of life, it looks like this fantasy is actually going to amount to something."

David's father, a natural sportsman and entrepreneur, had always favoured David's brother, leaving David feeling inadequate, despite getting to Cambridge and building a stable career and a happy home with Jacqueline. His father's death in 2006, which could not come soon enough for Jacqueline, had come too soon for David, who had longed to see approval in his father's eyes. His mother had been sweet, but she had died of breast cancer in 2004, and his brother had gone to Canada and lost touch. Jacqueline was his pillar of support.

"Then you should be happy," she coaxed him, recognising the familiar signs of a crisis of confidence, to which he was prone so often. She rubbed his shoulders.

David sat back, more relaxed. "The thing is, first it was just ideas, then Jeffrey persuaded me to let him grow some of his trees in a corner of the estate, then it was the research workshop, then the engineering workshop. During all these stages, it was somehow proportional to the rest of life. It merged with everything else that we were doing. I can't get my head round the fact that Jeffrey has actually bought the tanker. Suddenly, life has entered a new dimension."

"Well, good," Jacqueline exclaimed, encouragingly. "You need this, David. This is the chance you've been looking for all your life. Go for it. Jeffrey Harvey is the partner you need."

"You have a sort of love-hate opinion of Jeffrey, don't you? I never thought you really trusted him," David said, mildly surprised at Jacqueline's support.

"I can't help being fond of him," Jacqueline admitted. "He's always been a good friend to us, especially where Lucy's concerned, but he did treat Helen Crawley shockingly, with that awful affair with Raja Johar's niece. Thank God, Raja brought him to his senses before he got sacked.

The point, David darling, is he's ingenious, and he gets things done. He's not frightened of being unorthodox."

David nodded. "Do you know, he took his new girlfriend to the meeting when he officially bought the tanker? He hasn't let me meet her yet, but apparently she's a personal trainer, so I don't suppose her intellect is her main attraction." He sipped his tea.

"She won't last," Jacqueline replied dismissively. "He just likes a beautiful woman on his arm."

"He wouldn't let *me* go with him. He said I was too principled. I might upset his negotiations. He even calls me 'Honest David.' It makes me so mad."

"Why? What makes you so mad?" Jacqueline was amused, quite approving the nickname.

"Well, I do believe in honesty and integrity, but all the time I've tried to do things by the book, I've become so ensnared by bureaucracy that I've hardly been able to continue. It's only through Jeffrey and others like him, with his complete disregard for officialdom, that the likes of me get anywhere. But that puts us, then, right on the edge of the law too. Life shouldn't have to be such a gamble."

"But that's why the two of you make such a good team," Jacqueline pointed out. "He's not living any differently from how he's always lived. He's a free spirit, a risk-taker, but he's intelligent, and so are you. A venture like this needs someone anchored in reality to see it through, just as it needs a buccaneer like him. You're both entrepreneurs, each in your own way." Her eyes were glowing with enthusiasm.

"Jackie, love, you do realise, don't you, that I'm gambling with your future and that of the kids? It's not my future that worries me; it's what I'm risking for you."

"Oh, darling, they're not kids anymore. They're adults, ready and able to make their own way in the world. And if I have to go to prison for aiding and abetting you, then I will."

David smiled. "It won't ever come to that," he said.

"I'm so excited," Jacqueline continued. "I can't get over it. You've actually bought the tanker. It's really happening."

"Well, Jeffrey has, with his venture capitalist backers – and his girlfriend."

"Oh, that man, he's such a poser," Jacqueline said, laughing.

"Did you tell Tom and Lucy – about the tanker, I mean?"

Jacqueline looked him steadily in the eyes. "No, my sweet, I've never talked to them about the project. But now that it's going ahead, I think you should. They deserve that. They deserve your trust. I suspect they'll be even more impressed and supportive than me."

David squeezed her hand and then stood up decisively. "Come on, let's tell them together," he said.

Jacqueline and he walked from his study across the hall and into the drawing room, where the family was gathered. Conversation stopped when David walked in.

"Sorry if we were making too much noise, David," Howard said. "I've been trying to get Dot to shut up, but nothing doing."

"There's been nothing doing from Howie for most of our married life," Dorothy replied drily.

Jacqueline, though unable to stop herself from laughing, stepped in to call the family to order. "Mum, Dad, the lot of you, quiet. David's got some exciting news, and he's got to go to a meeting soon, so listen."

"Well, it's a bit hard to know where to begin. It's, er ..." David stumbled into his announcement.

"Oh, for goodness sake, Dad, just spit it out," Lucy scolded him. "What are you doing, leaving Mum or something?"

Everyone laughed at the absurdity of the suggestion, except David, who shut them up very effectively by saying, "Well, yes." There was silence and he had their full attention. "All being well, I probably am, for a few months."

Lucy glanced fearfully at her mother and was perplexed to see her relaxed and smiling.

"I haven't told you this before, because it was all so uncertain, but now that we know it's happening, I am going to bring you up to date. You mustn't divulge it to anyone just yet, but there's no reason you shouldn't know."

David glanced at each of them in turn to underline his words.

He continued, "Every year, thousands of people and animals die from drought and contaminated water in Africa, and every year, millions of litres of water, fresh water, are released as icebergs to melt in the oceans around Antarctica."

"Tom, is that the North Pole or the South Pole? I never remember," Howard asked in a whisper that everyone else heard too.

25

"South Pole, Grandpa," Tom said, without taking his eyes off David. Clearly, something awesome was coming.

"I am a lead member of a consortium which is testing the feasibility of transporting that water to Africa. We thought about it for years but never had the money such a project needs. To cut a long story short, we do now have the money, and a few weeks ago, we purchased an oil tanker. We have now taken possession of it, and it's on its way to a shipyard in India to be converted into a research vessel capable of carrying several million litres of water. It's a big ship – very big. Our vision is to set up water depots at strategic sites around the globe where fresh polar water can be stored rather than letting it just disappear into the ocean. This expedition will be a pilot study to see whether our ideas work."

There was a momentary silence as the news sunk in.

Then Tom spoke: "So let me get this right," he said, slowly. "My cool Dad owns an oil tanker?"

"Well, part-ownership; I suppose that I do, in a way; yes," David replied, not having seen himself in that light.

"Fucking respect, Dad. Forgive my French, but fucking respect." Tom got up and gave him a man-hug, and they broke into laughter.

"David, darling, this must be costing a fortune. How can you afford it?" Dorothy asked, knowing that she was voicing both her own and Howard's concerns for their daughter's future, even though Jacqueline, herself, seemed unperturbed.

"We have the financial backing we need. I can't tell you more than that, Dot; I'm sorry."

"I think it's cool, but where do you fit into all this?" Lucy asked. "I've not heard anything about it in the university."

"The university isn't involved, Lucy, sweet, at least not directly," David replied. "It wasn't prepared to help. It's for that reason, as well as commercial interests, that I must ask all of you not to say anything to anyone else. You see, it's not only water shortage; it's also water contamination that kills so many people in Africa. So we've developed a biological method of purifying the water that's both affordable and beneficial, using moringas."

"Moringas?" Lucy repeated excitedly. "That's my boss's special area of interest. He's an expert."

"Moringas?" Howard chipped in. "Aren't they those shush-shush things that Mexican dance bands have?"

"No, Howard," David replied patiently. "Those are maracas." He waited for the laughter to die down. "I am talking about the tree, Moringa oleifera. We've got some on the estate. One of us can take you to see them later."

"Anyone can make a mistake. What's so special about moringas, anyway?" Howard asked, ruffled by everyone's undisguised amusement at his error.

David realised that he would just have to explain: "Moringa oleifera is a tree that grows across the tropical regions of the world. Its commercial potential was never discovered during colonial times, or it would be as familiar to us as rubber, or palm trees, or tea. You can do lots of things with it. Our interest is that it produces seeds that have near-magical properties. Crush them in a cup of dirty Nile water, and over a period of a few minutes, the water becomes pure enough to drink. It was a German chemist, a woman, who worked out the biological process, but nothing came of it. It was Jeffrey Harvey who took it up and researched it. He went out to East Africa to study different methods of cultivation, looking to enhance the trees' properties. We went into business together as a result. As you know, we have our own, licensed research centre here, to see how we can genetically modify different cereals to improve their bio-resistance. Well, he's been working on the moringa genetic code to enhance its water purification qualities."

"That last bit is news to me," Lucy muttered.

David glanced at her but continued speaking.

"If we are going to store vast lakes of water to be used at a moment's notice, we have to be able to keep it pure. We think we have a biological way of doing this. We have genetically modified the seed to be able to remove every common pathogen that we are likely to encounter. A sediment is created that sinks, just leaving pure water."

"I don't understand," Lucy said, now sounding quite cross. "I'm his scientific assistant. Why don't I know anything about this?"

"Because you are university staff, and the university has refused to give its support to this work. We had to keep you out of it, Lucy."

Lucy stayed quiet, but the family recognised all the signs of a volcano building inside her.

"Dad, that means you are involved in GM research that's not approved by the university," Tom commented, sounding somewhat negative.

"Tom, dear boy, we are held back by officialdom. All the time, officialdom blocks things for no better reason than public sentiment or political bias – not on any rational scientific basis. You'll find that out soon enough when you're trying to earn a living. I'm not a lawbreaker by nature. I'm not going to risk the future of the estate. So we're circumventing EU law. We are germinating seeds on an estate in India. There'll be a glorified greenhouse on the ship, where we shall grow moringa saplings. By the time they reach Kenya, the trees will be big enough to plant as a commercial plantation, if we can get them ashore. If not, I guess we just keep growing them on board ship until we can. In any case, we'll harvest the seeds, and they'll do their work of saving lives without anyone bothering about it. Once we get official approval, then we can let the trees spread."

"Do you mean to tell me," Lucy began slowly, "that you and Professor Harvey have been planning a voyage of scientific importance, a voyage that could transform my career, without telling me, your own daughter, and his assistant?' Her voice had now risen appreciably.

Howard caught David's eye. "Oops," he said.

David sprang up. "Lucy, darling, I think you and I should have a few words together in private."

Lucy, too, sprang up. "I bloody well say we should!" she exclaimed, seizing him by the arm and virtually pushing him into the study.

She slammed the door behind them.

The following day, while Jeffrey was making what contingency plans he could, the *Moringa* cleared the Straits of Hormuz and sailed into the Gulf of Oman. She still bore the name *Empress Oil* on her hull, and her superstructure was that of an oil tanker, but below decks, the changes were under way. Raja was on board to experience the awesome size of the ship. He had seen no point in wasting the ten days involved in bringing the agency crew aboard, powering up the vessel, and sailing her from the Gulf and through the Arabian Sea to his shipyards, near Bhavnagar. He had chartered a plane and flown from Mumbai with twenty of his workers, under the able command of Arnesh. They had landed in Bahrain about three hours later and transferred at once to the *Empress Oil*.

It was an enormous project for the men. They had been working in shifts for seven days now, making their way along the ship, preparing the way for the army of workers who would descend on her in Bhavnagar, identifying what should be removed and what would stay. Such selective dismemberment would be a new skill for the shipyard workers. From the cavernous spaces of the oil tanks, they were going to construct new tanks and add a new deck from midships to the bows: the storage deck. It would consist of an open plan space for flexible storage with strong wire-mesh containers and a helicopter hangar in the bows.

Between it and the stern of the vessel would be the Grand Chamber for the moringa saplings, and above it, between it and the main deck, would be the corridor deck: a deck extending the length of the vessel, with a long, wide corridor on one side and smaller corridors extending off it, where there would be rooms available as workshops, stores, or recreational areas.

Raja preferred crossing the ocean at forty thousand feet in great comfort and had never been on such a huge vessel, or for so many days at sea, but he was so excited that he often forgot he was at sea. Sometimes, the ocean was so still, and the ship so large, that he might just as well have been on shore. There were just moments when a slight break in the rhythmic vibrations or sound would take him from the minutiae of particular details to awareness of the surrounding ocean. One such moment made him glance up nervously as he and Arnesh studied computerised projections of the alterations. He laughed at his own reflexes.

"I am an engineer, not a sailor," he said in their native Punjabi.

"That's all right, boss. I'm sometimes nervous too."

"You, with all your experience, Arnesh? How can you be nervous?"

"Because I know what oceans can do, even to a ship like this," Arnesh replied, giving Raja another pang of anxiety.

Talking in Punjabi pleased them both. Raja spoke Hindi to many of his workers and English to the crew.

"Well, I won't be on the ship when she sails for the South Pole, but you will be," Raja said with a laugh. "Your life will depend on the quality of your work. I cannot think of a better incentive to do well."

Soon, both of them were again visualising the helicopter hangar, the Grand Chamber, and the water tanks and irrigation pipes they would create over the coming weeks.

29

Chapter 4

THE TANGLED WEB

Mid-May 2010

"It's gone nine! It's time we got up."

Jeffrey heard Anna's firm voice through the duvet as he nestled comfortably beside her. He knew that she was right; indeed, it was way beyond getting-up time. He kissed her tummy and then rose, carrying the duvet with him, so both of them were exposed to the cool air in the room. It was a decisive move that neither of them could disregard. Giving him a loving smile, Anna swung her legs to the floor and moved gracefully to the bathroom, with Jeffrey following her.

"I wouldn't be too worried, darling," she said as she concentrated on dabbing lightly between her thighs with a tissue and then flushing the bowl. "I don't think you should do anything more about it. Just reply to the university if they ask any more questions. 'Scuse me." She pushed past him to the shower and slipped off her tee-shirt.

"I'm not sure, but maybe you're right," Jeffrey said, stepping into the shower after her as he spoke, and they commenced a gentle, almost ritual wash of each other's bodies as they continued chatting.

Jeffrey was getting anxious at the way the university authorities kept asking him to clarify events in his academic record, but gave him no information as to what action they were taking.

"Mmmm, do that bit again," Anna murmured. "Obviously, nothing's going to happen in a hurry. They may contact the university in East Africa, and they'll probably study that paper that your friend published, but I can't see them or the Ugandan police charging you with anything serious after all this time. The only real threat I can see is from Tyro himself. He sounds the sort of man who could really commit murder, so just stay on your guard, and hope he doesn't come back. You've got me to protect you if he does."

Jeffrey realised this last remark was made with complete sincerity. He had let his hand play over her stomach as she was talking. She looked at his eyes, saw that his attention was solidly fixed on her body, and decided that she need not give him further reassurance.

"That's an abdomen any top athlete would be proud of," he said admiringly. "You're not just gorgeous, you're fit with it, aren't you?"

"Not as fit as when I was competing, but yes. Does it meet with your approval?"

"There's still room for improvement," Jeffrey lied impishly, having stroked her perfect physique. "It's weird finding myself with a partner who's almost my equal physically."

Anna, in response to this remark, squeezed a bit of flab just above his hips in a way that made him wince.

"I'm fitter, stronger, and younger than you. I was in the army, the Norwegian army, and you're very lucky that I'm in a good mood," she chided him. Then she kissed him and added, "I admit you are largely responsible for that, but don't fool with me." The mix of kindness and menace was not lost on Jeffrey. He had accepted that he was now in a relationship where he had to watch himself.

"Getting back to the project," he said quickly as the water cascaded over them. "Turn round. I'll do your back. I'm meeting David Emmerson this afternoon: dear old Honest David. He's been getting really worried just recently."

"Don't stop. There's no problem with David. He's a strong friend and a strong ally," she replied confidently. "He's not a risk-taker like us. That's why he needs you. He doesn't like risks."

"That's true," Jeffrey said with a laugh. "What would you say about Gary?"

"No, that tickles. Gary? I've only met him briefly: that one time when you and I had just started dating. He seemed very like you, but"— she looked at him provocatively and added—"you know, taller, stronger, younger, more handsome—"

31

Jeffrey turned the temperature fully to cold and directed the power-shower straight onto her body, while she spluttered and ducked and shrieked. Then he relented and switched off the water, and she stumbled out of the cubicle.

"Ooh, that was evil," Anna said crossly, as she grabbed her towel and dabbed the water from her eyes, her nose, and off her dripping body.

"Just because you've discovered men doesn't mean that you can have us all," Jeffrey replied as he dried himself off and tossed the towel on the floor.

"Correction. I have discovered one man, but I don't like him very much at the moment. Now pick your towel up," she ordered.

"Fat chance," he replied and had taken two steps out of the bathroom when the whiplash of a wet towel-end stung his bottom like a bee.

The second one stung him while he was getting over his surprise, and the third stung his left thigh as he turned, clutching his bottom. The fourth one would have hit his undefended scrotum and floored him, but it never arrived. Instead, Anna tossed his towel playfully into his face and winked at him.

"I learnt to use all sorts of weapons in the army," she said as he grinned foolishly. "I do not like wet towels on my floor or bed. By the way, if you want to shave, you can use my razor. There are new blades in the cupboard."

"I was only joking," he said contritely, as he walked back past her, and she responded by giving him a sumptuous kiss on the lips.

She went through to the bedroom, leaving him to shave.

They left the flat about twenty minutes later, walking together downstairs before each going their separate ways for the day. Anna's hand was already on the street-door latch, about to open it, when Jeffrey placed his hand on her shoulder, causing her to pause for a moment.

"When I came to this flat last October, I was so desperate I didn't know what to do," he told her. "Now I have so many things to do, I'm not sure how to fit them all into one day."

She saw the love in his eyes. More than that, she saw his admiration. "I told you," she whispered. "Stick with me; you're going to win a Nobel Prize."

"If I don't get shot," he retorted. "Come on. Time to go."

"Good luck," she said.

"Hope things are working out all right with Maggie," he replied, striding away and giving a brief wave.

She watched him go and realised how easy it would be to repeat her mother's mistake and make a man the centre of her life, at the cost of all her own ambition and freedom.

"You're not the master of my life," Anna muttered as she watched him go. "My darling, I must not let that happen." Then she went quickly to her car and telephoned Maggie.

The first stop for Jeffrey was Professor Taylor's office, to be followed by a pub lunch with David. Mike Taylor, his head of department, had texted him to say he needed an update on Tyro Mukasa. Jeffrey was relieved to find that he still had Mike's confidence, but he knew he was not totally above suspicion. Jeffrey had not heard from Tyro since their meeting and could only go over the same ground as he and Mike had already discussed.

He emerged from Mike's office with the normal front of goodwill between them, but he was actually quite troubled, knowing that this meeting would not be the end of Mike's enquiries. He wondered whether Tyro would return to Cambridge and what further damage he was doing in the meantime. Jeffrey made his way along the river bank to the Green Man in Grantchester. He was glad when David texted him to say he was running late, as it gave him a chance to sit alone in the beer-garden of the pub, in the cool brightness of the day, and think about the three friends with whom he had created the Warlocks, almost twenty years ago:

Jimmy Moule, in Boston, Massachusetts, would have all the legal issues under control. Jeffrey felt the warmest affection for his quiet-spoken American friend, who was a keen explorer and an illustrious lawyer with it.

Raja Johar owned the shipyards in Bhavnagar, among several other enterprises. He was a widower; his beloved Sunita had died, leaving him childless, with only his work, and his brother's family, to comfort him. He would deliver the ship; there were no worries here, either.

David. When Jeffrey had fled Uganda, David provided land on his estate to grow a small plantation of moringas, so Jeffrey could continue his research. David's laboratory made it possible to carry out research free of university constraints. His engineering teams had devised economically viable means to harvest the polar ice, based on the agricultural engineering that was the family business. He was a truly dedicated friend, with a delightful family, who had invested generously in the project. However, his crisis of conscience every time Jeffrey wanted to do something covert was frustrating. It was a paradox that David's intense need for honesty and transparency actually made him less trustworthy.

Then Jeffrey's mind shifted to the wild card, Gary Murdoch. Gary took risk to its limits. He had that super-confidence typical of Americans. It often undoes them but sometimes produces champions. You can never be quite sure which, and that was the problem with Gary. He was several years junior to the others, a late addition to the team. Gary arrived at the university to complete his PhD, sponsored by the oil company for which he worked. Jeffrey was his tutor and recruited him for the project. Within weeks, Gary's flair and expertise had spawned ideas and a prototype to work on. In his own time, he was a free-fall fanatic, a stunt-pilot, and an all-round great guy. When Jeffrey was trying to extricate himself from a mad affair with Raja's niece, he introduced her to Gary. It was love at first sight for them both. Gary satiated her desire to sample freedom in all its forms, and she was equal to all his needs. Months later, she followed him back to the States, saving Jeffrey's job and reputation in the process. But Gary was wild. He did mad things.

While deep in his thoughts, Jeffrey's mobile rang. He expected it would be David, but instead, a Welsh voice he barely remembered began speaking.

"Jeffrey, hello. This is Alan Mills. I wonder if you remember me."

"Oh, hello," he said. "Yes, you were our college chaplain, a friend of Arthur Mukasa. How are you?"

"I like to think that you and I were friends too. Anyway, be that as it may, I am ringing on behalf of his brother, Tyro."

Jeffrey sat up at the sound of the name. "How do you know him?" he asked nervously, convinced that this was a new angle of attack about to start.

Alan chuckled. "He and I got on very well together when he was last over. We've remained in contact. He told me that you and he had some differences, and he's asked me to phone you, just to say that he's returning here today. He'll be staying with me, and I thought you might like to have dinner with us tomorrow evening."

Jeffrey felt a surge of anger at this virtual stranger wading into his personal life. He kept his voice courteous but firm as he said, "I know you're trying to do the right thing, and I appreciate your involvement, but this is an intensely personal matter. I'll save your number and contact him through you if necessary, but please don't try to arrange a meeting. All right? Thank you. Goodbye."

Jeffrey left Alan with no chance to reply, pressing the Call End button and putting the phone back in his pocket. He slammed his hand down on the roughly hewn table in a gesture of frustration, just as David arrived.

"You've been waiting for me that long, have you?" David said, tactfully pretending that he had not detected the deep concern in his friend's action.

"Hi, David, good to see you. I think you've arrived in the nick of time to stop me going mad."

"Do you want to talk about it?" David asked.

Jeffrey sighed. "Not really. A ghost from the past has come back to haunt me, and it's all gathering momentum."

David, beer in one hand and plate of sandwiches in the other, shrugged. "It's about time your past caught up with you," he said. "Your girlfriends change, but not you."

He sat down with the affable indifference of great friendship. He could either be perpetually concerned about Jeffrey or hope for the best. He chose the latter. "Let me add to your problems by telling you that Lucy is thinking of handing in her notice sometime soon – and kicking you in the shins for good measure."

Jeffrey mockingly raised his glass to David. "Thanks. Why?"

"You still haven't asked her to join the project. I told you," David said simply, taking another sip of his beer. "She has a right to know whether she's coming or not. She's your responsibility. She's been waiting months for you to ask her."

"Of course I'm going to ask her," Jeffrey admitted with a smile. "Eventually. Right now, she's the best scientific assistant ever. It'd be a pity to lose that. She can team up with Anna. Anna's in her twenties too, and I think Lucy would like her. Lucy will have to accept some fitness training from Anna, mind you, but if she agrees, then I'll tell her she can come."

"This Anna," David said diffidently, "no offence, but will she still be with you by the time we sail?" He took a good bite of his sandwich and raised his eyebrows enquiringly.

Jeffrey hesitated a moment and then replied, "David, I hope to marry Anna before we go."

"Ah, now that's a surprise," David replied, just managing to keep his mouthful of sandwich from spluttering onto the table. He swallowed hard. "Marriage? Is that right? The last bastion of slavery, as you once referred to it."

"That was in the days of Carrie," Jeffrey muttered. "This is Anna – it's different."

"All the same," David exclaimed, unconvinced. "This is a bit sudden, isn't it? Does she know you feel like this?"

"I'm not sure. Incredibly, I think she feels the same about me. If I lose her, I know I'll never find another woman like her," Jeffrey sighed and ran his hand through his hair.

David saw a line of conversation developing that he normally left to Jacqueline, who was much better at these sort of things. "Well, no, of course," he said enigmatically, then added quietly, "I came here to discuss finance."

Jeffrey reacted with self-annoyance. "You see what I mean, David? I'm obsessed. Sorry, mate, let's concentrate on the matter in hand. Can I have one of your sandwiches?"

He helped himself without waiting for David's reply. David disregarded the theft.

"We now have a workable ice-harvester," David said, readily changing subjects to discuss his team's progress. "My young engineer, Roland Muller, has solved the problem of the distance factor."

"What do you mean, the distance factor?" Jeffrey asked, desperately trying to stay focused on the new line of conversation.

"You know. The safe distance between the ship and the iceberg. We've had all sorts of problems with hoses of different types. Well, he's come up with a new, more powerful compressor, and—"

"Spare me the details, David; this is your part of the operation. As long as I know that it's all going to schedule, that's as much as I want at this stage."

"All right, if that's what you want," David had hoped Jeffrey might show some appreciation of the engineering achievement, but he was resigned to

Jeffrey's perpetual lack of interest in details and kept his disappointment to himself. "The point is that we now need more funds in order to produce the six harvesters proposed. Their unit cost is going to be about a hundred thousand pounds each, even using the resources of my own workshops. I hope our backers realise what they are getting themselves into."

"Well, you must contact Gary about that, and soon. You and he can discuss the details. He'll have to seek permission from the Finance Director for that expenditure, but he'll get it."

"Gary isn't all that easy to contact," David muttered. "He's currently somewhere in the United States. Are you sure he's the best man to handle our finances? He's a bit of an adventurer, if you ask me."

"He's got the personal touch," Jeffrey replied. "He's an oilman, and they like that. He's got expertise in both the management and delivery of this type of project. He'll get you what you need, you'll see."

"Well, there's something else too. In the old days, I'd have called it manpower, but I suppose these days, they're called human resources. But on the iceberg, it's going to be beef we need. Personnel to construct, maintain, handle, and dismantle all the gear, in adverse, possibly dangerous conditions; more helpers, Jeffrey." David looked doubtfully at Jeffrey, thinking he was presenting a significant hurdle to overcome.

Jeffrey shrugged to indicate that the matter was inconsequential. "We'll have four teams," he said, "led by Jimmy Moule, Gary, Maggie Robinson, and Anna Jensen. Don't raise your eyebrows like that. They all have a lot of experience of Arctic conditions. They all have management expertise. Maggie and Anna have both received military training and are tougher than most men. I don't need to look further for my team leaders. As for the beef, as you put it, I'll ask Raja to help. His workforce is enormous. He can afford to let us have the men we need."

"They'll be Indian, though," David protested, then added hastily, "I'm not being racist, Jeffrey; it's simply they'll be used to hot weather, not freezing cold. I mean, what mountains do you know in India?"

"The Himalayas … parts of them."

David blinked. "That's true," he said softly. "Oh well," he continued and then added, in a perplexed way, "I still can't get over what you've talked me into doing."

"Are you regretting it?"

David chuckled and shook his head. "I should be, but I'm not. I would never have had the confidence to do what you do, but I wouldn't miss this for anything, nor would Jackie. I mean, if this comes off, we'll change the world." He looked round to check that nobody was listening to them. "Jeffrey," he said in a low voice. "As a token of my trust, I've not pushed you further on the matter of how you raised the money, but I want to know if there's something else you should tell me."

"Frankly, I think it's better not to ask questions. Even Klaus Huber, the missionary doctor, referred to the project as turning dirty money into clean water. I'm just thankful we have a backer at all."

David reflected on this a moment and then asked, "What do they get in return for their investment – our backers?"

"If we fail, they get the *Moringa*, assuming she's still afloat."

"And if we succeed?"

"If we succeed in showing there's a commercially viable way of growing the modified moringas and harvesting Antarctic ice, and set up the company to do it, then all of us become very rich," Jeffrey said emphatically.

David looked at him steadily. "Why do I get the feeling that you're not telling me everything? Still, I'll do my bit, and if everyone else does theirs, what can go wrong?"

Jeffrey was well aware of the irony in David's voice but ignored it. "That's probably the best attitude," he agreed.

Sunday night, 30 May 2010, was a delicious gift to a woman madly in love. After a relaxing weekend, the May bank holiday was still to come, so there was no reason to spare her lover's energy, as he had all the next day to recover. It was well past midnight. Jeffrey had just staggered to the bathroom, and Anna was still spread-eagled in naked abandon on the bed, when his mobile started its cool melody. Anna rolled onto her side and picked up the phone to find out who was calling. Seeing the caller's name, her disinterest disappeared. With malicious satisfaction, she took the call and said, "Yes?" very tersely.

"Oh, uh, my name is Leena."

"I know exactly what your name is," Anna replied, very pleased with the effect of her ambush. "What do you want?"

"Jeffrey, please."

"You're too late. He's already had his orgasm. There's nothing left."

"Don't be disgusting," Leena hissed. "I'm in trouble. Please. I've been kidnapped."

Anna sounded disinterested. "Really?" she said, without any conviction, and then she got up from the bed, following Jeffrey to the bathroom. He was at the basin. "Here you are," she said, handing the phone to him. "It's one of your forty-three. She says she's been kidnapped or something."

With that, Anna went and sat wearily on the loo, letting the waters drain out of her with pleasurable relief. Jeffrey took the phone and went into the bedroom. Anna heard his occasional exclamations as she cleaned her teeth and straightened her hair – she did not take a shower, so as to retain the smell of sex on her body. She wandered back into the bedroom, still naked and feeling refreshed; he was propped up on the bed, waiting for her, the phone on the table beside him. He reached out for her, but she avoided his touch.

"You don't get off that lightly," she said, plumping up her pillows, to lean against them more comfortably, with a clear gap between him and her. "At one o'clock in the morning, a young woman named Leena – one of your forty-three, yes?"

"Look, you've got this all wrong—" he started.

"So the answer is yes, one of your forty-three," Anna continued relentlessly. "A young woman named Leena, with the cutest Indian accent, phones you at one o'clock in the morning, fully expecting to be invited round, only she is surprised to find me here and comes up with a pathetic story in an attempt to arouse some sympathetic male instincts in you. Is she beautiful? How silly of me to ask – of course she is. Is she coming round? Should I go?"

Saying this, she showed not the slightest intention to move. She was taunting him mercilessly and enjoying every moment of her jealousy.

"She didn't know it was one o'clock," he said patiently, appreciating how the call must seem to Anna.

"Why? Can't she tell the time?"

"Because she was in Las Vegas, that's why."

"Why would one of your girlfriends phone you from Las Vegas?" Anna persisted, dismissive of such a lame excuse for the timing of the call.

"She's not my girlfriend," Jeffrey said, sounding contrite and desperate. "It was a mistake that she ever was. I promise. Actually, she's now Gary Murdoch's girlfriend, and heaven help any man who tries to get between them. He's mad about her – and she would never have called me if she hadn't had to."

Anna stayed silently regarding him, and her face softened. "Go on," she said more gently. "I'm listening." She accepted a caress on her thigh.

"There was no time to get details," Jeffrey explained. "Something went wrong at the airport. Gary was arrested by security staff. She was being led away by a lady official when she became suspicious of her, so she ran to a police officer, and the bogus official disappeared. She doesn't know what's happened, but Gary has the tickets, so she is now sitting, petrified, in the Las Vegas airport."

"So why did she phone you?" Anna no longer sounded angry but curious.

"She's got joint British-Indian citizenship. She doesn't have residency in the States, doesn't know anyone other than Gary. I guess she saw me as the best person to get her out of a mess."

Anna pondered a moment and then said, "Good choice. If I had a crisis, I'd turn to you from the other side of the world too." She leant over and kissed his chest. "All right. You're in the clear. I suspect that, even for a woman lost in America, you have someone to help her out."

"Well, I think so, yes," Jeffrey said modestly.

Anna sat back delightedly. "You see? I knew it. Who?"

"Jimmy Moule. I've mentioned him to you. He's the lawyer in our consortium. He's based in Massachusetts, but he runs a big law firm. I'll text him. Now will you please come here and show me how much you forgive me?"

"But what about that text?" Anna protested, limply, before allowing his arms to fold around her. With Anna curled up against him, Jeffrey composed the text, pressed "Send," and turned out the light.

"There weren't really forty-three others before you," he murmured to her in the darkness. "I was just boasting that night."

"Do you think I don't know that?" she whispered in light-hearted reply. "I've been doing some checking."

"So you knew who Leena was?"

40

"Oh, yes."

"That's not fair," he complained sleepily and, feeling truly at peace, fell asleep.

Tuesday, 1 June

The end of the academic year was only a few days away, loose ends were being tied down, but one was still whipping around in the breeze, and Jeffrey was, once again, having to justify himself to a woman. In this case, Lucy, and her wish to sail on the *Moringa*.

"Look, all I'm saying is that I can't guarantee that you can come. Yours is a university-funded post; the university is nothing to do with this project."

Lucy put the coffee down that she had brought him and took a sip of her own. Her demeanour was one of sullen respect, the maximum level of resentment she could safely exhibit towards her chief. "I think it's a bit unfair, boss," she said, while her body language conveyed, "I think you're a real pig, and I hope your bloody boat sinks."

"If it's any consolation to you, we've hit a real snag," he said. "A man named Gary Murdoch has been arrested in America, and he's handling all the financial matters to do with the project. I'll have to phone your father later, but I'm waiting for more news."

"Can I do anything to help?"

"Not at the moment, thanks," Jeffrey replied, then he reflected a moment. "Well, actually, there is something. I'm not a Facebook user, but has there been anything about me on it, or any of these other networks I hear about?"

"What sort of things?" Lucy probed him, her interest awakened by the hint of a secret.

"Nothing specific," Jeffrey said without looking up. Lucy sat down opposite him, cradling her coffee mug with both hands, and stared fixedly at him, smiling with excitement. He was hiding something.

Jeffrey held out for another few seconds and then gave in. "A few months ago, someone threatened to publish something about me. Nothing's happened. He went back to Africa and hasn't contacted me since. But I've had word that he's coming back to the UK, and I just want to be sure that there are no rumours going round. I think he mentioned something

41

about Facebook, but I haven't the time to do anything about it. I never use it. There's nothing scandalous appearing about me, is there?" he ended, nervously.

"You don't really know what Facebook is, do you? Without me, you wouldn't know where to start looking, would you?" Lucy teased him, knowing that his computer skills hardly stretched beyond word processing. "Which is why you appointed me as your scientific assistant: to do your literature searches, to prepare your lecture presentations, and generally look after your interests in the age of instant communication. Actually, you have your own Facebook page, which I run for you."

"You what?" Jeffrey blurted out.

Lucy continued her annoyingly sweet smile "You agreed to it months ago. It keeps up your image on campus. That's how I know the gossip."

"Even if I did, I had no idea you were using it. I should have an input into what's on it."

"No. Bad idea." Lucy said decisively. "Better leave it to me, but I'm just reminding you why you can't do without me. Will that be all, boss?"

"For the moment, thank you, Lucy, yes," Jeffrey said, keeping his face expressionless as she left the room and then smiling to himself at her audacity.

However, it was a mystery, why he had heard nothing from Tyro Mukasa. He thought yet again of Tyro's brother, Arthur. Not a week passed that he did not think of Arthur. Though he had been Arthur's tutor, there had only been three years' difference in their ages. Arthur had been lonely, an outcast, and had responded readily to Jeffrey's admiration with a sensuality that Jeffrey had found irresistible. Arthur was so evidently different. He had a calm, quiet nature, a mental strength with the impression of physical fragility. He had an eye for colour and an attention to detail, which showed that his mind absorbed the minutest sensory stimuli and interpreted them with great clarity. He had a gentle sense of humour but a piercing shrewdness, and Jeffrey often felt that Arthur seemed to know his thoughts almost better than he, himself. Arthur was exceptional, an utterly beautiful forbidden love, who shared his passionate belief that biology could provide the answer to drought and disease. Their friendship could have survived if Arthur had lived. Arthur would have forgiven him his other loves. Together, they would have taken their work forward. Instead, Jeffrey had been forced to manage without him.

"You're not dead, my dear friend," Jeffrey muttered quietly into space, by way of atonement for his thoughts. "As long as this project lives, you live. I'll see to that."

Jeffrey forced himself to focus on some administrative issues and a paper he was keen to read. He was studying this when he heard the telephone ringing in the secretary's office, and Lucy answered it. Seconds later, the phone rang on his desk as she transferred the call.

"Jimmy Moule wishes to speak to you."

"Put him through."

The news was mixed. Jimmy had contacted a friend in Las Vegas. Within thirty minutes, a lawyer had reached Leena, and they had approached the airport security service together. Her passport had been taken away, but she had been released and was in a secure hotel under a different name. There was no clue as to who the supposed abductors might have been. They had not been allowed to see Gary, who was under investigation for some very serious crime.

"How serious?" Jeffrey asked, stunned by the news.

"I've got nothing to add on that point," Jimmy replied in his calm, authoritative voice. "Perhaps you might know."

"What could I possibly know?" Jeffrey asked, perplexed.

"Leena said he made $22,000 in one visit to the craps table."

"How much?" Jeffrey interrupted.

"Twenty-two thousand," Jimmy repeated patiently. "He made $22,000. He was betting thousands of dollars on single throws. Where would he have got that much money to throw around?"

"No idea," Jeffrey lied blandly, while thinking of the Moringa project budget and wondering how much had gone on Gary's gambling debts.

"Leena said it was his life savings, and that he had risked them to give her enough money to live off." Jimmy paused and then added drily, "It makes a touching story."

"But they can't arrest him for that, surely; certainly not in the gambling capital of the world?"

"If they think he's involved in crime, they can," Jimmy corrected him. "The police are always on the look-out."

"So what happens now?" Jeffrey asked, deciding to shut up about Gary's role in the Moringa project.

Jimmy answered his question with a question. "Jeffrey, can I ask you something? Is this man, Gary Murdoch, the same man we've always had doubts about?"

"Yes."

"Mmmm," Jimmy murmured in contemplation. "Jeffrey, would you let me advise you on this matter?"

"How much for?" Jeffrey half-joked.

Jimmy gave a short laugh but continued, "Gary Murdoch was a maverick, Jeffrey, and probably still is. Likeable, competent, but he's a maverick. Don't get involved in Gary Murdoch's problems. If he's dealing in narcotics, and your name gets linked to his, then you may find yourself facing extradition to the USA."

Jeffrey felt a wave of panic sweep over him. "Well, shouldn't we do something about lawyers and so on?" he asked, trying to think of the right thing to say.

"Jeffrey, I mean it. Leave Murdoch to sort himself out. You're a great guy, but, well, it's probably best that the CIA doesn't take too much interest in your life, from what I know of you. Leena's different. She's not implicated. The authorities are satisfied that she is not a threat. With proper representation, she'll have her passport back in forty-eight hours. Would you like me to arrange it?"

"Yes, please, Jimmy. Don't let her worry about the cost. I'll help her with that."

"I better help you with that too," Jimmy said, chuckling, "or you'll be bankrupt. Don't worry; I'll sort it out. You know, Jeffrey, talking to you always makes me glad that I've got a legitimate line of business. You look after yourself now. G'bye."

Jeffrey put down the phone and held his head in his hands. "Dear God," he muttered, more in prayer than exclamation.

Lucy, standing in the doorway, politely cleared her throat to let Jeffrey know that she was there. He looked up at her. "I need to talk to your father, urgently."

"I'll give him a call," she replied nonchalantly, pulling out her phone.

"No, no, absolutely not," Jeffrey said hurriedly. "I want you to be extremely careful about sending anything to anyone from your computer, as well."

Lucy had never seen him so agitated. "Are you all right, boss?" she asked.

"I'm fine. I'm fine," he said, tetchily. Then he thought of the fly-on-the-wall listening device so recently in the news. "If you see a fly in the office, I want you to crush it and throw it out. Is that clear?" he added, thinking he made good sense.

"Yes," Lucy said obediently, convinced that Jeffrey now needed very gentle handling. "Look, why not go home, boss?" she suggested.

Jeffrey looked down at his desk. There was not much on it. "I think that's a good idea. It's a bit early. Anna might be free. I'll drop by her place."

"You could call her," Lucy suggested.

"I've gone off phones," Jeffrey said, picking up his raincoat from the chair where he had dropped it. He reckoned it was fanciful to think that the secret services might be logging every phone call made, but at the moment, he would not take chances. He walked out, with a wave to Lucy.

He and Anna still lived separately, but they had exchanged keys so she had access to his house and he to her first floor flat. It was a happy, liberating way to live. He made his way to her flat and up the stairs, his spirits lifting with each step as he anticipated his welcome. He was truly excited as he slipped the key into her front door and swept in, calling her name, "Anna!"

To his astonishment, she was standing naked, outside her bedroom, looking taken aback by his sudden appearance.

He laughed. "Sorry, gorgeous," he said. "I should have phoned. I'll wait in here." And before she could reply, he stepped briskly into the living room, to be confronted by another naked woman, with short fair hair, standing still and holding the newspaper she had been reading by her side.

"Dear Lord," he blurted out. "Maggie!" His eyes were fixed on the statuesque woman.

"Jeffrey," she replied coolly, overcoming her surprise. An embarrassed smile began to appear on her face, along with a red flush from throat to hair-line. She raised the newspaper over her torso.

"I've always thought you very attractive," he said, still facing her awkwardly, not quite sure what he should do next.

"Thank you," she replied softly.

45

Meantime, Anna had sprung into action, diving into her bedroom and pulling on a tee-shirt and knickers; she ran her fingers through her hair and called Jeffrey as she did so.

"Jeffrey, darling, come here please."

Jeffrey nodded to Maggie. "You really do look beautiful like that – if I may say so – and I'm glad you read the *Independent*."

"Why?" she asked, surprised.

"It hides less of you than if you read the *Daily Telegraph*," he murmured, as he backed out of the living room, and outraged, she mouthed "Go away!"

He went obediently to Anna's room. When he reached the doorway, she pulled him into her room by both arms, slammed the door shut behind them, and locked it.

"I love you, Jeffrey Harvey, even when you arrive unannounced when you're supposed to be working," she said, kissing his unresponsive lips. "Let's get that coat off you and sit on the bed." He looked uncertain but did not resist as she took his raincoat off him. She pushed him backwards so that he sat on the bed. At the same time, a knock came from the door.

"Not now, Maggie," Anna said, not taking her eyes off Jeffrey.

"I need my clothes," Maggie whispered, plaintively.

"I love you," Anna repeated, looking into Jeffrey's eyes before turning to a neat pile of clothes on the chair with a sigh of exasperation and taking them over to the door. She unlocked the door, opened it slightly, and a disembodied, naked arm reached round, took the pile, and disappeared. She heard a whispered thanks through the door. When she turned round, Jeffrey was sitting with a bemused expression, not showing any sign of affection.

She walked back to him and extended her fingers. "Look," she said, "do you like my nails? And look at my toes – how beautiful the nails are." They were, indeed, a rich, enticing red. She put her right foot onto his left thigh so that her naked leg led his gaze from her knee to her vulva. "Feel my leg. Go on, touch It," she ordered. "Feel how smooth and freshly waxed it is." He gently ran his hand up her calf, round the smooth contours of her knee, and along the inner surface of her thigh to the fragile border of her knickers. "You see," she said, placing her hand soothingly on his shoulder, "this is what Maggs and I were doing. We were making each other look beautiful, feel beautiful. But for me, it was always with you in mind, my darling. I was doing it for you."

He looked up at her, quizzically. "Maggie was naked. You were naked."

Anna put her foot back on the ground and stared at him with her piercing gaze. "Nakedness is good," she said. "It's healthy. How many times do I have to say this to you? It's good when families and close friends can be naked in each other's company. You are so prudish, Jeffrey." She bit her lip and averted her eyes, unable to hold his gaze with candour. "We massaged each other. That's why," she explained hesitantly. "It was nice and very relaxing."

They stayed as they were, while he silently absorbed the facts as he found them; he thought of the value of his relationship with Anna and what might become of it if he sought further explanations now. In the silence, they heard the muffled sounds of Maggie moving down the corridor and letting herself out. The door latch clicked, and she was gone. Anna looked up, and Jeffrey saw the desperate entreaty for forgiveness in her eyes.

"You know," he said gently, "I've had one hell of an afternoon. I don't suppose you could give me a massage as well, could you?"

She exhaled with a great sigh of relief. "Yes, my love, the very best of massages," she replied. Crisis over, she re-asserted herself. She made to embrace him but then drew back. "But not until you've showered. You're all sweaty."

"Then undress me," he commanded her. He let her undress him, blotting everything from his mind save the pleasure of the moment. He showered while she remade the bed and, a few minutes later, lay stretched full-length on the bed on his stomach, while Anna sat astride the base of his spine and worked on his muscles with her strong, slender fingers. She did not ask any questions but let him choose when to re-engage with the world. Instead, he drifted into sleep and amused her by his gentle snores. She slipped out of the room, sent a soothing text to Maggie, and then sat on the bed, reading, until Jeffrey awoke.

"What time is it?" he asked.

"About twenty past six in the evening."

"I feel as if I have been asleep for hours."

"About one hour," she corrected him. "I love you."

He raised his head enough to kiss her thigh. "I know, and I love you."

He sat up and told her what Jimmy Moule had said. Leena seemed to be in the clear, but Gary was in custody. He had probably embezzled the project funds. He could be involved in money laundering. The whole project could come under CIA scrutiny.

Anna saw the signs of stress creeping back over Jeffrey; she brought him back to reality with a finger placed delicately over his lips. "Gary was just being Gary," she said quietly. "You can't be surprised about it. Your guess that he's used the project's account to finance his gambling is almost certainly right. I was wrong to think he would be good in a crisis," she chided herself. "He obviously can't be trusted."

"Well, I think you were right. I still think he can be," Jeffrey said, reaching for his shirt and then setting it aside. "That shirt's a bit sweaty. Have you got something I could wear?"

She looked slightly surprised. "Which dress did you have in mind?" she asked.

"No, a pullover or something."

"I'll find you something," she said and came back with a tee-shirt. "It's the biggest I've got. It's a bit girly, but wear your coat over it, and nobody will notice."

As he was putting it on, Jeffrey focused on the subject of Gary. "Gary's a risk-taker. That's how he likes to live, and he's good at it. Nobody could be that lucky for so long without having an innate skill. Mad, but competent. You might as well say I was mad for involving him, but I don't think I was."

"But you *are* mad, darling," Anna said lovingly. "If you weren't, you wouldn't have even started this whole thing. I'll do my best to keep you safe, just as Leena was probably trying to do for Gary."

"You think I need protecting, do you?" Jeffrey smiled.

"I know you do. Everyone I speak to thinks you are going to come to some sort of sticky end. Their views only differ about the type of end it will be. It's only you who doesn't seem to realise it."

"Maybe I'm beginning to," he said to her surprise.

Two days later, at about ten o'clock in the morning in Mumbai, India, and eleven thirty in the evening in Boston, a phone rang in Cambridge, England. It was four thirty in the morning. Jeffrey struggled into consciousness while Anna put a pillow over her head.

"Ngh," Jeffrey said by way of greeting.

"Good morning, Jeffrey," Jimmy's calm and friendly voice greeted him. "It seems you're not the early riser you once were."

"Jimmy, mate, I've never got up this early. What's the time, anyway?" Jeffrey said, rubbing the sleep from his eyes.

"For me, it's almost midnight and time I was heading to bed. For you, it's five o'clock in the morning, and it's time you were up anyway. You've got to be at Heathrow Airport in about three hours."

Jeffrey sat up, trying to clear his thoughts. "Airport? What do you mean?"

"Leena took off about five hours ago. She couldn't stay here, Jeffrey, she was too much at risk. We arranged for her to go straight from the hotel onto a plane. She has a British passport so it had to be Britain, and she said you're the one person she'd feel really safe with."

"You mean I've got to meet Leena?" At the sound of that name, Anna, who had seemed asleep, suddenly raised the pillow from over her head and stared coldly at Jeffrey.

"It would be the right thing to do, Jeffrey. She's badly shaken by what's happened, and with good reason. She needs to be with you for a couple of days just—"

"Leena, stay here?" Jeffrey exclaimed.

Anna seemed to glide like a snake as her stony face rose to confront Jeffrey. "Over my dead body," she warned him venomously.

Jimmy plainly heard her voice in the background and laughed gently. "You know, Jeffrey, talking to you always makes me glad that I'm safely married. I'll text you the flight number. You have a good day now."

"But Jimmy—"

"I'm off to bed now, Jeffrey, with Karen; twenty-six years of keeping each other warm. Good night."

As the phone went dead, Jeffrey felt deserted by his dear friend.

"I don't think I can cope with this," he sighed and collapsed back onto his pillow. Anna relented, coiling her arms around him and stroking his hair, becoming his ally in a moment of need.

"I've got to meet with David today. I've got to sort out the mess Gary has left. How can I spend half the day going to Heathrow and back?" he complained.

"You can't," Anna said soothingly. "So when she phones, you just tell her to grow up and to deal with it like any normal adult. Problem solved."

Jeffrey lay looking up at the ceiling a moment. "Nah, I can't do that; not in the circumstances." Anna shrugged as if she was finished with the subject. Jeffrey turned to her. "Would you go?" he asked.

"Would I go where?" she asked and then looked into his eyes, realising what he meant. "You mean collect your Indian girlfriend? No, I will not. You have a Norwegian girlfriend now. Too bad. If you wanted a sultry, dark-skinned hero-worshipper who falls into your arms with some heart-rending story, you should have grabbed her while you had the chance. Absolutely not."

Three hours later, still angry with herself for giving in, Anna was standing in the arrivals hall at Terminal 3 and had no trouble at all in identifying Leena, who fitted all her pre-conceptions. There she was, a slender, rather diminutive figure, with high cheekbones, large brown eyes, an annoyingly beautiful body, and a detestably perfect dress sense, in easy-casual contrasts, emerging from her transatlantic flight as if she had just stepped out of a chauffeur-driven car. Because Leena was from Jeffrey's past, Anna had imagined someone older than herself, but she realised in horror that, if anything, Leena was younger. Anna saw her as a direct threat and hated her. She had sent Leena a text, so Leena had come out looking for her, not Jeffrey. Anna was gratified to see Leena's eyes fix on her with catlike aggression, as she identified Anna amid the welcoming crowd in the arrivals hall.

"You must be Anna," Leena said. "Everyone else is smiling."

"Let's get one thing straight," Anna replied without any greeting. "I'm only here because he needed me to come. He needed me. He needs me. He's mine. Understood?"

"What do you think I'm going to do?" Leena asked scornfully. "Strip naked?"

"Don't bother," Anna retorted. "After a night with me, he wouldn't even be looking."

"You're pathetic," Leena countered.

So, pleasantries over, the two women, unwittingly making a stunning impression, walked Leena's trolley to the car park, where she caught sight of Jeffrey's Land Rover Defender. "I don't believe it," she gasped. "It's still the same car." Seething with the insult that even the car held memories of Leena, Anna reluctantly heaved the bags into the back, and they were under way, onto the M25, M11, and home.

The M25 is a tedious road. At five o'clock in the morning, it is almost as clear as a race-track, but by ten o'clock, the traffic seems set in cement. The tedium wore away at the angry silence. A sense of shared misfortune started to grow between the two women. Anna was the first to break the ice by silently offering a mint to Leena.

"Thanks," Leena mumbled, taking the proffered sweet. Then, after a moment's further silence, "I like your top, by the way. Well chosen. The colour really suits you."

"Thank you. I did not expect a compliment from you," Anna replied, and Leena looked at her uncertainly, not quite sure of her sincerity, until Anna added, "I hated you for looking as good as you did when you walked into the arrivals hall."

After that, the conversation flowed. They tested each other's intellect, physical ability, networking potential, dress-sense, and personality profiles in a friendly way. Once clear of the M1 intersection, even the Defender growled along at seventy-five miles an hour, and they trundled easily up the M11, calling off at the Stansted services for diesel and, by mutual consent, further conversation over a cup of coffee. At last, as they climbed back into the Defender, Anna raised the subject they had both avoided: "Look, in an hour's time, we'll be home, and Jeffrey will probably be waiting. I want to know, what's your interest in him? Why would you phone him, of all people, when you are in trouble so far away, in Las Vegas?"

"I promise, I promise, I promise I don't have any interest in Jeffrey," Leena said in desperation. "I'm so sorry I disturbed you when I phoned. My interest is getting Gary back. That's all. I had more confidence in Jeffrey at that moment than anyone else in the world. I knew he would find a way to help me."

"Yes, he's wonderful at helping others," agreed Anna. "But he can't help himself. He is who he is."

"I won't encourage him, don't worry."

"He won't need encouragement," Anna said in frustration. "One look at you ... he's mine now. I accept him for who he is, not what he ought to be. Just don't be the one I catch him with. Is that clear? I like you. I didn't want to, but I do. We can be friends, but it's up to you."

With that, Anna started the engine, and they commenced the final part of the journey. "You're much younger than I had thought you'd be,"

Anna continued, once they had re-joined the motorway. "You must have been a kid when you were with Jeffrey."

"Hasn't he told you?" Leena said in surprise.

"He's been wise enough to avoid all mention of you," Anna replied with some vehemence.

"It was five years ago," Leena explained. "It was my very first term at Cambridge. I developed a crush on Jeffrey and flirted with him in a tutorial. He responded, and that was the start of eight weeks of absolute madness. At the start, I was a virgin and believed myself to be in total love. He was so mature and exciting."

"I don't believe it," Anna exclaimed. "How old were you?"

"I turned nineteen that term."

"So you're only twenty-four now," Anna deduced, alarm bells ringing in her brain.

"Well, I'm twenty-three now, twenty-four in October," Leena corrected her, innocently, and nearly sent Anna spinning off into the embankment.

"You better finish your story," Anna replied. "How did it end?"

"People started to talk. I learnt what happens to students and their tutors who have affairs. I felt my whole career, and his, about to disappear in ruins. Thank God we survived to the end of term. He asked me to stay for Christmas, but I flew back to my parents and remembered all that I had worked for. I couldn't talk to my parents, they were so angry, but my Uncle Raja, who is a good friend of Jeffrey, persuaded them to let me return. Uncle Raja spoke to Jeffrey, and when I returned for the spring term, we were back to normal."

"Well, clearly you weren't," Anna commented, staggered by what Leena had said. "If you were totally over him, you wouldn't have been phoning him four years later from Las Vegas."

"We were no longer lovers," Leena replied. "But he's a wonderful man. He inspired me to follow my own path, to be independent and not hemmed in by cultural traditions. And it was through him that I met Gary. Gary fell madly in love with me. He was very exciting, and I followed him back to the States. I think Jeffrey intended it."

"Jeffrey doesn't have time for that sort of thing," Anna said dismissively, but Leena was not offended.

She just gave a gentle smile and said wisely, "He'll never stop surprising you."

Anna laughed. "Given what we've found out about each other this past week, he probably thinks the same about me." Then she deftly changed the subject.

Jeffrey had cleared most of his petty tasks and spoken by phone to David by mid-morning, still undressed. He made himself a cup of coffee and sat back on his sofa to play a favourite game, The Road of Destiny. He closed his eyes and suddenly thought of a road. The image was of a road running through a forest, but the canopy of the trees was high, and sunlight filtered through. The road, itself, was narrow, straight, and deserted, and in the distance, the trees came to an end, and it was flooded in sunlight. He opened his eyes, encouraged by what he had seen. He let his mind drift as he sipped his drink. Then, realising that more time had passed than he had planned, he rose, shaved, and showered. When he stepped out of the shower, he towelled himself and then, dutifully, hung up his towel, as was now his custom. He felt bright. He felt fit.

"You've still got it," he muttered to himself approvingly and threw open his clothes cupboard.

At that moment, his phone rang. It was Anna. "Where are you?" she asked.

"Still at home. Have you got Leena?"

"Yes, and we're just parking. Are you decent? Can we come in?"

"I've just finished dressing," he lied. "Let yourselves in, and I'll be down."

Jeffrey heard them enter as he snatched some garments, threw them on, and briskly came downstairs to see them. Both women looked at him with happiness and then in complete surprise.

"Very pretty," Leena said to Anna with a little laugh, and then she walked forward and kissed Jeffrey fondly on his cheek. "Hello," she said simply.

"Hello," he said. "I'm glad you're safe."

"Can I just use your shower to freshen up?" she asked.

"Yes, do. Top of the stairs on the right. Take a towel from the cupboard." Jeffrey watched her go up the stairs and then turned back to

Anna, who was looking unamused. "Everything went all right, didn't it?" he whispered, hopefully.

"Jeffrey, take that tee-shirt off," she whispered back tersely.

"But it's fresh on," he said, indignant at her telling-off.

"It's mine," she hissed. "It's the one I lent you to put on under your coat last week."

"Oh hell," Jeffrey replied, and then a thought struck him. "Do you think Leena noticed?"

"Of course she noticed, you chump," Anna replied. "Any woman would notice, Leena especially." Then she came forward and put her arms round him. "You and I have some serious talking to do." She smiled an exasperated smile and stroked his cheek.

"It's already on my list," he said, in self-defence.

"You don't keep lists, remember?" she whispered in his ear, feeling thankful Jeffrey was hers. "I'm moving in with you, darling; don't argue. I'm moving in with you." She pulled her face back to look him in the eyes, so that her playful body language was obvious. "Then you'll be able to wear any of my clothes you like."

"And you, mine," he replied, and they laughed and tussled noisily together.

She'll have heard that, Anna thought to herself with satisfaction, as the sound of Leena starting the shower reached them.

Leena's back in my life, Jeffrey thought to himself, as his day disintegrated. *This is going to take some sorting out.*

Chapter 5

FRIENDS AND FOES

Anna was several steps ahead of Jeffrey in her plans for their relationship. Having established that, in principle, she would be moving in with him, she felt more relaxed about Leena's presence. She was not having Leena stay with Jeffrey, or in her flat, but she could lodge with Maggie. Maggie immediately consented to the plan and, completely overlooking the ten years' difference between them, welcomed Leena like a sister.

Leaving the two of them to get to know each other, Anna texted Jeffrey to meet her at her flat after work, to choose what to bring with her when moving in. She greeted him after he slipped his key into the door, and they briefly sorted through her things. Then she stretched herself out on her bed, without looking at him, and allowed him to strip her nude and massage her, as a reminder to him of how lucky he was. She playfully refused sexual contact, to keep him keen; knowing she had done enough to outflank any threat from Leena, she flirted with him mercilessly. Eventually, all else driven from his mind, he suggested that they walk to his place, have supper, and sleep together. Anna felt triumphant. She jumped up nimbly and slipped out of the door, returning a few moments later, ready to go, in her raincoat and trainers. Jeffrey still loved her, despite her naughty afternoon with Maggie and the arrival of Leena. Life was very good.

The lane Jeffrey lived down was quiet and respectable, with grass verges and trees. There was nobody in sight as they entered the lane and walked the last few steps to his home. Then a figure emerged from the other side. Jeffrey stopped abruptly, almost throwing Anna off-balance.

"Tyro Mukasa." There was fear in Jeffrey's voice, as he looked into the big man's eyes. "Get behind me, Anna. He wants me, not you. That's right, isn't it, Tyro?"

Tyro stood in front of them. "Good evening, Jeffrey. I have been waiting for you. I thought that if I warned you of my coming, you might try to avoid me. I waited two hours, but it has now been worth it."

Anna instantly went into action. Her military training took over as she sprang lightly to one side, undoing her raincoat as she did so, revealing that she had nothing on underneath. The sudden, dramatic flash she gave both men astonished Jeffrey and caused Tyro to raise his arms to block out the sight, and he cried out, "Oh no. Please, madam, for the love of God—"

Jeffrey was quick to recover his senses; seeing his enemy distracted, he gave him a sharp kick on the right shin and then kicked his left leg from under him, sending him into the road.

"Mercy! Mercy! I am not here to harm you," the big man bellowed in his deep voice.

Jeffrey threw himself on top of Tyro, but in such an inexpert manner that they just rolled over and over, shouting at each other. Anna ran up menacingly, trying to keep her raincoat about her and then, getting her left arm caught in the belt, threw off the raincoat entirely, literally stripped and poised to defend her lover with her own life, if necessary.

Tyro once again cried out, "Madam! Please put some clothes on," as he tried to grapple with Jeffrey's flailing arms.

There was such desperation in Tyro's voice and such submission in his struggles that Jeffrey reined in his own aggression and looked up; he said, "Bloody hell, Anna! You're naked again. He's right. Put something on before you get us all arrested."

"Me get us arrested? Oh, bugger off, both of you," Anna retorted angrily.

She was hurt by Jeffrey's lack of appreciation for her support and frustrated not to have had some of the action, but seeing that peace had descended on the two men sitting in the road, she returned to her discarded raincoat and put it on. The men picked themselves up and brushed off the dirt. They were just in time: A police car appeared at the end of the lane, blue lights flashing, and drew up beside them.

There was no damage to property, there were no visible injuries, and they managed, between them, to concoct an impromptu story that Jeffrey and Tyro were just having a friendly wrestle that had been louder than intended, having been out drinking (though they were both sober). They meekly accepted the police warning about disturbing the peace and stood contritely in line as the police car drew away. There were now lights visible in the windows and doors along the lane.

"You better come inside with us," Jeffrey muttered to Tyro. "We'll sort out our differences in there."

After they went indoors, Anna disappeared upstairs to put some clothes on, and Jeffrey turned to Tyro and asked him if he would like something to drink.

"A cup of tea, thank you," Tyro replied hesitantly.

Jeffrey felt his own hostility ebb away. "What would you like in it: milk or rum?"

Tyro smiled slightly. "Rum? Yes, rum would be good."

Tyro was on his own in the front room while Jeffrey was making tea, when Anna came downstairs. Her hair was tousled. She was still deeply suspicious of Tyro and feared for Jeffrey while she was not close to protect him, so she had not wasted time over changing.

"I'm sorry for causing you any concerns," Tyro said. "But you did not need to behave so dramatically."

"I will be the judge of that," Anna replied coldly, still standing on the stairs.

Tyro was reminded of a lioness protecting her cubs and spoke carefully: "We have not met. Why are you so much my enemy?"

"He has told me about you," she replied. "You threatened to kill him. You threatened to shoot him."

At that moment, Jeffrey came back with the tea; sensing the dangerous tension in the room, he turned to Anna and kissed her arm. "To be honest, honey, you've threatened to shoot me as well," he muttered.

Both Anna and Tyro smiled.

"If it has to be done, it is for me to do, and nobody else," Anna retorted, while Jeffrey passed Tyro his rum-fortified tea. "Is that clear?" she asked firmly.

"Yes, madam," Tyro replied, with a glint of humour in his eyes.

"In that case, you can call me Anna," she said, descending the last steps. "And I will share your cup, Jeffrey." She took it out of his hands, had a sip, and passed it back. With that, all enmity ceased.

"I knew you were coming back. Alan Mills told me," Jeffrey said to Tyro, easing himself into a comfy chair while Anna perched on its arm.

"I went, and I came back, as I said I would. The Reverend Mills has offered me a room for as long as I wish to stay." Tyro paused. "He's a very good man. We have some long conversations."

"What about?" Jeffrey asked.

"About? Well, about Arthur. He remembers my brother. About you, though it seems he knows about you from what others have told him." Tyro took a sip of tea while Jeffrey grimaced. "And about anger, grief, shame, vengeance, and hatred. Those are long conversations."

Jeffrey and Anna watched silently as the big man grappled with the emotion evoked by these thoughts.

"Man-to-man sexual love seems acceptable in your culture," Tyro continued slowly, looking at his cup.

Anna felt Jeffrey's body become tense, even though he sat motionless. She could not understand the relevance of this unexpected comment.

"Even the Christian churches are starting to accept practices that Moses damned," Tyro mused. Then he chuckled and added, "But Alan, he said something to me so simple, but so brilliant in its clarity. He told me that I was better than Moses. Yes, really. Through Moses came the commandment that we should love God with all our heart, soul, and strength, but through Jesus, he reminded me, came the commandment to love our neighbour as ourselves."

With these words, Tyro finished his musing, looked up, and focused again on Jeffrey. "I came here this evening because I needed to say something to you, face-to-face. That's why I did not send you any message, so you didn't try to avoid me. I need to say this face-to-face so you know it's true. It is this: I now understand about you and Arthur. I cannot accept it, but it no longer angers me, or shames me, to think about it. We both loved Arthur in our own way. That is the thing I came to tell you. I no longer bear hatred because you are a homosexual."

"Well, that is good news," Jeffrey said quietly, acutely aware of Anna staring at him.

Anna turned to Tyro. "Aren't you overlooking someone?" she asked. "Me, for example?"

"And a few others," Jeffrey muttered, not looking up at her but thankful for her intervention.

"I am not overlooking Jeffrey and my brother," Tyro replied emphatically. "That is something you two may wish to discuss later."

"And what about the letters you wrote to the university authorities? Have you done anything about them?"

"I think you stole my brother's work, but I may be wrong," Tyro conceded. "I have given the evidence to the university to decide. Did you kill him? How can I tell? I saw his wounds, and yet, now my hatred is gone. I don't see you as a murderer. Perhaps more conversations with Reverend Mills will help me to decide."

Anna's brain had been focused for the past few seconds on the startling revelation that Jeffrey and Arthur had been lovers. Unanswered questions were buzzing through her mind. She was dying to know what else Tyro had up his sleeve. Jeffrey seemed lost for words.

"Darling, aren't you going to say something?" she prompted him.

"So what have the police said?" Jeffrey asked.

"The police? What do you mean, the police?"

"When we met, you said you were informing the university authorities and the Ugandan police."

"The police? Did I really threaten you with the police?" Tyro smiled. "Jeff, if I went to the police with the story of a suspicious death, they would arrest me long before they arrested you. I wouldn't send the police a Christmas card."

This seemed to Jeffrey and Anna, at that moment, the best joke they had heard, and the three of them laughed together.

Curiosity was tugging Jeffrey's sleeve. How had Tyro discovered Arthur's paper? A friend in the university had come across it by chance, he said, and sent it to him, not realising its full implications. Then Jeffrey asked how he had become so rich, and Tyro told him about the money to be made on the black market in Central Africa; about learning to fly to move the contraband; about inheriting the plane when its owner fled the country; about the two brothers who entered into business with him and died together in a car accident that left him in sole control, and so on.

"JAC even has an airship," Jeffrey added, sounding impressed.

"Ah, so you have been doing some research on me," Tyro said, sounding pleased. "Yes, we have an airship, a prototype from a bankrupt Canadian company that hoped to sell them for Arctic oil exploration. I bought it for the price of scrap. It can fly long distances and drop and pick up cargo where a plane can't land."

Useful for poachers and smuggling, Anna thought.

Jeffrey was thinking in a different direction. "So it could fly in cold air?"

"Yes," Tyro replied cautiously. This was the moment to hook the fish.

"How would you like to provide the air support for a three-month mission to Antarctica?"

"Why would I want to do that?" Tyro asked.

Jeffrey had his answer ready. "In honour of Arthur," he said, his voice impassioned with zeal. The fish was hooked. Quickly, he continued, "This project represents the culmination of Arthur's research. At least think about it. Your support is just what I've been hoping for. It's like you've been sent to us."

Tyro shifted uncomfortably at this last remark. "It will cost you a lot of money. Do you have that?" he asked.

"I'm sure we can pay for what we need," Jeffrey replied. "I'll put you in touch with a man called Gary Murdoch. You'll like him. He's a pilot, like yourself. He's in charge of logistics. He'll make a direct appeal to our investors. Say you'll do it."

"I'm always open to money," Tyro said. "If the money's right, I'll do it."

Tyro should have felt elated, but he didn't. He waited while Jeffrey wrote down some contact details for Gary. He felt Anna's watchful eyes on him and sensed her wariness, so he avoided her gaze, looking at his fingernails and wondering what path he had set himself on.

"I must go now," Tyro said.

He was tempted to stay longer, to tell Jeffrey of the danger he was in, but to do so now would be to put his own life in danger. He had accepted this man's hospitality, acted as a friend, but was betraying him even as he did so. This was not better than Moses; this was worse than Judas. The Angels were closing in on Jeffrey, ready to dispossess him of his project and his reputation, and he, Tyro, was watching it happen.

As Tyro stepped out of the door and turned to take his final leave, Jeffrey felt moved to throw a rope of friendship. "Tyro, I want you to know that not a day passes without me thinking of Arthur. One day, the dream we shared will come to pass, and he will be properly remembered. I'll make sure of that."

To Jeffrey's disappointment, Tyro looked at him but said nothing in return. Then he turned and walked away, leaving Jeffrey to go back to Anna.

"I'm glad he's gone. I don't trust him," she remarked, as he came to sit down again beside her on the sofa. "Now what about you?" she asked, nudging him, clearly amused.

"I'm not gay," he muttered.

"I know that better than anyone, my love," she said. "But are you bisexual?"

"Stop it, Anna," he begged. "Please just stop it before you ruin everything."

"I mean it, my sweet. I'm not laughing at you. You had a love affair with a man. You can't deny it to me. You have to face up to what has happened. I'll love you for it, I promise."

"Will you?" he asked.

"Yes. It's such a relief. Don't you see? The two of us, facing up to who we are and who we've been. We have nothing to hide from each other. I understand your feelings."

Now that his fear of rejection had eased, he realised that she was being totally genuine. She was still with him.

"You're about the only person who could, if that's the case," he replied.

"We are so close, you and me. I told you: I am meant to be with you, to love you and protect you, while you do amazing things."

Anna snuggled up against him and pulled his arm across her. They sat like that for a while, saying nothing, but thinking hard, and an awesome certainty came to Anna that she knew what his next words would be, and she did not know how to respond.

"Anna, whatever I've been in the past, I'm different now. I never thought I would ask this of anyone, but life without you seems impossible. So will you marry me?" Jeffrey could hardly believe that he had just uttered these words.

"Jeffrey, darling, I can't—" Anna began gently but was interrupted.

"Oh God. I'm so sorry, Anna. I shouldn't have asked that. I'm so sorry. I understand, after what you've just heard."

Jeffrey started to get up, embarrassed, but as quick as a cat, she gripped his shoulder and forced him back into the sofa. He looked at her, perplexed, as she fixed him with her eyes.

"Jeffrey Harvey, shut up and listen," Anna said firmly. "I can't give you children. I have no womb. I have no ovaries. I lost them to cancer." Seeing that Jeffrey was fully focused, open-mouthed, and not going anywhere, she settled back on the sofa and took both his hands. "I told you about the battle with my father. As soon as I turned sixteen, he threw me out of the house. I became the tart of a much older man, for my own protection. But I got a virus from him."

"HIV?"

"HPV, a virus that affects the neck of the womb. It causes cancer, if you're unlucky, and I was. I was careless. By the time I got symptoms and went to the doctor, it was all too late. They thought I would die. But here I am, still alive, six years later."

Jeffrey was appalled at the news. "But where's the scar? Surely there should be a big scar on your abdomen."

She looked down, demurely, letting her hair fall forward, framing her face, in a way she knew enticed him. "There are two small dots near my bikini line, but the womb came out from down below."

"Oh," he gasped, realising that he had asked for more information than he really wanted to know. "But now that it's done, it's all over. Right? No kids but no cancer – that's the deal?"

"I'm still here. That's the deal," she replied, glancing at him lovingly.

"I still want to marry you," he said, after a moment's pause, but the tone of his voice had changed.

"No, you don't. Don't pretend. We both need time to think," she replied. "There's no hurry. I'm not going anywhere. I want to live with you and go to Antarctica with you, but right now, I just want to go to bed with you. Would you settle for that?"

"You just say when you're ready," he whispered, keeping his confusion to himself.

"Mike, do you have a moment?"

Professor Mike Taylor looked up to see Steven McPherson standing in the doorway, obviously very keen to speak to him. "Yes, I think so. What's on your mind?" he asked affably.

Steven came rapidly over to his desk and placed a sheet of paper in front of him. "You recall that strange business with Professor Harvey that I brought to your attention, and you asked me to look into?"

Mike was instantly attentive. "Yes, of course: the Case of the Curious Dossier, as sent by the brother of one of our graduates. What have you found out?"

"Regarding the published paper in question, there still isn't much news, but there's some mystery about Professor Harvey, himself."

"That doesn't surprise me in the least," Mike muttered.

"During correspondence with Makerere University, I noticed they referred to Harvey as a visiting professor."

"Well, that's what he is: a visiting professor in eco-systemic psychology."

"Yes, but he's that in Uganda as well. I checked. He's a visiting professor there."

"But he's a visiting professor here," Mike said, perplexed. 'If he's a visiting professor there, and a visiting professor here, where has he actually attained academic status?"

"Exactly," Steven said. "I'm trying to find out more. He's what you might call a virtual professor. He's achieved professorial recognition here with about as much solidarity as the Cheshire cat."

"The harder you look, the less you see. That's a good analogy," Mike agreed, then grimaced hopelessly and rubbed his brow. "He seems a nice man when you meet him, but you can never pin him down. I had nothing to do with his appointment, I hasten to add. That was Jake Aspel, my predecessor. He and Harvey seemed to get on especially well."

"I never really got to know him," Steven commented diffidently. "I never quite know what he's doing."

"That's my point. He plays his part, in a way, but I can't really link him with any particular aspect of the university's life. There's something detached about him. He's very convincing at the time you talk to him, and then, about five minutes later, you feel robbed in some way. Does anyone else know about this?"

"No, I don't think so."

"Well, keep it like that. This could be very damaging for the university – and me. Find out what you can about him. We are sure about his academic credentials at least, aren't we? We're not harbouring a complete impostor?"

"If he's plagiarised other people's work in the past, as these documents contend, we can't even be sure of that."

Mike grimaced again. "This has the makings of a monumental scandal," he said. "You're going to have to be very careful. We need to know about him and this enterprise he's rumoured to be on, but if you go digging round too obviously, you're bound to stir interest in why you're doing it. Perhaps you could get somebody you trust to help you."

Steven looked doubtful for a moment, and then a thought hit him. "Perhaps I can," he replied, and Mike looked at him with surprise. "Do you know Maggie Robinson, by any chance?"

Mike thought for a moment. "Yes, I think I do. She's a botanist, isn't she?"

"No," Steven said, "a psychologist, but no matter. I bumped into her in the street on Saturday and found out that she's come to live quite close to me, because her relationship has broken up. It was a same-sex affair with a Norwegian woman, a personal trainer, Anna Jensen. Anna recently left her for a man – a certain man."

"Such things happen. Oh, hold on. You're not going to tell me it's Jeffrey Harvey, are you?" Mike asked.

"Well guessed," Steven said.

Mike whooped in joy, and his face lit up. "What a scoundrel," he exclaimed, with a hint of admiration in his voice.

"The point is that Maggie is still on good terms with her ex, apparently, and I think she might well be prepared to find out a few things for us."

The sun was now shining on Mike's rainy day of problems; it had transformed into an exciting rainbow of subterfuge, espionage, romance, and intrigue, and he loved it.

"Excellent. She sounds ideal. If you think you can get her to help without giving anything away, you should do so. The more information I have to present to the Academic Board, the better, but only when the time comes, and that's not yet."

"I'll sound her out. In the meantime, what do you want me to do with this email?"

"Placate Makerere. Tell them that we have sorted out the misunderstanding. I'm sure you can think of the right words." Mike sat back contentedly. "I don't know, Steven; *he's* a virtual professor with a life full of man-eating crocodiles, mystery ships, and shady lovers, and *I'm* a bona fide professor with a desk-load of petty admin. Which of us would you rather be?"

"You, Mike," Steven said; his envy of Jeffrey ate at his soul.

Hundreds of workers were moving along the walkways or were clustered in groups along the internal ironwork of the ship's hull. The dim gleam coming from the far reaches of the bows was emblazoned with the dancing sparks of metal-cutting saws and the fearsome glow of acetylene torches and arc-welders. Arnesh was standing under one of the lamps, where the lights were brightest, the huge cavern stretching away from him. Awed by the sight and the pounding sound that came from all around, he moved to where he could hear himself speak and called Raja.

"Boss," he yelled into his phone. "You must come."

Raja had to move the phone quickly from his ear. "Arnesh, my friend, don't shout, don't shout," he laughed. "Now, what is this you are saying?"

"The *Moringa*. I have found a place in the hull where you can feel the immensity of creation. It is magnificent. You must come today to feel it."

"All right," Raja said, capturing the enthusiasm in Arnesh's voice. "I'll come, but they are all to keep working."

Arnesh returned to the hull and gave instructions to his foremen. About ten minutes later, Raja appeared with the new deputy finance director and the members of the design team. Arnesh handed them earmuffs and guided them into the ship. In an instant, their expressions changed from interest to amazement, even alarm. They continued to stare in every direction as Arnesh guided them to the spot where he had been standing. He saw the smiles of wonderment, most satisfying on Raja's face, and knew he had been right to make his call. After a couple of minutes, Raja caught Arnesh's eye, and he led them away, into the sun again.

"Truly magnificent," Raja said approvingly. "Only the eye can do justice to such sights. A camera cannot capture it all."

"Well said, boss," Arnesh said.

"It's you, Arnesh," Raja said. "It's your influence. You are turning us all into poets and artists."

The designers laughed. The deputy finance director merely smiled and muttered something to Raja, who shrugged and put his hand on Arnesh's shoulder.

"Now, my friend, back to business. My colleagues and I were having a meeting when you called, and if you had not phoned me, I was about to call you. We have a further load to put on your shoulders."

"To do with the *Moringa*?"

"Of course," said Raja. "It is this. I require you to find room for an airship: a forty-three-metre-long airship."

Just for a moment, a look of astonishment came over Arnesh's face, and then his smile returned.

"Boss, the *Moringa* is such a beautiful ship; it will not only have an airship, but I will find room for the space shuttle launchpad as well, and then you won't even need to ask me."

Raja laughed. "There is no need for that. They have not asked for a space shuttle. I had my doubts, but you have reassured me. Can I tell them the airship is possible?"

"I will need the specifications, of course. I doubt we shall find room below deck, but there is plenty of space on deck." Arnesh thought a moment and then added hastily, "A change like this will reduce the time for sea trials. I will need to be with the ship when she sails, to see that she behaves herself."

"She better behave herself. I have promised my friend, Jeffrey Harvey, that she will do so. I warn you: If she sinks, you better go down with her. Don't come floating back here, expecting your job back."

"She will float, boss, but we have modernised her steering gear, as you know, and that we shall have to check."

"Very well. Pick the necessary men to go with you. They will be away from their families for over two months, and Professor Harvey has now asked that they not only look after the ship but are prepared to help with setting up the ice-harvester machines. They may even have to walk on the iceberg. Do you think you will find volunteers for such work?"

"Boss, if I put it to the men, as you have said it to me, you will have to ask for volunteers to stay behind. They will all want to come."

"You can have five men."

"Oh boss," Arnesh reasoned with him. "We are Indian. At least let me have enough for a cricket team."

"All right, you can have ten men; you are the team captain, so that makes eleven."

"I will take twelve men," Arnesh said, adding, before Raja could remonstrate, "All good cricket teams have a twelfth man, and I am the team manager."

Raja shook his head, content to have negotiated with his excellent subordinate the number they had both had in mind. "Sort it out. You always do," he said.

Then he walked away with his business secretary, leaving the design team to work out the altered conformation of the *Moringa* and with other specifications from the new deputy finance director, which were to be undertaken at the same time.

Raja texted Jeffrey: "Support team as agreed. Airship acceptable."

Anna was accustomed to sleeping in stages when she shared a bed with Jeffrey. She made a point of staying awake until he had drifted off, and she was quickly roused by any changes in his movements that meant he was awake. She would lie very still to see whether she was needed. If not, she would stay quiet in the darkness as he muttered to himself. If he seemed truly restless, then she would glide her body against him, so that he knew she was conscious, and leave the rest to him. If he needed to talk, she would listen; if he needed sex, she would encourage him. If he just needed her company in the stillness, she would take his hand. At the moment, he was awake and silent. Gently, she reached for his hand.

"Did I wake you?" he whispered.

She moved close beside him and said, "Your body movements change when you are up, and that wakes me. I like it when you are awake."

"I suppose that's something else you learnt in the Norwegian army."

"What?"

"Detecting whether your enemy is asleep by checking his body movements."

He sniggered at his own joke. Seductively, she caressed his earlobe with her mouth but then bit it sharply.

"Ouch! Stop it," he grumbled. "What did you do that for?"

"To remind you that you should never tease Norwegian girlfriends at three o'clock in the morning, when their sense of humour is at its lowest."

He rolled towards her and kissed her neck and throat, but he was not in an aroused state, so she did not flirt further.

"What woke you?" she asked tenderly.

He sighed and replied, "I've got to find a way out. The whole thing's madness."

Anna kissed where previously she had bitten and laid her head on his chest. "My darling, what do you mean?" she asked.

"The whole Moringa project is madness. It's a fantasy that's got completely out of hand."

Anna raised herself, perplexed. "What do you mean? Wait; I'm going to the bathroom, then you must tell me."

She disappeared, quickly dabbed her face with cold water, brushed her hair, and picked a long tee-shirt from off a shelf before returning to bed. She propped herself on pillows and pulled him to her, his head resting on her lap, and his arm round the top of her thighs.

"My sweet," she continued from where she had left off, "what can possibly have disturbed you like this?"

"I was talking to Steve McPherson yesterday afternoon, and he ran rings round me."

Anna scoffed at the sound of the name. "That introvert? What does he know about the Moringa project?"

"Nothing, specifically, but I saw him in college yesterday. I got the feeling that it wasn't coincidence. We went and had coffee together, and indirectly, without mentioning the Moringa project by name, he rubbished it."

"So indirectly, you put him right, I should think."

"No," Jeffrey said, sitting up, agitated. "No, you see, that's the point. I couldn't. He's got a background in economics. I don't have the detailed figures in my head that he does. He has all sorts of equations and figures to do with global commodities and environmental sustainability and ... I don't know what else. The very fact that he raised the subject made me realise that he knows a lot more than he's been letting on."

Anna stroked his face. "Jeffrey, you don't need such figures. People only need figures like that when they have nothing else. They produce figures to support their arguments. Did he mention any figures that support the project? Of course not. He envies you. You don't need figures like that. You have inspiration. You see the big picture. He has no such gifts."

"But I couldn't tell you whether it makes economic sense. He could, and apparently, it doesn't."

Anna looked at him, perplexed, not knowing quite how far to take this conversation at half past three in the morning; she relied on the calming effect of her hand on his cheek to retain some control of the situation.

"The Moringa project was never about economics," she said gently. "It has always been about making the best use of the earth's resources and saving lives. Antarctica's loss is Africa's gain – you once said those very words to me – and despite all the Steven McPhersons of the world, you have never lost sight of your goal. I don't understand why you suddenly doubt yourself now. You know it's financially possible. That's all it needs to be."

"But if he's right, how is it that we have the finance? Our investors are experts."

"And he's not. I don't see the problem," she responded firmly.

Jeffrey thought about that for a moment. Then he continued, more calmly, "It was the whole tone of the conversation. In the past, I always had the feeling that he was envious of me, as you say. Yesterday, I got the feeling that he was gloating – almost pitying me. I'm worried that he's about to do something which will bring down the whole project, and me with it."

"He can't bring down the project. The university doesn't have any financial or scientific involvement. The worst he can do is produce figures, like he's done."

"No, that's not the worst," Jeffrey replied, morosely.

"Oh, I give up." Anna sighed and removed her tee-shirt in a deliberatively provocative manner. "I'm going back to sleep. You can curl up next to me if you want."

The offer was too tempting, and Jeffrey lay down as if welded to her from chest to thighs. "Perhaps I ought—" he started.

"Shush," she said unsympathetically. "Think where you are, count your blessings, and go to sleep."

He kissed her gratefully and drifted back to sleep. Anna listened to his steady breathing, worked out a suitable action plan, and with her life in good order, fell asleep herself.

Saturday: Anna was up and dressed and on the telephone to David by eight o'clock, while Jeffrey was still asleep.

She had thought so deeply about the matter that she disregarded the need to give David time to adjust his thought processes to her own. David was still in his pyjamas and dressing gown, contemplating the pleasures of a lazy morning and a leisurely breakfast in the conservatory with Jacqueline, when he picked up the phone and was instantly assailed by Anna.

"This is Anna, Anna Jensen. Jeffrey was very restless last night. I need you to speak to him. It will make him feel much better."

"Good morning, Anna. Nice to hear you so early," David replied, caught off guard by Anna's assault on his senses.

Anna calmed down and told David something of Jeffrey's lost confidence, and David found himself adopting the role of a counsellor.

"Well, he's like an actor waiting to go on stage," he said. "It's nothing to worry about. Wait until he wakes up, then you and he come round here about eleven o'clock, and we can go and have a look at the new ice harvester. Good idea, hey? I'll have a word with Roly Muller, who designed it. We've been testing it on the estate, so Jeffrey can see it in action. There's no need to mention what you've just told me. I'm sure he'll be back to his normal self. Splendid. See you later; cheerio." He put down the phone and picked up the newspaper.

"You've perked up," Jaqueline commented nonchalantly, sipping at her tea as she watched him with amusement. "What is it about middle-aged men that they go virile when a young woman speaks to them?"

"I'm always virile. I'm every bit as virile as Jeffrey," David protested. "I warn you: You doubt my virility at your peril." He vigorously snapped open the newspaper.

Jacqueline put down her cup and casually loosened the belt of her dressing-gown. "Oh, be your age, darling. What virility?" she demanded and made as if to get up from her chair, only to find herself in a clinch on the sofa and then, still laughing, on the floor, in a tussle in which honours were even until she suddenly did submit, and they indulged in marital intimacy that would have shocked the children, leaving paper strewn all over the conservatory and both of them very dishevelled on the rug.

Of course, by the time Anna and Jeffrey arrived, David, Jacqueline, and the house were all looking so respectable that they would never have guessed that such a conventional couple behaved like that.

David managed to seem pleasantly surprised about how well things were going, and Jacqueline joined in the morale-boosting exercise in a very convincing fashion. Despite her reservations about Jeffrey's moral character, she was impressed by how well he was behaving towards Anna and realised, very quickly, that David had been wrong to depict Anna as just another affair. Jeffrey was, at last, in love.

Jeffrey had seemed subdued when he arrived, and David understood why Anna had been concerned, but just as he predicted, Jeffrey became reanimated at the prospect of seeing the harvester in action. Jacqueline, now intrigued by Anna, decided to join them, so after morning refreshments of tea and coffee, all four climbed into David's Range Rover and headed along the tracks of the Emmerson estate to a long shed, tucked away in a copse. On the way, they passed a muck-spreader in action, a great jet of slurry shooting out some twenty to thirty metres over the ground.

"Take note, Jeffrey," David said. "That's one of our models. The harvester was based on that machine."

Jeffrey grimaced.

David drove to the back of the shed, where there was a concrete apron, on which stood a dark green tub, about the size of a minibus, with a gun barrel mounted off centre at the head end and a tail of four slender hoses, each ending in a shiny metallic device about the size of a lawn mower head or a vacuum cleaner. Two of these shiny heads lay on the concrete, while two had been placed on an ice rink about ten metres square, which had been wheeled into place by a big tractor that was parked nearby. The driver and another man were watching their approach.

"There's Roland," David said, "with Frank on the tractor. You haven't met Roland yet, have you, Jeffrey? This is excellent. We can get straight on with the demonstration."

Jeffrey knew that Roland was the main designer of the harvesters, but his attention was fixed wholly on the machine itself. Anna discreetly took his hand in hers and gave a reassuring squeeze. They all stepped briskly out and strode over to the small ice rink.

"They look like snakes with big heads," Anna remarked, pointing at the hoses.

"We call this machine a hydra. Do you know what the hydra was in Greek mythology?" Jeffrey asked her, without taking his gaze away from the contraption.

"No, I learnt Norse mythology, not Greek mythology." She tugged playfully at his arm. "So tell me: What was the hydra?"

"A monster with several heads, each of which acted independently of the others."

"I see. So this is your monster, and these are its heads. And do they all act independently of each other?"

"Here's the man to tell you," David interjected. "Jeffrey, this is Dr Roland Muller. Roly, meet Professor Harvey."

Anna saw that Roland was looking at Jeffrey with zeal, bordering on adulation.

"Herr Professor, it is a great honour to meet you at last. I can't tell you how lucky I feel to be a part of your venture."

"David's told me a lot about you, Roland," Jeffrey said, exaggerating. "I'm keen to see for myself what you've achieved."

He felt guilty not knowing more about the man. He vaguely remembered David saying that he was from East Germany, studied in Heidelberg, and came to David's attention as a postgraduate in Cambridge. But Jeffrey's interest in the harvester was all the reward Roland needed at the moment.

"Yes, yes, of course," Roland replied with nervous enthusiasm, but remembering his manners, he turned first to Anna and said, "Mrs Harvey, it's a pleasure to meet you too."

"Perhaps one day," David intervened quickly, as Anna blushed. "Come on, Jeffrey. You go ahead, Roly, and get started before the ice melts." Pushing Roland to go on ahead and following on with Jeffrey, he strode over to the tractor and climbed onto one of the big rear tyres, indicating that Jeffrey should do the same.

Jacqueline moved up beside Anna. "I'd stay here if I were you," she muttered. "I've seen this before, and you get just as good a view here."

Then she added, "Roly is a better engineer than he is a diplomat, you'll be glad to know."

The two women shared a smile of understanding.

"He meant no harm, I'm sure," Anna replied. "Actually, he called Jeffrey 'Herr Professor,' and that was just what he needed. He responds well to hero worship."

Jacqueline was impressed by Anna's worldly wisdom. "If I'm honest, I'm not sure I'd wish Jeffrey on any woman," she said gently. "But you seem to know what you're doing where he's concerned. Good luck, is all I can say."

At that moment, David called out, "Jackie, Anna! It's about to start."

A second later, lights lit up on the two heads on the ice rink, and they began to move, accompanied by a rasping noise and a hum. They were moving slowly over the rink in an orderly fashion, while the hoses connecting them to the body stretched out or collapsed back.

David started shouting, "Look! See how quickly the ice is disappearing? Do you notice? The heads are robots. They never touch, let alone collide. It's brilliant engineering. Brilliant. They don't even touch the sides. Do you see that? They can identify walls; they can identify drops. They could be on the edge of a precipice but won't go over it. Left to themselves, they just carry on working. Jackie! Jackie! Go and stand in the middle."

"Why me?" Jackie shouted with some indignation.

"Because you've got boots on," he called back.

"He could just as well do it himself," Jacqueline protested to Anna as she started to climb onto the ice.

"I'll do it with you," Anna offered, in a show of solidarity.

"Just be careful. It's slippery."

"Why are we doing this?"

"You'll see. Walk slowly into the middle."

The hoses snaked like anacondas, but while the pipes might stroke against their legs, the heads always veered away and then resumed their straight line.

"Oh, this is horrible. You pigs," Anna exclaimed to the four men, who were laughing at her and Jacqueline. And in that happy moment, it was Jeffrey's laughter that made it all worthwhile for her.

"But do you see?" David said, oblivious to anything beyond his demonstration. "The heads are so sensitive, they can even avoid a woman's legs on the move. There they are, just eating up the ice. Now for the next stage. This is the show-stopper."

Jeffrey leapt down from the tractor and strode over to help Anna clamber back over the rink onto firm ground, the proffering and accepting of that help having far more to do with mystical ritual than physical necessity.

As Anna leant against Jeffrey, Jacqueline gingerly stepped over the rim, unassisted, calling after David, "Don't mind me!"

She almost slipped over, and Jeffrey quickly offered his free arm for support.

"Come on, Jackie," David retorted cheerfully. "Jeffrey's got his hands full already."

"Ooh, he's going to get such a thump in the eye soon," Jacqueline mumbled crossly. Then she became aware of her grip on Jeffrey's arm. "It's a long time since I've let you get this close to me, Jeffrey. It must be Anna's influence."

She gave a wink of support to Anna, and they walked up to join David and Roland, closer to the harvester.

Roland held a radio-control unit in his hands, and Jeffrey whispered to Anna, "Look out for the toy helicopter," which made her giggle.

"Right, I am ready," Roland announced excitedly.

"Good. Good," David said, equally animated. "Now, Jeffrey, choose a target. It can be anything you like up, to a hundred metres away."

"All right, then I'll choose that oak tree by the fence."

"I knew you'd choose that," Roland announced. "Too easy. I'll show you." He pressed a button on his console, and a missile of ice, about twenty centimetres long, shot out of the barrel of the harvester and smashed against the oak tree a second or so later.

"Bullseye!" David called out. "Good shot, Roly." He applauded as he turned to look at Jeffrey. "Fantastic, hey? What do you think? Wait. There's more. Roly, give us the full blast."

"Certainly, David. We have enough ice for five seconds."

David explained, "In case any of you haven't worked it out, the heads have scraped up all the ice and fed it back into the body of the harvester, which condenses it into ice shells at just below the melting point. They then feed into the gun's barrel and can be discharged as single shells or as a stream, as Roly will now show us. You might also like to take note of the accuracy of the aiming system. Right, Roly: take it away."

"I've seen this before," Jacqueline whispered quickly to Anna. "I apologise for my husband."

At that moment, the barrel began to elongate and raise up a few degrees, in a way that so mimicked a man's penis that Anna whipped her hand up to her mouth. Suddenly, a white discharge pulsed out of the spout in three quick bursts, each accompanied by a grunt from the harvester.

"Oh!" Anna exclaimed, doubling up with laughter and embarrassment at having given herself away so obviously.

"They don't see it. They just don't see it," Jacqueline said sympathetically.

The ice hit the tree again.

David and Roly turned to each other in triumph, and David congratulated him, before walking back to Jeffrey, Anna, and Jacqueline. "Well what do you think?" he asked.

"Well, it's a bit rude, David," Jeffrey remarked, deliberately making Anna splutter through her nose and look to the ground again.

David took the teasing in good heart. "So Jackie tells me, but only undeveloped minds could possibly think that," he replied grandly.

"Presumably, when this is all up and running, there will be a hose connected to the barrel to take the ice, or slush, to the tanker."

Jeffrey felt that he was stating the obvious, but Roland immediately corrected him.

"We have done away with the hose, Professor. Hoses are too impractical. They are long, heavy, and easily damaged. That is why I have devised the howitzer. It will fire the ice shells in a continuous stream, under electronic guidance."

"You can't open fire on my ship with a bloody howitzer, Roland," Jeffrey said, aghast. "No, I won't hear of it. Have some sense. There'll be five or six of these things all firing at once. It'll be a bombardment."

"We thought you might say that, didn't we, Roly?" David laughed. "Put it this way, Jeffrey: we're still working on the collecting system, but it doesn't involve bombarding the *Moringa*, I assure you. There'll be floating reservoirs between the iceberg and the ship. We're getting there."

There was business to discuss and views to be expressed, but the morning had been a success, and to keep it so, Jeffrey warmly thanked Roland for his impressive work in keeping the project alive and on schedule, and then the two couples drove back to the house. Jeffrey and Anna left soon afterwards.

"But if he's right, how is it that we have the finance? Our investors are experts." Jeffrey's anxious question to Anna of the previous night was a lot more perceptive than either of them had appreciated. Stephen McPherson had raised a valid doubt in his mind. Investors do not waste their money on doing good.

Later that afternoon, Cherry Bonner enjoyed the sight of the Grande Époque ferry approaching the jetty, as she looked across Lake Geneva from the third floor balcony of her exquisite hotel suite, enjoying the sun of early July, which was bathing Lausanne in heat. It pleased her so much. The suite's living room was a luxurious combination of nineteenth-century elegance and twenty-first-century interior design, which went so well with the grandeur of the building itself. Inside the room, her partners, her fellow Angels, were lounging at ease and swapping anecdotes, while Jean-Pierre busied himself with papers and a laptop at an ornate ormolu table. Her late husband had founded the Clerkenwell Angels, best described, I suppose, as investors without sentiment, and when he died, she took control, building an organisation on their lack of principles, to their considerable profit.

They had convened in Lausanne to discuss a specific issue face-to-face. Their heroin interests were in crisis. The imminent departure of the Americans and their allies from Afghanistan meant that the poppy fields, and the factories they supplied, were under threat of takeover by the Taliban. They were undecided whether to pull out of their interests or to stay; whether to continue to hoard heroin in the region or to try to move it. Either option seemed hazardous and carried the risk that a trail of clues could lead to their doors. Then Jean-Pierre had a stroke of luck: A Swiss missionary friend of his father asked for help to raise money for a project to bring Antarctic water to the drought-stricken territories of East Africa in a giant tanker. The tanker was to set sail from India, pick up water in Antarctica, then head for Mombasa. Jean-Pierre realised that if they could take control of the ship, it would be the perfect cover for spiriting away heroin, leaving no trail. Cherry was delighted. She tasked an American partner, Duke Dukakis, with the mission, Jean-Pierre to help. This day in Lausanne was the moment to convince the others that the scheme could work.

Cherry returned to the sofa and brought the meeting to order, saying, "And now, finally, to the Moringa project itself, where my sources tell me there have been some interesting developments. One might call it the cherry on the cake of our investments," it was a bit childish, but it kept the meeting lively. "Jean-Pierre, would you explain?"

Jean-Pierre was a cultured, elegant man who could have responded eloquently to her request in any of five languages. He was in his early thirties, a man of Lausanne, born, raised, and trained there, and he exuded gracious arrogance as a natural part of his being. Jean-Pierre was not an Angel and was careful to make that known. He was head of the secretariat and wielded more influence over Cherry than all of them.

He thanked Cherry for the opportunity to speak and then gave the first word to Dukakis. What a contrast. There was nothing gracious or elegant about Duke. He was shorter, and square and powerful. He reached calmly into the bowl of boiled sweets, as he had the habit of doing, unwrapped one, and put it in his mouth, then addressed himself to business:

"You'll all recall that Professor Jeffrey Harvey is a liability to us, and he doesn't know shit about running a project," he began. "He's reliant on one of his team, named Gary Murdoch. The professor doesn't care about money, so he can't be bought. Murdoch is our chosen leader for this project. His strength is his risk management. His weakness is gambling. He likes the good things in life. So we set about getting Gary on our side. It wasn't that hard.

"We have all the evidence we need to prove that Murdoch was gambling with money embezzled from the funds we made available for the Moringa project. We filmed him in action at the gaming tables, in Vegas, and had him apprehended by some very persuasive guys in dark suits. We tried to grab his girlfriend too, but she got away. No matter; we got Murdoch. I won't go into details, but I spoke to him personally.

"The long and the short of it is that he's now one of us. He has agreed to become the leader of the Moringa project in place of Professor Harvey. He will do as we say. He will work with the ship's captain, Ernst Brage, to see that our needs are met. In return, we forget the embezzlement; we make him rich. He liked that offer very much. If he gives the game away, or tries to, we kill him. He knows that too. I told him if he didn't want to get involved, he could walk out the door and be arrested for embezzlement.

He chose to stay. He's ours. There are risks for us, sure, but I don't think we need worry. He'll deliver."

"What about the girlfriend you mentioned?" Cherry asked.

"Some lawyer friend turned up at the airport before we could do anything," Duke explained with a shrug. "She was taken to a secret place and then flew to England. She's a British citizen, but that's about all we know. Gary is crazy about her. He won't do anything to risk her. She's not part of the project, anyway."

"So what happens now?" Cherry put to him.

"We're letting him go, just as soon as we have a flight to London arranged. He will get his phone back at the departure gate."

Duke was quite reliable. Cherry congratulated him and asked Jean-Pierre to report on Professor Harvey.

Jean-Pierre smirked with patronizing disdain. "He is in a mess. He has been relying on everyone else's competence to pull the project together. His lack of project management skills has undermined confidence in him, even among his colleagues. When Murdoch makes his move, it will be well received by the other members of the Moringa project."

"That's not enough," Cherry intervened. "I don't want Harvey on the ship. He's too influential. He'll be trouble if we don't remove him. Do we need to arrange an accident?"

"No, in that respect, you've had some luck," Jean-Pierre continued. He always amused Cherry by distancing himself from the activities of the Angels. He was so adorable and useful to her, in so many ways, that she never teased him about it.

"Professor Harvey is in a mess for another reason. He is under investigation for stealing the work of one of his students, who died under mysterious circumstances. The accusation comes from a Ugandan, the brother of the dead student. His name is Tyro Mukasa. He hates Harvey. He even wanted to shoot him. He runs a small air-freight business sustained by black-market trading, so he was easy to bribe. He's working for us, now, to undermine Harvey's reputation. He had a meeting with Harvey, pretended that all was forgiven, and managed to mention that he ran an air transport company. Harvey swallowed the bait. He's engaged Mukasa to provide logistical air support for the project."

Cherry couldn't conceal her delight. "So our takeover is complete, is that right?" she exclaimed, while the other Angels laughed at this twist of fortune.

"Harvey's done for," Jean-Pierre ended. "His reputation is about to be blown apart, so Murdoch can insist that he resigns from the project. And you get control of the ship and its air support."

"So are we all agreed? The *Moringa* will carry our entire stock in one consignment. It's an all-or-nothing move." Cherry looked to the others for confirmation.

"It's brilliant," Duke added. "The Moringa project is the perfect disguise. Our cargo just disappears from sight and reappears all over Europe and the States, wherever we have our outlets."

An air of silent self-satisfaction descended over them.

"Perhaps you might find this a good moment to end the meeting, Madame President," Jean-Pierre suggested, gauging the mood. "May I propose that you end the day and commence the evening?"

"What a good idea," Cherry agreed. "Meeting over, everyone; we reconvene at eight."

The other members took their cue and left her suite, talking among themselves. With two hours of free time in that private suite with its lovely bed, Cherry whispered, "Jean-Pierre, have you a moment?"

He smiled. "For you, Cherry, I always have a moment. What would you like me to do?"

"Go and collect Abi from the station, there's an angel," she replied. Jean-Pierre's surprise was written all over his face. It was the first time that Cherry had invited her daughter to attend a meeting of the Clerkenwell Angels.

Chapter 6

THE WORM IN THE APPLE

Friday, 27 August 2010

Leena suffered vomiting and diarrhoea throughout the night. Maggie did her best to offer sympathetic support but, unable to do anything useful, went to bed. By six o'clock next morning, Maggie was fully dressed, and her backpack and sleeping bag were by the front door. Leena noticed them as she staggered weakly to the bathroom.

Maggie heard her and called through the bathroom door, "Are you all right in there?"

"No, but I'll cope," Leena replied, wishing desperately that Maggie would leave her in peace while she sat on the loo.

"Well, I'll have to be off soon," Maggie continued, oblivious to Leena's embarrassment at having to carry on a conversation while passing diarrhoea and urine without quite knowing which was which.

A wave of nausea passed over her, but there was nothing left to vomit.

"I'll be out in a minute," she muttered, in a voice that pleaded to Maggie to shut up.

"All right. I'll stay until you're out," Maggie replied, as if she were doing Leena a favour. "Don't be long." She walked to the kitchen.

Leena emerged two minutes later and stood in the kitchen doorway. "I shouldn't be in the kitchen. I'll contaminate everything. I'm sorry, but I can't come with you."

"So I gather. I'm sorry you're feeling so rotten, love. I've already told Anna. She sent her best, but we've enough to carry without setting up a stretcher for you."

Leena tottered back to bed as Maggie followed her, chatting sympathetically. "If you're not coming, we can leave the second tent behind and carry just the food packets to last the two of us. To be honest, we'll probably make quicker time."

"I'm sure you will," Leena agreed, lying motionless on the bed, feeling queasy just at the thought of a route march.

Maggie fussed over Leena a moment, straightening the duvet and rug. "Don't worry; it's just gastroenteritis. In twenty-four hours, you'll either be better or dead."

Maggie meant this as a joke, but as Leena was feeling closer to death than health, she failed to see the humour.

The route march was part of the training programme that Anna and Maggie had set themselves in preparation for the voyage. Anna had served three years in the Norwegian army and had been a successful biathlete (shooting and skiing). Maggie was a mountaineer, lean and muscular. Neither of them was as fit now as they had been when they met, but the excitement of the Antarctic challenge had grabbed them both.

Anna had stunned Maggie by asking Leena to join them on the march. Anna had decided that she would like to keep Leena away from Jeffrey, while she was not around to keep watch. Maggie, however, had drawn her own conclusions. She suspected, and hoped, that Anna still did not know her own mind, sexually, and had invited Leena as a chaperone. Leena would definitely not be on the *Moringa* when it sailed, so she had no reason to train for the harsh Antarctic conditions.

Maggie had felt resentment that she would be denied the time alone with Anna, on which her own plans relied. On a whim, she had bought some prawns and had left them, thawed, for three days before serving them. She did not know what subliminal thought had possessed her to behave in this way. She really liked Leena, and even as she served them, she told herself that they were probably all right. She gave the excuse of shellfish allergy to avoid eating them herself.

Leena's digestive system started ejecting all its contents by every means available a few hours later. Maggie, guilt-laden, had her wish, and she and Anna would be trekking over Exmoor on their own over the August bank holiday.

When Anna put the phone down after hearing about Leena's illness, she actually asked Jeffrey whether he would like to come with them. He made a suitably sarcastic comment in declining the invitation and continued downloading apps for his new tablet, while munching some toast. Several weeks had elapsed since his proposal of marriage, and each had much to ponder about the other.

Quietly, he thought to himself, *Three's a crowd. She is who she is.*

Soon afterwards, Maggie and Anna were under way in dismal weather, so typical of an August bank holiday weekend, taking Jeffrey's Land Rover and leaving him with Maggie's Peugeot. The first half-hour passed in rapid-fire conversation, as the two women caught up on each other's news and debated the weather prospects, but the conversation subsided as they progressed round the crowded corridor of the M25. The holiday traffic was as heavy as expected, and Anna almost missed the M4 turnoff, finding herself in the outermost of four lanes of jam-packed, slow-moving traffic, with nobody in a mood to give way.

"You should have moved across earlier, love," Maggie said, sticking her left arm out of the window and desperately signalling left. They crossed two lanes and then squeezed between two long container-lorries and onto the slip road. "Bloody hell."

"Sorry, Maggs, my mind drifted," Anna said. "I've got a guilty conscience."

"Oh yes?" Maggie smiled in anticipation of juicy gossip. "Well, come on, confess it all."

"I told Jeffrey that we'd have to be away for four days, even though I know we can do it in three."

"Well, you're the sneaky one. Why did you do that?" Maggie's hopes were raised. She sensed a real chance to win Anna back but said nothing.

"Because we've got four free days, and we should use them. We need all the training we can get."

"You won't hear me complaining," Maggie said, very pleased at the news.

"Yes, but I'm starting to think about it. That's what I was obsessing about just now. Jeffrey is Jeffrey, and leaving him alone for four days, and Leena on her own as well."

"Oh, I really wouldn't worry about that," Maggie said with a shrug of indifference.

"You've got a guilty secret too. I can tell," Anna exclaimed. "Come on, out with it."

So Maggie told her about the prawns. Anna was shocked and very stern in condemning her.

"You're right, you're absolutely right. I shouldn't have done it, and I'm very sorry," Maggie said contritely.

"I should think so; poor Leena."

"Of course, if Jeffrey does go round to see her, the sight and smell will kill his sex drive for a month."

Anna stayed serious for a second longer and then burst into laughter, and the two women, very content with life, continued on their way.

Maggie knew nothing about Jeffrey's sex drive. He resisted calling Leena by concentrating on the long list of matters demanding his attention, but she kept coming back to his mind as being alone and sick and, maybe, in need of attention. Loneliness crept up on him too, with the thought that Anna would not be around for several days. He let Lucy go home early and then made his way to Maggie's flat. He rang the bell and waited.

Eventually, Leena's voice came on the entry phone: "Who's there?" she asked in a weak whisper.

"Jeffrey."

"I'm in a dreadful state."

"That's why I came round."

"Come up," she said.

Her presence, weak and needing help, aroused all his manliness, initially in an honourable way. He tried to think what Anna would have done in the circumstances. He wanted to call her for advice, so as to involve her in his actions, but then Leena retched and gave a pleading glance in his direction, and Anna became unnecessary as he coped. He gently dabbed Leena's face with cold water and, when she shuffled through to the bathroom, stripped the stained and smelly sheet from the bed and laid a new one – new pillowcase too – so she rested herself back on clean linen with a citrus aroma. After sixteen hellish hours, something at last felt good, and she was no longer lonely. She lay on the fresh sheet, curled up under her duvet, and extended her hand for Jeffrey to hold. First, he gave her a few sips of water and then let her sink back, holding his hand as she drifted into sleep.

When she woke, at about one o' clock in the morning, the sickness had passed. Jeffrey was still beside her but had kicked off his shoes and was lying asleep on top of the duvet. He was still holding her hand protectively. The room was cool, and his face was cold to touch.

"Jeffrey, you'll get sick too, if you're not careful," she whispered endearingly, prodding him gently to rouse him. "At least come under the duvet."

Half-asleep, Jeffrey gratefully complied. The next four hours passed in semi-sleep and semi-arousal, each article of his clothing disappearing in logical sequence, as the bed warmed up and their bodies took control. Leena thought momentarily of Gary, far away and locked up, probably forever. Jeffrey thought momentarily of Anna, undoubtedly asleep in the arms of Maggie. Old feelings returned to them both.

At about five thirty, Leena thought overwhelmingly of how tenderly she felt to Jeffrey, and he could not resist the exquisite temptation of her body any longer. But poised at the gate, he hesitated.

"What's wrong?" she asked.

"No condom," he replied.

"It's all right," she said. "I'm on the pill."

He hesitated a moment more, and then he slipped into her, and she received him. All that followed was wickedly sublime, and he had no reason to leave the flat for the next three days; not even a change of clothes was required.

The expedition, although well-motivated, was a mistake. Maggie was much more in love with Anna than the latter had recognised. She, for her part, was resentful that Maggie had deliberately sabotaged her plans in such a reckless way. Anna's intention had been to leave Jeffrey alone to sort out his problems while she and Maggie took Leena out of harm's way. It would have been sufficient for Leena just to complete the trip while the other two carried the gear. Maggie had ruined all this with her selfishness.

They started walking in the late afternoon and made better-than-expected progress, but that night, in the intimacy of the tent, Maggie made unrestrained advances, and though Anna acquiesced out of past loyalty, her confusion was such that she could not bring herself to participate actively, leading to Maggie displaying shameless exhibitionism to satisfy her needs.

The next morning, neither of them spoke about it (or anything much else). Both women put their disturbed emotional energy into their physical task and, hardly stopping, had reached their planned campsite by mid-afternoon. They walked on for a further three hours before selecting a new campsite. That evening, Saturday, Maggie had been the complete opposite of the evening before, not even proffering a kiss or a hug and falling asleep in the foetal position, a lonely, isolated figure.

Anna could not sleep, tired though she was, and eventually reached out, felt for the long zip of Maggie's sleeping bag, and gently undid it. Maggie did not stir, even though Anna had to tug the zip round her curled thighs. She did not stir even when Anna caressed her buttocks through her pyjamas. She lay still when Anna whispered her name. Anna realised that Maggie was waiting for her to come to her and, this night, did not hold back.

For Maggie, it was erotic relief; for Anna, it was guilty bliss. They hardly slept, rose at first light, and pushed on, each enveloped in their own thoughts, striding out together.

It was just past eight o'clock Sunday morning. David was always glad to wake up and feel Jacqueline beside him, but this morning more so than usual.

"Thank you for last night," he murmured.

"You're welcome," Jacqueline replied, comfortably snuggling herself in David's arms. "You haven't lost your touch."

"You haven't lost your beauty," he said, nuzzling her.

"You once told me I was the sexiest girl in Cambridgeshire," she reminded him, yet again, of one of his clumsier compliments.

"For goodness sake, I was only eighteen," he said in mitigation. "It didn't put you off me."

"Of course not. It made me bloody angry, all the same."

"I haven't forgotten." They both laughed at the memory. "You've always been the most fabulous girl in the world to me, Jackie, you know that."

"I can think of one or two others who have caught your eye."

David hid his twinge of guilt with feigned surprise. "Who?"

"Anna, for example."

"Anna?"

"Yes, Anna. I saw the way you sized her up, when we went with Jeffrey and her to see that blessed ice-gathering machine of yours."

"The hydra, you mean. I didn't size her up – not really. It just seemed sensible to see what sort of a woman Jeffrey had acquired this time."

"What did you think of her?"

It sounded an innocent question, but David knew well enough not to give a straight answer to his wife when discussing a beautiful woman.

A suitable description came to mind: "She's a woman with hair in her armpits."

Jacqueline dissolved in laughter and looked at David with tolerant adoration in her eyes. "You do say the silliest things, but I understand exactly what you mean. He'd be foolish to mess with her."

"I've never seen her armpits, mind you, but metaphorically speaking."

"Metaphorically speaking," Jacqueline agreed, kissing his nose. "And now, metaphorically speaking, it's time to spread your wings, my love. We've got a free day ahead of us, and we shouldn't waste it."

While David's morning was taken up with administrative tasks, Anna and Maggie made such strong progress on their march that by noon, they only had a little over one hour's walking to do to complete the course, nine hours ahead of their schedule.

They sat together by the stream that runs along the Doone Valley, and just for a minute, Maggie thought her world was complete once more.

"Have we earned ourselves a night in a hotel, do you think?" she asked. "I could do with a shower instead of another night under canvas."

"At this rate, we'll be back at the car before one o'clock. That means we could get back to Cambridge by late evening," Anna replied, tightening the straps on her backpack.

"Cambridge! Why ever? We're not expected back until tomorrow evening at the earliest. If a hotel's too expensive, we can stay in a B & B, but we've got a night and a day, possibly two nights, when we're free to be with each other. We're back as a couple, love. Don't let's waste any more time about it."

Maggie smiled encouragingly as she spoke and shuffled her bottom over the grass to hug Anna, but she shrugged off the caress and met Maggie's kiss with her cheek, not her lips.

"I'm sorry, Maggie," Anna said in a firm voice. "It wasn't supposed to be like this."

Maggie instantly stood up and spun away in exasperation. "Oh, for Pete's sake, woman, get yourself sorted out," she shouted.

"Leena was supposed to be with us. If she had been, well …"

Anna found that she could not complete her own sentence. She realised she did not know what effect Leena might have had.

Maggie was unforgiving. She knelt down and, with her face only a few centimetres away from Anna, said contemptuously, "I'm so sorry. I'm so bloody sorry. I'm so bloody sorry that I fucked up your precious plans so you didn't have your Indian nursemaid here to protect you from wicked me, and to stop you doing all those wicked things which you bloody enjoyed, and you bloody well know it."

"I love Jeffrey," Anna said, reciting the words like an incantation to ward off an evil spirit. She was frightened.

Maggie sensed that Anna was in crisis. Still staring into her eyes, but with a softened gaze, she used her right hand to stroke Anna's neck. Anna looked down but did not pull away.

"Phone him, then. Tell him you'll be in his arms tonight." It was said as a challenge, but the anger was gone.

"Later," Anna muttered. "If you've got such a clear conscience, you telephone Leena and ask her if there are any prawns left."

Maggie smiled in spite of herself. "Like you said: later."

With that, the two women swung their backpacks into position and set off, with hardly another word spoken. When they reached the Land Rover, they both knew that they were heading back to Cambridge; Maggie did not even bother to discuss it, as Anna sat in the driving seat and started up the engine.

Halfway through the afternoon, David received a telephone call that surprised him. It was Gary Murdoch on the line: "Hi, David! Guess who?"

"Gary," David greeted him, delighted. "I'd given you up for lost. What the hell's been happening? We thought you'd been arrested by the CIA or something."

"Fucking scary, man," Gary replied happily. "I trebled my stake money one evening in a casino in Vegas, and they put their goons onto me. But it was a case of mistaken identity, and now I'm free. What can I say?"

Gary airbrushed out of the conversation the identity of the men who had really seized him, the hours of interrogation he had endured over the embezzlement of the Moringa project funds, and the contract he had made with Duke Dukakis to avoid going to jail. "Look, David, you and me, we've got to talk, in private. I don't mean over the phone. I mean face-to-face. You're Jeffrey's friend, and I wouldn't do anything to undermine his trust in you, but you and me, we've got to get a handle on what's going on. I'm concerned that Jeffrey hasn't the skills he needs to deliver this project."

"To be honest, I'm concerned too. When will that be possible?"

"There's someone I need to see first: my girl, Leena. I've tried her cell phone, but maybe she had to change her number in the UK. Do you know where I can find her?"

"What do you mean, find her?" David asked, perplexed. "You're not in England, are you?"

"Hell, yes. Landed at Heathrow four hours ago. The immigration guys had a lot of questions, but they let me in. I'm in a hire car now. I should be in Cambridge by eight, but I don't know where to head. Have you any ideas?"

David had no interest in Leena, but he sounded considerate over the telephone. He gave Gary directions to drive to Vicarage Farm and said that, meanwhile, he would make enquiries. Sometime later, he walked into the drawing room, where Jacqueline was browsing on her computer.

"Jackie, guess what? Gary's back in England. You wouldn't happen to know where his girlfriend Leena is staying, would you? He's been trying to contact her."

Jacqueline took a few seconds to absorb what David had said and then replied, "That's surprising news but quite welcome. Anna told me that Leena had taken a room with her friend, Maggie Robinson. I've got Maggie's address, if you give me a moment." She went to her contacts page and read it out.

"You never cease to amaze me," David said, kissing her. "I could phone Gary now. That would please him." With that, he went back to the house telephone in his study.

Gary answered as he drove the hired Jaguar XF. He was making steady progress. "Thanks, David; I owe you. Don't tell her. She's going to be so surprised to see me. I guess I'll stay with her tonight and call you tomorrow. Are you all right with that?"

David was happy to oblige. "Yes, of course. It would be much better to meet tomorrow morning. How about coming here for breakfast, at about nine?"

"Yeah, yeah," Gary agreed eagerly. "I'll see you then."

David felt he had done a good deed and went into the garden to pick some blackberries for his breakfast with Gary in the morning, and then he wandered back to the drawing room. Lucy was now on the sofa with the Sunday newspaper, keeping Jacqueline company.

"Gary's going straight there," he said to Jacqueline.

"Who's going where?" Lucy's antenna picked up conversations even in her sleep, let alone browsing a newspaper.

"Gary Murdoch is back. He's going round to Maggie Robinson's flat to see Leena," Jacqueline explained.

"I hope she's better," Lucy replied, continuing to scan the pages as she spoke.

"What do you mean?" David asked.

"She was ill on Friday. She was supposed to go with Anna and Maggie to Exmoor but was too ill with a tummy bug. Jeffrey went round to see her on Friday afternoon."

Jacqueline turned round to face Lucy, a look of alarm on her face. "So where is Anna now?" she asked.

Lucy glanced up from the newspaper. "In Devon."

"With Maggie Robinson, while Jeffrey and Leena are here," Jacqueline said, finishing Lucy's sentence for her. "Ye gods." Jacqueline's alarm was now evident. "David, phone Jeffrey. It doesn't matter what about. Just call him and find out where he is."

"Why should I disturb him on Sunday evening?"

"Darling, stop being naive. Jeffrey's alone, and Leena's alone. A leopard doesn't change its spots, not that much. We could be right back to where we were a few years ago. He's probably not there, but just check. If he is there, and Gary finds him, he will literally kill him. You know Gary. And if Gary doesn't, then Anna will."

"I'll phone him," Lucy said, partly to stop her parents bickering and partly out of aroused curiosity. "Just voicemail," she said a few seconds later. "That's interesting."

David's misgivings about Jeffrey, that he had been trying to suppress, now flooded his mind. "Jackie, I don't suppose you'd come with me on a drive into Cambridge, would you? We can knock on this Maggie Robinson's door, and if Jeffrey and Leena are there, you'll know better how to handle it than I will."

Some miles away, on the M25, the silence between Anna and Maggie was becoming overpowering. One of them had to say something, yet for mile after mile, neither of them could think what. The songs they both liked had the wrong words for the present circumstances, and they had mutually agreed to have no music rather than the wrong music.

"I'm just not made like you, that's all," Anna mumbled, as she concentrated on her driving.

"You're made exactly like me," Maggie corrected her bitterly.

"Not anymore."

"Are we talking about your sexual preferences or your body?"

"That wasn't a fair thing to say."

Maggie realised she had let her anger get the better of her tongue. "No, you're right. It was a horrible thing to say. I'm sorry," she said contritely. "I'm just a frustrated bitch."

Silence again, apart from the throbbing, guttural engine, and the whine of the wheels, and the hum of the passing traffic.

As they passed Stansted, Maggie tried again. "Does Jeffrey know about your operation?"

"Yes."

"You didn't do the self-condemnation routine again, did you?"

"Why not? It was the truth. I behaved like a tart, and I got what was coming to me," Anna said glumly.

"You weren't a tart, my poor love. You were a victim of your father's brutality to your mother. We've been over this," Maggie responded, desperate to put her arms round her beautiful, damaged friend.

"I sold my body to an older man I had no feelings for," Anna retorted and then continued, more soberly, "And if I'd used condoms, I'd have been fine."

"Don't go over that again," Maggie interjected, recognizing the beginnings of a familiar conversation. "And after all that, Jeffrey still says he loves you?"

"Mmmm, it must mean something, mustn't it?" Anna caught Maggie's eyes, and they smiled. Forgiveness replaced anger.

"He's mad. You're both mad. I ought to stop seeing you again," Maggie threatened and then gasped. "What am I saying? But I should, shouldn't I? Perhaps you better sail without me."

Anna gave Maggie's hand a reassuring squeeze. "Don't be silly. You're coming. The ship's big enough for the three of us."

"It must be enormous, if that's the case," Maggie replied sarcastically, but Anna was unruffled.

"Yes, it is. Just wait till you see her."

Gary was the first to arrive at Maggie's flat. When he pressed the entry phone bell at the front door of the building, a telephone rang in the hall of the flat. Leena, wearing only a tee-shirt and slips, rose from the bed, where she had been reading a magazine, and casually answered it, expecting to send the caller away.

On hearing his voice, her startled cry of "Gary!" came out like a shriek of terror.

The tone of her voice, and the sound of that name, had an instantaneous effect on Jeffrey, who shot, naked, out of the bed and started scrabbling urgently for his clothes, while Leena tried to buy time in making all sorts of cooing expressions of love and yearning down the receiver.

Jeffrey had not worn his trousers in two days and could not find them in his panic. Gary's laughing insistence on being allowed to come in cut into Leena's protestations. Professing her desperate desire to see him – true, but not in these circumstances – Leena bought a few more precious seconds by explaining to Gary that she was unwell after severe food-poisoning, and he must make allowances for her. Signalling to Jeffrey to jump out of the window, she pressed the entry buzzer and put down the telephone.

"Get out," she ordered. "You've got ten seconds."

"I can't find my trousers!"

"Too bad; just go."

She virtually pushed him out of the window onto a tiny balcony, from where he scrambled in the evening light for a drain-pipe and lowered himself past the window below, resting his feet on the narrow ledge above the front door, which Gary had just gone through. While he was balanced there, trouserless, thankful for the semi-darkness, two things happened: First, he heard Gary's whoop of joy as Leena opened the door of the flat to him and he scooped her into his arms; second, David and Jacqueline arrived.

They stood, arm in arm, looking at him, both with broad smiles on their faces, and he could tell they had no appreciation of the gravity of his situation. David was about to call up to him, but Jeffrey made urgent signals for silence; using the drainpipe, he let himself down as far as he could and leapt the last bit to the ground, landing sprawled out at their feet.

He stood up. "This is a miracle," he whispered to them, still aware of the open window above them. "Thank God you're here."

"Thank Jacqueline, more likely," David said. "She's the one who put two and two together." He looked at his disreputable friend with scornful amusement, while shielding him from view.

"It wasn't hard, given the facts," Jacqueline commented. "You haven't changed. You never will."

"Actually, I have changed, but I wouldn't expect you to understand," Jeffrey protested. "But regardless of what you think, please, can you get me away from here?"

"I gather you've heard that Gary's on his way," David said.

"He's already arrived," Jeffrey replied. "No warning."

"Ah, quicker than I thought," David commented, taking Jeffrey by the arm and preparing to guide him to the Range Rover. Jeffrey was about to ask David what he meant by that remark, when the last voice he wanted to hear at that moment stopped him, and he spun round, aghast.

"Jeffrey, what the hell are you doing without your trousers?"

"Anna! Not you as well – this isn't possible."

"Hello, Jeffrey," Maggie said sardonically. "Fancy seeing you here."

The two women stood together, looking rough and strong, but Anna was outraged while Maggie was just amused.

"Good evening, Maggie," Jeffrey said.

All eyes turned upwards as an unseen hand snapped shut the window above them. They could see a pair of trousers snagged on the parapet just outside the window, well out of reach.

"A fat lot of good that is," Jeffrey commented in exasperation.

"Don't worry," Maggie said. "I'll get them." She quickly scaled the drainpipe, retrieved the trousers, and sprang lightly down.

"Well, thank you for that, anyway," Jeffrey said as he struggled into them, while his lover and his friends looked on, in a protective circle round him.

"So who is in my flat, may I ask?" Maggie enquired while this was going on.

"Leena and Gary."

David immediately recognized the importance of getting Jeffrey away without being seen. He told Anna to take Jeffrey home and asked Maggie to wait two minutes so they could all clear the scene and then to go in, and say nothing to Gary of what had taken place.

Maggie was quite surprised to find Gary alone in the kitchen, rather than in Leena's room. Gary was surprised by her entrance. Neither exchanged a normal greeting.

"I'm just getting her some water," he explained. "She won't let me into her room. She says she can't let me see it in its present state. She says she's been really sick. Is that right?"

"Oh, dreadfully sick, poor girl," Maggie agreed sympathetically. "I'm not surprised she couldn't let you into her room. She's been flat on her back; all weekend, probably. I blame the prawns. I'm Maggie, by the way. Hello."

Anna spent a sleepless night and was woken early by a stretch of brooding, which darkened her mind until she could no longer think. Jeffrey got up in silence and sat, mute and ashamed, at the breakfast bar in his kitchen; she joined him, unwashed, walking like a zombie. The dam of anger blocking her thoughts burst as she was holding the milk carton, realising she couldn't choose between pouring milk into her coffee or over her cereals. Power flooded back into her being. She slammed the carton down, making Jeffrey stand up in alarm, took two steps to where he was standing, and landed a full-handed slap to the side of his face so hard that it stunned him.

He reeled against the sink as his legs gave way, and he collapsed towards the floor. But he did not fall, because she saved him. Supporting him under his drooping shoulders and helping him to a chair, she stroked his face, tears filling her eyes. After several seconds, the shock passed, and he focused on her, crouching beside him.

"I'm so sorry, Anna." Jeffrey's misery was in every word.

"You're forgiven, darling – until the next time. Then you'll get another one." She was crying now and kissed him on his lips, her cold tears moistening his face. "Now, you must do the same to me. Slap me as I slapped you."

"What?"

"Do it," she demanded urgently. "I need to feel forgiven. I'm just as guilty as you. Now do it. I'll despise you if you don't."

"Are you sure about this?"

"Yes," she said earnestly.

"Oh, very well," he replied, showing no sign of anger and using his hands to stroke her hair back away from her face rather than striking it.

"Don't torture me, just do it," she pleaded.

"I'll do it tonight, I promise," he said quietly, with a smile. "You will present your bare buttocks to me. Of course, other things may happen as well."

Instead of the sexy response he had expected, she shook her head, as if in disbelief. "Jeffrey, don't you think of anything else? What about the ship? What about the iceberg?"

"Why should I think about the *Titanic* at a moment like this?" he tried to joke.

Anna sprang up and said angrily, "For goodness sake, be serious. Do you know what first attracted me to you, Jeffrey? Do you know that? You're good looking, yes, but you were full of mystery and adventure."

Jeffrey stared at her, wondering what was coming next. Anna thought about her next words, wishing her English was better.

"What I hadn't seen was your pathetic side. You can't help yourself. You just do what pleases Jeffrey." She sniffed loudly after that and passed a finger across her nostrils. He handed her a tissue. She said thank you, blew into it, and sat on a stool by the bar. "No one else could make me cry," she mumbled defiantly.

Then she noticed him rubbing his cheek.

"Are you all right?" she asked. "I think I hit you harder than I meant."

"You certainly don't hide your feelings. That's something I've learnt about you," he replied, sombre again.

Anna sighed and said, "It's a wake-up call, my love. You nearly wrecked our lives this weekend, and Gary might have killed you. You have the university breathing down your neck, your academic reputation is on the edge of ruin, and then you make a fool of yourself, standing in the street without your trousers on. Wake up, Jeffrey. I worked so hard to persuade Jacqueline that you'd changed, and now you've undone all that." She sat on his lap and ran her hand through his hair. "I know I'm to blame. I should have told you on our first night that I'm no longer a complete woman. I still seem to be more confused about that than I have admitted to myself, but I've been working so hard to be the person you need."

He was sitting now, hands on his thighs, not touching her, listening to her condemnation, unable to disguise his dejection any longer. "You're the most complete woman I've ever met," he said gently. "It's nobody's fault but mine. Leena was sick and lonely. You were with Maggie. Gary was in prison, or so we thought, and old memories awoke. I'm so sorry. Both she and I knew it was just mutual comfort. It wasn't love. We didn't plan it. We thought nobody else would even know we'd been together."

"Well, you got that one wrong," Anna commented.

"Truly, I'm so sorry," he repeated. "I know it's over between us, you and me, and I'm not going to be so pathetic as to plead with you. I'll just say that I won't ever get over you. What a fool I've been. I just hope we can be friends."

"No," Anna retorted.

"What?" he replied, distraught at the menace in her voice.

"You are not my friend. You are my lover. Don't ever call me your friend again." She took his hands and put them round her. "When you finish at lunchtime, you are going to take me to London in the train. We are going to Hatton Garden, and you are going to buy me an engagement ring – a big one. Then I will forgive you. Do you accept my terms?"

"I can only promise to do my best," he said.

"Me too," she replied. "Do you accept?"

"Who told you about Hatton Garden?"

"Do you accept?" she repeated fiercely.

"I accept."

Anna, as if freed from a ton of despair, clutched herself to him, and they stayed like that, Jeffrey hardly daring to believe his luck.

At last, she released her grip and looked him in the eyes again. "Tonight," she said, "you may punish me just as you described. You must punish me – but after I have the ring."

Having set her conditions to her satisfaction, she presented her mouth for his kiss. He might not be all she had hoped for, but Leena was not going to take her man from her.

Gary had used a few hours of his flight to England to clarify what he saw as his objectives. He ended with a list:

1   Leena
2   Survive
3   Become rich
4   Become head of the Moringa project
5   Oust Jeffrey Harvey

He had counted down the hours until he could call her and hear the surprise in her voice.

He had not been disappointed. Leena's shriek when she heard him say, "Guess who?" was all that he had hoped for; no way was it faked. And the way she had just kept burbling her sweet nothings down the phone, as if he were still in America, when all she had to do was let him in, was really, really cute. It had made his sense of freedom complete.

He had not minded that she just wanted to be held last night. He was tired, and they had both fallen asleep in each other's arms. He was fresher for it, this morning. The jet lag was a bind, but it would wear off, and he wanted to start work right away.

He telephoned David and arrived for breakfast, forty minutes later, at about the time that Jeffrey was having his face slapped by Anna a few miles away.

He quickly managed to find common ground with David, having ascertained from their brief conversation of the day before that the latter was not confident in Jeffrey's management of the project. David soon warmed to Gary's informality and started to reveal the concerns he had been harbouring.

96

"I asked him time and again about how we were being financed," David said. "I never got a clear answer. He never included me in any of the key financial meetings."

After breakfast, they disappeared to David's study, and, over the next three hours, Gary gradually cut Jeffrey out of involvement of all events under David's control. Whenever David used a phrase like, "We should discuss that with Jeffrey" or "That's something Jeffrey will need to know," Gary found a way to remind him how Jeffrey had treated him. Gary showed professional competence in all the work David's team were doing, which contrasted so dramatically with Jeffrey's disinterest in engineering.

They discussed with Roland detailed aspects of the hydras – the ice harvesters – and the inclinometers they would use to gauge the slant on the iceberg and the sonars to detect cracks. Later, they went round the estate, and David showed Gary the moringa plantation.

"By rights, these trees shouldn't be here," David explained. "It's thanks to Jeffrey's research that they flourish in a much wider range of habitat than the original trees." He sighed and added, "Having said which, Jeffrey finds himself in hot water over possible plagiarism, and things don't look too good."

"Yep. Duke Dukakis told me."

"Isn't he one of our backers? You mean they know?" David gasped in consternation at this news.

Gary nodded. "They know all right. I spoke to Dukakis before I left. That's why they want me to take over the management of the project."

"You didn't tell me that," David said, more as a comment than an accusation.

"I wasn't sure how you'd respond," Gary replied. "But they are so worried, they are ready to withdraw their investment."

David was placated.

"I can't blame them losing confidence in Jeffrey," David admitted. "He's been a damn fool; more than that, he now comes across as a dishonest fool. He's not. He's a deeply caring, committed man, but he's eccentric, and he can't help himself doing some stupid things."

As they walked back to the car, Gary prepared his next move. "Do you want to run the project?" he asked, gambling with this question.

David hesitated only a moment before saying, "No. I think you are the right man for the job. You have a grasp of every aspect of it, from the financial aspects to what it will be like to be on the ice. We've got to be careful, though. Jeffrey's going through a worrying time. Losing control of the project could unhinge him. You'll have to discuss it with Raja Johar and Jimmy Moule too. Best to present it in a positive light, as taking a burden off his shoulders at this difficult time."

"I'll look after Jeffrey, don't worry," Gary replied. David's answer had been perfect.

They climbed back into the Range Rover, and Gary continued to ask questions as David drove. "So why do you need to take trees on the ship when you could fly seeds?"

"We're taking both," David explained. "You can't just fly agricultural products where you want. There are all sorts of restrictions. "It takes years to grow mature trees from seeds. We've only got limited stocks. We need to build them up. The young trees we take will be ready much sooner. There's a real commercial advantage if we can just get the patent for the change. Forests in the Sahara, that's Jeffrey's dream, Gary. I'm the pragmatist, but even I'm excited."

Further discussions followed back at Vicarage Farm. David admitted that there were some serious gaps in his risk assessments, but the inventories were meticulous. He enjoyed telling Jacqueline, later, how Gary had expressed his admiration by exclaiming, "Shit, David, you're anal."

"High praise, indeed," Jacqueline had commented, acidly.

The day's work came to an end at about ten thirty at night, after studying satellite images that Gary had brought with him of the iceberg, the size of a small island, where the predicted encounter with the *Moringa* would take place.

"Jeffrey suggested that we should call the iceberg Fortune," Gary muttered.

"I like that name. It's appropriate. Jeffrey's good at that sort of thing," Jacqueline replied.

They all fell into silence, contemplating what confronted them, and it seemed a fitting time to end. Gary felt that he was well placed to take over the project and oust Jeffrey: objectives 4 and 5. It was time objective 1, Leena, was in his grasp too. He said goodbye to Jacqueline and thanked her for her hospitality. He would have to work harder to impress her. David walked him over to his Audi.

After leaving Vicarage Farm, Gary rushed back to Maggie's flat. He was desperate for Leena. He did not care if Maggie heard them through the bedroom wall or not. He did not care if they roused the whole apartment block. Yet, as the previous night, though Leena seemed to respond to his searching hands and moved silkily beside him, she would not let him enter her pelvis but coaxed him until resistance to her moves was impossible, and he came in great convulsive surges over her stomach, and then lay still on top of her, pinning her to the bed.

"Gary, please move, my love, you're crushing me," she pleaded after giving him a few seconds to recover.

"Sorry, honey," he said, now as meek as a puppy. He raised his torso, and they looked down between their bodies together.

"There's no doubting you're an oilman," she commented. "When you come, you come by the gallon."

"I've been waiting for you so long, honey. There's nothing wrong between us, is there?"

"Wrong?" She put incredulity into the word as she reached for the tissues, handing one to him. "Can't you tell how much I love you?"

"Sure, but, you know—"

"My honey," she said, moving to sit astride his tummy and wiping hers gently dry, "I told you, I have been ill. Women get problems when they're ill. It will pass soon, I promise you. I want you so much."

That night, Anna, delighted with the ring being made for her by jewellers in the quirky London lane called Hatton Garden, allowed her punishment to take place from Jeffrey's skilful hands. They went to sleep, each thankful to have found the other. Neither made any reference to forever. They both felt that it was tempting fate. Anna made Jeffrey promise not to disclose their engagement until she had the ring on her finger, and he light-heartedly agreed.

The following day, Gary telephoned Jeffrey to organise a meeting. They were equally keen and looking forward to it. Gary suggested they should involve as many of the Warlocks as possible, and Jeffrey agreed. Gary was satisfied he had no idea that a coup was coming. Jeffrey said he had been in touch with Raja in Mumbai and Jimmy in Boston, so he expected them both to be on the satellite link, and there would be David, Gary, and himself in the room. His assistant, Lucy, would be there to take minutes. He spoke like a man in total control of events.

Gary was jubilant. He telephoned Jean-Pierre to inform him that the meeting to oust Jeffrey was ready to go ahead. Jean-Pierre told him to schedule the meeting the following Saturday, to give Tyro time to attend. The plans were made accordingly, and on Friday night, Gary spoke directly to Tyro for the first time. Tyro was actually sitting in conversation with Alan when he telephoned.

"I should not be at this meeting," Tyro said, sounding troubled. "Jeff Harvey doesn't know about my full role in all this."

"No," Gary said, "but he'll find out tomorrow. It will be another body-blow to him when he realises that his investors as well as the university know about his cheating. He'll learn that they've been behind you all along. Then he'll be told that you will be on the voyage, but he won't. That'll cut him up still more. Revenge is sweet, Tyro, buddy. See you at the meeting."

Tyro put down the phone. Alan saw that he was troubled and asked him why.

"Tomorrow a meeting of the Warlocks will take place, and I am ordered to attend. I do not want to go, Reverend."

"To the meeting?"

"I do not want to go on the voyage. I fear the ship."

Alan was amazed. "If you have the courage to fly, why be afraid to go by ship?"

"Because it takes weeks to cover the distance a plane will cover in hours, and a wave can swallow you up so quickly."

"What's going to sink a tanker?" Alan laughed. "A ship is a place of freedom. Away from land, you are free from all the everyday petty rules and regulations."

"Will I be free, or will I be trapped?" Tyro asked sombrely.

"Trapped? That's like saying I'm trapped in Cambridge. How much space do you need? You are setting off on an adventure I can't begin to contemplate. I envy you, Tyro. I truly envy you." Alan shifted comfortably in his armchair to take a sip of his whisky.

"Well then, come with me," Tyro suggested sharply.

"Ah, well." Alan's demeanour changed in an instant. "That's ... that's just not possible, you see," he replied nervously, almost spilling his drink as he put it down hurriedly.

"I'm making it possible," Tyro said. "I have six places to allocate. You can come as one of my team."

"Well, that's wonderful, of course." Alan began; he was clearly agitated and unable to think of any plausible reason to refuse the invitation. "But I just don't think my college responsibilities ... you know ..."

"You see, Alan, confronted with reality, you too are scared," Tyro pointed out. "That's all I needed to know. I was troubled by my fear. It made me doubt my faith as a Christian, but when I see you, with your much greater faith, respond with fear, that is much more comforting than a thousand words spoken from a place of security." The big man chuckled, with a hint of derision. "Thank you. Don't worry, my friend; you don't need to come."

Now Tyro felt able to talk about the conflict between justice and betrayal, which was really troubling his soul, as he thought of his role in Jeffrey's downfall, but Alan had ceased to concentrate and told him he could not help any more. He had to be up early for Holy Communion, he said. They parted to their own rooms shortly afterwards, Alan with cowardice on his mind, Tyro with guilt on his.

The meeting started at eleven, which made it a reasonable time in India and the States, as well. Tyro was grimly amused to find that, by pure coincidence, it was taking place in the same hotel, in the same room, where his confrontation with Jeffrey had occurred. The hotel was used to renting out its seminar rooms to academic meetings.

David, Lucy, Jeffrey, and Gary were already in the sunless room, seated at the table, while a member of the hotel staff fiddled with a video link system. The only empty chair was between the screen and Gary, so Tyro moved towards it.

"We'll have to do without it," David was saying. "Let's not risk the link we have established. The Indian link is the important one." When he caught sight of Tyro, he was surprised at the sight of a stranger. Tyro turned his attention to Jeffrey, expecting him to be nervous at his presence, but Jeffrey seemed to be relaxed and in good spirits.

"Perfect timing, Tyro," Jeffrey said affably, as if Tyro had been expected all along. "We are just waiting for the Skype link with Raja Johar in India, and then we can begin. We can't get the link with Jimmy Moule."

"As I don't know who he is, I will not miss him," Tyro replied, causing the others to chuckle.

"He's a big-shot lawyer and polar explorer," Gary intervened. "He keeps people like you and me out of prison, Tyro."

"Let's hope he stays on our side?" Tyro retorted pointedly, which kept the humour buoyant. Gary gave him a critical look, but Tyro disregarded it.

Tyro could not work out who knew what. Everyone was being so nice. Perhaps he and Gary were the only ones to be properly informed of the takeover. He sat back in his seat so that he could regard everyone more intently. And why, he wondered, had Jeffrey accepted his arrival so calmly? Gary had been wrong to think that Jeffrey would fall apart.

Raja came on the screen, and the meeting started with both sides working out who they were looking at.

"Hello, Raja," Gary called out, immediately putting his presence in the driving position.

"Hello, Jeffrey; hello, Gary," Raja replied, indicating his view of the hierarchy. "I have Arnesh, my shipyard director, with me, and we are speaking to you from Bhavnagar, where the sun shines and the days are hot – unlike Cambridge in September, as I recall."

"Hello, Raja," Jeffrey intervened. "Cambridge in September: There's nowhere better," he joked.

He could see that Gary was desperate to take control of the meeting, but he continued speaking, looking at Gary and making clear that he wanted the floor for a while longer.

"Now, I have a short announcement to make, before the meeting gets going." Everyone anticipated the usual announcements about fire alarms, toilets, mobile phones, and so on. But the inattention ended sharply as Jeffrey said, "Tyro Mukasa, here, presented to the university authorities some documents that have obliged them to question my academic credentials. Most of you know that I am under investigation, but you may not have known Tyro's part in this."

Tyro sat up, gripping the arms of his chair, ready to make a rapid exit. He cursed his foolishness in being guided to the chair farthest from the door. Jeffrey was quietly satisfied to see the look of a trapped animal but continued.

"It's all right, Tyro, relax. You did what you felt you had to do. Let me finish. Another thing: Gary was detained but released thanks to the intervention of Duke Dukakis, one of our investors. I used to think we were too small for them to notice us, but they are actually taking very great notice in everything about us – and me in particular – to see if there's anything there that could damage their investment. In a way, they know me better than you do. Another example of their interest is seeing Tyro here today; I didn't tell him about the meeting, so someone else told him to be here. Isn't that right, Tyro? It confirms, in a way, what I discussed with Anna last night. Our investors don't trust me. I've been made to realise that I'm putting this whole venture at risk, and maybe myself, by trying to remain in control. I'm no longer the right person to lead the enterprise. I'm heeding the warning signs and am going to step away from the project, before I ruin it."

Nobody said anything.

"Your silence tells me that you all agree."

"Not just us, Jeffrey," Gary said softly, as if sympathetic. "You're right. When I was being held by the men in dark suits, it was Duke Dukakis, one of the Clerkenwell Angels, who negotiated my release, in person. They've heard the allegations against you. They're sufficiently concerned that they're ready to withdraw funding from the project unless you're replaced. They want me to take over."

"That's the first I've been told of it," Jeffrey said, without malice, which even sent a twinge of guilt through Gary. "Which of you knew about this?"

"Tyro, myself, and David," Gary replied.

Jeffrey gave a small start at the sound of David's name.

"Jeffrey, I'm not against you; you know that," David intervened hurriedly. "I've great respect for your skills. It's you who kept the Moringa project alive right from the start, but ever since the purchase of the ship, frankly, I've been worried at our lack of expertise. Added to which, if this project hits the news, as it may well do, and the press gets hold of the allegations about you and unauthorised GM crop production, we could all be dragged down with you."

"Someone tell me, please, what the hell is going on?" Raja's voice rasped, urgently, from the speakers by the screen.

Jeffrey looked across at Gary. "You tell him, Gary. You seem to know more about it than I do. I'm going out for a while. I'll be on my phone if you need me."

Lucy looked at him, uncertain as to whether to follow him or not. "Stay here," Jeffrey ordered her firmly. "I'll see you back at the university after lunch."

"You can't just walk out of a meeting, Jeffrey," David protested. "That's very rude to Raja and the rest of us. We're your friends."

Jeffrey bit back the retort that was on his lips.

"Just leave him alone," Lucy whispered crossly to her father, and Jeffrey left the room.

Gary brought the meeting to order, apologised to Raja, and explained what had transpired. After getting his support, he received verbal reports from all those present. They all fed off each other's figures, voraciously, willingly, swapping information and advice, working through problems, and giving themselves renewed confidence that they would succeed in the mission.

They were about forty minutes into the meeting when Tyro felt his mobile phone vibrate. He glanced down, saw a text had arrived from Alan, and discreetly read the message. His exclamation of surprise, however, drew attention to himself.

"Something important?" Gary snapped.

"God is with us," Tyro replied, smiling. "The Reverend Mills will be on my team."

"What? Alan Mills, the chaplain? Really?" David's voice was full of surprise and delight.

"This," Tyro said, pointing to his phone, "was a message from him, asking to come. I challenged him to come with us, but I didn't think he would do so."

"We can't take passengers," Gary said firmly, staring aggressively at Tyro.

Tyro was unmoved. "I have six places allocated to me," he said calmly. "The Reverend Mills will be one of my team. We need a man of God."

Gary backed off. "I just hope you know what you're doing, for all our sakes."

"Does this mean you now need a cathedral built on the bloody ship?" Raja asked. "If so, Arnesh will have to tell the boys. I'm sure they can have it done by tomorrow."

"No cathedrals, gudjwaras, or mosques needed," Gary replied, glad of some light relief.

"Thank God for that," Raja continued. "Now let me tell you something: Gandhi was once an unknown lawyer, and so was Mandela. They were not always great men. They became great men because they could see things other men couldn't. They had vision, you see? My point is this, Gary: I accept you as the project leader because Jeffrey says you are the project leader, see? If Jeffrey says you are no longer project leader, then you are no longer the project leader. Jeffrey has vision. He may become a great man. We are all here because of him. Yes, let's be honest: He is a bloody awful leader, but he knows it. He knows that for his vision to succeed, he needs your skills. You are the leader, but he remains at the top."

"I hear you, Raja," Gary replied. "You own a multimillion-dollar business. Perhaps you should be the boss." Gary gambled again, as he had done with David.

"No, I know about business, not about oceans and icebergs. You are the man to direct the project now. I will provide the ship and the men to maintain her; that is my role. The shipyard director himself, Arnesh, here, will oversee them. You will be able to go on board the *Moringa* from the moment you get here. Arnesh will handle everything. Now I must go. Mr Mukasa, I hope you know what you are doing, threatening the reputation of Professor Harvey with your secret documents. This has been an exceptional meeting. I wish you well in the coming weeks."

"We'll meet again in eight weeks' time. That will be our last meeting before we begin our journey," Gary announced.

Raja disappeared from the screen, leaving Arnesh to tie up any loose ends. Gary was satisfied that he had fully achieved his fourth objective, becoming head of the Moringa project, and brought the meeting to an end soon afterwards.

Chapter 7

LUMPS, BUMPS, AND BRUISES

The next two weeks were a flurry of activity for all involved. After years in which the Moringa project had seemed to be a theoretical possibility, suddenly it was under way. It was as if Jeffrey's resignation had been the spark. From the moment Gary took over, there was never a day that he didn't contact each of the others for a progress report and to update them. David made room for him in his own office, which meant that the two of them could work in close partnership. He paid eight hundred pounds for an old Ford Fiesta and rented a room in town, which he hardly used. Leena continued to stay with Maggie, who turned a blind eye to Gary's perpetual overnight stays, and pretended to turn a deaf ear to the sounds that came through the wall. What she heard, though, touched her conscience, as it was clear that they were not enjoying the physical pleasures of a happily reunited couple, and she regretted, time and again, ever having bought the prawns, let alone giving them to Leena.

One morning, after Gary had gone, to Maggie's surprise, Leena reached out and touched her shoulder. "Maggie ..." she began.

Maggie turned round, took one look at Leena's face, and was shocked at the despairing look in her eyes. "Oh my God, love, you are in a mess," she said, getting up and putting her arms round Leena's thin torso. "What can possibly be so wrong?"

"I'm so ashamed I could kill myself."

"Oh, love, there are a good few people who deserve to die before you, believe me. You mustn't think like that."

"I've abused your kindness, I've deceived Gary, and I've betrayed my parents," Leena continued listlessly, as if speaking to herself.

"Let's not get eloquent. You fucked Jeffrey, and now you're fucked. Anything else?"

Leena smiled, her head resting comfortably on Maggie's shoulder. "You do have a way with words, Maggie."

"And with prawns," she said, ruefully.

"Prawns?" Leena repeated, puzzled at these words.

"Never mind," Maggie said quickly. "Look, I think I know the problem, and I think I know the solution. These walls are not exactly made of double-thick concrete. Put simply, love, why don't you just let Gary fuck you into a stupor tonight? He'll feel better, you'll feel better, I'll feel better, and we all can leave the past behind us."

"I can't. I haven't had my period yet. I won't feel clean until I've had it. I've been waiting. It has to be soon."

"I thought you were on the pill. I've seen the packets in the bathroom," Maggie responded.

Leena recovered her composure and walked back to the kitchen to pick up her mug of coffee, chatting as she did so.

"Yes, I am, well, sort of. I missed a day or two while Gary was away, but I'm always regular. It should have come ten days ago. It should all be over. I should be giving myself to Gary by now, like any normal woman." She came back into the living room with her coffee.

Maggie started to view the problem in a different light. "Are you properly back on the pill?" she asked.

Leena raised her free hand in a gesture of frustration. "No, I'm not. I always start the new pack after my period. Now, I don't know when to start it. I'm all over the place, Maggie. My whole life is chaos."

"You could be pregnant."

"I can't be," she exclaimed. "I am just emotional at the moment, and my hormones are playing havoc with my mind." She took a gulp of coffee, clumsily spilling some as she did so. "I'm sorry," she muttered and plucked a tissue from a box on the table, to wipe up the spilt drops.

Maggie stood looking at Leena, elegant even in distress. "You've got style, I'll give you that. Your world's collapsing about you, but you still apologise for slurping your coffee."

"Laugh at me. I deserve it," Leena said dejectedly.

"Stop pitying yourself," Maggie replied, irritated by the remark. "You know perfectly well that I'm not laughing at you. I'm trying to help. Now, here's my advice, take it or leave it, as I'm off to work, anyway. I'll take an overnight bag with me; you have the flat to yourself, and when Gary comes home tonight, you give him all he needs, but use a condom."

"I hate those things," Leena squirmed.

"Well, then, let *him* wear it," Maggie retorted. "They work better that way, anyway."

Leena turned her head away in embarrassment. "Oh, Maggie, stop it," she giggled. "I feel I want to laugh and cry at the same time."

Maggie drew her close, put an arm tenderly around her, and kissed her lightly on the bridge of her nose. "Don't try it, love; you'll choke to death. Go to the chemist and buy the condoms and a pregnancy testing kit. Hide it from Gary, obviously. Do as I've said, and by tomorrow morning, you and Gary will be as tight as peas in a pod. Now, I need the bathroom for a few minutes, then I'll be out of your way. When you're ready to do the pregnancy test, let me know."

"Where will you stay tonight?"

"I'll go back to Anna's flat. It's empty now. She won't say no."

Leena left the flat almost as soon as Maggie. She felt restless with her anxiety over Gary. He was angry with her. She had learnt not to let him get angry. Added to which, she now had this nagging doubt that she was pregnant. Maggie had given her the nudge she needed, to send her to the chemist. She was back home just in time.

Gary had left the flat in a bad mood and driven to Vicarage Farm without thinking too much about it, but rather, about Leena and her cultural purities. When he arrived, he saw there was plenty of activity, but he was not needed. David came over to him and, out of politeness, went through some of this and some of that, and though everyone was very engaging, Gary realised there was actually nothing useful he could do and nowhere to release the tension that was inside him. As he stood alone, outside the long shed, he heard a small aircraft approaching and looked up to watch it, and his eyes went beyond it to the scattered clouds. There, he saw freedom. Telling David he would be on his mobile if he were needed, Gary ran eagerly back to his car and phoned Leena. She had just come back from the chemist. Not surprisingly, given his anger two hours earlier, she sounded reserved, almost frightened, at the sound of his voice.

"Babe," he said, "I don't blame you for being mad at me. Can you forgive me?"

She was perplexed. She expected him to be angry still, but clearly, he was not. "What do I have to forgive you for? I'm the difficult one," she cooed.

"Do you remember our first meeting?" he asked.

"Falling out of a plane together – how could I forget?"

"Well, let's do it again."

"When?"

"Today. Now."

She felt a surge of excitement. The man Gary could be, if he tried, still aroused her.

"All right," she agreed. "But have you phoned the club? We'll need to hire rigs. And how do I get there? You've got the car."

"It's okay. We can sort it out. I'll come by and pick you up. Can you phone the club?"

"All right, but you'll have to pay for everything. I'm broke."

Gary drove back to Leena, hardly believing that she had agreed to jump. Deep down, at best, he had hoped she might come and watch him. When he parked, she saw him through the window and waved to him. The door was already ajar as he approached, and when he entered the flat, she was waiting for him in the sexiest short pants that he had seen, with a half-open blouse barely concealing her nipples. He stopped in his tracks, gawping at her, and then came to his senses.

"Damn, babe, you make one hell of a sight, but you can't go out like that."

Leena walked seductively up to him. "I've just slipped into something casual, but if you don't like it, you can always take it off me." She half-closed her eyes like a smiling cat, and as she put her face to his for a kiss, her tongue slipped lightly across the margin of his lips.

"Babe, it's mid-morning. What if Maggie walks in?"

"She won't be back until tomorrow," Leena purred, now moist-kissing his Adam's apple.

"What about the parachuting?" he pleaded, holding on to the last of his self-control.

"We're booked for three o'clock. That gives us four hours." Her eyes were downcast now, as she focused on undoing his belt. "What can we do with four hours?" Then she undid his trouser zip and slid her hand gently inside.

"Right now, I can't think," he whispered, gasping.

"Well," she said. "Let's start by taking off your shoes."

She hooked her thumbs over the waistband of his jeans, so as she slid down his body, she took jeans and boxer shorts with her, and her face was opposite his naked groin, but she did nothing except remove his shoes and socks, and then his jeans and boxers. Then, still crouched, she raised her eyes.

"Coming up," she said, and slithered back up his body, raising his shirt as she did so, and together, they flicked it free of his body. "Still no ideas?" she prompted him gently.

Her blouse seemed to melt off her body as he brushed it away, and the quick release of two buttons let her shorts drop to the floor, revealing her smooth and hairless skin, which was just the way he liked it.

"Babe," he muttered. "I don't want to do anything you don't want."

"Angel," she whispered back, "you couldn't do anything I don't want. I want everything."

With that, he lifted her up; she twined her legs about his thighs, and he carried her through to the bed.

Maggie was glad to be back in her one-time love nest with Anna. She had a relaxing shower and then walked briskly to Jeffrey and Anna's home, to spend the evening with them, as arranged. Anna was delighted to welcome her and gave her a big hug.

"How is he?" Maggie whispered while they were still at the door.

Anna grimaced by way of reply. Then she said, cheerfully, "There's so much to talk about."

It was true that there was much to talk about, but Maggie found Jeffrey so preoccupied by the threats facing him that he hardly spoke throughout the meal. He looked ill. After supper, she excused herself and sent a text to Leena while in the toilet: "Let me know if you need me." The answer came back before she had washed her hands: "Fab day. Stay away," with a smiley emoticon.

Reassured that she had put Leena's life straight, she went back to put Anna and Jeffrey's life straight too.

Jeffrey had put the television on, and there was enough background sound as she and Anna did the post-supper clearing up that Maggie felt free to talk about him.

"It's as if he has given up," she commented to Anna.

"He did what he had to do to," Anna said. "He knows there's a movement in the university to shame him and wreck the project. It's just envy, only envy. Now he has stepped back from the project, even if they discredit him, the project can survive. But he is deeply hurt."

"Who do you mean by 'they'?"

Anna gave a bitter laugh. "Officially, the university authorities, but it is all being stirred up by people who envy his freedom, and his enterprise, and his achievements." She saw a fly on a cupboard and flicked her dishcloth at it with such ferocity that she flattened it before it could move.

"Was that one of them?" Maggie asked, taken aback by the level of anger in the blow.

"I wish. He's such a wonderful man," Anna said, slumping against the sideboard, all aggression gone; she rubbed her neck to relieve an aching muscle. "Of course, he hasn't given up on the Moringa. It's been his ambition ever since he was a student. When you know him, then his whole life has meaning. You can understand him. If you don't know him, then yes, he could seem like as a playboy or a fraud."

Anna fell silent at this expression of her own doubts. Maggie came up and took over the neck massage, expertly working her hands over the nape of Anna's neck.

She let Anna absorb the benefit of the massage for a few moments before probing further: "Do you think there may be some truth in the allegations, then?" she asked.

Anna reached across her chest and took Maggie's hand in hers and kissed it lightly, to end the massage, keeping affectionate hold of it.

"I don't know, and I don't care," she replied. "This has been his life's work, and perhaps he did use his student's work along the way. But these people – they are out to destroy him. This is just an excuse to put a knife into him. The awful thing is they seem to know things he has kept confidential or didn't want the university to know. Things which are irrelevant to the accusations, but which can be used to embarrass him and undermine his reputation." They returned to the last of the clearing-up. "Little things like times he's been drunk at parties or had an affair. Things which, lumped together, could be used to accuse him of giving the university a bad name. We just don't know where it's all coming from. It has hurt him that one of his friends is betraying him. If they find out about his recent escape without his trousers, I think it will finish him."

"Well, surely he has got allies in the university who can help?"

"To be honest, he hasn't got many friends in the academic staff. The dean is involved in the disciplinary proceedings, and others are just keeping clear until everything's finished." By now, they had finished all that needed to be done. "We better go back to him, or he'll know we're talking about him," Anna said. "He hates me being away for too long at the moment; it's about the only good thing to come out of this business," she added with a smile.

"What about Steve McPherson?" Maggie suggested.

Anna stopped abruptly and looked round. "What about him?" she snapped.

"Well, he's a friend, isn't he? Can't he help?"

"You've got to be joking. Friend? He's the worst of the lot. He's a horrible creep. Anyway, how do you know him?"

Maggie had detected serious negative vibes in Anna's tone and tried to backtrack: "Oh, I don't really," she replied, hurriedly. "I just heard the name." She tried to walk on.

Anna's outstretched hand hit her in the chest, propelled her backwards, and pinned her to the same cupboard where the remains of the fly were stuck to the door beside her. "Hello, fly," Maggie said.

"Tell me," Anna said ferociously.

"Oh, Anna, love, I'm so sorry. He said he was a friend of Jeffrey's. He seemed to know him well."

"When did you meet him? Where?" Anna persisted, harshly.

"Soon after I moved into the new flat, really. In a way, I've known him for some time, but we've bumped into each other a lot just recently, as he lives quite close."

"So?"

"So we've come across each other in the supermarket, and I was sitting in Costa's one day, and he came and sat at my table. We chatted and found out we both knew Jeffrey. It was all very casual."

"I bet it was," Anna said bitterly, releasing the pressure on her ex-lover. "And has he just happened to be in Costa's on any other occasion?"

"Two or three times," Maggie responded, as light began to dawn. "And on another occasion, we stopped and chatted in the street." Her voice dwindled into nothing. "I've been had for a complete fool, haven't I? Bloody hell, it's another Prawngate, isn't it? I've gone and screwed up everything."

"I'm as much to blame as you," Anna conceded, with some reluctance. "I told you things I shouldn't have done." Then her frustration resurfaced. "But I didn't think you'd tell anyone else, and certainly not Steve McPherson." She pressed Maggie against the cupboard again and looked her straight in the eyes.

Jeffrey wandered into the kitchen and spied Maggie with her back to the cupboard, pinned by Anna's hand. "Care for a cup of tea, Maggie?" he asked, as if everything were normal. "Don't move. I'll bring it over to you."

Hearing Jeffrey's voice, Anna released her hold on Maggie and focused all her attention on him. "Don't worry, sweetheart," she said. "You go back and rest, and I'll bring it through."

He looked lovingly at her but his voice was firm: "Anna, darling, I am not an invalid, and I'm not deaf. I heard the name Steve McPherson mentioned as I came in, and judging by the way you were pushing Maggie through the cupboard, she's probably admitted that she's now straight and sleeping with the man."

"It's not that bad," Anna admitted, hugging him.

"It's worse," Maggie confessed, feeling sick with herself and ready for a verbal lashing. "I've been a complete fool, Jeffrey. I've let myself be tricked by this Steve McPherson into telling him things about you. I'm very sorry. You're not my favourite person, but I would never have done that to you on purpose."

Maggie looked so abject and lonely after this confession that Jeffrey had no heart to be cross with her. "Maggie, come over here, come on," he coaxed her, gently.

She moved hesitantly to where he and Anna were standing in comfortable union.

"Now," he said, "Group hug." He extended his free arm. Anna immediately extended her free arm, and Maggie glided between them, her arms around them both. For her part, Maggie decided that this was not the moment to tell them that Leena's period was overdue and gave herself up to being where she belonged.

The following morning, Tyro took off from Stansted for the airport at Bhavnagar, with a consignment of materials. His A320 airbus was mostly set up for carrying cargo but had a small, luxurious passenger cabin at the front. He flew with two of his pilots and made the journey with refuelling stops in Athens and Dubai along the way. He contacted Raja's office on landing and then made his way to the Bluehill Hotel, about twenty minutes' drive from the airport. He rested, washed and changed, and then went back to the airport to join Raja in his helicopter, and together, they flew on a sightseeing tour of the city and the docks, with Raja acting as his tour guide.

Naturally, the main focus of attention was the *Moringa*, looking magnificent, as the work continued on her. Tyro eyed her superstructure with expert attention to detail and discussed her flight deck design with Birindar, the pilot, by means of the headset. Raja pointed out the hulk of a largely dismembered aircraft carrier from which many parts had been taken. Tyro eyed the length of deck available for the airship to dock.

"You'll note that the airship shed is to the right side of the deck, not in the middle," Raja pointed out. "If you have to approach from over the rear of the ship, this will give you a better angle of descent and more deck space to aim for."

"Won't the ship tip over?" Tyro asked anxiously.

"No, there are ballast tanks to compensate for any uneven weight distribution," Raja replied, sensing that Tyro feared ships as much as he, himself, did. He checked with Tyro that he had seen all he wished to see and then directed the pilot: "Now, Birindar, the moment you have been waiting for. Take us down, please."

Birindar smiled broadly. "Yes, sir," he replied and glanced over his shoulder to see Tyro's look of surprise.

"Where are we landing?" Tyro asked as they descended in wide circles over the shipyard, drawing attention to themselves.

Raja replied, "On the flight deck of the *Moringa*, naturally. Where else would we land on such an occasion?" He was enjoying the excitement of the moment.

"Has it been tested?" Tyro asked as they hovered and then began the vertical descent.

"We are the test," Raja replied happily. "I've told Arnesh that if it collapses we may die, but he will be demoted. For Arnesh, that would be a fate worse than death."

The helicopter lightly touched the flight deck. Several hundred workmen, surveying the scene, started to wave.

Raja waved back. "My loyal workforce," he commented proudly. "All secretly longing to see a balls-up, but they have done too good a job. Arnesh has seen to that."

Birindar throttled back, and the helicopter's full weight transferred to the flight deck, as the rotor blades flickered round, slowly rotated, and stopped. Arnesh stepped forward to meet them as they clambered out.

Tyro's amazement overcame his politeness. His eyes kept looking this way and that, even as he was being introduced to various members of the management.

"I have arranged a full tour for you tomorrow," Raja told him. "I hope that you can stay for a day or two. It would be most helpful to have your advice as we complete the finishing touches. Now, it is very hot, so let's go to my office, where we can be cool and have our chat."

Arnesh escorted them off the *Moringa* to a waiting car that took them to the administrative buildings, where Raja had his top-floor office suite.

Tyro was beginning to feel tired, but the cool room and some warm tea revived him. They were alone, for the first time.

"I have been awaiting your arrival with great eagerness," Raja said as he settled into one of the luxurious armchairs in the room. "I am greatly interested in you and want to ask you certain things. I hope you will excuse my curiosity."

"Raja, my friend," Tyro answered. "You decide what to ask, and I will decide what to answer."

They both laughed.

"I do not remember you at Cambridge; were you there?"

"No, but my brother, Arthur, was there," Tyro replied, and there was silence for a moment as Raja absorbed this.

"What are the documents that Jeffrey referred to," he finally asked, "that you have provided to his university and which are so threatening to him?"

"My brother died violently. Jeff was the only other person with him at the time. I believed that he killed Arthur, but nobody would listen to me, because I could show no motive. Then, last year, documents were sent to me, showing that he had stolen Arthur's work. Arthur was his student. I had found the motive. I went to Cambridge to confront him with my brother's murder and with the theft. I sent copies of the documents to the university." Tyro withheld the fact that he had been sent to discredit Jeffrey.

Raja reflected a moment on what Tyro had said. "When we were at university, for me it was as if Jeffrey stood on a pedestal. You know, I was in awe of him. He was so free, so independent, so visionary, unlike me, with my strict upbringing, suppressed by parental rules and so on. It was his example that gave me the courage to challenge my father, so that I could choose my own path. Do you really think Jeffrey capable of murdering a friend?"

"It was more than friendship. They were lovers. My brother was a homosexual, God spare his soul." There was silence again. Even Raja's sharp intellect needed time to assimilate this information. "Did you love him?" Tyro's question was so direct that Raja laughed in childish embarrassment.

"No, no. Well, in a way, yes, but not in any physical sense, you understand."

"My brother did." The pain in Tyro's words found an echo in Raja's heart, who thought of his niece, Leena, and her relationship with Jeffrey.

"So did my niece," he replied. "She was a student of his too. It was unacceptable. He almost wrecked her life."

"My brother died," Tyro repeated.

"I'm truly sorry. I don't defend him for his weaknesses, but could he ever kill? I don't think so. Could it be possible that your abhorrence of Jeffrey's intimacy with your brother clouds your view of his guilt in this tragedy?"

116

"It doesn't matter now," Tyro said, shrugging. "I made a new friend in Cambridge, a true man of God. He made me realise that I could not live forever with my hatred. I went to see Jeff and forgave him his homosexual acts with Arthur. He told me that he did not kill Arthur, but he has lied about Arthur's death; I'm sure of it. No matter. All that matters to me is to see Arthur's work succeed."

Raja picked his words with great care, trying not to offend or alienate Tyro: "Tyro, I respect what that you say. I trust you. I ask you, please, to trust me, as one of the founders of this project." Then he began to reason with Tyro, finding out what the papers were that he had received, who had sent them, and where Gary Murdoch fit into the picture. As the talking came to an end, they were both better informed men.

"Our investors – by which you mean the Clerkenwell Angels, yes? They are really that ruthless? You know this?" Raja was intrigued. He had the sense of invulnerability that belongs to very rich people. "Are you not forgetting me, and David Emmerson, and Jimmy Moule? The investors do not control us."

Tyro smiled. "You are three good men. Gary and me – we are bad men, each of us in their debt, Gary for his freedom, me for my business. You can be sure that the captain is a bad man too. He has done something which puts him in their debt in a way that is useful to them."

"And don't you think three good men can overcome three bad men?" Raja asked. "What if I decided not to release the ship from my yard, for example?"

"They know you would not do that. But if you did anything to threaten their investment, they would eliminate you."

"Like they eliminated Jeffrey?" Raja smirked. "I'd like to see them try."

"No. More probably, they would do it as my business partners were eliminated: in a car crash."

Raja pondered a moment. "Tell me," he said. "Jeffrey Harvey: Is he a good man or a bad man?"

Tyro gave a wry smile. "Raja, my friend, I have been asking myself that question for many months. He is his own man. He has his own way of doing things. Nobody controls him."

Raja paused. "Let me be honest, since you value honesty, and tell you that I have a motive behind our conversation."

"I had already suspected that, but thank you," Tyro said, his body language showing appreciation of Raja's admission.

"I have kept close contact with my beloved university, where I spent some of the happiest days of my life, with my beloved bride, Sunita, whose death nothing can ever replace. I have much to be grateful for, and through my endowments, it has something to be grateful to me for, in return. If, as a result of our conversation, you did feel like writing another letter withdrawing your accusations, I could ensure that it reached the appropriate authorities. I am sure that Jeffrey did not rob your late brother but, rather, took back data that they had shared so that nobody else would steal it."

"You are a good friend."

"I hope so. And Jeffrey is a good man. We need him. We all need him, and just now, he needs us. There isn't much time."

When Tyro was ready to take his leave, Raja summoned Arnesh, who arranged a suitable meeting time with Tyro for the following day, and then saw him off in Raja's chauffeured Rolls Royce. As soon as Tyro left the room, Raja telephoned his sister-in-law, Leena's mother, in Jodhpur, to whom he always spoke Punjabi.

"You know Leena called you from America a few months ago to tell you that she was now financially secure, and that you and Ravi did not need to worry?"

"Yes. We agreed that she could stay in America."

"Do you know how she got that money?"

"No."

"Her boyfriend stole the money from a group of ruthless investors and gambled it in Las Vegas. That's how."

"Oh my, oh my," she replied softly; Raja could almost feel her palpitations as she responded to the news.

"I just learnt this a few minutes ago. Do you know where she is at the moment?"

"No. She is not a good daughter in that respect. She is always quite vague."

"Well, she is living with her boyfriend, who has escaped to England."

"Oh my, oh my."

Raja gauged that he had softened his sister-in-law enough for her to comply with his instructions.

"You and Ravi have been very tolerant parents. It is now time for you to find her a husband and to call her back to India."

The conversation went on for several minutes, mostly going over the old ground of how Raja had encouraged them to let Leena return to England to finish her studies, but in the end, it was agreed that Leena would be instructed to leave her boyfriend and to return to India to marry a suitor chosen by her parents. Raja had always liked Leena for her initiative and spirit, and he was sad to end her freedom. However, away from home, she was vulnerable, and that made him vulnerable. She could be kidnapped by Tyro's "bad men" as a means of coercing him to do as they wanted. Tyro, he thought, had a very simplistic view of life, but it made for great clarity.

Leena had no idea what was coming her way. She simply did not know. She held the pregnancy test stick in her right hand, with her eyes closed tight, as she counted the passing seconds out loud. The morning of the parachute jumps, her seduction of Gary had been so successful that their embrace, and all that followed, had satisfied his desires for two whole days, but she could tell by the way he went off to work that she was in for a late night again. It was time to face up to the pregnancy test. When she reached one hundred and twenty seconds, she was supposed to open her eyes, but she kept them closed and carried on counting beyond one hundred and fifty, until curiosity overcame her cowardice, and she looked.

That evening, Maggie, sitting in a lecture theatre waiting for the presentation to start, felt her phone vibrate in her hip pocket. Leena had sent her a text which stated, "Did preg test today. All well. Thanks for being there for me."

It was a relief to Maggie, who only now appreciated the level of anxiety she had endured as a result of her trick with the prawns. Prawngate was over, her guilt absolved, and no permanent damage had been caused. She texted back, "Good news," then she settled back to spend an hour on "the Feminine Role and the Feminine Gender in Ancient Greece." She looked round the audience to confirm that she was still in the younger half, a practice that she found strangely comforting, and found herself looking straight into the eyes of Steven McPherson, who immediately averted his gaze. He was one of the very few men in the audience and was sitting at the end of the row two behind hers. He must have come in as the speaker, Dr

Debbie Gannet, arrived. While Dr Gannet was being introduced, Maggie sent a quick text to Anna: "Bloody Steve here! Don't worry."

The anger Maggie felt at Steve's presence did not detract from the pleasure of the evening. Indeed, it galvanised her and helped her to focus. Debbie Gannet led her audience into a world of complex inter-relationships where the feminine role and the feminine gender overlapped but were not the same. The feminine roles in the great dramas of the Grecian dramatists, for example, were central to the plot but not played by female actors. The men selected to play them would certainly have been seductively feminine. Love was symbolised by a goddess, Aphrodite, but defensive war was also symbolised by a goddess: Athena. Women would fight to defend their children and their homes. Men were, similarly, adopting a feminine role in defending their homelands and families. Women were the civilising force in society. The true feminine role was one of virtue, in contrast to the masculine role, which was belligerent, irresponsible, and frivolous. This was reflected in many myths, where love affairs or fighting so often brought harm to the gods. Intellectuals were adopting the feminine role in advancing civilisation through thought. Socrates believed in the equality of the sexes, likened himself to a midwife in assisting the birth of ideas in others, extolled virtue, and helped defend Athens in war. He epitomised the feminine role, at a time when the women of Athens had no vote and could not own property.

Maggie became engrossed in the talk as it progressed and hoped to learn more about the masculine role in the feminine gender and ancient awareness of trans-sexuality and cross-gender identity, which was evident from what was being revealed, and yet Dr Gannet touched only briefly on these topics. She wondered whether this was indicative of ancient prejudices or of Gannet's range of expertise. By the end, she realised that as enlightening as the talk had been, her search for an explanation of her own identity, and what she could say to help Anna, had not been satisfied.

She applauded but had no real interest in the questions that followed. She judged the third one to be so banal that she joined the trickle of early leavers. As she walked casually away, Steven made his way to her side.

"Hello," he said. "Fancy meeting you here."

Maggie looked at him but said nothing and carried on walking. He was clearly uncertain about what to say or do next. When she was outside the building and he was still beside her, she turned and faced him. "Are you stalking me, Steven?" Her tone was humorous and gentle, because that was her nature, but the question was serious.

"No, absolutely not," he replied hurriedly.

"What possible interest could you have in a talk about the feminine role in ancient Greece?" she quizzed him.

"I could ask you the same question, I suppose."

"I'm a woman, and I'm in love with a woman, so I'm lesbian. As far as I know, you don't have either of those attributes," she answered, with withering charm.

"You mentioned the lecture the last time we met," he proffered weakly. "I don't attend these open lectures very often, so I thought I'd give it a try."

"Then why didn't you say so the first time? Are you here in the hope of meeting me? If so, why not let me know?"

"I didn't feel I knew you well enough. This was part of trying to get to know you better."

She found his words quite touching and, in different circumstances, might have responded, but she was angry enough with him to disregard any of his qualities. "Yes, well, I don't want to get to know you better. You're not a friend, and I don't want you as one."

"Could you tell me why you're being so unfriendly?" he asked, hesitantly, seeming genuinely hurt that he was being rejected.

"You know why I am. I don't need to tell you. Good night, and don't even think of following me." Having dismissed him with this curt put-down, she walked off, without giving him a backward glance.

Steven cursed himself for being too eager. He could not continue pretending to bump into her in the street, but what had started out as amateur detective work had become more than that to him. He found her very attractive. She was undeniably good-looking, smart, humorous, and adventurous. He was legally separated from Vicky, who had left him for being too boring, but he lived in the vain hope of reconciliation. In the meantime, he had found the female companionship that he craved in the coffee-time chats with Maggie.

He had barely entered his home when his doorbell rang. It was almost ten thirty at night, but on the basis that nothing exciting ever happened in his life, he had no hesitation in opening the door. He was pleasantly surprised to find a beautiful, dark-haired woman who spoke with a Scandinavian accent asking to come in, as she had some information he might find useful.

"Who might you be?" he asked.

"Oh, Steven, we've met twice before. Surely you recognise me?" Steven peered in the low light. "Let me in, before anyone sees me," the woman said, pushing past him in a moment. "There, now you can see me in the light," she said.

"Yes, I know – you're Anna, Maggie Robinson's friend."

Anna stood slightly beyond his reach, but very close.

"We both know that I was her lover, Steve. There's no need to be polite to me," she said in a soft, provocative voice, with a tempting look in her eyes. "And now I am sometimes her lover and sometimes Jeffrey Harvey's lover. That is the information I wanted to give you. Jeffrey has had many lovers, and so have I, so I am free to give myself to anyone I choose."

"That is certainly very interesting," Steven said, hardly able to contain his delight. Here was more fuel to burn Jeffrey's reputation.

"The thing is, Steven, I don't want anyone else knowing about this. Maggie and Jeffrey are still my friends. You understand, don't you?"

"I think I do, yes," he said cautiously.

"I could, for example, give myself to you."

"Why would you do that?" Steven asked, astounded, yet curious about the possibility.

"Because you are lonely, and I like sex. Maggie is sweet but indiscreet. She has told me that you have bumped into her several times, but too often for it to be by chance. Poor you; you are chasing the wrong woman. She feels no arousal with men, but I do. I live for it. That's why I'm here. I'm free, in all senses."

"In return, I say nothing about this to Maggie or Jeffrey or anyone else. Is that it?"

"I don't talk about you, and you don't talk about me," Anna said. "Nobody talks about anybody." She turned and moved farther away from Steven, towards his bookcase, where she took out a big, leather-bound volume and gently stroked its cover with gloved hands.

"Do you know what I'm wearing under this coat?" she asked, keeping her eyes on the book. Then she looked up. "Nothing, except these gloves that go all the way to my elbows."

"Is that all?" he asked, as the effect of many weeks of loneliness began to undermine his caution.

"I don't think there's anything else. Shall we take a look?"

"Are you trying to compromise me? Is that it?"

"Steven, you are already compromised by me being here. All I have to do is scream. I'm trying to have sex with you. I'm here to sleep with you. I fancy you, all right? We can bring a little excitement into each other's lives, a bit of risk. I have all night to give to you. I'm offering myself to you, for the sheer excitement of doing so. It's a chance for guilt-free sex, if you like."

"Supposing I like what I see?" Steven asked, his self-control melting away at the prospect of a real adventure.

"I come again," Anna said, coming close to him. "So will you. Can't we at least take this chance together? It's not been easy to make myself this ready."

Steven reached out to her coat, but Anna took a step back. "I'm not a whore," she said with gentle reproof. "I'm not to be spread-eagled on the sofa. Take me to your bedroom. Then, if what you see is what you want, we can do it as it should be done."

"You don't need to take the book with you," he said. "I'm not that boring."

She smiled, provocatively. "I'm expecting it to be a long night," she said. "I'll need something to do after I've exhausted you."

"Is that so?" he said with a laugh, starting towards her.

She gave a giggle of laughter herself and ran ahead of him up the stairs. At the top, she stopped and said, "Which way?"

He caught right up with her but never had time to answer. The book hit him under the chin, and because she kicked his leading leg away, he was free in space, somersaulting backwards. She watched carefully as his head hit the steps. His body's force twisted his neck intolerably. He crumpled into another half-somersault, and his head hit the base of the wall at the bottom of the stairs. It was as quick as that, and all over. She came down the stairs, looked at the broken head, avoided the body, and returned the book to the shelf.

"Nobody threatens the man I love," she said in her normal voice, then, touching nothing but the lock on the door, let herself out and made her way unobtrusively to her flat, where she let herself in and opened the door of Maggie's bedroom.

Maggie heard the creak of the door, stirred, and switched on her bedside light. "Anna? Anna, my love, what are you doing here?"

"Jeffrey was asleep, and I was awake. I felt I needed to see you and, perhaps, you needed to see me, so—"

"Well, what are you waiting for? Get undressed, and come to bed."

"Undressed?" Anna queried innocently, slipping off her coat to reveal that she was wearing only her white gloves. She adopted a model's pose. "Don't you like me dressed like this?"

"Well, apparently Vicky was coming home from some Law Society party at about two in the morning, and she noticed that the lights were still on in the home, but the bedroom curtains weren't drawn. She went in and found him slumped at the foot of the stairs." Lucy was giving Jeffrey the latest hot gossip.

"The poor man; are there any details about his condition?"

"Nobody knows yet," Lucy replied. "But he was unconscious when he was taken away."

"I thought he and Vicky had separated," Jeffrey said.

"Yes, they did, two years ago. It seems sheer luck that she happened to be passing by," Lucy said, filling in the details.

"It doesn't sound as if he's going to get back to work in the next week, anyway. I better see what help I can offer." It was already past three o'clock in the afternoon, so he contacted the dean's office to let the admin staff know that he was available, if needed, but that was all. When he went home, he told Anna that Steven McPherson was in hospital after an accident at home.

"In hospital?" she said with surprise and then added, "That sounds serious."

"I think it is," Jeffrey replied. "Vicky found him unconscious at the foot of the stairs."

"His wife? She was there?" Anna asked.

"Apparently not." Jeffrey answered, lying back on the sofa. "They separated some time ago. Interesting, though, isn't it? Vicky still had a key to the house. He hadn't changed the lock. And they were still obviously watching out for each other. She was going home after a party. Do you know what I think? I think they were still in love, without being able to live with each other."

She came over and stood looking down on him. "There's no escaping love, Jeffrey, not true love. You just have to learn to live with it."

"Suppose so," he said.

"Love requires constant vigilance for the happiness of the one you love. Like Steven's wife showed him, and like I will always show you," she added.

He stroked her thighs in silence. "Do you really meant that?"

"Of course," she said.

"In that case, what are you cooking me for dinner?"

"Me," she replied, jumping on top of him. "I am already hot for you and ready to serve."

She concentrated entirely on Jeffrey for the next ten minutes, but then, as they settled and lay uncomfortably but snug together, she thought only of Steven, broken, perhaps dying, and of his distraught wife beside him. "We are both vigilant, you and I," Anna said to herself and then realised that she had inadvertently spoken aloud.

"Yes, I suppose we are," Jeffrey muttered, assuming the remark had been addressed to him.

The following week, Jeffrey received a letter from the office of the vice-chancellor. He waited until Anna was back from her daily training session so he could open it with her. He anticipated that it would be formal notification of the start of disciplinary proceedings, what evidence he was expected to provide, when and where to present himself, and so on. In fact, it was simply to say that allegations of serious misconduct had been made against him but had now been withdrawn. As the documents referred to the university authorities did not, themselves, support any case against him, the university had suspended further action, pending the outcome of any last minute enquiries.

"Who'd have thought I would get a letter like this?" he asked. "What's that saying about a week being a long time in politics?"

"Go and see Mike Taylor at once, sweetheart," Anna advised him. "Don't give anyone the chance to say anything further against you. He must make clear to everyone that your reputation is untouched."

Jeffrey knew that only his most ardent supporter could see him as having an untouched reputation. He was aware of his own level of guilt. But he said nothing because he realised the advice was good. The threat to his work had been unjust, and there was a valuable chance, now, to change the vice-chancellor's verdict of "not proven" to one of "innocent" by acting decisively.

Mike was affable, even apologetic, for the problems Jeffrey had faced. Going through Steven McPherson's work to reschedule it, he had handled the dossier Steven had put together against Jeffrey as one of the first items.

"You'll understand, Jeffrey, that in the light of what we received from Mr Mukasa, we had to make further enquiries. I put poor Steven in charge of this, and I understood from him that some irregularities had come to light. You are, if I may say so, a rather colourful character, and not, how shall I put it, mainstream. But he hadn't mentioned to me a letter he had received from Mr Mukasa, withdrawing all allegations of theft of his brother's work, and stating that you were a man to be trusted – his own words – and a true friend to his brother at the time he died."

"Why would Steven have withheld that letter?"

Mike reflected and said, "I think I can understand it. It was, perhaps, an error on my part to have given him the task. The file was full of anecdotes. He had been like a terrier in hunting evidence against you, Jeffrey. Steven is a meticulous and hard-working man, but reading his draft report and comparing it to the information on which he was basing it, I think his prejudices were getting the better of him."

"So what happens to all the information now?"

Mike sounded nervous as he spoke: "Would you trust me to destroy everything in it except the letters from Makerere University and the letter from Mr Mukasa withdrawing his allegations?"

"If I refuse?"

"The documents will have to be passed to the vice-chancellor's office, I'm afraid. They may rescind the letter they have sent you. There'll be an official enquiry. It'll go on for months before the committee reaches a conclusion. It'll be very inconvenient for all of us, to say the least, and I'm not all that sure of the outcome."

"And if I agree to your proposal?"

"I have already sent a copy of Mr Mukasa's letter to the vice-chancellor's office. It was on that basis they wrote to you. I confirmed that we have no suggestion of irregularity from Makerere University. It only remains for me to answer their final enquiries by stating that your reputation as one of our most accomplished and, er, free-thinking members of staff is beyond reproach. If you agree, then it's all settled, and we are all in the clear. I'm sure the vice-chancellor's office will write to you to that effect."

"I can live with that," Jeffrey agreed.

"Good," Mike said, sounding very relieved. "And you'll forget what I told you about Steven withholding Mr Mukasa's letter? I don't want Steven's reputation blemished by this matter."

"Provided you give me your full support, I will do the same for Steven."

"Well," Mike said amicably, "I think that concludes a very fruitful meeting; no hard feelings?"

"No hard feelings," Jeffrey replied.

"We must have a game of squash sometime," Mike said as they stood up, thereby making one of those nebulous arrangements that never come to anything, but indicate sociability.

"Good idea," Jeffrey replied, knowing they would never arrange it. Then, more sincerely, he asked, "What's the news on Steven?"

"Oh, quite encouraging; he's starting to regain consciousness," Mike replied.

They shook hands, good colleagues if not close friends. Then Jeffrey walked out of the office, feeling triumphant. "I'm in the clear!" he texted Anna.

Jacqueline was perched on a stool by the kitchen island, hot mug of coffee to hand. The clocks were soon to go back an hour, the oak tree leaves were becoming bronze and gold, and she was turning the pages of her diary, planning the family's Christmas preparations and counting the days between David leaving and returning to her.

"It's over three months, David; we've never been apart for so long."

"We'll manage. We'll have to," David replied, continuing to peel an apple, without any show of concern at Jacqueline's calculations.

"What if you fall ill or something?"

"That's all covered. There'll be a medical officer on board. I thought you knew that."

"I do, but that's hardly the same thing as having Addenbrooke's hospital just up the road, is it?"

"When have I ever needed to go to Addenbrooke's?" David demanded.

"All right," Jacqueline conceded. "It was years ago, for a cut hand. All the same, if you need a hospital, Addenbrooke's is there, and it won't be once you're on the ship." She was silent a moment and then added, "What about, you know, being without me?"

"Jackie, really darling, must you?" David muttered uncomfortably.

"Well, let's face it, my sweet, it could be a hundred days. The most I've ever made you wait was thirty-nine, and that was when Tom was born."

"Others cope," David said tersely, trying to concentrate on his apple.

"Well, would you like me to buy you one of those inflatable women?" Jacqueline persisted naughtily.

"Jackie, really," David protested and then added, "I wouldn't mind a rubber one, if you modelled it, of course."

"In your dreams, David Emmerson," Jackie snapped back, shocked at having her bluff called.

Just at that moment, Lucy came into the room, barefoot, in shorts and tank-top, her fair hair curling over her shoulders.

"What are you two squabbling about now?" she asked affably. She looked at her parents, who both averted their eyes. "Well, judging by the way you've both gone silent, it was either money or sex," she said, took a yoghurt from the fridge, and went for a spoon from the drawer. "Aha. That little smile on your face, Mum, tells me it was sex."

"Or not," Jacqueline said pointedly.

"Thank you, Mummy, I don't want to know," Lucy said hurriedly.

"Tell her you offered to buy me an inflatable woman," David mumbled, knowing he was on dangerous ground. Fortunately for him, Lucy didn't hear.

"David," Jacqueline whispered angrily, as Lucy glided away again, her lips tightly pursed round the spoonful of yoghurt she had just taken. "That wasn't for sharing."

A little later, when David had returned to the estate, Lucy sought out her mother in the study and gave her a kiss and a hug. "You're not really worried about Daddy, are you?" she asked.

"Oh, I don't know," Jacqueline said, sighing. "I find myself worrying about all sorts of things as the voyage gets closer. I haven't slept properly for several nights, but don't tell your father. Actually, I'm just as worried about you, darling, probably more so."

"Me?" Lucy exclaimed, genuinely surprised. "What could possibly happen to me?"

"For a start, you're going to be sailing through shark-infested waters."

"Oh Mum, I'm hardly going to be taking a quick swim off the side of the boat."

"Well, there's at least one shark *on* the boat."

"I suppose you mean Jeffrey. You don't have a very high opinion of him, do you?"

"I just know what he's like, that's all. It's not even his fault, necessarily." Jacqueline had not forgiven Jeffrey for his affair with Carrie Peters, which ended his relationship with Helen Crawley, let alone his affair with Leena, not to mention their recent exploits, and now he had this much younger woman, Anna, whom none of her friends knew much about. Lucy saw that her mother was truly agitated.

"Mummy," she said consolingly, "there are some very good reasons why you shouldn't worry about Jeffrey. Firstly, Anna will be with him, and he's besotted with her. Secondly, if Jeffrey was mad enough to kiss any other woman, Anna would chuck him overboard. I just don't see the problem."

Jacqueline clasped Lucy's hands in her own. "Silly me," she said with a smile.

Then she changed the subject and asked Lucy what, exactly, she would be doing aboard ship, and Lucy told her about all the research she would be doing to identify the range of organic matter to be found in the water as the *Moringa's* tanks were filled and how she would monitor the purification of the water. She also told her about the university diving course she had been on, so that she could dive in the ocean near the iceberg with Jeffrey and Anna. Her mother needed reassurance at the moment, and Lucy felt that telling her that she was fully trained and prepared for the voyage would be a good move.

"It sounds very exciting, but won't you freeze to death?" Jacqueline asked, her imagination stirred by Lucy's description.

"No. I think it's warmer in the ocean than out."

"Well, whatever you do, make the most of the trip, darling," Jackie responded, wistfully. "Because one day, you'll find yourself minding the farm while others do the exciting things – just like me."

As Anna walked beside Jeffrey along the hospital corridors, she felt the proximity of fate but was not anxious. They were going to see Steven, at Jeffrey's suggestion, to show support and goodwill for a colleague. Fate had placed her at Jeffrey's side. She did not fear the meeting.

They walked into the small side ward, with its four beds. Steven was in the bed by the window, sitting up and fully conscious, head shaved, with a surgical dressing, and wearing a neck brace. Vicky was sitting beside him. He smiled in welcome as he caught sight of Jeffrey and Anna, and shook hands with them both, in a clumsy fashion. Vicky shared a polite kiss with them, and they drew up some chairs. Steven said nothing about the dossier on Jeffrey, and Jeffrey did not mention it, either. They talked about what was going on in the university, and it took them several minutes to get to the subject that Anna was longing to find out. Steven was upbeat, looking forward to his discharge, thankful for the use of his arms and remarkably stoic about the weakness in his legs that still had time to improve. He owed his life to Vicky, he said. She had found him at the foot of the stairs where he had fallen. The brain haemorrhage had been operated on in time to save his life and much of his mobility. Vicky never let go of his hand throughout the conversation and gave it a gentle squeeze.

"I think I had been out that evening," Steven explained. "But I don't remember anything about it, or the fall, or what followed after that; nothing, until waking up in hospital three days ago. It's a weird feeling, losing a chunk of your life like that."

Vicky was looking adoringly into Steven's eyes. "The main thing is we'll still be able to have children," she added, at which point she and Steven went all soft and kissed, and it became evident to Jeffrey and Anna that the reconciliation had happened.

"We'll leave you to it," Jeffrey muttered, and he and Anna quietly made their way out.

They walked arm in arm out of the hospital, lost in their own happy thoughts, and headed back to the multi-storey car park. "You know, it's funny how life works," Jeffrey said at last, as if he had made a great discovery. "I honestly think that his accident was a blessing for him. They're back together again."

"Oh Jeffrey," Anna said, hugging his arm tightly. "You're such a romantic, and I'm such a realist; how are we going to survive?"

Chapter 8

FIRST STEPS

The pregnancy test had been positive. As Leena looked at the two blue lines on the testing strip, a leaden weight had descended on her mind, making it hard to think or move for several minutes. But she had not panicked. She had retained the wisdom not to disclose the news to anyone. Life had taught her that a secret shared is not a secret, and she needed to keep her options open. She sent an ambiguous text message to Maggie. She hid all evidence of the test and spent a routine evening with Gary, talking about the things he would need while he was away and what she would do while he was gone. She let him use her body in the darkness and drifted into sleep, cradled in his arms. When she woke three hours later, her faculty of thought returned to her, and she lay comfortable and warm on the opposite side of the bed to him, as she debated what to do.

Jeffrey was the father; there was no real doubt about that, but to tell him so could bring disaster to both of them. Anna's threat to her, not to be caught with Jeffrey, and Gary's short temper both frightened her. Jeffrey would never be acceptable to her parents as a husband, and he would hate her for causing a break-up with Anna. Maggie would support Anna. It would be disastrous, and Leena could see that she might be left assaulted, homeless, and alone.

If she proclaimed Gary the father, he would be shocked, but no more than that. It would hardly be a surprise, given the nature and extent of their recent lovemaking. He would support her, the others would support her, and she would be treated with respect instead of shame. Her parents would probably accept him, with reluctance, provided she lived outside

India. One little deceit was all that was required. But the thought of being married to Gary horrified her. He was a dangerous man. He made life exciting, and his passion was intoxicating in short bursts, but he was unpredictable and had to be handled very gently. She might live in fear for the rest of her life.

The chances she would have a miscarriage were negligible. Neither the three parachute jumps she had done with Gary, nor the vigorous lovemaking that she had encouraged, had done anything to disturb the pregnancy. In fact, apart from mild queasiness, and a need to be asleep by nine o'clock, she was feeling radiantly healthy and invigorated. In the space of these few days since doing the test, her feelings for the child had changed from rejection to deep attachment: recognition that the two of them were growing in health together. Thoughts of abortion were out of the question. She would protect the child at all costs.

She reasoned that the pregnancy should remain a secret until the *Moringa* had sailed. She would retain the flat and do agency work to support herself. The ship's voyage was so full of uncertainty that it was pointless to look beyond it. Whatever happened, she would not be alone. She gave her body a gentle rub where she estimated her uterus to be, wished her baby good night, and calmly fell asleep again.

She felt very lethargic the following morning and hardly stirred when Gary rose, bathed, dressed, and left the flat, kissing her as he departed. Eventually, she crawled out of bed, lazily made herself some tea and toast, and went to check her emails. In a second, her life was plunged into crisis again. She was devastated by what she found. For several minutes, she really thought she would have a miscarriage after all, and to control her desire to scream, she returned to bed, put her earphones in her ears, and listened to her MP3 player.

The email that Leena received was from her father. It instructed her to return to India immediately. She was to set aside her relationship to the American oilman. He was a criminal, and her attachment to him discredited her. She should prepare herself to be the most appealing bride possible to a suitor that her father and mother would organise. Any disobedience on her part would bring shame on the family and make suitable marriages for her two younger sisters almost impossible. Her family would not forgive her. Uncle Raja was in full agreement with these instructions, so she was not to trouble him. She should be grateful to her parents for their tolerance, and now that she had gained the education and experience she had sought, it was time to grow up and marry a man they could all honour.

Leena realised at once, from her father's implacable words, that her parents had learnt about Gary's arrest in Las Vegas. They had excused her crush on Jeffrey a few years previously, thanks to Uncle Raja's intervention, but now that tolerance was gone. She reflected, miserably, that it was Gary's behaviour that had been her undoing. Clearly, her father had not learnt about her own behaviour in sharing a sexual weekend with Jeffrey, or else his email would have already disowned her for disobedience and cut her off from further contact. At least that had not happened. She felt trapped. She could not go back to India in her pregnant state, and yet only divine intervention could prevent her from having to return to her parents.

There is no point in being rich if you are not going to enjoy it; hence, the *Clarissa*. The Clerkenwell Angels commissioned her, at Cherry's suggestion, and she provided them with endless satisfaction. Cherry found that the Angels were less mistrustful of one another when on board the yacht, and the pleasures readily to hand made it one of their favourite locations to do business. While they were in the air-conditioned comfort of the saloon or their cabins, the ship would cruise between islands and anchor far enough away to ensure privacy, but in easy reach for the launch to take them into the little harbours for evening saunters along the promenades. She was big enough to carry a squad of eight bodyguards, a captain, four strong crewmen, four young women for domestic duties and escorts ashore, and an excellent cook.

The *Clarissa* was a fitting location to find themselves discussing the Moringa project. It was in early October, close to the time that she would leave the Mediterranean region and head across the Atlantic to the West Indies, but Cherry proposed an exciting alternative: Instead of crossing the Atlantic, she would cruise through the Suez Canal, and they could all fly to Mauritius in March 2011, board her there, and watch the *Moringa* sail up from Antarctica on its way to Mombasa. None of the partners knew anything about seamanship, but they liked the idea, and they all voted for it.

Having allowed time for discussion, Cherry brought the meeting to order again. "Now, Jean-Pierre, an update on the whole Moringa project for everyone please, starting with the cargo. Has it arrived safely from Pakistan?"

Jean-Pierre complied, with his usual impeccable manners. "Our stockpiles have all reached Bhavnagar, and the sacks are ready for loading, disguised as fertiliser for the trees. Loading will begin in about four weeks' time."

"Is the cargo safe where it is?" Cherry persisted.

"Yes; I am reliably informed that it has not aroused interest, and it is dry and cool in one of the warehouses."

He then went on to assure the Angels that the venture was going well. They had control of the project. "The ship's captain is Ernst Brage, a Norwegian at the top of his skills. He knows about the cargo, but we know things about him, so he will shut up. Plus, he is getting a big bonus if he delivers it safely. He advised our agents on the selection of the ship, and he has picked the crew."

"Except for the first officer," Duke Dukakis barged in, rudely, much to Cherry's irritation. "I picked him on the recommendation of my associates in Houston. His name is Ramos Hernandez. He's an Argentinian. Known members of his family are involved in a drug cartel – I won't say where – but he knows the full picture. He'll be of real value to us once the heroin, that is to say, the cargo, reaches its destination."

"Does Ramos know how to sail a ship?" Cherry asked, to taunt him.

"Yeah, he knows how to sail a ship," Duke replied.

"That's all we require of him for the moment," she asserted. The others all smiled. Duke shut up, and put a sweet in his mouth.

Jean-Pierre continued, "As we are on the subject of the crew, there will also be a medical officer on board, Dr Emily Ross. She's an agency doctor, of no consequence."

Jean-Pierre then took questions from different Angels, reassuring themselves on individual points. When the questions ceased, he continued, "In summary, your investment looks sound and has the potential to provide substantial returns. Your backing for the Moringa project has solved the problem of transporting the cargo out of India in one shipment, with very low risk of detection. The venture is expected to cover its costs and provide substantial returns in the medium to long term. The recovery of Antarctic water is a research programme, a delay of a few weeks only. It does not matter to you if the water reaches its destination or not."

"So Jean-Pierre," Cherry said, bringing everyone's full attention to her, "from what you tell us, all is going to plan. Is that right?"

"Yes," he replied simply. "It is currently going to plan."

Cherry knew him too well. She probed deeper. "Is anything not going to plan?" she asked.

He shrugged and gave in, saying, "Professor Harvey is still more involved than we intended."

"I thought we had nailed Harvey," she said, with some surprise. She was not at all pleased.

"Tyro Mukasa sent a letter to the university exonerating him. I don't understand it, nor do my subordinates. He hated Harvey – even threatened to kill him. He seems to have had a complete change of character which, to us, is inexplicable."

"So he acted without instructions from us. Indeed, he disobeyed our instructions, which were to denounce Harvey. Is that right?" Cherry said, checking that she had the facts right.

"That's right," Jean-Pierre replied. The Angels could sense his discomfort.

"Mukasa has a finite value to the project, doesn't he?" Cherry asked. "I don't think he's a major player."

"After they have disengaged from the iceberg, he has no further role of any significance," Jean-Pierre replied impassively.

"I don't like people I can't trust," Cherry mused aloud; they all knew it, anyway. She turned her attention from Jean-Pierre to her partners: "I think we should terminate Tyro Mukasa. Once he has done his bit, we should dispose of him. Are we agreed? He's too unreliable."

The seven other Angels nodded agreement, looking from one to another, as if anyone would not agree.

Duke spoke up again: "I'll see to it myself when I return to Geneva. With Ramos on board, on a big ship, on a wide ocean, it shouldn't be too difficult." If he wanted the responsibility, he could have it.

"And what of Professor Harvey?" Jean-Pierre asked.

"What? You want to kill him too?" Duke snapped.

135

Cherry detected that his derision of Jean-Pierre was supported by the others. Duke continued after a moment's silence, during which Jean-Pierre looked very uncomfortable: "In my book, that guy is a saint. We've got all the control we need. Leave him alone."

"I quite agree," Cherry said. It was good to see Jean-Pierre reminded of his place in the pecking order.

It was typical of Jeffrey's approach to life that he had not prepared a plan for embarkation. Gary, when he took over, drew up a plan, negotiated embarkation arrangements, and set the departure date for the twenty-first of January 2011, the absolute limit if they were to complete their work before the end of the Antarctic summer. There was not to be a big farewell party. Nobody wanted one, anyway. They just wanted to be left to get on with the tasks in hand, without drawing any attention to themselves.

On Friday, 19 November, there was a final meeting, attended by everyone except Jimmy Moule and Tyro, who had asked Alan to represent him. Jimmy sent his apologies from Boston, not only for the meeting, but for the voyage itself, and wished everyone well. He had a busy law firm to run and could not afford to take the time off. It would be unfair on his partners. With great regret, he would not be coming.

Jeffrey was at the meeting. Gary had been angered by Jeffrey's reinstatement by the university, which meant that he could come on the voyage, though Gary would remain the project manager. It would cause complications on the trip.

For his part, Jeffrey was stunned to discover that Ernst Brage was to be captain of the *Moringa*. Ernst, the Norwegian who had flirted with Anna on the day he had bought the ship. Yet again, as with Tyro, a man Jeffrey had disparaged had come back into his life.

Ernst was there. He nodded in recognition to Jeffrey and smiled warmly to Anna. He then outlined the course they would take: virtually due south. He did not anticipate any problems from the weather at this time of year. He reminded them that he was responsible for the safety of the *Moringa* and everyone on board, and his word would be law in any crisis. He caused laughter by saying that he loved ships and hated passengers. Gary intervened to say that nobody was a passenger. The project team was a scientific group and would be referred to as the Warlocks. Ernst stayed affable and said that the ship's crew would be there to help but should be allowed to get on with their own jobs. He inspired confidence but was clearly not interested in making friends. When asked what he thought of the voyage, he said it was heroism worthy of Vikings. The idea of filling his tanks from an iceberg was madness, but maybe they would succeed. The fight against drought made him ready to try. Jeffrey was impressed but felt that it was wiser, at this time, to say nothing. He saw Ernst as a threat.

When asked about the length of time the voyage would take, Ernst said the maximum time they could be at sea would be ten weeks, but he envisaged about eight weeks. Even allowing for bad weather, the journey south should not take more than three weeks, and the journey from the iceberg to Mombasa, also about three weeks. That left up to four weeks to harvest water from the iceberg, depending on the weather and other factors.

Where was the iceberg? Gary stepped in here to say that it was in the Southern Ocean, almost due south of Heard Island, for anyone wanting to look it up. It was near latitude 60 degrees south, outside the Antarctic Circle but in the Southern Ocean. There would be other icebergs in the vicinity, but this one was the target because it was so big, and seemed stable, according to the satellite views from the National Ice Center.

Did it have a name? All icebergs are given a letter and a number by the National Ice Center, Gary replied. This iceberg was D something, but he could not remember. Anyway, to the Warlocks, this was the ice island of Fortune. Fortune was its name.

On a different topic, Alan announced that Tyro would be flying from Stansted to Entebbe, Uganda on the second of January. There, he would spend time with his family and then fly to Bhavnagar. Tyro and Alan would be on the flight as passengers, so there were still four places, if anyone wanted to come. They would have about ten days in which to visit Kampala and a Ugandan game park. Tyro would contact some of his game ranger friends and arrange it all. Lucy jumped at the opportunity, even as Alan was still speaking. She turned to Anna for support. Anna was just as keen, so she offered to go, and when Maggie said she would go too, that left one last place. Everyone expected Jeffrey to say he would go too, but he stayed silent, and Leena grabbed her chance.

Leena had been going steadily mad, trying to stall her parents and find a way out of her predicament. Now had come this godsend.

Gary was furious. He had taken it for granted, without asking her, that she would go with him to see him off from Bhavnagar, and he had booked flights for himself and her. He wanted to be ahead of the others, and she would be with him.

"That's not possible, sorry," he announced coldly.

Leena felt frightened but held her ground. "It is possible," she said, "and I wish to take that place. Four ladies together can look after each other. It makes up for not being able to go to Devon, don't you think, Maggie, Anna?"

"Sure," Anna replied at once. "Why not?"

"But I've bought our tickets," Gary protested.

"It would be fun to have Leena with us," Maggie quickly intervened, and that settled the matter. Gary had been outvoted.

"Looks like it's agreed, then," David concluded.

"I will tell your parents that you are on your way to India, with three women friends. That will please them," Raja added. There was firmness in his voice, but it was not disapproval.

From this meeting onwards, though, Gary perceived that it was him against the rest and allied himself to Ernst Brage, until well into the voyage.

Everyone marked their departure on the first leg of their journey in their own way. Gary and Leena chose to be alone. Leena had already told Gary about her father's edict, that her relationship with him must end, and Gary had put the whole blame on his own shoulders, cursing his gambling habit, and the embezzlement of funds, for robbing him of a future with Leena. Neither of them felt like being in company that night.

David and Jacqueline organised a send-off dinner for Lucy, but she told them she already had a party organised with a bunch of friends. Their disappointment lasted about three minutes, until they realised that they were free to do as they chose. They not only confirmed their table at the Hotel Felix but reserved a luxury room as well, so they could drink what they liked and make the most of the night.

Jeffrey and Anna invited Tyro and Alan to have dinner with them in their home. Maggie was staying the night with them.

At the end of dinner, Tyro raised his glass, looked at Jeffrey, and said, "To Arthur."

"To Arthur," came the response from everyone around the table.

Sometime later, Jeffrey managed to find time to talk to Tyro on his own. "You know," he began, "I'm not sure whether you're my friend or not."

"I think we understand each other," Tyro replied.

"In any case, I'm grateful to you for writing to the university to withdraw the allegations against me. Why did you do it?"

"A conversation I had with Raja. It made me realise you inspire people, Jeff, as you inspired Arthur to do the work that he did. Whatever it was you stole, I think he would have wanted you to have it. You generate strong feelings in people, one way or another."

Jeffrey said, "That letter saved me. I was staring ruin in the face, but that letter changed everything. It turned out that my chief accuser was hiding it, but it was discovered in his files when he fell down some stairs and had to be carted off to hospital."

Tyro noticed Anna standing quietly behind Jeffrey, listening to their conversation. "Your chief accuser fell downstairs. That was a lucky coincidence," Tyro said, but he was looking at Anna as he said it.

"I'll say so," Jeffrey said, oblivious to Anna's presence and concentrating on the coffee machine. Over his shoulder, Anna held Tyro's gaze and gave a slight smile. Tyro returned the smile. The lioness had pounced.

"You're a lucky man, Jeff."

"What, to have me?" Anna said brightly, as if she had just come within hearing. "I agree with that."

The flight from England to Uganda was highly enjoyable in the luxurious passenger section of Tyro's airbus. Mostly, they talked, ate, read novels, and dozed, with short re-fuelling stops in Rome and Cairo. On arrival at Entebbe airport, they were not hampered by any heavy luggage, as it was able to stay on board, and they went quickly through immigration and stepped into Africa.

Alan was not interested in game parks. He was looking forward to visiting Tyro's church in Jinja and attending a prayer meeting there, and he and Tyro were leaving the four women at the airport. However, Tyro had made sure that they would see Uganda in its best light. He saw them off in his Twin-Otter, and they were flown, at his own expense, directly to the airstrip in the game park. They stayed three days in the game lodge, going on the morning and evening game drives, taking a motor launch along the channel between the big lakes, and sunbathing beside the swimming pool. Each evening, after the game drive, they showered and sat on the veranda, sipping *waragi* cocktails before dinner and a sound sleep.

Having allowed them three days to acclimatise to their new environment, Tyro had arranged for the tempo of the tour to change. They left the tourist trail behind. Nicholas, a friend from Tyro's youth, now a senior game ranger, collected them from the lodge and drove them about forty kilometres to the small town where he lived. Although all four women were determined to have an exciting time, they all felt the underlying tension between Anna and Leena and found it easier to be compatible by pairing up. Maggie felt protective towards Leena, and by coming to her support when Anna made some of her barbed comments, she became Leena's natural ally. Lucy, for her part, adored Anna. She knew it was Anna's influence on Jeffrey that had made it possible for her to overcome the doubts of David and Jacqueline. Also, it was Anna who had organised the diving lessons.

Nicholas explained on the journey to the village that the inhabitants mainly spoke a form of Swahili; they would not all understand English. Foreigners, he said, were known as *Wazungu*, and his wife and her female relatives and friends were all looking forward to welcoming the Wazungu ladies. His wife, Birungi, was very suspicious that her husband had gone to pick up four strange women. Two of them were to stay with his wife and family, and two with a widowed cousin, Sarah, and her children. Her husband had died of AIDS, but she had been wise and followed the advice of health visitors in answer to her husband's needs, and God had spared her.

"Tyro told me that one of you is a soldier. Is that you?" he asked Anna, sitting beside him as the Land Rover Defender kicked up a cloud of dust along the dirt road.

"There are two of us," Anna replied, indicating Maggie, sitting in the back with Lucy and Leena, the bags on the floor behind them.

"But you are the real soldier, yes? You are the one who guards the professor?"

Anna and Maggie shared a quick glance, and both knew they wanted to be around for the action. "We'll stay with you," Anna said. "Maggie and I are both trained soldiers. We won't be in your way, and it's possible you will need our help."

"Yes, that might be good," Nicholas replied. "But please, it could be a risk for you to be here," he said, turning politely to Lucy and Leena. Clearly, he was right. Nowhere in the village offered much protection from a rampaging hippo. It was agreed that Anna and Maggie would stay, while Lucy and Leena returned to the town by bus with Danny, who took over Anna's rifle. Lucy became the spear bearer; they made an odd sight as they boarded the bus to town.

The village was set on top of a gentle slope about sixty metres from the water's edge. The buildings were made of wood and mud, with elephant-grass roofing. Some walls were made of single layers of brick, but any of them could collapse under attack from an angry bull hippo. The biggest structure was the bar, with a long roof supported by wooden posts, and walls waist-height without doors in the doorways. It was the first building the fishermen came to as they walked up from the water's edge, and from its benches, there was a commanding view of the boats. Nicholas placed himself there with his rifle and prepared to wait. The bar owner brought him a beer, and the two of them started chatting quietly. The vigil started at about ten o'clock in the evening.

Anna and Maggie sat on the far side of the bar, partly to give Nicholas a full view of the shore, and partly for their own privacy. They had gone back to their makeshift camp for a supper of fish they had bought, followed by a short rest, and had returned to the bar with a thermos flask of coffee. The village was quiet. There was no movement. The only light was from a sliver of moon, and their eyes had grown accustomed to the dark. In the background were the ever-present trills of the cicadas and the occasional sounds of owls and big mammals.

"It's quite like old times: the two of us in the darkness on a night exercise," Anna said quietly, as they sat, leaning over their plastic mugs.

"Don't get me started," Maggie replied. "Have you heard from Jeffrey?"

"Just a text to say they've arrived in Mumbai, and that he's missing me." A little smile passed over Anna's face.

"Oh yes," Maggie said sceptically. "Which part of you?"

Anna passed her phone over to Maggie, with the text brightly lit: "Arrived Mumbai. nlp. xx"

"It's not the most caring of messages, is it?" Maggie said, passing back the phone.

Anna extinguished the screen. "Actually, it's quite romantic. It stands for '*Ne lavez pas.*'

"That means 'Don't wash,' doesn't it?"

"Something like that," Anna cooed, her mind drifting fondly to intimacy with Jeffrey. "It's our coded message to each other – one of them."

"That's not romantic, that's disgusting," Maggie protested.

"I disagree. It's nice that he likes my womanly smell. He doesn't mean it too literally," she giggled. "I love it when I wake in the night, feeling his warmth and getting the manly scent of his body."

"Not for me, thank you," Maggie said firmly.

There was silence between the two of them following this remark, broken by Anna saying in a very low voice, "Maggie, have you something you want to tell me about Leena?"

"Like what?" Maggie bluffed. It was on the tip of her tongue to say, "Leena is pregnant," but she just managed to stop herself.

"Are you falling in love with her?"

"What? No! Why do you ask?" Maggie shot back at her. Anna detected guilt.

"She's very beautiful," Anna cooed supportively. "You seemed very pleased to be with her last night, and today you were so protective of her. It has to mean something is going on. Is she receptive to your interest?"

Maggie could not confess total innocence. "Yes and no. She's a bit fed up with men at the moment, and she's glad of my friendship. It's platonic."

"Oh Maggs, it's such a relief that you've told me. I won't interfere, and I won't tell anyone else, I promise." Anna took Maggie's left hand by the index finger and ran it across her closed lips in the darkness. "Sealed," she said.

They started to listen more attentively to the sounds of the night and continued to talk sporadically. The barman went to bed, leaving a cluster of empty beer bottles on the table and several full ones at Nicholas's side. They watched him over the space of half an hour slump, and rouse himself, and then slump and slumber, empty beer bottles clinking as they rolled and dropped off the table.

"Well, that's the end of the hippo hunt," Maggie muttered. "We might as well bed down here."

Anna agreed, and they were just stretching out on the benches when a huffing and a grunting came from the direction of the water.

"That's the hippo. It's coming back," Maggie whispered.

As she spoke, Anna was zigzagging round benches and tables to the snoring Nicholas. She started to shake him, urgently, whispering to him to wake up and pinching his earlobes, but to no avail.

"It's no good. *You'll* have to shoot it," Maggie murmured, moving to be beside her.

"I can't do that. I'm not licensed."

"Bugger the licence. If that hippo ruins any more boats, this village goes hungry, and Nicholas gets sacked. Here's the rifle. Now, use it."

They scrambled over the low wall. Anna checked there was a bullet in the breech, and with Maggie close behind her, she started tentatively to the water's edge.

"We could be in real trouble, Maggs." Anna sounded deeply worried.

"Only if you miss him, and you're not going to do that," Maggie replied calmly, trying to keep Anna relaxed.

"I need to see its head. Do something to attract its attention," Anna whispered, anxiously, but there was no need. At that moment, the hippo became aware of their presence and turned towards them, offering Anna the perfect shot. She raised the rifle but there was no bang.

"I can't do it." Anna was aiming between the hippo's eyes, but she was paralysed by her anxiety. It began to lurch forward, heaving its weight up the slope.

"Yes, you can. Leena's pregnant with Jeffrey's baby."

Only in the deepest recesses of Maggie's mind was there any logic to these urgent words; they just spilled out of her mouth. Their effect, however, was electric.

"He is so dead," Anna muttered, all tension gone, and as if she had all the time in the world, she squeezed the trigger. Roosting birds flew squawking from the nearby trees at the sound. The hippo collapsed without so much as a twitch.

"Good girl, job done, now give me the gun. Quickly."

Maggie almost tore the gun from Anna's grasp, ran to the bar, and threw it down beside Nicholas, and then she rushed back to Anna, who was staring at the hippo. The first villagers were already nervously approaching the bar.

"Did you mean—" Anna began, but Maggie cut her short.

"Now is not the time, love. Follow me. Keep your head down," Maggie gave the orders, and Anna obediently followed her as they made their way, in the shadow of the bushes, to where the bus was parked, ready for the morning. They clambered into it and sat huddled side by side.

"I can't believe we just did that," Anna whispered.

"I can't believe we just got away with it," Maggie replied. They looked at each other and burst into suppressed laughter.

"Did you mean what you said? Leena's having Jeffrey's baby?"

"Yes. But it was better for the hippo to get the bullet than Jeffrey."

"Who says they won't both get one?" Anna asked ominously.

"Well, don't blame me," Maggie muttered unsympathetically. "I warned you when you first got involved with him that you'd be crying on my shoulder because you'd found him with another woman."

Anna nestled her head comfortably against Maggie's shoulder. "Am I crying?" she challenged Maggie, sleepily.

"No, you wretch, you're in seventh heaven, more like," Maggie conceded. Then, after a pause, she added, "But you're not to hurt Leena. You made a promise. I made a promise, and I've broken it already, but only to make you shoot that damned hippo."

"Lips sealed, like I said." Anna was very close to sleep now, but she gave Maggie another squeeze to counter the bitter pang of sorrow that had swept over her. "He's mine. She'll never get him. We'll sort it out."

Elated and exhausted, they dozed off. They were discovered by the bus driver at about seven o'clock, much to the relief of the village. Their empty camp site, and the thermos flask in the bar, had raised fears that the Wazungu women had been carried off by the leopard known to frequent the area.

"We went crawling through the bushes with a leopard on the loose," Maggie whispered, horrified, a little later.

148

Nicholas was the hero of the village. There was amusement that he had been found unconscious amid the beer bottles just after the shooting, but he had done his duty, shot the hippo, and saved the boats, so nobody begrudged him the beer. Anna and Maggie were led down to see the hippo. The process of butchering it had begun, and the maribou storks and the vultures were spiralling around and landing close by, but Maggie still managed to take the photo she wanted of the hippo's head close-up.

Be scared, Jeffrey, she thought as she looked with satisfaction at the photograph. *Be very scared.*

Danny came with the Land Rover to pick them all up at about nine o'clock. He had Lucy and Leena with him. Although there was much excited chatter when they first arrived and saw the hippo, a strange contented silence fell over the occupants of the Land Rover on the way back into town, as each savoured their own special secret: Anna and Maggie knew Leena's secret. Nicholas's secret was that he could not remember the night's events, but he had seen the bullet wound in the hippo's skull and knew that he could not have fired the fatal shot from his position in the bar. Lucy's secret was only known to Danny, and vice versa – and they would treasure it forever.

They spent most of the day in town, but in late afternoon, after farewells and presents of appreciation from the ladies to their hostesses, Nicholas drove them back to the park rangers' quarters near the airstrip, ready for a flight to Kampala in the morning. Danny came too and particularly enjoyed sitting with Lucy and pointing out the wildlife as he and Nicholas took them on a privileged late-evening drive, after the tourist vehicles had gone. They spent several minutes beside a big hippo wallow, where the beasts lay benign and placid or hauled their massive frames through the muddy goo and onto bare ground. It really was dark as Nicholas started up the engine for what they all thought was the last time, but he turned off the main route and headed about two hundred metres across the scrub to a solitary tree and switched off the engine again.

He turned to Anna and said, "And now I have something especially for you."

He turned on the spotlight, pointing it into the tree. There, on the lowest branch, about five metres from the ground, lay a young, maned lion, looking down on them.

"I was told about him this afternoon. Grassland lions do not often climb trees, but there are some which do," Nicholas murmured.

"He is so beautiful," Anna said adoringly.

"A lion for a lioness," Nicholas said, and this time, nobody thought it funny. It was a touching tribute, and Anna appreciated its true significance.

They all watched in silence for about half a minute, and then Anna turned to Nicholas and said, "Thank you," in a way that spoke of mutual respect. The silence in the car continued as he doused the light, turned on the engine, and headed back to the main route. But as he swung the Land Rover onto it, he called out, "Isn't Africa exciting?"

There was a cry of "Yes" from everyone in the car, and Nicholas gave his high-pitched laugh, and the chatter and raucous laughter continued until the journey's end.

Chapter 9

BHAVNAGAR

Throughout early January 2011, the teams and equipment arrived at the docks of Bhavnagar, and the loading of the *Moringa* took place, including the sacks of fertiliser that nobody bothered about.

The airship caused great interest. It had a rigid framework, the parts being brought on a flight from Entebbe. Putting it together fired the enthusiasm of every man in the shipyard, and Tyro had a continual stream of helpers, though his confidence rested with Solomon, his engineer, and his three groundsmen/mechanics: Henry, Council, and Jomo. They set to work in the bitter cold, with a week to go. It was a design feature of the airship that it could be taken apart and reconstructed in areas of wilderness where there were only basic facilities, and Solomon had been trained by the company in Canada, when Tyro had attended the flying course, so they erected it while it was within the perimeter of the shipyard and protected with guards. It was a hybrid craft, kept aloft by the contained gas and the action of the two engines at the back of the gondola. Its engines were capable of taking additional energy from solar panels built into the fabric of the shell. The controls were very similar to those of a conventional aeroplane, except that the craft had a hover facility and could rise or fall almost vertically when needed, especially when docking. The gondola, for the crew and equipment, was part of the shell. The gas to provide lift was helium from a local shipping agent, and the containers were clearly marked "Helium." Tyro showed excellent health and safety credentials by insisting that nobody smoked and only non-spark tools were used on connecting the pipes. The gas inflated several separate collapsible cells within the shell.

These were filled initially from a road tanker, but two large tanks had been built into the bows of the ship so that, on the voyage, the gas cells on the airship could be partially deflated by pumping gas under pressure into the tanks, when the airship was moored, and then reinflated as required. When finished, it looked futuristic and awesome.

Not everything went to plan in the last few days before the *Moringa* set sail. David was not at all sympathetic when he received a message the day before departure, to tell him that two team members had been in a Laurel-and-Hardy mess-up at Heathrow, and neither would be coming. One had lost his passport between home and the airport, and the other had delayed too long to try and help him; running for the aircraft, he tripped, fell, and broke his right arm. David had an emergency meeting with Arnesh, who immediately offered the services of his team to help with the lagoons.

There was a welcome surprise, though, in the late arrival of Jimmy Moule. When he had written to say he could not come, he did not realise that his wife, Karen, had been in discussion with his partners, and that they had agreed to award Jimmy a leave of absence. He was so highly principled that he felt unable to accept, until Karen, against her own wishes, persuaded him to go. At the last possible moment, he sent a text message to Jeffrey to check that there was still room for him, arriving heavily jet-lagged. He went straight to bed and was still fast asleep as the *Moringa* left port.

The day before sailing, Raja forced Leena to say her farewell to her friends. He was not prepared to let her be anywhere near the *Moringa* as it left harbour. He stood, virtually on guard, as they held a small lunchtime reception at the Bluehill Hotel, at the end of which she went up to each of them to wish them a safe and successful voyage. Alan was there, but not Tyro; Gary stayed away as well. When the ship left harbour, Leena would be asleep in Raja's villa, several kilometres out of town, and later in the day, she would fly with him to Delhi to be reunited with her parents.

That afternoon, Tyro and Lothar, another pilot, practised their helicopter landings. Both of them took the helicopter, a Russian-built thug of a machine called a Hind, liberated in the Sudanese civil war, on a series of circuits, the noise of which drummed into the ears of everyone on the ground as they finished loading the ship and commenced boarding.

There was a silence, and the news spread that Tyro was taking the airship up. Crowds gathered at the shipyard to watch him walk across the barren ground to the tethered craft. He took Solomon with him, and they created a sensation as they took off from the shipyard and circled the town and the harbour, while the ground crew made their way to the *Moringa*.

The docking, however, was another matter. Tyro had trouble with the buoyancy and weight distribution as he approached the *Moringa*, and his ground crew watched in horror as it seemed the airship, the chief pilot, and the chief engineer were going to be wiped out before the expedition had set sail. He released the mooring ropes from too high up, and it took tremendous effort from the ground crew, and others, to manhandle the craft, secure the ropes to the winches, and bring it to the deck.

It was still night-time, and very cold, on the morning of Friday, 21 January 2011, as the *Moringa* was released from her moorings and made her way into the Arabian Sea. There was just the faintest light of dawn, which was lost in the blaze of floodlights from the shore, the ship herself, and the tug which helped her navigate the narrow channel. Jacqueline was on the dockside to wave them off. She and David had gone to bed together in his cabin, knowing that she had to be ashore by four o'clock. She was strongly tempted to stay on board and lingered by the gangway with David and Lucy until the very last minute. As she stepped ashore, the gangway was removed. She was as excited about the trip as they were and waved to them both, then stood and watched with a small group of workers from the night shift. Jeffrey and Anna appeared on deck and then Maggie. The maintenance crew appeared from their quarters further towards the bow, and they received cheers and waves from their friends on the quayside. Then there was such activity and so many people coming and going that she had to accept that the parting had taken place, and it was time for her to leave, as well.

One of the dockyard managers had been charged with looking after Jacqueline and accompanied her back to central office for warmth and tea. After half an hour or so, Raja's pilot, Birindar, met her as arranged and flew her the short hop to Bhavnagar airport. By now, it was daylight. Alighting from the elegant Squirrel, after waiting for the rotor to stop, she saw Tyro walking out to the Hind. He had arranged to fly out to join the ship, having completed some final matters that needed his attention.

"G'morning, Tyro," she called cheerfully, feeling comforted that he represented a last link with the departing ship.

"*Jambo*, Jacqueline," Tyro greeted her. They had seen so much of each other over the past few days that they felt true friendship. He waited for her to join him, although she noticed him look at his watch and realised that she should not delay him.

"I'm sure you want to be under way," she said. "Has anything turned up which they left behind?"

"One or two things," Tyro replied in a noncommittal way.

"Isn't that always the case?" Jacqueline responded in the hackneyed manner that indicated her lack of interest. "Still, this will be exciting for you – your first landing on the ship."

"First landing on the moving ship; I was practising yesterday, you know."

That was stating the obvious.

"I saw Alan on the ship last night," Jacqueline continued.

"Yes, he and Roly have been discussing the beauty of machines ever since they met. He had no wish to fly with me this morning."

"I would happily go with you," Jacqueline said with a laugh. "In fact, if you stay any longer, I might beg you to take me with you."

Tyro smiled respectfully. "That would give us both problems," he replied. "I must go, Jacqueline. I have no time to waste. I'm sorry."

"Of course, you need to be off. Good luck."

They did not shake hands. It seemed too formal. He climbed into the Hind and appeared a few moments later in the pilot's seat, and they waved to each other. She stood back to watch, but the noise and down-currents of air made her step into the heliport terminal. The brutish machine rose and hovered, reminding her of a predatory dragonfly, as Tyro sought out his direction and then flew tugger-tugger-tugger into the distance.

She was fully prepared to take a taxi back to her hotel and so was surprised to see Raja draw up in his chauffeured car as she was about to go. She thought it was charming of him to be so considerate. Yet when he saw her, he did not smile. He walked rapidly over to her, asked her to go with him, and continued onto the heliport tarmac, where he looked around in an agitated way. Birindar, having spotted him from an office window, ran out to see what the matter was.

Raja turned to Jacqueline and asked, "How long ago did Tyro Mukasa take off?"

"About five minutes ago," Jacqueline said, uncertain about this turn of events. "What has he forgotten?"

"Any sense of decency. I knew he was a thief. I should never have trusted him. Birindar, five minutes – can we catch him?" He spoke in English so that Jacqueline could follow the conversation.

"We can try, sir."

"Then let's do so. He's aiming for the *Moringa*. Jacqueline, please, I beg you to come with us."

"Hold on," Jacqueline said with natural hesitancy. "I must know what all this is about."

"He has my niece with him. I must try to get her back at once, or she will be ruined. You are a wise woman, Jacqueline; you can talk sense into her which a heavy-handed uncle cannot do. Now, please, any delay, and they will be too far away."

"This is all too exciting; I must just run to the loo," Jacqueline exclaimed, jogging back into the heliport as Raja voiced his exasperation in vain.

She came dashing out again within two minutes, smiling and apologising, and told him if he was going to be cross, she wouldn't come. She had plenty of experience in handling bad-tempered men. Inside the helicopter, they could only communicate by microphone, but the moment she and Raja had their headphones in place, she started firing questions.

"Are you saying Tyro's kidnapped her?"

"No, no, they must have planned this together. I deliberately kept her away from the ship to prevent her trying to get on board."

"But I don't understand. She's Gary's partner. It's for them to decide whether she goes or not."

"No," Raja said abruptly, without any of his normal courtesy. "She knows very well that it is over. It has to be. Her parents have ordered her to go back home. I am responsible to see that it happens."

Raja was beginning to regret his hasty decision to ask Jacqueline to accompany him, and they had not even taken off.

"But she's a grown woman. She doesn't have to listen to her parents." Jacqueline felt she was stating the obvious.

"She is a most irresponsible woman. She is highly intelligent, and she begged her parents for the chance to study at Cambridge. Naturally, I supported her. But this is typical of her behaviour," Raja exclaimed.

"She's a vivacious, independent young woman. She's seized life with both hands, and like all young people, she's made a few mistakes."

"Her parents will find her a suitable husband."

"Oh, that's ridiculous," Jacqueline said fiercely. "You might as well send her to prison."

The two of them were now as heated as each other.

"If she disobeys her parents, she brings shame on the whole family. Her sisters will never find good husbands," Raja argued.

"If they are even half as beautiful as she is, they will have no trouble at all," Jacqueline said dismissively. "I've heard that there's a shortage of women in India. Young men will be falling over themselves to marry them."

An angry gap in the conversation ensued as they took off and flew in pursuit of Tyro. It was broken by Raja: "Whose side are you on, Jacqueline?" He was unable to contain his exasperation. "I asked you to come because I thought you would help me to talk reason into the girl. I thought you would be on my side and the side of her parents, who are doing their best to save her reputation."

"I am on the side of feminine emancipation, Raja," Jacqueline said with conviction. "A just society treats women as equals." Then her tone softened, coaxing him out of his anger. "Raja, give her this last chance. With her intelligence and the experience she's gaining, in twenty years' time, she could be one of India's inspirational leaders, whether in business or politics."

"I most respectfully intervene, sir," Birindar said, his voice coming over their headsets, and they realised that he would have heard their conversation. "But the helicopter ahead is landing on the big ship. Should I seek permission to land as well?"

"Raja, David is on board," Jacqueline said urgently. "He's the most dependable man you could ever hope to find. I'll send him a message to look after Leena and to make sure she shares a cabin with Lucy or Maggie Robinson. That way, she will not bring disrespect to her name, or you, or your family. Please, don't let's make a scene now."

Raja sat silently a moment, reflecting on her words, then a weight seemed to lift from his mind. "On that point, I fully agree with you," he said in a change of mood that surprised and delighted her. "This great adventure deserves a great send-off. Birindar, we shall not land. We shall give them a fly-past. Can you do that?"

"Yes sir, we shall give them a fly past," Birindar replied with such enthusiasm that it made Jacqueline grip her shoulder straps, in anticipation of what was to come.

"And Jacqueline," Raja said happily, "you and I, we shall wave and wave, and wish them a safe and wonderful journey. My sister will not speak to me ever again, but— My God, Jacqueline, can you see the ship? What a magnificent sight."

On board the *Moringa*, Anna had just said to Maggie, as they looked out on the ocean, what a relief it was to have seen the last of Leena, so she could work out her feelings for Jeffrey, but then Tyro's helicopter came into view, landed, and disgorged Leena. Everyone ran on deck to witness Tyro's landing, and a general cheer had greeted him and Leena as they stepped out, when suddenly, they became aware of another helicopter approaching fast and diving towards them. Tyro stood transfixed, recognising Raja's helicopter instantly, and wondered whether it had a machine gun in the nose. However, instead of releasing a volley of bullets, it commenced a series of swoops, figures of eight, and low passes, just off the port and starboard beams, and the passengers inside could be seen waving hard.

David and Lucy recognised Jacqueline and waved back in amazement. Leena saw Raja staring straight at her on one low pass, and she put her hands together in supplication, then realised he was waving; on the next pass, she waved back, joyfully, with great love. All the ship's company managed a moment on deck to see the display, and Ernst ordered the sounding of the ship's horn in response. Then with a final pass, the helicopter continued astern without turning and, rising gently, disappeared towards land.

The *Moringa* had started her voyage.

Maggie was ecstatic to see Leena and, despite offending Anna, Jeffrey, and Gary, who were all thoroughly displeased, welcomed her and offered to share her cabin, which had two bunks. Leena accepted gladly.

The depth of Gary's anger was too deep for anyone else to comprehend. He had been able to rationalise the loss of Leena as a girlfriend, because of his deceit and dishonesty in stealing money to go gambling. He blamed himself and could see that a respectable Indian family could not forgive such behaviour in a prospective son-in-law. It explained why Leena could still find him sexy but not want to marry him. But now, he could rationalise her actions only by assuming that he had been ditched so that she could be with Maggie. She must have been planning this all the time she was pretending that she was a dutiful daughter. Worse, her new affair would take place in front of him and everyone else who knew them, rubbing salt into his wound. Then and there, he lost all affection for her.

"If that's what you want, that's fine by me," Gary snapped at Leena when she accepted Maggie's offer of cabin space. "I've got work to do. I don't want you around. Is that clear? You stay out of my sight, you little bitch."

Leena was clearly upset by the vehemence of Gary's words; Maggie was furious. Anna seized the initiative, disregarding her own misgivings, and determined to prevent the project disintegrating into violence on the first day. She offered Leena the use of any clothes or toiletries she might need. It was a gesture of support that showed whose side she was on.

Gary looked as if he would hit Anna, so Alan hastily tried to defuse the situation by quoting from the Bible: "It is the time when Kings go forth to battle."

"What the hell does that mean?" Gary asked.

"It means that you have work to do, and we should respect that. It is not the time for leaders to be worrying about women, or else you could end up like David and Bathsheba."

Gary now looked confused as well as angry. "What the hell are you on about? Fuck off. Butt out," he spat at Alan.

This brought Tyro into the dispute. He stood face to face with Gary, and the two big men squared their shoulders and clenched their fists; as neither was going to back down, a violent punch-up seemed imminent, when Jimmy Moule said in his calm, reflective voice that the two of them reminded him of a pair of bull-moose that he had seen in Alaska. He spoke as if he had all the time in the world. Jeffrey asked Jimmy what happened to the moose. Though nobody was moving, they were all dying of curiosity.

"Their antlers were locked – ridiculous. There they were, two fine creatures, no use to anybody," Jimmy drawled. "I had to shoot them both."

They were no longer frightening. They were ridiculous. While the others tried to hide their smiles, Gary repeated that he had work to do, Tyro said so did he, and that was the end of the matter. The *Moringa* was so large that once the teams settled into their different tasks, it was not hard to avoid each other.

That evening, Maggie and Leena were undressing together. "You're taking a big risk," Maggie said to her. "There's no escape from this ship for ten weeks, and no maternity unit, either."

Leena turned to her happily, undoing her bra as she did so. "I don't want to escape, Maggie. This is where I want to be. It was India I had to escape from. Don't you understand?" She tossed her head to clear her long black hair from her eyes and then slipped her nightdress over her head.

Maggie watched appreciatively. "What are you going to tell Jeffrey and Gary when they start noticing your change of shape?"

"They won't notice. And if they do, we just say I'm putting on weight. I'll wear loose clothes; they won't know the difference."

"You just said 'we' then. You're not expecting to involve me in all this subterfuge, are you?" Maggie asked as she slipped her pants off; naked, she reached for a towel to wrap round herself. The width of the cabin being partially taken up by the two bunk beds made it necessary for her and Leena to stand in close proximity.

"You are involved, Maggie," Leena said as she removed her own pants from under her nightdress. "I think you've been involved for some weeks."

Maggie dropped her gaze in embarrassment at Leena's words. "Well, I'm trying not to be," she said. "Gary will be back sometime, when he's not so busy and has time on his hands. You better work out what you're going to say to him."

Then she shuffled into the tiny en suite bathroom, and Leena realised they would just have to accustom themselves to the sound of each other's ablutions.

When Maggie came out, she grimaced apologetically. "Sorry you had to hear that; your turn."

Leena did not get up from where she was reclining on the lower bunk. "Maggie," she said quietly. "Please just sit beside me."

Maggie dabbed her face a few times with her face towel to give her some seconds to think. She had her bath towel around her, but it was constricting as she tried to sit, so she loosened it and just kept it draped over the front of her firm, lanky body with her hand, as she settled herself by Leena.

"I can't keep Gary, and I can't keep my baby," Leena said simply, with a maturity and gravity that told Maggie not to waste time on empty expostulations of disbelief. Instead, she reached out and took one of Leena's hands in her free hand. She saw that Leena was sad, but there were no tears, no signs of frailty.

"Did your uncle find out about the baby?" Maggie asked, trying to deduce events from the things she knew. "I actually wondered, this morning, as he flew around us, whether he'd been chasing you rather than coming to see you off."

"Yes, he was chasing me, but only because he loves me. He has always protected me from my parents. They are so strict."

"So you had to escape India to escape your parents, is that it?"

"Yes."

"Do they know about the baby too?"

Leena kissed Maggie's hand affectionately.

"Nobody knows, except you," she replied. "Not my uncle, not my family, nobody. It's our secret, yours and mine."

"Why was Jacqueline with your uncle, do you think?"

"Pure chance. Tyro and I had everything planned. I had just got into the helicopter when my uncle's helicopter landed and Jacqueline got out. It was awful. She saw Tyro and came over to speak with him. I expected my uncle to turn up at any moment, but Tyro was clever, and we got away in time."

Maggie stood up and folded the bath towel. "I think you and I have had enough excitement for one day. I sleep naked, by the way, so you better close your eyes if that offends you."

Leena watched her climb the small ladder beside her bed, and saw the bunk above her give slightly as it took Maggie's weight.

Leena started to get up to go to the bathroom, when Maggie's voice floated down to her again: "I still don't understand why you're breaking up with Gary."

"Because my parents called me back to India to marry a man by arrangement."

"What would they do if they found out about your pregnancy?"

"They would force me to have an abortion, for the sake of family honour. It would all be in secret. Now can I go to the bathroom?"

"It's getting a bit late for that."

"Going to the bathroom?" Leena repeated, sounding perplexed.

"No, no, having an abortion," Maggie explained hastily. "Sorry, I'm asking too many questions. I don't mean to be nosey."

"I like you being nosey. It shows that you care," Leena said, shuffling quickly to the loo.

When she came back, she saw that Maggie's light was still on above her bunk. As she climbed into her own bunk, Maggie's voice came from above, again: "I can't go to sleep without telling you something first."

Leena resigned herself to further conversation, while longing for sleep. "What do you want to tell me?" she asked, settling herself into her bunk.

"The secret about your baby: You know it, I know it, and so does Anna."

Leena felt disappointment more than anger at these words. "Why did you tell her? You promised not to tell anyone."

Maggie's head appeared upside down as she leant over her bunk. "I told her so as to save my life and hers," she said. "It was Anna who shot the hippo. Nicholas was too drunk. It was charging us, and she couldn't bring herself to pull the trigger."

"And that was the moment you decided to tell her my secret?" Leena asked, in disbelief.

"I'm a psychologist, love; I do these things. It worked. I told her that you were having Jeffrey's baby, and she immediately shot the hippo through the head."

"Oh," Leena said at this revelation; she lay back, staring up at the inverted Maggie. "Am I next, then?"

"You're the last person she'd shoot. Didn't you notice how she came to your defence when Gary shouted at you this morning? Hold on, I'm getting dizzy. Stay there."

With that, her head disappeared, and a second later, her whole body reappeared, coming down the ladder with the total lack of inhibition of a true naturist.

"Look, this time you've got to make a promise to me that you'll keep a secret," she said, sitting at the foot of Leena's bunk and pulling a towel over her legs.

"In the same way you kept my secret?" Leena queried.

"Even more so; even in the face of a charging tiger."

"I promise."

The two women looked at each other, aware of mutual affection, as Maggie explained, "Anna can't have children. She had her womb removed due to cancer. So you see, your child is quite possibly the only child that Jeffrey is going to father."

Leena was upset by the news. "Poor Anna," she said sadly.

"Anna's mad at you for having it off with Jeffrey, but she'll protect you with her life as long as you're carrying his child."

Leena absorbed this for a few seconds and then asked, "What about you?"

Maggie was surprised. "What about me?"

"We've talked about me. We've talked about Anna. What about you?"

"There's nothing to tell," Maggie said with a shrug. "I'm not pregnant, and I'm not the lover of an eccentric womaniser. It seems I'm here to pick up the pieces."

"Do you miss Anna as a partner?"

Maggie paused a moment to consider the question. "Anna doesn't know her own sexuality. She has had a very complicated life. I'm not totally excluded. I think she will always need me, one way or another."

Both women had unconsciously adopted the same pose, sitting with their chins resting on flexed knees.

"I love you. You told me once that I was beautiful," Leena said quietly. "Well, I think you are beautiful – and wise. You understand people."

"I should do – it's my job. And I like your compliment, even if I don't believe it. Thank you." Both women stayed silently where they were, glancing into each other's eyes. "I think it's time I went to my own bed," Maggie eventually declared. "It's not too far away, if you get my meaning."

She swung her legs to the floor, ducked her head forwards under the bunk, and their lips met softly.

"You could teach me yoga," Maggie commented lightly, as if the kiss had been an ordinary good night kiss, which both of them knew it was not.

She gave her excitement away by rising too quickly from the bunk and hitting her head on the side of the ladder.

"Oh shit, shit, shit," she exclaimed, clutching at her head and then murmuring profuse apologies for her profanity as she sank back onto the bunk.

Leena put her arm round Maggie's shoulders, unable to suppress a laugh. "Are you all right?"

Maggie laughed too, despite the pain. "Yeah, I'm fine; it was my own fault. But another kiss like that, and I might not get back to my own bunk, and I don't think that should happen until we have talked through a few things."

She was now aware of her nakedness, plus a lump on her head, and moisture between her thighs that she preferred to hide.

"I will teach you yoga, and you can give me counselling," Leena replied.

On that note, Maggie climbed up into her bunk, and they switched out their lights and muttered good night to each other.

That same evening, Raja entertained Jacqueline to dinner, prior to her departure for London the following day. During the evening, she noticed that he seemed restless and kept rubbing his stomach. Then he began to look worried, and he reached out to her, asking for help. He had a severe chest pain. Jacqueline's nursing skills came back to her, at once. She gave Raja an aspirin, called his physician, and arranged an emergency admission at the clinic, only a few minutes' drive in the chauffeured Rolls.

Two hours later, a stent was placed in the left anterior descending artery of Raja's heart, and he was admitted for the rest of the night. While he was undergoing the procedure, Jacqueline texted David to tell him that Raja had suffered a heart attack and then cancelled her flight. Raja would need to be properly looked after, and she was not needed urgently, anywhere else. Investigations showed that Raja's heart muscle was undamaged. The following day his condition was stable enough that he could be released, so she escorted him back home, soothed away his fears for Leena, and began to look after him in a way that nobody else had done since Sunita died.

So that is how everyone on board the *Moringa* came to be there.

How they all got off again is another matter.

163

Part 2

THE VOYAGE OF
THE MORINGA

Chapter 10

THE JOURNEY SOUTH

Jeffrey Harvey was impatient to be in Antarctica. What he looked on as *his* ship, the *Moringa*, was clear of the Indian coastline, having sailed almost the whole length of the west coast of the subcontinent. He really had nothing to do, except try to stay out of other people's way as they trained in the use of the equipment, made sure that everything was in order, and became familiar with the ship and everyone else aboard. The sense of team spirit strengthened, and the climatic changes that occurred every few days as they entered equatorial waters and headed down towards Antarctica meant constant discussion and planning as to what would be required and when.

The Warlocks quickly discovered that Ernst Brage the captain, was taciturn and business-like, and not inclined to socialise. Ramos Hernandez, the first officer, and Hans, the bosun, were extroverted, sociable men who were always willing to give advice and assistance. The ship's crew had little time for more than brief greetings. Most of them had worked under Ernst before, and they functioned as a close team, keeping to themselves, but Stefan and Silvio were two new crewmen he had selected. They were both in their early twenties, best friends, with the dream of starting a shipping business together. They were well qualified and had crewed everything from yachts to liners, trying to save money so that one day, they could lease their own yacht with which to start a business. The trouble was that life always seemed to have yet another woman on which to spend their cash. They had truly thought that by coming on this voyage, they were keeping away from temptation, and then Lucy had stepped aboard.

In the first few days of the voyage, Lucy flirted light-heartedly, pretending not to notice that both were watching her: running her hand gently through her hair, baring flesh in the tropical heat, that sort of thing. Then, about ten days into the voyage, they came to her as she left her laboratory and said they had to speak with her. She led them back to the laboratory, strictly off-limits to them, where they told her that she was ruining their friendship. She had to tell them which one she preferred.

She was speechless. She did not have any interest in either of them, but she now learnt that their passion had led them close to violence, without her having any knowledge of the depth of their feelings. She sat between them on the counter and gave them her decision: grow up, sex with neither, friendship with both. There were a few seconds of contemplative silence, but ten minutes later, they were all chatting happily together like old friends.

The other exception was the medical officer, Emily Ross. She initially felt that she did not belong anywhere, but in a way, that suited her. She quite often fell into conversation with Roly, who was much the same age and shared an interest in how things worked, whether the human body or a machine. They found that they could talk openly about themselves and the things that interested them. Emily had spent three years married to a doctor, who had focused on his career at the expense of hers, their marriage, and her health. A few months as a ship's doctor seemed to her a good first step in returning to professional life. Roly was very considerate and would sometimes call by the medical unit just to keep her company. She liked those visits.

It took several days for Emily to summon the courage to talk to Jeffrey, whom she saw as an eminent Cambridge professor, but one morning, he was standing alone on the main deck after she had completed her morning surgery: the normal selection of minor infections and injuries, which had taken about forty minutes to sort out.

"Good morning, Professor," she said, respectfully.

"Good morning, Dr Ross," he replied, teasing her for her formality. He liked Emily. She had a natural air of intelligence about her. "I'd prefer to be called Jeffrey," he said, sauntering over to the guardrail.

"Jeffrey," she corrected herself with a demure smile. "Could you tell me exactly where we are heading? Apart from the fact that it's an iceberg in Antarctica, I really have no idea."

Jeffrey pointed to a pod of dolphins near the ship, but the sight was common enough, now, not to stop the conversation.

"Antarctica is covered in ice," he began, "with a number of ice shelves stretching out into the ocean; the ice is hundreds of metres deep."

"Everyone knows that," Emily replied, unimpressed.

Jeffrey smiled at her scorn. "All right. Well, in the mid-nineties, one ice shelf started to crack. It's called the Amery ice shelf. This was probably just a natural occurrence and nothing to do with global warming. Then, in the Antarctic summer of 2004, a huge chunk broke away. I mean huge. If your vision of an iceberg is the sort of thing that sunk the Titanic, then think again. For a start, it's flat. Icebergs are divided into the flat and non-flat variety, and this one is flat. Secondly, it's over ten kilometres long and about eight kilometres wide."

"Oh, my God, that's an island," Emily exclaimed.

"There's enough water in it for the whole human population for a day. We've named it Fortune. So that's where we're going: to the iceberg of Fortune."

"How will you know where to find it? Won't it have melted by now?"

"We'll find it because it's always in the same place, and we have its GPS location. You know how 90 percent of an iceberg is under water? Well, Fortune is about two hundred feet or more above the surface, so there's well over a thousand feet below the surface. Having escaped from the Amery shelf, Fortune bobbed along for a while and then bumped into a raised part of the ocean-bed. Basically, it's stuck there, against the Montagu Ridge, at the southern tip of the Kerguelen Plateau. It's a raised part of the ocean-bed, vaguely horseshoe shaped. Fortune is stuck there."

"I see."

"And in those temperatures, it's not melting significantly either, and smaller icebergs bump into it, helping to keep it frozen."

"What will be the effect of gouging a big hole in it?"

"It's a tiny divot, not a big hole," Jeffrey corrected. "A thousand cubic metres, if we're lucky. I promised my missionary friend, Klaus Huber, that I'd bring him back enough for his town, so that if ever there's an outbreak of cholera again, he'll have enough pure water to keep them safe." He stopped talking, took in the beauty of the ocean, and continued in a kindlier fashion, "We're out to prove a point. If we can convince our backers to invest heavily, then, sure, we would expect the whole iceberg to disappear. But the point is that it's going to disappear one day, anyway, splitting into smaller chunks. We think it would be much better to harvest it as a resource, and store it for when it's needed, rather than let it disappear into the ocean."

"That sounds reasonable," Emily agreed; she hesitated and then asked tentatively, "What about our carbon footprint?"

Jeffrey shook his head in good-humoured exasperation. "That jargon, again; look, I'm a tree man. We're bringing trees and water to Africa. That means we're bringing oxygen to Africa. Hopefully, in two centuries' time or so, the conservationists will be calling for a national park to protect the last remnants of the Sahara Desert. Warmth, carbon dioxide, and sunshine are just what trees need."

"Hmm," Emily mused. "I might want to discuss that point of view." They laughed in friendship.

"Anytime. By the way, have you had a chance to talk to Anna yet? She's my fiancée."

"I didn't know she was your fiancée. Congratulations."

"I'm not supposed to call her that yet," Jeffrey confessed. "Please keep it to yourself. We've brought the ring with us, but she's still waiting for the right moment to announce it. It must be sometime on this trip; perhaps when we reach Fortune." He sounded bemused.

Emily was empathetic. "It's a big step isn't it?" she commented softly.

"You could say that. Any advice?" he asked, appreciative of her understanding.

Emily just smiled and shook her head.

The *Moringa* went through a year of seasonal changes in the space of two weeks. Ernst Brage slowed their progress near the Tropic of Capricorn so that he could carry out manoeuvres and familiarise himself with the ship's new steering gear and GPS system, that would enable him to keep her on station, close to Fortune, for days at a time, provided the weather was not too extreme. The boat crews practised their skills with the fast, rigid-hulled inflatable boats (RHIBs) and zodiacs which would be used in deploying and managing the floating lagoons into which the hydras, on the top of Fortune, would fire the ice from their cannons.

On 11 February 2011, they passed close to the Kerguelen Islands, which had a French scientific base. By this stage, the ocean was icy and menacing. The weather that day was cloudy, the ocean grey, and the waves were topped with foam. This would be their closest human contact in the event of a catastrophe, and yet as they passed the outline of the islands, they felt incredibly thankful to be on the *Moringa*, which would take them back to the tropics, rather than with the scientists ashore, facing the long, dark Antarctic winter. Shortly after that, they caught a glimpse of Heard Island. The *Moringa* slowed to half its cruising speed as it encountered pack ice and icebergs, and passed from the Indian to the Southern Ocean.

On the morning of Valentine's Day, the fourteenth of February, Jeffrey and Anna were up at five o'clock, and went straight out on the upper stern deck, beside the ship's funnel, well wrapped up against the cold morning air. They scanned the ocean to the southwest, with the morning sun casting the *Moringa's* shadow immediately before them and lighting up, with sparkling brilliance, everything beyond.

While it was Jeffrey's turn to use the binoculars, Anna regarded the ocean around them and noted the icebergs. "We shall look very silly if we get a hole in our boat now," she mused.

"It's a ship, honey-child, not a boat, and it's not going to get a hole in it," Jeffrey replied without lowering the glasses. "I've had that experience already. I'm not having it again."

Suddenly, the ship's loudspeaker system crackled into action. Ernst's voice boomed out: "Good morning. The iceberg called Fortune is just off the port bow, near the horizon. We are approaching Fortune."

"Is it?" muttered Jeffrey.

"Oh, Jeffrey," Anna exclaimed in frustration. "Don't tell me you missed it. Look! I can see it even without the binoculars."

"Blasted things. Yes, I see it."

"At last," Anna commented drily.

Jimmy appeared on deck, with his Canon camera and long telephoto lens. He snapped the couple as they turned, their faces alight with happiness.

"Good morning, children," he said amiably as he walked to the rail. "Ah yes," he said. "I see."

Then he raised his camera and took a swift series of shots, experimenting with different settings. After that, the three of them stood silently, looking at the ocean, which that day was a blue reflection of the sky.

"Jeffrey," Jimmy said, "that evening in college, when all this started: Did you seriously get up the following morning, thinking this day would really come?"

"No, not really, but I dreamed that it might." Jeffrey sounded very content. "There was a logic about it. I just thought, then, that I should keep the ball rolling until something stopped us. So far, nothing has."

Jimmy nodded. "I can believe it of you. There are times I don't know how you live with yourself, but I'm very glad you're my friend."

Jeffrey raised his binoculars and pointed them towards Fortune. "My God, it's beautiful," he said. "I've never seen a cliff face like it. It's blues and whites and crystal and water – pure water."

Anna's curiosity had been aroused by Jimmy seeming to identify the actual moment, the big bang, of the Moringa project. "You mean you can actually remember the moment that this all came about?" she asked Jimmy, fascinated by the thought.

"The moment? That's probably too precise," Jimmy said in his slow, reflective manner. "But the time and the place? Sure."

"Well then, tell me," Anna badgered him playfully. "Was he really to blame?" she said, speaking about Jeffrey as if he weren't there.

"If I was to apportion blame for us being here, I guess I'd lay about 80 percent of it on Jeffrey's shoulders and 20 percent on Raja, David, and myself."

"I might disagree," Jeffrey said quietly, not wanting to disturb Jimmy's version of events.

"Go on, Jimmy," Anna coaxed, aware that they might be disturbed at any moment. She cast a glance towards Fortune.

"It was sometime in early February 1991, and we were all in the graduates Common Room, which was a sort of post-grad club, and it was evening. The four of us used to meet there quite regularly to watch the news on TV and play a few hands of bridge and pass around the port."

172

"Port?" Anna echoed. "Do you mean the drink, port? What age were you – twenty going on eighty?"

"We were all in our early to late twenties, and it was a very civilised way to end the day," Jimmy replied with dignity. "Shall I go on?"

"Yes please. Sorry," Anna quickly apologised, contrite for her interruption.

"Well, this particular evening, we were playing cards when the television news started, and David said, 'Here we go again: war, pestilence, and famine.' You see, the war in Kuwait, the first Gulf War, had just ended. Saddam had sent his troops, fresh from defeat in Kuwait, to knock the hell out of the Kurds instead. Somalia and Sudan – that part of the world – were in famine due to drought, and it was threatening the lives of about twenty million people. Jeffrey had just come back from there, a few months before. Well, when David just rattled off 'war, pestilence, and famine' while looking at his cards, Jeffrey got uppity with him and the rest of us. He said that we were the brains of the world, and we ought to sort it out. We laughed at him and asked if he had any ideas. And Jeffrey came right back at us and said yes, he had. He said we should take some of the tankers doing nothing in the Gulf, send them to the South Pole to collect all the ice melting due to global warming, and take the water to Africa. That was the big bang moment, I guess. Just for a laugh, we put away the cards, turned off the TV, and spent the rest of the evening talking over his idea. David was a chemist, so we agreed he could work on the purification of water. Raja was an engineer, heir to his father's industrial dynasty, so we said he could adapt the tankers. I had already been on three expeditions in the northern Polar regions, so I was to develop ways to collect the ice. Jeffrey knew about East Africa, so he would be our drought expert.

"We went to bed that night full of port, feeling we had sorted out the world, and woke up next morning, not remembering much about it. But the next time we met, Jeffrey presented us all with a written record of what we had said. A lot of it was nonsense, but some bits were mighty good. So most nights after that, when we met, we would add a few more ideas to the mix. It was all light-hearted, but when time allowed, one of us would do some research. Meanwhile, Jeffrey was already learning about the water-purifying properties of the moringa trees. Under the pretence of an intellectual game, he was actually getting us to formulate a real plan."

David's voice broke in from behind them: "We became known as the Warlocks by our fellow postgrads. We were the magicians who were going to solve the world's problems." He and Lucy had joined the others on deck, unseen. "And here we are, after twenty years. So that's our iceberg? It makes quite a sight."

The interruption Anna had feared had occurred. They all greeted each other, and talk turned excitedly to Fortune. Lucy, who seemed resentful at having to be up so early, stood trying to fathom what she was seeing.

"That's an island, not an iceberg," she muttered.

"It's an island *and* an iceberg," Jeffrey replied. "It's time we were getting ourselves ready. I wonder where Gary is. He should be up by now."

Jeffrey felt vindictive satisfaction as he said these words and a sense of superiority over the man circumstances had placed above him in what was rightfully his domain. He called Ernst on his handset: "Ernst, have you heard anything from Gary?"

"Yes, of course," Ernst replied. "He's with me here on the bridge. We have made plans. I will slow the engines, and he is about to call a meeting. Do you want to speak to him?"

"No, no, I'll see him soon," Jeffrey replied hastily, adding, "It's a fantastic view here, that's all."

It sounded a lame reason for asking about Gary's whereabouts. Elation to dejection had taken one brief exchange. Gary was up, Gary was doing the planning, Gary was ahead of him, and Gary had excluded him.

"It's a good view from here too," Ernst said in a patronizing voice and rang off.

Anna smiled sympathetically into his eyes and gave his arm an affectionate squeeze. "Damn," she whispered.

At that moment, Gary's voice came over the ship's speaker system, reaching from bow to stern, announcing a meeting in the stern mess in one hour, everybody to be ready for action.

"Just before you go," Anna said as Jimmy and David turned to leave, "I just want to say that I think the three of you should be very proud."

The three men looked at each other, childishly abashed. The thought that they had achieved something remarkable together had not really dawned on them.

"That's kind of you, Anna," David replied, "but just at the moment, I think 'very worried' is closer to the mark."

They all laughed and strode back inside, leaving Lucy, who seemed lost in her own dream world, looking out over the ocean.

Anna went back to collect her. "Come on, Lucy; wake up, sleepy-head, action stations. There's work to be done."

Lucy, tousle-haired, turned her bleary eyes towards her. Anna knew the look well.

"How much sleep did you get last night?" she asked.

"Sleep didn't come into it," Lucy replied with a slow, sad shake of the head and ambled off the deck. Under the Valentine's effect, she had changed the rules with Silvio and Stefan. They were wonderful, very capable lovers, she had discovered.

Roland was halfway along the deck when Gary's announcement came. He wanted the drones to be ready to fly the moment the command was given, and he felt that if he hurried, he could complete the inspection he had set out to do and still be back in time for the meeting. He set out with a flat-footed, waddling run to reach the hangar. By the time he arrived, the flight crew were fully occupied. The Hind was already on the lift, ready to be brought up from the hangar. He went down the spiral staircase and into the hangar to where his drones were housed. Alan was waiting for him, and together they quickly completed the inspection of the meticulously cared-for drones.

Just as they finished, and as Roly was expressing his satisfaction, Tyro and Lothar appeared in their flying gear and walked to the flight deck.

"Are they flying now?" Roly asked in surprise, mindful of how little time there was left before the meeting.

"I think so," Alan replied.

"Then I want to go with them. A view from the helicopter before I send the drones could be most helpful." He ran to the lift, calling out, "Can I come with you, please?"

About five minutes later, they were airborne. Gary would have stopped them had he seen them, but he was already on his way to the meeting room. Ernst didn't care, as he watched from the bridge. They flew at one hundred metres, across the short expanse of ocean, and keeping this height, crossed the cliff edge of Fortune, so that it was barely fifteen metres below them. Roly gasped as he saw the precipitous cliffs and the vast expanse of ice; he felt his heart thumping with the shock of that first moment, as he sat by the open door. None of the aerial views he had seen had conveyed the immensity of the iceberg. He pressed himself back against the solidity of the helicopter bulkhead for a few seconds to gather his senses and start again.

They spent ten minutes over the iceberg, checking possible dropping zones for the hydras, then Tyro veered away and headed back to the *Moringa*. Landing on the ship had once seemed an adventure in itself, but now, it had all the reassurance of home.

When they walked into the meeting, everyone else was present and talking avidly among themselves. Although there were some good-natured greetings as they were noticed, Gary's voice subdued them all with an aggressive challenge: "You're late," he snapped. "This operation is now under way and needs discipline if it's to succeed. In future, be on time."

Tyro remained good-natured as he explained, "Gary, for us, your meeting was a few minutes too early – just a few minutes. But we are here now, with photos of sites for us to land the harvesters, which we thought might be useful for the meeting."

"Well done. Good thinking," David said. "Perhaps we can put them up on the screen." He started to get up to fiddle with the connections.

"Shut up, and sit down," Gary ordered. David sat down immediately, stupefied at Gary's language. "Ernst has control of the ship, and I have control of operations, so what we say goes. That's where safety and success lie for everybody. You can all forget your prima donna roles in bringing this to life. From now on, until it's over, you listen to the two of us." Gary glanced round with some satisfaction at the shocked looks on the faces confronting him. "Now, Ernst has something to say."

Ernst stepped forward and spoke with assured authority. "Gary is an oilman. He knows what he is doing. For him, this is a calculated risk, and you better listen to him. He knows the oceans. He knows what they can do. The rest of you," he added, grimacing disdainfully, "if you really knew the risks, you'd be begging me to leave right now." He paused, as if he'd had a second thought, and his voice softened. "Anna, you, of course, are the exception. You are a Norwegian soldier, disciplined, and trained to survive in arctic conditions. You are an asset to any expedition. We have three days of good weather ahead of us. Beyond that, I don't know. During this time, you will be doing whatever you have to do. If, at any time, I order you back to the ship, you must leave whatever you are doing and return. If I consider the vessel is at risk, and I have given the necessary orders, then I will steer the ship to safety, regardless of the consequence to any individuals who have not obeyed my instructions. I may also order you to cease any activity I believe to be endangering the ship. If you do not do so, I can, and I will, arrest you. That is all I have to say." He glanced round them all one last time. "I leave you to your madness," he ended with a grim smile to Gary and walked out, returning to the bridge.

"Thank you, Ernst, that's made the situation very clear for all of us," Gary continued as the captain left the room. "Right, we all know the drill. We stick to it. No more freelance activities, however well-intentioned. One last matter: Ernst and I have agreed to cut all personal communications with the outside world." He was ready for the protests that followed. "Cool it. Cool it. The world still knows where we are, and routine ship-to-shore contact is being maintained. But we've got to concentrate on our own close-range communication. There's no place for Facebook chit-chat or photos that arouse too much interest. We just need to get on with our work. Now, let's go, people."

"Just a mo—" David started to protest, but he found that he had no support as the meeting broke up, with jostling activity and a burst of noise. Arnesh and his men pushed their way out of the room, with cheerful rudeness and a chorus of chatter, to set up the two huge barges that would float as freshwater lagoons between Fortune and the *Moringa*.

"Come on, David, join in, mate. It's happening. It's really happening." Jeffrey's excited voice and stimulating slap on David's shoulder made the latter realise that he just had to bury his outrage.

"I really think he went too far, too far," he protested to Jeffrey as he stood up and joined in the move to the door.

To his surprise, Jeffrey was unsympathetic. "Gary's just doing what we wanted him to do: He's licking us into shape." But as he was talking, Jeffrey cast a glance in Gary's direction, and their eyes met.

"You're the boss, but watch yourself," Jeffrey's gaze conveyed.

"I'm the boss," Gary's gaze replied.

Then Jeffrey, in turn, felt a light tap on his shoulder and looked round to see Anna disappearing towards the door. "Got to go."

"What about – you know," he called, thinking of the ring still in her drawer.

She mouthed the word "Later," blew him a kiss, and was gone.

He noticed Maggie give a kiss to Leena and then join Anna, while Leena's eyes stayed on her, disregarding Gary's presence altogether. Gary noticed too. Tyro and Lothar had already gone through the door. Alan and the three ground crew – Council, Jomo, and Henry – were in the throng, the same as Jeffrey and David. Jimmy, Gary, and Leena were bringing up the rear. Jeffrey had never known Jimmy to exhibit excitement, but there was a pitch to his voice and vitality in his eyes that belied his outward calmness, as he engaged in small talk in moving towards the door.

"These meetings don't concern you," Gary snapped coldly to Leena as he caught up with her. They had not spoken to each other throughout the journey south.

"Good morning, Gary," Leena mumbled back, giving him the briefest of glances, and then they were all out, the room empty, their energy pulsing through the *Moringa*, like the vibration of her engines as she approached Fortune.

Gary and Jimmy set off together for the flight deck, while Jeffrey and David made their way to the Grand Chamber. Jeffrey suddenly turned to David. "Hold on," he said. "Where's Lucy? It's just dawned on me that she wasn't at the meeting."

"I sent her back to bed," David replied. "She looked exhausted this morning. I don't think she slept well. She'll join us later."

Ernst brought the *Moringa* to rest about eight hundred metres from Fortune. It was essential to have the proper instrumentation set up on the surface of Fortune, so they knew where the fault lines were and could detect the angle of tilt. They feared a wall of ice breaking away, sending the hydras into the ocean and creating a wave that would swamp the ship. Jimmy, Anna, and Maggie were dropped by helicopter onto the surface of the ice, while Roland's drones flew overhead and landed at pre-set points on the ice, several hundred metres apart; from there, their tilt meters started sending back data to Roland on the *Moringa*. The three team leaders had all gone together to get an initial feel of the terrain and to set an example. The helicopter was kept busy as it ferried personnel and equipment. This stage was so dangerous and crucial to the mission that nobody on the ship was able to disregard it, but kept glancing at the Hind, dropping out of sight and rising again. Jeffrey had gone back to the observation deck with David, so as to follow events through his binoculars as much as possible. He knew that Jimmy was in constant touch with Gary, but he felt very uneasy about Anna and Maggie, so vulnerable on the ice.

"They are all highly experienced mountaineers, Jeffrey, and they all know about ice and its danger," David said to bolster Jeffrey's confidence and to stifle his own doubts. "We couldn't have wished for a better-trained team."

"It doesn't matter how good their training is, if the ice gives way under their feet now," Jeffrey replied, watching as Lothar flew back to the ship. He felt a burning pain in his stomach and a thumping pulse in his chest. "They're taking too long," he said irritably.

"No, they're not," David said quietly. "It's going remarkably well. This isn't like you, Jeffrey. You're usually the one to calm me." Then he spotted a useful distraction. "Look, the airship's coming out. They must be ready to launch it."

He pointed up the deck to where the airship was beginning to emerge from its hangar, with men clustered round the ropes and curious gulls circling and swooping above.

"David, this isn't right. I'm responsible for everyone being here. I want to be up there with them. I want to know what's going on."

"A fat lot of good that would be," David replied. "You know Africa, not Antarctica. If they find elephant tracks, I'm sure they'll let you know." He was finding Jeffrey's self-pity distracting, as he tried to watch the exhilarating sight of the airship.

"I want to be in charge," Jeffrey said, at which David faced him sharply.

"Well, you lost that battle. Remember? Frankly, Jeffrey, until we get to Africa, you haven't got a role. Leave it to Gary."

Then he immediately regretted what he'd said.

"I didn't mean that. You're our inspiration," he added hurriedly.

Jeffrey smiled at David's haste to correct himself. "What the hell; I'm being a fool," he said. "Anna can look after herself. They all can."

He too looked at the airship, now being held at the far end of the deck, its nose pointing towards the ocean. Then a flurry of activity caught his attention.

"There seems to be something going on up front. I think Tyro's got problems."

"Yes, let's get there," David replied.

As they jogged to the bow, they saw the airship catch the breeze like a young stallion, pulling at its weighted cables and coaxing its handlers to release it from its bonds and let it be free. The engines were idling, yet there was barely any noise.

"It's so silent," Jeffrey said, stating the obvious in comparison to the noise of the helicopter.

"That's hybrid technology for you." David puffed with satisfaction. "Tyro will be able to hover at peace all day in that beauty, if needed."

A small group was huddled round the airship's gondola, and the crewmen on the rope were showing signs of concern. Jeffrey hurried the remaining short distance, leaving David behind him, and he saw that Gary was standing on the steps of the gondola, shouting at Tyro, who was in the pilot's seat, with Roland sitting on the seat by the entrance, his bank of equipment in front of him.

"What's going on?" Jeffrey demanded as he reached the gondola.

Immediately, Gary answered, "The bastard won't let me on," but he remained staring into the gondola.

"Gary wants to come. That's not the plan," Tyro shouted angrily.

Whether or not this was Tyro getting back for Gary's ill manners at the meeting, Jeffrey could not tell, but Tyro was the pilot. His word was final.

"You'll have to back off, Gary," he said in a friendly tone. "Next time, hey?"

But tempers were running higher than he had appreciated.

"Mind your own bloody business," Gary shouted at him, not letting go of the gondola.

"Come on, mate," Jeffrey said firmly. "We don't want an accident on the first day."

As he said this, he put a restraining arm on Gary's shoulder and pulled him backwards. It was only a gentle tug, but Gary's grasp slipped from the gondola before he was ready, and he fell to the ground, on his side.

Tyro seized his moment and shouted, "Launch! Launch!"

It was too late for Gary to try to board again, and the three men, Gary, Jeffrey, and David, stood out of the way while the ground crew released the ropes, which recoiled into the fuselage as the airship lifted off over the bows, rising rapidly into the clear sky, and performed a graceful arc to fly, majestically, over the iceberg.

As it did so, Gary turned his back on his former friend and called Ernst on his intercom.

"Ernst. We have a problem. You better come." He turned to David. "David, you have work to do. Get your butt out of here."

David stayed put. "I'm staying right here. I think I've had enough orders this morning."

"David, please go," Jeffrey urged him. "The sooner those machines are on the ice, the sooner we can get them working. Please. It's really important. Gary and I will sort this out."

David hesitated. "Well, Jeffrey, if you're sure, but you know where to find me if necessary." Then he turned to Gary. "My goodness, I was wrong about you," he said vehemently. "I can't believe I thought you were the right man for the job."

"Yep, well, in case you haven't worked it out, you and Jeffrey were the prima donnas that I was talking about this morning," Gary replied with provocative intent, tempting David to take him on.

David knew he was unable to match Gary physically or verbally in a brawl and backed away cautiously.

As David left, Gary turned to Jeffrey and said, "We'll get this over quicker if we go to meet Ernst."

Jeffrey shrugged and said, "He can come here. You're the one messing up his day."

The captain arrived five minutes later.

"Ernst—" Gary began, but Ernst interrupted him.

"You don't have to explain, Gary. I saw it for myself from the bridge: Professor Harvey pulled you off the airship while your back was turned. It was a dangerous and unprovoked attack." Although he was speaking to Gary, he was looking directly at Jeffrey.

"You said it," Gary agreed, looking directly at Jeffrey.

"You were endangering the airship," Jeffrey retorted.

181

"What do you know about airships, Jeffrey?" Gary taunted him. "You pulled me back when I was giving Tyro his orders. You don't think that was endangering *me*? You just don't get it, do you? You're nothing on this ship, Jeffrey. Nothing."

Before Jeffrey could reply, Ernst broke in. "Professor Harvey, you will go back to your cabin. My men will escort you. You are not to leave your cabin without my permission. Is that understood?"

Jeffrey saw that refusing to comply would achieve nothing. He was being watched by David, the ground crew, and several of the ship's crew, among others. He turned and walked back, flanked by two of Ernst's men, to the tower, with Ernst behind him. It was a walk of shame, deliberately engineered by Ernst to show the ship's company his absolute power and Jeffrey's total absence of authority. Once inside the tower, Ernst returned to the bridge, where he could be seen by everyone, and Jeffrey disappeared from view to his cabin.

Chapter 11

HOT WATER

Arnesh and his men were making good progress with the inflatable lagoons. Each lagoon, twenty-five metres long and twelve metres wide, lay extended on the ocean, being tended by the men in their powerboats: two RHIBs commanded by Ewan and Hans from the *Moringa's* crew, and two smaller zodiacs, which buzzed round like sheepdogs controlling two flocks of sheep. Once completed, with splash-guards, sea anchors, ropes, and navigation lights attached, each lagoon would become a target into which the hydras would fire their ice and out of which water would be pumped into the *Moringa's* chambers.

The sound of the helicopter's engine made Gary turn and walk to the flight deck. It took off and hovered while the first of the hydras was attached, then pulled away with its heavy load swinging beneath it. The airship was gliding by, about two hundred metres above that. Gary realised that he wanted to be in two places at once. His first impulse had been to jump aboard the airship, to monitor operations from the air. Now he was desperate to be on the iceberg, to experience the awesome excitement and assess the surface for himself, as originally planned.

When the Hind returned, it brought Jimmy, Anna, and Maggie, who had paved the way for Gary, Frank, and Baljeet (one of Arnesh's men). The returning trio had checked the safety and suitability of the ice, placed anchor points for safety ropes, set up contact with the airship, and unloaded the first cargo. After three hours on the ice, they were exhilarated and exhausted.

Jimmy was the first to step out of the helicopter. He had a beaming smile on his face. "That was intense," he said slowly, as he shook David's hand. David was there to greet them all and could see the exhaustion in Jimmy's features.

David had not time to reply before Gary strode up, shouting out, "Great show, you guys, great show. Go and get showered and changed. See you in the mess in three hours." Then, he and his team climbed in; Lothar, the pilot, waved in acknowledgement to David, and they were under way.

As the Hind moved off and its noise subsided, Maggie muttered to David, "Still giving orders, I see. Not much changed, then, while we were away."

Anna turned to David with disappointment in her voice. "Where's Jeffrey, David? I thought he'd be here."

David was aware that several of Brage's crewmen were within earshot and that he should be careful what he said. "Actually, there have been a few changes while you've been gone," he replied, "but well done, all of you. Anna, you will find Jeffrey waiting for you in your cabin."

David's tone and body language told them all, at once, that something was wrong.

"What's going on?" Anna asked, pushing brusquely past him to jog to the stern.

David's downcast look indicated that he didn't want any further questions from Jimmy or Maggie.

Jimmy took his cue. "I guess I'll go take a shower and maybe have a cup of soup. I should be ready for rational conversation after that," he said amiably.

"I'll join you in the shower, Jimmy," Maggie said. "That way, we can save on water."

"Yeah, we really need to do that, don't we, Maggie?" Jimmy replied, and the two of them nudged each other in good humour.

Anna had just reached the tower when Ernst's voice came over the loudspeaker system, telling her to report to the bridge.

"What the hell? Who does he think he is? He can't order me around," Anna said, stopping angrily and turning to a nearby crewman, Silvio.

"He's the captain, and with respect, he can, madam," Silvio replied, politely. "Don't make mistakes with this captain. The professor has made a mistake, I think."

Anna felt alarmed and sensed Silvio knew exactly what was happening. "Silvio, please tell me what's going on. Is the professor in some sort of trouble? I want to see him."

"Please go and see the captain first. You'll just make it worse for the professor, otherwise," Silvio replied nervously.

On the way up to the bridge, Anna thought rapidly. Gary and Ernst were working as a pair. She had to split them. This would be an ideal opportunity, while Gary was off the ship. Gary seemed to see Ernst as the dominant force. She would ally herself to Ernst, indeed flirt with him. As she approached the door, a crewman spotted her through the glass, unlocked the door, and let her in.

Anna walked briskly over to Ernst with a broad smile. "Ernst, we've done it; we've established a base on the ice," she said in Norwegian. She put her arms around his neck and gave him a kiss on the cheek, which he acknowledged with a light hug. "So," she said, still in Norwegian, disengaging from him, "we have something to celebrate."

"Well done, Anna, but it's too early for celebrations." Ernst, too, spoke in Norwegian, looking at Anna intently, unsure of her body language. "Jeffrey assaulted Gary this morning. It could have been very dangerous. Did Gary tell you?"

Anna looked perplexed: "There must be some mistake. Jeffrey has no idea how to fight. What happened? Where are the bruises?"

"There aren't any bruises, luckily," Ernst replied, though her taunt against Gary made him smile. "He pulled Gary backwards off the airship as it was about to take off."

"What a ridiculous thing to do. How stupid," Anna exclaimed and gave a sigh of exasperation. "Jeffrey is frustrated. He isn't master of anything right now, including himself." She walked over to the window to look across to the iceberg, fatigue creeping over her. "He needs me, and that is nice, but he isn't the alpha man I thought." She paused, reflecting on her own words. "If I am truthful, I have room for an alpha man in my life."

These last words were supposed to be flirtatious, but they were spoken with an honesty that surprised even her. She did not know quite why she said them. Startled by her own admission, she turned suddenly, shaking herself into full wakefulness, and saw Ernst staring at her quizzically.

She broke into English to continue the conversation: "I'm sorry. I should not be saying such things. Jeffrey was stupid to do that, I agree. What have you done about it?"

Ernst stood there, master of his ship, and spoke with quiet authority: "I just had him confined to his cabin for the day. His behaviour was a risk to the lives of others on board. You must talk to him, Anna. He has no position on board this ship. I know he has difficulty understanding this, but if he tries to take charge again, I will take whatever steps I consider necessary."

"That sounds fair," Anna replied. "But there won't be any further trouble. I will speak to him, as you ask. Now may I return to my cabin? If nothing else, I need to see the loo."

Ernst smiled at this. "Please don't let me detain you," he said and walked with her to the door.

In turning to go, Anna looked at him. "If not today, then someday, perhaps," she said quietly, in Norwegian, and in her heart of hearts, she knew that she meant it.

"You aren't playing with me, are you, Anna?" he asked, in kind.

"Just a Norwegian farewell," she replied, with a dismissive smile. She had taken a risk with Ernst, one that she now felt had been wickedly exciting. She would have to control the amount of lust she permitted herself as well as in him, she realised. In return, she could influence him and protect Jeffrey; Gary would not get the better of her.

She really did need Jeffrey and the loo. In fact, she needed them in reverse order, and reaching their cabin, she dived straight past him before he could get up from the bunk, pulled urgently at her clothes, and sank onto the loo. She let out a sigh of intense relief.

Jeffrey laughed as Anna and happiness returned so abruptly. "That's the second-best feeling in the world: finding a loo when you need one," he said with understanding, as he gently closed the door to give her some privacy.

She called back to him, "My poor love, you've had a dreadful day. Give me a moment, then I'm all yours."

After she finished and washed up, she stood looking down at herself, deciding if he would prefer her with her knickers on or off. She decided knickers on, bra and tee-shirt on, but nothing else, and walked back into the cabin. It was warm, and he was sitting on his bunk in denim shirt and jeans. She sat beside him and rested her head on his shoulder, one hand on his thigh and the other hand clasped in his.

"I think I'm in love," she said, sleepiness now overwhelming her.

"Oh," he said. "Who with?"

"You, only you," she replied, as if offended, but a stab of doubt pierced her conscience.

"It takes two to be in love," he murmured.

She stayed silent and pretended she had drifted into her dreams. He turned and gave her the lightest of kisses and lay her on the bed.

She roused herself. "I've got to meet Gary and the others when everyone's back, and I still don't know what happened to you," she said in a worried tone.

"It'll wait," he whispered, pushing her gently back to lie down again.

"My love, please promise me not to do anything else that gives Ernst an excuse to hurt you – not Ernst, not Gary," she pleaded. "I need to find out more, but I think you are in danger."

"Anna, love, you spent half the day on top of an iceberg, while I've been sitting in a cabin. You have a strange perception of danger," he replied, giving her a fond squeeze. "I'll wake you in forty minutes."

She took a deep breath in and slowly out. "It was wonderful," she murmured. "It wasn't dangerous, not really." Then, she drifted into genuine sleep.

David and Lucy were tending the moringa saplings in the Grand Chamber. They were not alone; Arnesh and his team had shown great enthusiasm and skill in caring for the plants in their off-duty periods, moving placidly and patiently, talking with subdued voices to each other and to the saplings, as if nursing sleeping children, offering them encouragement and describing colourful images of the Eden they were going to become when they grew up. The peace of the Grand Chamber contrasted pleasantly with the bustle that seemed to be everywhere else in the ship.

"It frightened me to see Jeffrey being marched off by Captain Brage. I wanted to run up and hug him," Lucy said.

"I'm glad you didn't," David confided. "Brage might have put his hands on you, and if he'd done that, I couldn't have restrained myself. I was livid enough to see Jeffrey detained. I was ready to intervene, but he wanted me to stay out of it. He was right, of course."

"Frank said that you were angry even at the meeting," Lucy replied, supportively.

"I was shocked at the meeting," David admitted. "The way Gary and Ernst just wrested all power from the rest of us was incredible." He was speaking calmly, but Lucy knew the distress that he was hiding.

"What are you going to do now?"

"To be honest, I'm not quite sure," David admitted. "I can't believe Gary's behaviour. I'd never have given him my support if I'd known what a Jekyll-and-Hyde personality he has." He paused and sighed. "I wish your mother were here. She'd know what to do."

Lucy stopped tending the shrubs to tend to her father instead. She rested her head on his shoulder. "You miss her, don't you, Daddy dear?" she said soothingly.

"Frankly, yes," David confessed. "I can go three or four days hardly thinking about her, and then something happens, and I suddenly want to tell her about it or just give her a hug."

"What about the other times, when you could happily wring her neck? You're not missing those, surely," Lucy teased him.

"Oh, for goodness sake, you're as bad as your mother," David protested, but he laughed, and that was Lucy's intention. "And as good," he added. "Having you on board has made a huge difference to me." He gave her a fatherly hug. "No, what's really got to me today is this bloody communication ban that Ernst and Gary have imposed. They've effectively imprisoned the whole of the rest of us. Ernst and his crew have us at their mercy, especially with Gary alongside, and we can't do a thing about it."

"Oh well, let's not think about it. We're here, and that's the main thing. A dream come true. You and Jeffrey should feel very proud."

"Thank you, my dear. I am proud of it, to be honest. I'm proud that we all stayed true to the ideal and then had the massive support of others like you. I just hope that the price of getting here hasn't been more than Jeffrey bargained for. He told me himself that he had gone to some bad people."

"Dad, stop worrying and be happy. That's an order."

"Orders, orders. First Gary and Ernst, and now you," David exclaimed. "We can finish now. Frank can carry on from here in the morning." He stuck a peg in the earth.

Lucy loved her father dearly but knew that he lacked guile. You could not tell him secrets because he so easily gave them away, in the spirit of honesty and openness. So she kept many thoughts to herself.

"Good idea," she said. "It'll be another big day tomorrow. With luck, everyone will have calmed down."

Tyro had missed Alan. Three hours in the airship with Roland had not enriched his life. There had not been any conversation or challenging thoughts or pertinent quotes from the Bible. There had been no laughter. There had been no comradeship. Roland had focused on the task allocated to him and had mapped fissures and cracks, and taken soundings of the ice, leaving Tyro to do his job: flying the airship to and fro. They had stood ready, as emergency backup, when the hydras were landed, but all had gone smoothly.

"This has been a very successful flight," Roland said. "You are a good pilot, a very good pilot. I have not felt nervous at all." They watched the activity on the ship beneath them. "Tomorrow, if the weather is good, I will be able to control all the hydras, all day, from here."

Tyro shut his mind to the following day and concentrated on the docking. It was as exciting as the first time, approaching from the stern of the *Moringa*, clearing the tower, and sinking towards the bows, with some solid metalwork to hit if he veered off course. Docking the airship was not his strong point, and he was relieved when the ground crew managed to seize the guy ropes at the first attempt and tethered the craft to its winches.

Once safely down, Tyro acknowledged Roland with a cursory nod, as if the docking had been a formality, and put away his logbook, while Roland, with help from Council, went about the task of carrying various pieces of equipment away from the airship. Tyro left them to it, disembarked, and found Alan waiting for him. After the initial greetings, their conversation turned immediately to the start of the flight.

"Jeff was trying to protect me," he said to Alan. "He did what he thought best. Gary was a danger to us. I had the right to refuse him. I did not expect Jeff to seize hold of him, though."

189

"I think Jeffrey could be in serious trouble," Alan said, thinking of how he had been virtually frog-marched up the deck with guards either side.

"You are right," Tyro replied soberly. "Wait, I must see the airship into the shed."

Both he and Alan took part in guiding it backwards into its shed, barely longer or higher than the airship itself, set to the starboard side of the main deck, just forward of the roof of the Grand Chamber. Then, they walked across the deck, and, instead of taking the spiral staircase, they took the lift from the main deck down to the storage deck, two floors below. The lift was designed to take heavy equipment between the two decks, so it did not have doors to the corridor deck in between. They left Roland loading his black boxes onto one of the motorised trolleys, to follow on. When the lift doors opened onto the storage deck, they sauntered along the wide central avenue to the main hangar in the bows, past the wire cages and secured containers full of stores, resuming their conversation in Tyro's small office, where Tyro, once again, could relax with some intelligent conversation.

Raja had not felt so cared for since Sunita's death. The combination of Jacqueline's nursing skills and her deep, long-standing friendship meant that they could share intimacy in complete trust. He had not felt any embarrassment when she had helped him to bathe and dress in the first days following his heart attack, while he had felt so shaken, weak, and vulnerable. She had moved into his bedroom at home, different beds, of course, so that if he awoke in the night, she could be on hand to reassure him. He had quickly regained his self-confidence and began to discuss returning to work, but she kept talking of places to see in India that even he had not visited, and before he had realised what was happening, she presented him with an itinerary of a six-week tour they could make together, in his private jet.

"Only Sunita could make me take time off like that," he grumbled, with feigned reluctance.

"I think she's been helping me put this trip together," Jacqueline replied innocently.

After that, Raja offered no more resistance but gave in to having a woman in his life again, as she gave instructions to his secretary and house staff about what they would need, while he contentedly authorised it. The destinations were not as important to Jacqueline as her main aim of encouraging Raja to relax and making him a healthier man in the process. She was brilliantly successful, and somewhere in India, they were lost in happiness, neither quite sure where they were, leaving that to their pilots and guides.

One night, just after they had gone to bed, she was roused by a text message from Lucy's mobile:

"Communications blackout. Jeffrey arrested. Dad outraged. Prisoners. Help."

Jacqueline read the text message out loud, with intense frustration. "Oh, I give up, I really do. It's this modern generation's need to be in permanent contact with somebody. When I was Lucy's age, we were expected when we arrived. You remember those days." Raja dutifully nodded his sleepy head while Jacqueline continued her rant. "There weren't any phones where we went. My parents might get a postcard, if they were lucky – weeks late. It doesn't surprise me in the least that Jeffrey's been arrested; he deserves to be permanently locked up, as far as I'm concerned. And David is always outraged about something. They've probably had an argument, and Lucy's blowing her top, as usual." Jacqueline was very cross that Raja had been disturbed and flounced back to her bed, with her mobile phone in her hand. "Even texts like this are becoming outdated. It's all instantaneous messaging on Facebook or something."

"So what do you intend to do?" Raja asked calmly, as he lay, comfortably propped up on his pillows.

"Nothing, that's what," Jacqueline replied, climbing back into her own bed. "I'm fed up with the lot of them. I've been mothering Lucy and Tom – and David – for twenty years, and at last I thought I was getting a break. I haven't felt so free to be myself since before I got married – when David and I, and you and Sunita, were all young singles together. Do you remember us all having to share that one room in a house in Crete?"

"Oh, one of my happiest memories," Raja chuckled drowsily. "All of us so embarrassed we hardly dared undress the first night, and after two days, we were walking round naked and not even noticing. It was too hot for clothes, even for Sunita and me."

"And we could just walk out straight onto that lovely beach in the early morning, before anyone else arrived." Jacqueline lay back on her pillows, as she thought of that holiday and calmed down. "In the morning, I'll contact Davina Mason. Her husband, Tony, works in something called the International Maritime Organisation, based in London. I'll tell her about the text; she can tell Tony, and if they're interested, they can handle it. But that is all I'm doing. Now, let's get back to sleep."

With that, Jacqueline switched off her phone and her light. At about the same moment, Stefan switched off Lucy's phone, having sent the message she had given him, and put it back in his pocket to give to her in the morning. That message was all he dared to send in the circumstances.

At just after four o'clock in the morning, the *Moringa* came rapidly to life as the different teams went into action in their respective parts of the ship. The aim was to have all five hydras firing their howitzers by six o'clock. Their generators had been on all night to keep all working parts from freezing up. Crews would have to go in to refuel the generators later, but right now, all that mattered was that the howitzers fired and were on target to hit the lagoons. Roland, in his vantage point from the airship, would refine his aim so that the lagoons were filled in turn, while the ends of long hoses from the ship would be transferred from one lagoon to the other, and the water pumped into the ship's tanks. The process would be one of continuous motion for several days. It would use the entire ship's complement, and even if it ran smoothly, it would be utterly exhausting for everyone.

The airship came grudgingly out of its shed, unimpressed at having to function in such cold temperatures. Tyro was at the controls; Roland and Alan were waiting on the flight deck. Ernst and Gary had let it be known that they would be working on the bridge together during the day, to orchestrate events; there would not be a repetition of yesterday's stand-off. After the airship took off, Ernst would begin the complex task of turning the ship so that it was stern-on to Fortune. A long hawser would be unwound and attached to each lagoon.

Anna, Maggie, and Jimmy were returning to Fortune's plateau to oversee the process, ensuring that the hydra heads were working as intended. Anna and Jeffrey were still struggling to get dressed in their confined cabin when there was knock on their door. Anna opened it to find Lucy standing there.

"Hello, Lucy. You're up early," Anna remarked.

Lucy gave a shrug and whispered wickedly that at the moment, there wasn't much difference between night and day in her life; catching sight of Jeffrey struggling to pull up his trousers, she called out cheerfully, "Good morning, boss."

"Morning, Lucy. You don't have to call me boss anymore."

"I've never had to," Lucy replied. "I choose to. It's who you are."

"Well, thank you for that," Jeffrey said, evidently pleased by her compliment.

Anna and Lucy shared a wink.

"In our past life," he continued, "when you were nice to me, it was because you were buttering me up to ask for a favour. What is it this time?"

"If all goes well this morning, do you think we could go diving this afternoon?" Lucy asked, unashamed at being found out.

"If you can get us a zodiac, yes, but *you*'ll have to ask Gary. I don't want to talk to him at the moment." Jeffrey sounded happy and relaxed. "Now, let's get upstairs and see those howitzers open up."

"We've still got several minutes; the airship still hasn't taken off," Lucy reassured him.

One deck below, in their shared cabin, Leena was finishing Maggie's massage with the final effleurage. For this stroke, her palms started below Maggie's buttocks, pushed them firmly upwards, and let them slide back as her hands slowly proceeded over the pelvis and up to the neck, her fingers cupped over the ridge of her shoulders, out to the shoulder joints and the upper arms, then sinuously glided down, her fingertips stimulating Maggie's armpits and the margins of her breasts and coming to a stop over her hips. During the course of thirty minutes, the massage had warmed Maggie's skin and loosened her muscles from toes to head. She had anticipated those pleasures. This final, long stroke was a surprise that was as blissful as it was perplexing. Maggie stayed silently where she was lying, with Leena's palms resting on her waist.

Further along the corridor, Jimmy was preparing to leave his cabin. He kissed his small photograph of Karen, his one and only love of twenty-eight years (married for twenty-six of them), and tucked it back in the credit-card sheath in which he protected it, slipping it back into his trouser pocket. He stood looking at his cabin door before opening it. His insatiable need for snow, ice, cliffs, and wilderness had not killed him yet, but the near-misses were mounting. Karen had been able to stop. She had delayed having kids as long as possible so that she and Jimmy could share their love of the wilderness together, but after twelve years of marriage, when she was thirty-two and he was thirty-three, she had chosen to be a mother. He had never chosen to be a father. She acknowledged that. The twins were almost teenagers now. He had lost count of the weekends that he had been away from them, alone or with buddies, testing the physical limits, but never three months away, until now. Only this one expedition could have tempted him away from them, he had told himself, but when he said this to Karen, she had just patted him on the chest and said there always had been one last expedition, and there always would be.

"Each time I go," he explained to her, "it releases a spirit inside me that's been calling out to be heard. Once all that tension is out of me, I'm free, and then I come home to you, and I feel normal. And then, one day, the spirit returns, and the tension starts building again."

"That call you hear," Karen replied softly, "how does it compare to the sound of a crying widow with her fatherless kids?"

"Come on, now, that's not fair. I promise I'll be careful," he said. *I promise I'll be careful,* he said to himself, now. *I'll only stand on the edge of a two-hundred-foot-high iceberg that could sheer off under me at any moment and stare across the ocean and feel the awesomeness of nature. Christ, I'm mad. I need to be home.* With that thought in his mind, he opened the door. David was passing along the corridor, and they greeted each other, but David showed no inclination to linger.

"Where are you off to, David?" Jimmy asked him with his soft mellow voice. "Have you got Jackie stowed away somewhere?"

"I must say good morning to my moringas. They'll be waiting for me," David replied with cheerful enthusiasm.

"Well, talk to them nicely," Jimmy replied, reassured to find somebody else madder than he was on board the ship.

"I always do," David called back as he disappeared down the stairs.

Jimmy walked out onto the main deck. He could have taken the long corridor but wanted to feel the cold morning air. He walked past the roof of the Grand Chamber and past the airship's shed, to the staircase and lift amidships. He noted the activity on the flight deck and prepared himself for the day ahead.

David found the Grand Chamber still in the same good order as he had left it six hours previously. Of course it was. The moringas didn't need him as much as he needed them. He walked proudly along the gantries, fondly chatting to the saplings and stroking them. Much of the touching and soft words that should have been for Jacqueline were lavished on these plants. Not that he was short of female company. Emily, the medical officer, and Lucy would both be round to help during the day.

Recalling that Arnesh and some of his gang had been tending one of the lines of plants, he walked along to see their work. To his surprise, he came across a weed at the base of one of the trunks. Firstly, he could not think how the weed had got there, and secondly, he was surprised that they hadn't seen it and removed it. It was a good size, and David had not had any trouble spotting it. Just at that moment, Frank came into the chamber, saw him, and waved. This was the voyage of a lifetime for Frank, and he was loving every minute of it. David hailed him.

"Morning, Frank; could you come over here a moment?"

"Morning, boss; something interesting there? What you got there, then?"

"Well, it's some sort of a weed that seems to be growing under this—"

"Some sort of a weed?" Frank echoed in disbelief. "Where were you when the rest of us were growing up? I'll say it's some sort of weed. It's marijuana, boss. Where did you get that?"

"I didn't get it. It was growing here," David said tetchily.

Frank was amused. "Oh, you're a dark horse, you are," he taunted his boss. "You've only been away from Mrs Emmerson five weeks, and you're already smoking pot. I'll have to tell her, you know."

"If I go down, I'm taking you with me," David retorted.

"Look, there's another one there – and there," Frank said, walking slowly along the lines. Altogether, there were twelve, carefully planted tufts.

David stood looking at them a moment and then sighed; he said, "They've obviously been planted deliberately. It must be Arnesh and his bunch who did this yesterday evening. We have to pull them out, of course. If this marijuana is found when we dock, it'll put the whole project in jeopardy."

195

"Do you want me to do that now?" Frank asked.

"No, but don't talk about it to anyone. I'll have a word with Arnesh and ask him to remove them. He and the others must have been growing it in their cabins since they came aboard. It looks like there's one bunch per person, so it's probably their whole crop."

"What? You mean you're going to allow them to keep it?" Frank asked with some surprise.

"Yes, yes, I'm not going to be judge and jury on this, Frank. The Indian team have been invaluable on this trip. It's just a difference in cultures. They've each got their little pot of marijuana, and we've got a boat-load of unlicensed moringas. Who are the greater criminals?"

"Oh well, boss, put like that, I think I'll join the Indians," Frank said enviously, looking at the weed growing at their feet.

"To work, Frank, to work," David said sternly. "I can't afford to have you drifting off on cloud nine."

On the bridge, Gary and Ernst were discussing the latest satellite weather reports, working out their significance for the day's operations. A low-pressure trough had deepened more than anticipated, making the risk of high winds that much greater.

"If we don't tell Tyro about this, he will launch in the next two minutes," Gary said. "He needs to know."

"What will that do to the start of the cannons?" Ernst asked.

"Plan B is for Roland to start them from the ship," Gary replied. "He will not have such good control, and it will take time to set up. It is definitely second best, but possible. We can't set up a base on the ice; it's too risky. The airship gives us a stable platform and the best view."

"Then launch the airship and get the cannons started. I've no time for airships if they can't fly," Ernst said impatiently.

"That decision is mine," Gary replied. "I'll call Tyro, and see what he thinks."

Ernst put his hand over the headset so Gary could not pick it up. "Don't radio him. If he's going, let him go. We shall just waste time if you chat about the weather." Ernst, himself, picked up the headset. "Bridge to airship: You are clear to go. What's delaying you?"

"Airship to bridge," Tyro's voice came through, calm and dignified. "Good morning, Captain. I hope you are well and looking forward to a beautiful day. My flight checks are now complete, and we are about to fly."

"Good luck," Ernst signed off, sounding as if he didn't care if they flew or crashed, as long as the airship left the *Moringa*, so he could get on with his manoeuvre. He handed the headset to Stefan, who was on bridge duty, and went to watch from the bridge window.

"Let's not have a turf war, Ernst," Gary muttered, as he stood beside him. "Yours is the ship, mine is the mission. Remember?"

"Take-offs and landings are a matter for the ship," Ernst said scathingly. "Therefore, they are my responsibility. The rest is yours. Good luck with it."

They watched as the airship caught the breeze, lifted its nose, and rose over the ocean.

"This is the stupidest part of a stupid exercise of a stupid man," Ernst continued as they watched the airship turn and pass over them. "How has he trapped you into it?" He gave a derisory snort.

Gary turned to him. "How do you think it feels to stand on an oil rig in the middle of the North Sea during a storm? I've done that too. How did some stupid man dream that up? Huh? It's enterprise, Ernst; it's exploration. One day, there may be technology that you and I can't even imagine to harvest polar ice on a commercial scale, but right now, there are men like Jeffrey to dream things up, and men like me to make them happen, along with Tyro up there, and David Emmerson, and even you."

Ernst smirked and raised a hand dismissively. "No need to include me in your bunch of idealists. However, I am under orders and must do what I can to protect my ship while you carry out your heroics."

Having made his position clear, Ernst walked out onto the small bridge deck opposite Fortune. Gary decided it wasn't worth bothering to remonstrate with him any longer. Instead, he went over to Stefan and held out his hand for the headphones.

"I want to speak to the airship," he said.

"Go ahead," Stefan replied, handing them over. "You're connected."

"Tyro, how's it going?"

"Good morning, Gary," Tyro replied in a slow, relaxed deep voice. "How are you this morning? We are doing well here. We are feeling the wind today, but the sky is bright, the ocean is blue, and Fortune is glistening. It is a beautiful sight, Gary. We are indeed blessed at this moment."

Gary curbed his impatience. He knew Tyro was right. These were moments to savour. "If you'd let me fly with you yesterday, I might know what you're talking about," he replied, half-joking.

"How is Jeffrey today? Have you settled your differences?"

"We will, Tyro, we will. Now, how soon before we see the harvesters in action?"

There was a pause, as Tyro checked with Roland. "About one minute. And Gary?" Tyro paused again.

"Yes?"

"Nothing is to happen to Jeffrey," Tyro said in a firm voice.

Gary was utterly perplexed.

"Like what, man? He stepped out of line. He's back in line. No hard feelings."

"We'll speak later," Tyro replied. "Let's enjoy the moment."

Gary handed the headphones back to Stefan. "One minute to go." He called to Ernst, "May I join you to watch?"

"If you like," Ernst replied with indifference.

Standing beside Ernst, Gary muttered to him, "Tyro just said to me that nothing must happen to Jeffrey. I don't know what he meant. You're not planning anything, are you? The Angels haven't given instructions, have they?"

"Against Jeffrey Harvey?" Ernst asked, surprised. "No." He turned to Ramos, the first officer, standing beside him, who had heard Gary's question. "Do you know of any plans to harm the professor?"

Ramos gazed seaward, apparently uninterested. "Plans to harm Professor Harvey? What a strange idea for Tyro Mukasa to have," he commented drily.

Anna and Jeffrey had chosen to watch from the stern deck, on top of the tower. Lucy had gone to find David, Jimmy was making his way to the bows, and Maggie and Leena had not emerged yet from their cabin, so Anna and Jeffrey had the deck to themselves. They were standing, snuggled against each other, leaning on the railing.

"I was noticing that we are about half as high here as the top of Fortune," Jeffrey remarked.

"That's true," Anna replied. "I stood near the edge and watched the gulls over the ship."

"That was foolhardy," Jeffrey muttered calmly. "Brave, but foolhardy."

Anna was unconcerned. "I knew the ice could take my weight, and I felt so alive as I stepped back. You must come. I'll keep you safe, I promise."

Jeffrey looked through his binoculars. "Tyro has been holding position for some time. Roland is probably arranging for the hydras to start in unison."

Actually, a discussion had started on the airship, the outcome of which was of such interest to Roland that the firing of the howitzers, which was a simple formality, had been set aside for a few moments.

Wanting some light conversation, while waiting for Roland to be ready, Tyro had asked Alan what he had mumbled as they took off. "It was my prayer for take-offs," Alan replied. "I always pray 'Lord, we are about to take off. Amen.'"

Tyro shrugged. "How does that help? You haven't asked for anything," he pointed out.

"Because then I know that the Lord is watching, and I can relax," Alan replied.

Tyro concentrated on his flying and then asked, "Supposing some disaster happens, and you are about to crash. Would you feel anger that your prayer had not been answered?"

"No, because I board a plane – or an airship – in the knowledge that it could crash. The Lord provides us with options in life, not with certainty."

"Well then, why bother to pray at all?" Roland asked. "Only science provides certainty." He continued to fiddle with the selection of controls in front of him as he said this.

"The state of our present-day scientific knowledge has been reached by scientists, over the centuries, taking different options that the Lord has provided," Alan countered gently.

"Jesus did not need science," Tyro said to them. "He said to a lame man, 'Walk,' and the lame man walked. He fed five thousand people with a few loaves and fishes. He walked on water without anything that floated. Jesus did not need science to have certainty."

"I am not a Christian," Roland said, turning away from his instruments to face the others, "so I do not understand your logic. Was Christ a man or God? If Christ was a man, he would have needed science to achieve the things you just mentioned. That level of scientific knowledge was not available in his day; therefore, they are myths and did not happen. If he was God, he did not die, and the resurrection did not happen. Therefore, we should abolish Easter."

"Ah, but your logic overlooks faith," Alan said. "Jesus taught us to have faith."

"But was Christ a man or God?" Roland persisted, certain that he had the checkmate question, and the howitzers lost their importance.

"Christ was a man," Alan replied without any sign of discomfort.

"But Alan," Tyro sounded troubled. "Why then do I pray to God the Father, God the Son, and God the Holy Ghost?"

"And if he was a man, he couldn't have done all the things he was supposed to have done," Roland said triumphantly.

"He didn't," Alan said with a smile. "God made all the miracles happen. God rewarded the supernatural faith of Jesus."

"Jesus walked on water. He had to be God to do that," Tyro said, looking down at the vast, cold ocean.

"Well, not really," Alan said. "According to the story, Peter did it too. The disciples saw Jesus walking towards them, and Peter, presumably worried for Jesus's safety, gets out of the boat and starts walking towards him. Then, after he's gone some of the way, he starts to sink, and Jesus gets to him and pulls him back up. Jesus was a man. He saw Peter walking on the water and knew God was rewarding Peter's faith. Then he saw Peter's faith waiver, and that was when he sank and cried out to be saved. And as Jesus pulled Peter up again, he didn't say, 'Peter, you fool'; he said to him, 'Peter, why doubt?' It wasn't science. It was faith."

"I don't know," Tyro muttered. "It's not what they preach in my church. You really believe that?"

"I do, and one day, I may persuade you."

There was silence in the gondola for a second or two, then Tyro re-focused on the job in hand, in a relaxed and contemplative way. "Roly," he said, "I think we should start the howitzers."

He was more correct than he knew. Cocooned in their warm, secure gondola, they had been oblivious to the consternation the delay was causing on the *Moringa*. People move through time at different rates, and the rate in the gondola, where time stretched in front of them, was significantly different from that on the *Moringa*, where each second was being accounted for. Jeffrey was convinced that all four howitzers had failed and was on the edge of despair that his twenty-year dream was in jeopardy. Anna had told him that she and Maggie would go at once, and bugger the risks. On the bridge, Ernst was smirking as Gary shouted obscenities and threats down the radio, which Tyro had switched off in the gondola, so as to be free of intrusion from the ship. All work had stopped, and the different crews were lining the railings.

The start-up procedures began, and the hydra heads all seemed to be moving. Roland and Alan looked down on the ice with great joy, one with the certainty of science and the other with the certainty of faith. Tyro concentrated on maintaining station. On the *Moringa*, every eye was on them.

"The pressure is high enough in all the howitzers. We can open fire," Roland shouted in his excitement.

"Then open fire, my friend," Tyro commanded in his majestic voice, and Roland pressed the button.

"They're firing! They're all firing. Yep, all of them." There was huge relief in Jeffrey's voice as he scanned Fortune's cliff face with his binoculars.

Anna could make out the direction of the parabolas from where she stood. "They seem to be on target," she said.

"Yes, they are. Roland's got it absolutely right. That's fantastic."

Anna was less impressed. "He's been practising often enough. I should bloody well hope so."

Jeffrey passed her the binoculars so she could assess the situation for herself.

"Now the hard work begins," Jeffrey proclaimed, as if he had become Winston Churchill.

"Is that so?" Anna lowered the binoculars and eyed him scathingly. "What do you think yesterday was?"

"A warm-up," he said cheerfully.

"You ungrateful bastard." Anna went back to watching the water splashing into the lagoons. "I'll tell Jimmy you said that – and Maggie. By the way, those howitzers seem to be filling both the pools at once." She passed the binoculars back to Jeffrey to verify this.

"Roland wanted this to happen to start with, so that he can refine the aim later. In a while, he'll have them all firing into one lagoon," Jeffrey explained. Then he let out a sigh. "This process seemed fine in theory, but there'll be long delays in reality. Now I see the full picture. We're going to waste all the good weather like this. It's a great pity."

"The ship should be closer to the lagoons, then you could empty them as fast as they are filled," Anna said, stating the obvious.

Jeffrey gave a dismissive puff of the lips. "It's too great a risk to the ship. If a big enough piece of ice broke away from Fortune, the wave it created could swamp us. That's why we came up with this idea in the first place."

"It's not too great a risk," Anna said dismissively. "I've been up there. I should know. You should tell Ernst. He would be delighted to get away from here sooner than later."

"I can't tell Ernst anything. Anyway, he would never risk his ship."

"It's your ship, Jeffrey, not his. I was with you when you bought it. Remember?" Anna reminded him tersely. "This is your dream, this is your consortium, the moringas are your research, and this is your ship. With the possible exception of David, the rest of us are all risk-takers. We accept what's coming. If bad weather sets in, then that's it. The main purpose of this voyage has gone. You won't arouse any interest in your idea at all. So do you want the ship laid close to the lagoons or not?"

Jeffrey had withered before this onslaught, realising that Anna was exhibiting the spirit that he had once had but had lost along the way. "If I were in charge, then yes," Jeffrey replied. "But it was made very clear to me yesterday that I have no power at all."

"Leave it to me," Anna said firmly.

"Forget it, Anna," Jeffrey replied, sounding cross. "If you stir things up, Ernst will assume I'm behind it. It was you who said last night that I should avoid giving him any excuse to harm me, and I think you're right."

"Fifty pounds says that I can get Ernst to move the ship to the lagoons without any harm coming to you at all," Anna challenged him.

"Put like that, how can I resist? You've got yourself a bet. I'll go and read in our cabin. When they come to arrest me, they can bring your fifty pounds with them," Jeffrey muttered, but he was feeling much more optimistic than he sounded. He sensed he shouldn't ask any more questions, but as he reached the door, he turned and said, "Take care," then went down to their cabin.

She gave him a few seconds to get clear and then made her way to the bridge door and knocked.

Ernst saw her and came to the door himself. They spoke in Norwegian. "Is Gary here?" she asked.

"He's just gone," Ernst said, looking at her in a way that made his interest in her quite apparent.

She looked away coyly. "So has Jeffrey. He's gone to have a rest, poor thing." Then she looked into his eyes. "I'm bored," she said. "Have you a little time to spare?"

"Alone?" he asked.

"In return for a small favour, yes. I was thinking we could be stuck here for days at the rate things are going. Why don't you take the ship closer to the lagoons? It'll be so much quicker. It's stupid having such long hoses."

"Yes, it's stupid, but perhaps less stupid than risking the ship if the iceberg cracks."

Anna put a hint of disdain into her voice at his anxiety: "I've stood on Fortune. It's not going to break up. I'll camp up there all day and all night if it makes you feel any better. We're Norwegians, Ernst. We know about the seas and about ice. I mean it. In return for your promise, I'll spend forty minutes with you now, and you can try to impress me. So, alpha man, what do you think?" He hesitated. "You're wasting time," she prompted. "Let's get the job done and get away from here. You'll get the credit for the idea and for getting us away from here sooner." She passed a hand through her hair, tossing it in an alluring way.

"Why are you doing this? Are you seriously interested in me?" There was obvious hope in his voice.

"You can decide for yourself," she said, as if she were open to persuasion.

"One moment," he said. Then he closed the door and walked back to the first officer. He soon returned to Anna. "Ramos will look after things in my absence. I have told him that he has not seen you, and I need an hour's undisturbed rest. Now, if you please, my cabin is just here."

Anna had not expected to be so successful. She had presumed that Ernst would be difficult to shift, that he would offer resistance, probably a refusal, to her idea. Ernst noticed.

"Now you're wasting time," he teased her.

"No, I'm not," she answered sharply, stepping into his cabin and closing the door behind her.

Just over an hour later, she was back in her own cabin. "Come on, Jeffrey, sweetheart; wake up. Gary's calling a meeting."

Jeffrey woke up with a familiar ear-tingling and realised he had fallen asleep waiting for Anna.

"I wish you wouldn't do that," he mumbled, rubbing his ear as full consciousness returned. Anna looked on, smiling unrepentantly. His looked at her through bleary eyes and wondered how anyone could look as fresh and vivacious as she did. "How long have I been asleep?"

"Nearly two hours," she kissed him. "Now go and freshen up, then we can go along to the meeting."

He didn't move. Memory returned. "Hold on," he said. "First things first. Do you owe me fifty pounds, or do I owe you?"

"You owe me," she replied, ruffling his hair, "big time. Now, come on, or we'll be late."

"I won't ask how you managed it. I don't want to know," he said, walking to the shower room.

"Do you mind how I did it?" she asked him, as he came out.

"No. I trust you," he said, turning to the mirror and brushing his hair.

"Good," she said briskly.

He put an arm on her shoulder and said admiringly, "You are incredible. You've achieved the impossible."

She put her arms round his waist and hugged herself to him.

"Would you like me to do a striptease for you this evening?" she cooed. "How good would that be?"

"As long as I get the best seat in the house, pretty good."

"Well, slip that fifty you owe me into my panties, and you might get lucky, good sir," she flirted.

"I haven't got fifty pounds," he replied with a kiss to her forehead. "You're going to have to keep your clothes on for the rest of the voyage."

"That could be a problem," she said. "Let's go."

She hid well that, to her surprise, Ernst was not the womaniser she had taken him to be. He was actually serious about wanting her to leave Jeffrey. He said he had never forgotten their first meeting. He told her how much he had hoped for fate to bring them back together, saying he had watched her with Jeffrey and noticed that things were not entirely right. He spoke of all this, and his touch, when it came, had not been as unwelcome to her as she had imagined it. He had delicately stroked her neck. She had asked him not to touch. She had treated him to a striptease, to taunt him, but when she bared her breasts, he had asked her to stop. He said he loved her, which made her very angry, because that was a lie. In her anger, she had insisted on continuing further than she had planned, pulling down her trousers and knickers together, and twisting all the way round with them round her ankles in front of him, and it was meant to make him feel like a client with a tart, and shut him up. Only it hadn't felt like that at all, but something very confusing. And she had dressed again and apologised for treating him so badly and begged him not to tell anyone. And he had apologised too and clasped her hand as she opened the door, calling her name, as if wanting her to stay. And she had smiled at him, nervously, and said she had to go. It was very confusing.

The meeting hadn't yet started. Anna spotted Maggie and Leena, and immediately went to sit next to them, Jeffrey following her. They were glad to see each other and shared kisses.

"Where were you this morning?" Anna asked Maggie. "Everyone else was watching the start of the water-jets."

"Leena and I were meditating," Maggie replied, looking very relaxed and content. "Arnesh has let us into a secret. He showed Leena a meditation room that he incorporated into the design of the ship. It's ideal."

"A meditation room?" David asked from behind her. "What's it like?"

"Well, I suppose it's big enough for ten or twelve people. It's hidden away, dimly lit, calming, with mats and cushions scattered around."

"Does it happen to smell of anything?" David asked casually. He saw Leena cast a quick glance at Maggie as he asked this.

Maggie cocked her head to one side in thought. "Yes, I suppose it does," she said. "Let's say it has an exotic, Eastern smell."

"Ah yes, I rather thought it might," David said, sitting back with a satisfied smile on his face. Maggie and Anna continued to chat.

"What was that about?" Jeffrey muttered.

"I'll tell you later," David replied.

205

Gary entered the room. Lucy came in hurriedly, just behind him, and sat by her father.

Gary looked round the twenty or so people in the audience, indicating that he was ready to start, and summed up each character as he did so. Wherever he glanced, Gary felt superiority over everyone he saw – except over Jimmy Moule. Jimmy was American. Jimmy was a sharp lawyer disguised behind a benign nature. He seemed to know that something was not right about the voyage. He never seemed quite satisfied by anything that he saw or anything that he was told. He never said much, but there wasn't a loose cover that Jimmy wouldn't look under or a careless remark that he wouldn't ponder over for a moment.

It was time to start. Gary explained the change of plan; Ernst was going to bring the *Moringa* closer to Fortune. He said he hadn't been consulted about it but gave no hint of anger. He made this lack of consultation seem like a regrettable oversight, but it pleased everyone else that Ernst had given him a dose of his own medicine.

"So that's it. There's a trade-off. We'll get the job done quicker, but we'll be more at risk doing it. If you are out in one of the launches, stay alert. Be ready to take evasive action. Those of us on board – it's not impossible that if a big chunk of ice breaks away, a wave could sweep across the deck, so don't be complacent. To ensure that we don't get caught out, Anna Jensen is going to be on top of the iceberg. As long as she feels it is safe to be there, we'll stay here. If she feels it's time to leave, we'll move away immediately. Any questions?"

While Gary answered questions from others in the room, Jeffrey had a few for Anna. "I suppose that little detail slipped your mind earlier, did it?" he whispered.

"It wasn't important," she whispered back.

"Who's going with you?"

"Nobody," she said dismissively.

"What?" Jeffrey blurted out so loudly that everyone in the room turned to him, including Gary, who stopped speaking in mid-sentence. As happens at such times, Jeffrey muttered, "Sorry," and crouched back in his chair.

Gary gave him a pointed look, finished what he was saying, and concluded the meeting.

Anna went off to prepare for her vigil, leaving Jeffrey alone and disgruntled. He saw David talking to Lucy, remembered something that David had said, and went over to them.

"What was so interesting about the incense in the meditation room?" Jeffrey asked.

David said, "I don't think it was incense that Maggie and Leena smelt, or if it was, it was there to hide the smell of marijuana. Last night, Lucy and I were tending the moringa trees, and Arnesh and his team were helping. They've been showing great interest in the shrubs. This morning, when Frank and I looked where they had been working, we found twelve plants of marijuana neatly dug into the soil."

Jeffrey's eyebrows raised at the news, but that was all. "Twelve plants can't do that much harm. Did you dig them up?" he asked.

"No, we left them," David replied. "I'd feel more comfortable if Arnesh did it himself."

Jeffrey nodded approvingly. "I'll have a word with him," he said.

As he spoke, he saw Stefan slip into the room and seek out Lucy, who was standing behind her father. He saw how her face lit up when she noticed Stefan, and a mobile phone slipped quickly from his hand to hers, and then he was gone. Nobody else seemed to notice anything, but as she looked round, Lucy caught Jeffrey's eye and gave him an impish, conspiratorial smile. Jeffrey winked at her, not quite sure what he had witnessed, but certain that romance was involved.

"I'd be grateful if you would, Jeffrey," David said, still talking about Arnesh and the marijuana, oblivious to what had happened behind him. "You've got a better grasp of cultural differences than I have. I might come across as a bit racist, which I'd hate to do. You know that I'm not like that at all."

Jeffrey laughed and said, "Lucy, talk some sense into your father, will you? I've got to go. By the way, about the dive: Have you spoken to Gary?"

"Don't bother about it, boss," Lucy replied with a shrug of resignation. "It's obviously not going to happen today. There's plenty for me to get on with."

"Sorry about that," Jeffrey replied, and then he added wickedly, "But Stefan looks nice."

"Stefan? Who is Stefan?" David asked, while Lucy glowered at Jeffrey, who mimed a little kiss at her and headed back to the cabin, where Anna had almost finished dressing for her vigil on the ice.

He was truly anxious for her, and she was scared, yet neither could find the soft words that might have changed the course of events.

"This is bloody madness," he criticised her, cruelly.

"Bugger off," she retorted. "For goodness sake, try to be of some use while I'm gone." She moved him out of her way so she could pick up her gloves.

"Ernst had not right to force you to do this," he said, disregarding her jibe.

"He didn't force me; I offered to do it," Anna retorted. "I do things my way. You got what you wanted."

"I didn't want a human sacrifice."

She stopped and looked at him. "Actually, now I think about it, that's quite typical of you, Jeffrey. You know what you want, but you don't think about the consequences on others of getting it."

"Don't be ridiculous," he retorted.

Anna made final adjustments to her clothing with renewed vigour. "All right. So now I'm ridiculous," she said crossly. "I've got to go – and I will be back." She gave him a light peck of affection on the cheek and left him. "Striptease will be tomorrow night."

It took only a few seconds from the time she left the cabin for his anger to turn to guilt and frustration. Cursing himself, he put on his additional layers and, when he was ready, went on deck to watch her take off. Ernst was watching from the bridge, and Maggie and Leena emerged from the midships doorway and came over to him.

"Has she gone yet?" Maggie asked.

"Any moment now. It's crazy, isn't it?" he replied.

Maggie turned to Leena. "Leena, love, could I just have a few minutes alone with Jeffrey?"

"Of course," Leena said, flashing a smile to Maggie and nodding to Jeffrey. "I'll watch from further up." She slipped away, towards the flight deck. The other two watched her until she was out of hearing range, then Jeffrey turned to Maggie.

"All right," he said. "What did you want to say to me?"

"Oh, don't tempt me," Maggie burst out. "Jeffrey, you wouldn't believe what I have to say to you. However, that'll have to wait. No, I want you to tell me whether you've noticed any change in Anna."

"In what way?"

"Anything."

"Anna is Anna," Jeffrey replied. "She does things her own way. I don't know where her limits are. Living with her, I've come to expect the unexpected. Sometimes it's fun. Sometimes, like today, it scares me."

"Yesterday, on Fortune, she was the same. It was as if she no longer cared whether she lived or died. Jimmy is more experienced on ice than any of us, but even he wouldn't do some of the things she did."

"Do you think she's showing signs of mental illness?" he asked, troubled by the idea.

Maggie grimaced. "Not mental illness, no. There's a well-known saying that you shouldn't make a lover of your patient or a patient of your lover, but I can't help using my skills. This fatalism she's been exhibiting; well, it makes me wonder if her cancer has returned."

Jeffrey looked perplexed. "But that's not possible. She told me, she showed me, that she's had everything surgically removed. No kids, but no more cancer; that was the deal."

"She didn't tell you everything, then. I thought that was the case," Maggie replied. "They wanted to take her lymph nodes, as well. It meant having a large scar from her breastbone to her pubic bone, all the way down the middle. She was very young and sensationally beautiful. She wouldn't let them do it. There's a very real chance that the cancer is still inside her. The lymph nodes are a sort of defensive barrier, but eventually, the cancer could break through and she'll die."

"And you think that could be happening now?" Jeffrey asked quietly.

"It would explain tempting a sudden death without really wanting to die."

"Does she really think I'm so shallow that I wouldn't love her if she had a scar on her abdomen?" he asked, ashamed at the thought.

Maggie touched his arm reassuringly. "She loves you, Jeffrey, though I hate to admit it, and she wants to be beautiful for you, just as she once did for me. She wants to be as beautiful as she can be. My guess is that she feels guilty enough that she can't give you children, so she's made her choice to be beautiful instead, rather than safe, and she may be paying the price."

"Isn't there anything that can be done?"

"Once the cancer breaks out again? No, it will be all over her body, carried in the bloodstream."

"And that could be happening now; that's what you're saying?"

"It's in my mind. She seems healthy but unsettled. I don't know."

They became aware of the helicopter engine, which had been part of the background hum, now beginning a crescendo. They turned to watch it rise, steady itself just clear of the deck, turn to the ocean, and rapidly gain height as it left the ship behind.

"Thank you, Maggie. Thank you for telling me." Jeffrey tried to think of something cheerful on which to end their brief conversation. "You and Leena seem to be getting on quite well."

"What do you mean by that?" Maggie's retort was sharp and instant.

"Oh ... well ... I ... er ..." Jeffrey faltered.

"Leena and I are two lonely people who are finding mutual comfort in each other's company. We are not a couple, Jeffrey."

"Sorry."

"You're forgiven. See you later." Maggie gave him an unexpected kiss on the cheek and, as she walked away, turned to look at Fortune. "She's almost there, already."

Jeffrey looked at the helicopter and immediately recalled Anna's voice telling him to find something useful to do while she was gone. So without wasting further time looking forlornly at the iceberg, he went looking for Arnesh, instead.

Chapter 12

SMOKE SCREEN

Arnesh delighted in reminding everyone that he and his team had built the ship. They had taken care to design some comfortable quarters for themselves, too, including a kitchen for their needs. It was now mid-afternoon, but Jeffrey, being near the middle of the ship, felt this would be a likely place to find Arnesh, and, sure enough, he was there, having a mug of tea with two of his mates; they welcomed Jeffrey and encouraged him to join them.

"So Professor, what can we do for you?" he asked.

"Arnesh, would you happen to know anything about the marijuana plants that are growing beside the moringas in the Grand Chamber?"

"Oh yes, we put them there, Professor," Arnesh said cheerfully, while his two friends smiled with him. Jeffrey was unsure how much English the latter understood. "Let me explain, Professor. When we were constructing the ship, its name was a mystery to us. The boss explained to us that it was the name of a mysterious tree that grows in Africa that can purify the waters of the Nile. He said you had taken the seed from these trees and changed them to be even better, and this ship would take these trees back to Africa. But he told us these changes were not legal yet, so we were not to talk about the trees. See?"

"Not really," Jeffrey said, perplexed.

"Moringa, marijuana – magic plants, not legal – they sound very alike. Indeed, there is hardly any difference at all," Arnesh explained, without any sign of guilt.

Jeffrey was beginning to see the connection. "I agree the names sound similar, but you must have seen that they look very different."

"Ah, but when we were constructing the ship, we had not seen the trees, Professor. We thought if you were bringing your magical and not-very-lawful moringa aboard, we might bring some of our magical and not-very-lawful marijuana aboard to help us through the long voyage, and we could all have a fine time together."

Arnesh's logic was so crafty and so simple that Jeffrey could not fault it. He thought how everyone had commented on the calm way the Indian crew were always going about their business on the voyage down, as well as in the risky environment of the Antarctic, and realised that he could now explain why. They were all stoned.

"Fair enough," Jeffrey said pensively. "But why, after so many weeks, have you now planted your marijuana in the Grand Chamber?"

"Well, we were having a discussion about your moringas and our marijuana as to whether they could be related. So we decided to plant some of our marijuana next to your moringa to look more closely and work it out for ourselves. We have more than enough to spare, now."

"You mean you have more?"

"Oh yes, Professor," Arnesh said with an evident sense of pride. "We are as good at farming as we are at building ships."

"So just how many do you have?"

"We have a good patch, now."

"What? You have an area set aside for it?"

"Oh, indeed," Arnesh said, laughing. 'We built this ship, don't forget," he said. "We don't just know its nooks and crannies; we made them. There was space for us. Wherever this ship takes your moringa, it takes our marijuana too." He translated his words to his two mates, who laughed happily and nodded their heads in agreement.

Jeffrey was not at all amused. He was now quite concerned as to the extent of Arnesh's patch. "Arnesh, you must understand, moringas and marijuana are totally different. You have seen the moringas. May I see the marijuana?"

Arnesh explained Jeffrey's request to the others, and a short debate in Punjabi took place while Jeffrey looked on. "They are worried that you will tell everyone on the ship where it is."

"I won't, and nor must you. If you are growing marijuana on the ship, it must remain a total secret. Other than the plants in the Grand Chamber, do you think anyone else knows?"

Arnesh looked doubtful. "Well, Professor, until this moment, we weren't worried. That is why we were pleased to plant some of our crop with yours. We thought that, with all the money you will make with your trees, it would not matter the little bit of money we make with our marijuana. Now, I see we made a mistake. We must become very secret. We are not rich men. This money will be most welcome to our families."

"Arnesh, please, don't say anything more. Please, at least let me see the patch you've got."

They all finished their tea, and then Jeffrey was led to a part of the ship he had never visited before.

It was not in Ernst Brage's interest for Anna to get frostbite. He needed her strong fingers and toes all in one piece. Whether he was looking out over the ocean or staring at the deck, his mind's eye kept returning to the vision of Anna, naked in his cabin, rotating angrily with her trousers around her ankles. It was so exciting, so ridiculous, so unlike anything anyone had ever done for him, that he wanted her with him very much. Life with her, by its very nature, would be an adventure. He had known it from the moment he had first set eyes on her, the day she came with Jeffrey to buy the ship. That day, she had seemed so inaccessible, but fate had brought them together. Yesterday had proved that she was not inaccessible, and that she was even more incredible than he had realised. She had changed from a fantasy to reality. He had tried to stop her undressing, for fear of losing her respect – he would have moved the ship, anyway – but after her angry gyration, she had been gentle and had not taunted him for the arousal he could not hide. She had given him hope. He now kept telling himself that there had to be a next time.

Gary came onto the bridge, and Ernst's first words to him were "I'm worried about Anna."

Gary was surprised and looked at him with interest. "Why would you be worried about Anna? Yours is the ship, mine is the project. Remember? She's part of my crew, not yours."

"She's Norwegian," Ernst replied hastily, as if this was adequate to explain his concern.

"She's also Jeffrey's," Gary said pointedly. "If I was concerned, I would talk to him, and if he was concerned, he could talk to me."

"Perhaps you should be concerned," Ernst said haughtily, trying to regain the moral high ground, but Gary shrugged off his comment.

"Take my advice, Ernst: Don't chase after Anna. If you step out of line with her, she'll wipe the floor with you." Gary turned away, disdainfully. Ernst thought again of Anna in his cabin and said nothing.

Gary walked over to Stefan to take the headset and contact Tyro, but Stefan was listening intently to a message and held up his hand to indicate that he must not be disturbed. Then he turned to Ernst. "We are being contacted by another ship, sir."

"That's interesting, Ernst," Gary said suspiciously. This was not part of any plan he knew about, but Ernst seemed just as surprised.

"Do you know its name?" Ernst asked.

"It's a British destroyer, sir, HMS *Cornwall*."

"What do they want?"

"Under orders of the International Maritime Organisation, they are sending a boarding party. They require us to maintain our position."

"It must be something to do with the moringa trees," Gary said. "I'll warn David at once." He pulled out the walkie-talkie from his pocket and moved to the far side of the bridge, away from Ernst's activity zone.

Ernst had moved over to Stefan. "They may be sending a helicopter, so warn them that we've got an airship and a helicopter in the air. It's not up yet, but it will be soon."

Gary made contact with David. "David, the Royal Navy's sending a boarding party. It's due any time. It's on the authority of the International Maritime Organisation, whoever they are. I suggest that you contact Jimmy Moule. You may need his legal advice."

"Why me?" David sounded victimised.

"It must be something to do with your moringa trees. I can't think what else they would want to board us for."

"Maybe," David said drily, with one or two other reasons coming to his mind.

"Well, I'm leaving it in your hands, David. Be ready."

David was standing in Lucy's laboratory and had been chatting to her when Gary's call interrupted them. Lucy saw the look of annoyance on David's face.

"What's Gary done now?" she asked sympathetically.

"It's not Gary, Lucy darling," David replied. "It's the Royal Navy. They're sending a boarding party, for crying out loud."

Lucy gave a shout of "Hurrah!" followed by a stifling hug round David's neck, which caught him completely by surprise, as did her next words: "Good for Mum."

David disentangled himself from Lucy's grasp, wondering if he was going mad or she was. "Lucy, get off me," he said, while she laughed at his dishevelled state. "What on earth has your mother to do with this?"

"She'll have told them to send a boarding party," Lucy replied as if it was the most obvious fact in the world.

David shook his head in disbelief. "You can't just phone the Royal Navy and order a boarding party," he protested. "Why should she want to do so, anyway?"

"When Ernst and Gary tried to enforce a communications blackout, it felt like we were prisoners. You said so, yourself. So I gave my phone to Stefan, and when he found the right moment, he sent Mum a text message I had prepared."

"There's that name Stefan again," David observed. "I don't know what you and he are up to, but there'll be hell to pay if Ernst and Gary get to hear about that. Fortunately, even if Jackie did get your message, she was hardly in a position to send in the navy. Sorry, darling, but I have to tell you that you're being rather silly at the moment."

Before Lucy had a chance to reply, Jeffrey appeared in the room, with Arnesh following along behind him. "Hello, David, I hoped I'd find you here. I have something rather urgent to discuss with you."

"Yes, well, it will have to wait, old son. One of Her Majesty's ships is sending a boarding party any time now, and Gary thinks they're unhappy about the moringas."

"I think they're coming because I got a message to Mum saying we were being held like prisoners," Lucy added defiantly.

Jeffrey gave her a quick, surprised glance and then said, "Lucy, please contact Jimmy Moule and ask him to be here in five minutes. Tell him this takes priority over everything." Then he turned back to David. "David, I really need you to go with Arnesh. Now."

"Jeffrey, the boarding party," David reiterated.

"Especially if a boarding party is coming. You need to see this, David. It'll take less than ten minutes. Jimmy will be here when you get back. Just go."

Still muttering about everyone giving him orders, David set off with Arnesh. On the bridge, Ernst was watching, intently, on his radar screen, the approach of HMS *Cornwall*. Ramos was with him. Gary was on the flight deck, organising the take-off of the helicopter with cylinders for the compressors, and Maggie had volunteered to fly with it to assist Anna in the refuelling operation. Some of the ship's company were resting between shifts, others were going about their tasks. Arnesh's team were dotted about the ship, carrying out maintenance work on the vessel and its engines. Frank and Leena were tending the saplings, and crew members were overseeing the pumps sucking the water out of the lagoons into the *Moringa*'s tanks.

It took Arnesh just under five minutes to lead David to a part of the ship he had not known existed and show him a small door that he would not have noticed in the semi-darkness of a dimly lit, narrow corridor. They went down some steps to another narrow door.

"I don't know what we're doing here," David said anxiously. "We ought to be getting back."

"First, you must open this door, sir, because Professor Harvey says so, though I, personally, prefer that you don't."

"If I must, I will. Open up."

"Then please put these on first, sir," Arnesh said, handing David some dark goggles.

"What on earth do I need these for? I can barely see in the gloom as it is." But he saw that Arnesh was slipping on goggles as well and realised why. "Oh, I see. This is your marijuana patch, is it? All right, open up."

Arnesh pushed open the door.

A light that dazzled David even through his goggles burst onto them. David crouched and thrust himself through the door, into a low-roofed deck of endless green. "Oh, my God! Oh, my God! Arnesh, what have you done?" David heard his own voice escaping from him in a reflex shout he could not contain. He spun on his own axis, staggered out of the door, pressed his back to the stair wall, and shouted, "Shut it! Shut it!"

Removing his goggles restored his vision, and his eyes readjusted to the gloom. He took a few deep breaths, turned to Arnesh, and berated him with venomous anger. "Arnesh, that is not a patch of marijuana. That is a field of marijuana, a field that is little short of a prairie. How you manage to have that much light without blowing the electrics of the ship astounds me."

"We have our own generator," Arnesh tried to explain.

"Shut up. I'm not interested. Do you realise that we have the Royal Navy bearing down on us at this very moment? They're not interested in my moringas. They're not interested in my wife. They're interested in your marijuana. And because your marijuana is on our ship, they'll arrest the bloody lot of us. We are all going to be put in irons because of you."

"Yes sir," Arnesh said gently, "but I think we should go back to Professor Harvey."

A broader sense of reality returned to David's stunned mind. "Yes, yes, lead the way, but don't get too far ahead. God help us if the navy's here already."

A few minutes later, they were back at the laboratory. Jeffrey was already explaining the situation to Jimmy, who was listening with his normal, calm nature.

David disrupted the scene by his appearance. "That's it! We've had it. We're all going to jail," he announced loudly, without any regard for Jeffrey and Jimmy's conversation.

"Just take it easy there, David," Jimmy said, slipping into the reassuring tones of an attorney advising his client. "We are on the high seas, outside any national jurisdiction. A naval vessel working on behalf of the International Maritime Organisation can send a boarding party, and can even impound contraband, but the crew doesn't have the powers of arrest, so just relax."

"In that case," David retorted, "let's own up to the marijuana the moment they step aboard. Then they can take the whole lot away, though they'll need a battleship to do it, and they can leave us alone."

"David, calm down and stop gabbling." Jeffrey's firm, critical tone made David reflect on how he was behaving.

Jimmy intervened. "You'll need to establish, from them, the reason they're here. At the moment, you have no idea. It may not have anything to do with you. Jeffrey, you said there was some marijuana planted in the Grand Chamber."

"Oh hell," David interrupted. "I'd forgotten all about that."

Lucy put a comforting arm about his waist, as Jimmy said something that surprised them all: "Arnesh, I think you planted twelve plants. Just leave them there."

"Why would we want to do that, sir?" Arnesh asked. "Why don't we just remove them?"

"Whatever their reason for coming, they are going to do a routine search of the ship. They are experienced. If you try to hide what is already there, you're likely to leave clues in your haste, and that will make them nosy. If they find a small crop, neatly planted, they won't look further. If they find the whole crop, as you describe, you'll go onto every list of major drug dealers in the world. Best avoid that."

It was the only explanation Arnesh needed. He was on his radio to his mate and best friend, Anwar, as he left the room, with David and Lucy following him.

"What do you think Gary and Ernst know of the marijuana?" Jimmy asked.

"Probably nothing," Jeffrey replied. "Gary should be all right, but none of us know what sort of link there is between the two of them, and Ernst is bad news. If he finds out there's a crop of marijuana on board, he could use it as a reason to end the whole mission."

"All the same, he's the captain, and marijuana is about to be found on his ship." A helicopter passed overhead. "The helicopter – it sounds different."

"You're right. That's not ours. I guess the navy's here," Jimmy commented. "Let's see what's happening."

Outside, it looked like an air display was in progress, with two helicopters and an airship in the sky together. The machine that caught their immediate attention was the blue-grey helicopter with the blue, white, and red roundels flying low, its fuselage door open and the two pilots and a crewman looking down on them, observing the scene beneath them. Then its pattern of flight changed, and it began a series of hovers and swoops, the occupants looking down to left and right, clearly fascinated by what they were seeing.

"I don't think they can quite believe their eyes," Jimmy said, smiling.

"Who can blame them?" Jeffrey replied, casting a quick glance at the howitzer salvoes, three of which were currently firing into the lagoons, and then looking along the deck to the flight deck. "Look, that's Gary on the flight deck. I think he's making sure that the naval helicopter doesn't land."

"Good thinking. It looks like Tyro is bringing the airship down," Jimmy remarked, looking round to where the less-noisy airship was completing a circuit of the *Moringa* and descending. The airship now held their attention as it completed its final turn and faced the stern of the ship head-on.

"We mustn't leave here until I've had a ride in that thing," Jimmy remarked as he admired the sleek silvery craft, coming low towards the tower.

"How can you think of joyrides at a time like this?" Jeffrey asked, distracted for a moment by the naval helicopter, which was hovering out of the airship's way.

"Look out!" The alarm in Jimmy's voice made Jeffrey glance back to the airship again.

The turbulent breeze had caught the airship. With only seconds to go, it suddenly became clear that the gondola could hit the stern.

Inside the gondola, the imminent crash caused Alan to panic. "Rise up, Tyro! Rise up," he shouted in alarm, as all three occupants stared at the ironwork ahead of them.

Tyro could do no more. "First you tell me to be better than Moses, now you want a resurrection. You are a very demanding friend, Alan," he said calmly.

The gondola rose, and cleared the tower by a hand's breadth. The airship floated, clumsily swaying over Jimmy and Jeffrey, still instinctively crouching, and sank gently above the landing deck, while Gary and some deckhands seized the ropes, secured the airship to the winches, and brought it down. Alan and Roland staggered out.

Gary put his head in at the door, smiling broadly. "Tyro, buddy, that was one hell of a landing. Don't ever do another one like it. You scared the shit out of me," he called out.

"I think Alan needs to pray harder," Tyro shouted in reply.

Gary laughed and said, "Ah, so Alan was to blame. I should have guessed. It's always the quiet guys who cause the biggest problems."

"In that case, I blame Roly," Alan called back, and they all laughed in a welcome release of tension. They knew how close death had been. Its awesome proximity had put their petty differences into perspective and strengthened their common bond.

"We saw the warship and its helicopter," Tyro said. "Are we in trouble?"

"I don't know, but we need to clear the flight deck. We'll bring the Hind back, and they may want to send a boarding party. I just don't know."

Tyro climbed out, and the two men helped to move the airship into the shed, under the Royal Navy's watchful gaze.

HMS *Cornwall* took station across the *Moringa's* bows about an hour later, and two boat-loads of marines came across and boarded her via the entrance to the storage deck, halfway up the hull. Ramos and Gary were waiting to meet them. David, Lucy, and Leena were watching behind Gary. Under instructions from Ernst, all others aboard ship were at their respective posts. Three steady streams of water were filling the lagoons. All was in order. Jimmy, Anna, and Maggie were back on Fortune, where they wanted to be, having flown out with a second consignment of fuel.

Ramos and Gary went up the stairways to the main deck with the lieutenant in command and one of the marines, and from there to the bridge. A sergeant remained on the storage deck, and he sent the men out in twos to scout around. They held their guns at the ready, despite David, Lucy, and Leena standing on the deck, watching them.

The sergeant approached Lucy, as she had caught his eye the most. "Are you all right, miss?" he asked in a manner far friendlier than his bearing.

"Yes, thanks, but it's lovely to see you. I'm dying to know why you're here," Lucy replied, with an excited smile and a flick of her head, which tossed her fair hair.

"We understand some of those on board are being held against their will. Does that include the three of you?"

Now that marines had arrived, Lucy began to think that her text message had been a bit excessive. However, given the circumstances, she felt it was better to stick to her theme and make the most of it. "Sort of; my boss was imprisoned by the captain for several hours, and he's taken away our right to communicate with the outside world, without any agreement to do so. Ask my father," Lucy said, deftly passing the situation to David to handle.

"Is that right? What sort of ship is this?" The marine fired his questions at David, looking along the storage deck to the aircraft hangars. "I've never seen anything like it," he added.

"This is a research vessel," David explained proudly. "We've developed the means of harvesting melting Antarctic ice, and a biological means of keeping water safe for human consumption. Combine those two factors as we have done, and you have a potent means of overcoming drought anywhere in the world. It's taken us over twenty years, and now we've done it. And yes, my daughter is right. I'm not sure it required a destroyer to sort out the problem, but my colleagues and I, who are supposedly in charge of this venture, have been subjected to draconian treatment by the captain, aided and abetted by our own project leader, I might add, in a way that suggests some sort of takeover is going on."

"Where do you fit into this?" the sergeant asked, looking around him as David was talking, not really concentrating on David at all.

"I'm one of the founders of the project, along with my daughter's boss, as she just mentioned. We've just been cut out of all decision-making. It's utterly unreasonable," David said angrily, his self-esteem now badly dented.

The marine smiled and turned back to Lucy. "When the chopper crew came back and reported what they'd seen, everyone wanted to be on the boarding party. They said there were ice-firing guns, an airship, and a lone woman on a giant iceberg. It's wild." He noticed two of his men nosing around the distant hangar and turned round to look at the wall behind him, with its locked double doorway. "What's behind there?" he asked, expecting to be told of fluid containers of some sort.

"He didn't listen to a word I said," David mumbled to Leena.

"That's the Grand Chamber," Lucy replied nonchalantly. The marine looked perplexed. "That's where we have the moringas," she added, trying vainly to clarify its purpose.

"Moringas? What's moringas?" the marine asked, unsure that he had heard correctly.

"Moringas, man, moringas," David interrupted crossly, inadvertently challenging the sergeant's intellect in front of his men. "They're the trees that purify the water."

The marine was back on duty, all familiarity gone. "How many do you have?"

"About a thousand – in various stages of growth," David replied, wishing he had said rather less.

"A thousand trees," the marine repeated, "growing in this ship. Just a moment." He moved a few paces away and radioed the lieutenant. He returned moments later. "I'm to carry out a search of the Grand Chamber, as you call it."

David had already regretted his outburst and cursed himself for his stupidity. He spoke much more contritely now: "I'd like to have the head of the science project with us, my daughter's boss, the one who was imprisoned," he said, nervously.

"Who is he?" the marine asked. "Where is he? I've got to do this now."

"Professor Harvey," David replied. It pleased Lucy and Leena to hear him give Jeffrey his proper title, even under such circumstances.

"I'll find him for you," Lucy offered. "He'll be in the lab or in the canteen."

"Mason, go with this lady, find the professor, and bring him to the Grand Chamber," the sergeant ordered, putting a mocking emphasis on the word "Grand." "Balcombe, Martin, come with me." Then he turned to David and said, "Right, sir, lead on."

Everyone set off as directed. Leena tagged on to David, sensing he needed some support, but the sergeant turned to her: "You can stay here, miss," he said curtly.

"I'm needed for interpreting," she replied with quick-thinking. "Some of our assistants are from India and don't speak English."

"All right, but from now on, you stay with us all the time. Understood?" the sergeant retorted.

"Fully understood; yes," Leena replied submissively.

The Grand Chamber could only be entered from the storage deck's big double doors, or the corridor deck's pedestrian entrance, just above it, so David led the way up the stairs along the deck and into the upper gantries of the Grand Chamber, so the marines had the opportunity to see whole impressive vista of the moringas circulating in regimented lines along the walls with the lattice-work of walkways and ladders in between and the service deck halfway down. The air was warm, and water dripped down the walls from above.

The marines had not imagined any such sight, and Balcombe let slip an expletive before he knew it. "Fucking hell," he whispered in admiration.

"Shut up, Balcombe," the sergeant said, suppressing his own sense of wonder.

"Sorry, Sergeant, but it's Babylon, isn't it: the hanging gardens and all that?"

"I'll hang you if you say anything else," the sergeant said firmly. Then he noticed three men standing, looking at them from the other end of the gantry. "Who are they?" he asked David.

"Oh, that's the head gardener and two of the Indian personnel," David replied.

"Who don't speak English, as I was explaining," Leena added sweetly. Then she called to Arnesh in Punjabi: "Arnesh, for the love of my uncle and all you hold dear on this earth, you do not speak English. Now, come over here and bring Anwar with you."

Then she turned to the sergeant: "I told them you are not going to hurt them and they should come to meet you," she said.

"Frank, come on over," David called, following Leena's lead.

When the three men had joined them, the sergeant said, "Look, you can all make this a lot easier if you cooperate. The International Maritime Organisation has a drug-busting role, and we're part of its initiative. Suddenly, we come across a ship growing trees in mid-ocean. What the hell else are you growing? Are you growing something here you shouldn't be?"

"Anwar, the soldier is asking about what we are growing in here. Give him an innocent smile," Leena said.

Anwar's face broke into a salacious leer, but at that dramatic moment, a rumbling noise started above them.

"What's happening?" the sergeant demanded, and he, Balcombe, and Martin raised their guns defensively, as if expecting an attack.

"I'm just opening the skylights to give you more light," Frank explained helpfully.

He had the control in his pocket and had deliberately pressed it to disturb the sergeant, which it did. The warning beeps followed by the deep rumbling as the roof panels folded back prevented the sergeant from talking for about thirty seconds. During the enforced lull, Leena took the opportunity to introduce Arnesh, who pretended to speak no English, and Anwar, who really didn't speak any.

"That was very thoughtful of you, Frank. Well done," David said loudly as the noise died down, preventing the sergeant from saying something much less complimentary.

David was glad of any delay that gave Jeffrey time to join them. His guile was needed, David knew that. His own painful honesty was highly likely to make matters worse, especially if they found the marijuana before Jeffrey arrived.

By the time he could speak loudly again, the sergeant had lost all patience. "If we have to go searching for anything that shouldn't be here, we can make life very unpleasant for you, believe me. You'd do much better to come clean," he said, standing in the face of one thousand trees, genetically modified without any internationally acceptable authorisation.

At that moment Jeffrey appeared and joined the group. "Hello, David," he said. "Hello, Leena."

Before he could say another word, Leena stopped him: "Hello Jeffrey, don't mind me. I'm just here to act as interpreter for Anwar and Arnesh. I thought it might be useful. This is the sergeant in charge of the search."

Jeffrey extended his hand, but the sergeant disregarded it.

"Who are you?" the sergeant challenged him.

"I'm Professor Harvey. I think you sent for me."

"You're head of this science project, are you, sir?" the sergeant queried.

Behind his back, David caught Jeffrey's eye and nodded. Balcombe and Martin noticed, but they were enjoying themselves by now and said nothing.

"Yes, that's right," Jeffrey said, and, as he spoke, he felt back where he belonged.

"Well, put bluntly, as nobody else seems prepared to answer me, are you growing any plant material you know to be illegal? Are you trafficking, sir?"

"Why do you even ask?" Jeffrey seemed the picture of hurt innocence. "This is a respectable analytical scientific project."

The sergeant was unimpressed by Jeffrey's assertion. "Answer the question, sir. Since our attention was drawn to this ship, we have learnt that you started out from Bhavnagar, in northwest India. I now find you are full of strange plants. If you tell me that, after this little detour to Antarctica, you are headed for East Africa, I shall be very interested."

"That was a good guess," Jeffrey replied.

The sergeant looked at him, trying to work out whether Jeffrey was sincere or facetious. "The route from Pakistan to East Africa is now a main drug route, or didn't you know that? Now, do we uproot every precious tree you've got, or do you cooperate?"

"We are not traffickers. We are not concealing what we have. This is it. Our cargo is these trees and Antarctic water." Jeffrey then paused, and everyone wondered, for different reasons, what he would say next. "We do, however, have a small amount of marijuana on board for medicinal purposes."

The effect was electric. The sergeant said a triumphant, "Thank you," as he, at last, got the confession he had anticipated, while Arnesh exploded into Punjabi, saying to Leena, "What did he have to say that for, the bloody fool?"

Leena turned to the sergeant, saying, "Mr Singh is cross. It is time for tea. He suggests that you join him."

The sergeant looked astonished at this interruption. "No, thank you, and you tell him he's not to leave for tea until I say so," he said curtly.

Leena smiled sweetly to Arnesh: "That was close. Think before you speak."

The sergeant dismissed what he couldn't understand. Instead, he looked at Jeffrey and said, "I want to see the marijuana – all of it – now."

"Of course," Jeffrey replied politely. "It's growing on one of the terraces."

"Growing? You're growing marijuana?"

"Purely for medicinal purposes," Jeffrey repeated. "Our Indian colleagues are liable to intense pains from working in these temperatures. The marijuana eases this type of pain more effectively than opioids or ordinary painkillers."

"Our medical officer can explain if you like," David volunteered, wondering what Emily Ross would say at being compromised in this way.

Jeffrey and the sergeant disregarded him.

"Please tell me," Jeffrey continued, "have you really come across us by accident or have you been tracking us across thousands of miles of ocean because of a few leaves of marijuana?"

The sergeant, flushed with success, opened up a little. "It was chance, really. We were on a goodwill visit to Fremantle. We'd just left when we received orders to divert to investigate a report of suspected abduction and piracy on board this ship."

"Ah," David exclaimed in happy surprise. "So it *was* down to my wife. Lucy will be chuffed." Then he realised that everyone was looking at him in open-mouthed bewilderment. "Well, good for Jackie," he said defiantly, followed by a humble "Sorry," and he shut up.

The sergeant exchanged glances of mutual astonishment with Jeffrey and then said quietly, "You better lead on."

"What a load of nutters," Balcombe muttered to Martin, as they followed along at the back.

Frank stopped the rotation mechanism, and they walked down to where the recently planted marijuana had been placed beside the moringas, along one of the terraces.

"That's a lot of marijuana for medicinal purposes," the sergeant commented.

"Oh, it's really not that much. Our Indian colleagues provided our store. Each arrived with a couple of plants. That's all. It's really their personal supply," Jeffrey replied diffidently.

"Then you're not the person I should be talking to," the sergeant said; he beckoned Arnesh and Anwar closer and attempted to ask them questions to probe how the marijuana had come into their possession and other such matters. Arnesh and Anwar were notorious jokers when they were together, always egging each other on at the best of times. Now, with their sense of militancy and indignation, they started to give ever more provocative answers to the sergeant's questions to see how well Leena could convert them into polite replies.

When the sergeant asked how, exactly, the marijuana had a medicinal effect, and Leena translated his words, Anwar immediately replied that they could rub it over each other's naked arses and warm their hands. Leena translated this by saying that the marijuana was very beneficial in removing the pain of cold hands, to which Indian men are prone in cold climates. The problem was that she broke into spluttering laughter just as she finished saying this. One glance at Arnesh and Anwar's faces confirmed in the sergeant's mind that there was no point in continuing.

There had been no piracy. The reported abduction amounted to nothing more than a denial of outside contact, which could be quickly rectified with a warning to the captain, and the drug smuggling was a small amount of marijuana. The only matter nagging at him was whether there might be a further cache of marijuana, or heroin, even, somewhere, but the story he had heard was consistent with what he had seen. Drug traffickers came in many shapes and sizes, including types like Arnesh, Anwar, and Jeffrey, but there was something so sincerely honest about the indignant toff who kept going on about his wife and was in charge of the trees that he had to be believed.

The sergeant turned to David and said, "Can you give me your assurance that there is no other hoard of marijuana or any other illicit substance on this ship? Can you give me that assurance?"

Jeffrey, Lucy, Leena, Frank, and Arnesh all felt their stomachs knot.

"I can and I do," Honest David replied, looking the sergeant straight in the eyes.

The sergeant looked at him a moment longer, then looked round at the trees above, below, and around him, and felt a pang of sadness at having to leave such a unique and beautiful space. He thought, *How could anyone have imagined all this, let alone have created it? Yet here it is, on the edge of Antarctica. Of course, they're all mad. Only the mad and good would be involved in such a project.*

"Can we close the skylight now?" David asked gently. "The trees may get cold."

The request made up the sergeant's mind.

"Martin, Balcombe, pull up half the marijuana plants and bring them up on deck. Yes, you can close the skylight and whatever else you have to do." Turning to Leena, he said, "You can tell your friends they can be thankful we're not taking the whole lot. What's left should be more than enough for their cold toes."

Anwar, who had not understood the sergeant's words, saw the plants being uprooted and shouted at him, "Soldiers are the same, everywhere: rapists and looters."

Leena said quickly, "He thanks you most sincerely for your generous wisdom."

"You must think I was born yesterday," the sergeant replied quietly to her. "He didn't say any such thing." Then he turned to the marines pulling up the last of the plants: "Come on, Balcombe; come on, Martin. That's enough. Let's get back on deck. If I stay any longer down here, I'll turn into a hippy."

Frank used the remote to close the skylights. The rumbling noise from the roof of the Grand Chamber prevented further conversation, and after a few seconds, Frank, Arnesh, and Anwar found themselves alone, surveying the mess where the plants had been roughly uprooted.

"It could have been worse," Frank said cheerfully.

"It could have been much, much worse," Arnesh agreed. He pointed to the remaining marijuana. "Would you like some?" he asked.

Frank sighed. "Better not," he said. "Now what did you really tell that nice marine?"

Ernst was reprimanded and warned about charges of abduction and piracy. The lieutenant should also have warned him about murder. It was clear to Ernst that one of his crew had betrayed him, and apart from Ramos, there were only two crew members who might have had the opportunity: Otto, who had been with him on a previous ship, and Stefan, the love-struck new boy. So that was the traitor. The stupid young man had, unknowingly, put them all in danger, thanks to his disobedience. Ernst knew that he had to report this incident to the Angels and that he would be held responsible. He knew what he would be ordered to do, and it sickened him, but he would have no option if he, himself, were to survive. Otto and Ramos would only be loyal to him as long as he was loyal to the Angels. A successful mission would bring real wealth to all of them. He watched the marines, strongly tempted to send Stefan with them, but there was no way to do so without raising their suspicions all over again.

David was also wrestling with his conscience. He went to the lab and sat with a cup of tea in his hands, agonising over whether he should have disclosed the existence of the marijuana farm on board. "No good ever comes of telling a lie," he kept mumbling, and Lucy rolled her eyes at hearing this old mantra again. "The sergeant was there to help us, damn it. In the long run, I'll live to regret this. I know I will." So his monologue continued, while Lucy busied herself with catching up on some slide preparations.

"Dad, stop worrying," she interrupted him when she had heard enough. "Jeffrey has been bending the truth forever, and he's doing just fine. We were all really proud of you." She leaned over from her bar stool and gave him a motherly kiss on his forehead. "Now, I've got things to do."

"Thank you, Lucy; I'm not a child," David retorted, goaded out of his self-pity. "I happen to have things to do, as well."

Further along the ship, in the maintenance workshop, Arnesh and Anwar were regaling their compatriots with the story of how their marijuana crop was saved. At the point of the story where Leena was interpreting for the sergeant, one of the men went weak at the knees with laughter and sank to the floor, while the rest offered exciting suggestions of even lewder alternatives that made the story impossible to complete.

In the hangar, the mood was less jubilant. The four brothers were serious in their maintenance of the helicopters and airship. For as long as there was a job to do on the ice, they had to work, day and night, to make sure that all the aircraft were serviceable at all times. They were disciplined and well-trained veterans of the Sudanese civil war and understood better than almost anyone else on board the importance of readiness for the unexpected. There was, however, some cause for celebration, and Alan, Tyro, and Roland took time to share tea together, talking over their flight and their near-catastrophic landing.

"So who was it who saved us today?" Roland asked Alan. "Was it you or was it Tyro?"

"How do you mean?" Alan asked, mildly perplexed by the question.

"I could hear you praying for our survival when you realised we were in trouble. So was it your prayers which saved us or was it the airship following the scientific principles that govern flight?"

"You don't have to answer that, Reverend," Tyro said, annoyed by Roland's persistent teasing of his friend, but Alan seemed unperturbed.

"I wasn't praying for our survival," he replied amiably. "I was reciting the Lord's Prayer. Do you know it? It's the prayer that Jesus taught us, made into a beautiful poem."

229

"Yes, I know it," Roland said, "in German, but I couldn't recite it. How was it supposed to help in that situation anyway?"

"It was a great help to me," Alan replied with a smile. "Thy kingdom come, Thy will be done. I reminded myself of God's will, not mine, in such circumstances, and let Tyro do the rest – with a little request on my part for some more height." All three of them laughed at the memory.

"To me, it was the application of science that saved us," Roland continued, unconvinced by Alan's explanation. "What about you, Tyro: What difference do you think prayer made to saving us? Did you pray?"

"Oh yes, Roly, I prayed," Tyro said sombrely, nodding his head. "I said to God, 'Dear Lord, if I throw Roly and all his scientific equipment out of the door, will you save Alan and me?' And the Lord replied, 'You should be so lucky. You have sinned too much to be released of all your burdens. I'll save you and Alan, but Roly stays.' And even as Alan asked me for the resurrection, we rose clear of the tower. So who's to say how any of us was saved today?"

Then he winked at Alan, and the three of them sat in friendly silence, not really understanding each other, but grateful for their deliverance.

Chapter 13

MENACE

Five days later, Tyro looked up at the twilight sky. The air was clear, and there was just a slight breeze. Take-off would be easy in the morning, and there would be good visibility. The *Moringa* was sitting lower in the water now, as her tanks were filled. The airship would need to be launched only a few more times, and then it would be time for the journey home. He estimated that they would need about three more days of good weather to reach their target of a million litres. That meant three more days of security, after which he would need to be highly vigilant if he were to survive, and three days to put into action the plan he had devised.

He turned to find Alan standing, looking at him a few paces away. "Jambo, Alan; how long have you been standing there?"

"A few moments, that's all. Thinking about tomorrow's flight, hey?" Alan replied in his lilting voice.

"Yes, my friend, but would you do me a favour and fly with Lothar tomorrow?"

Alan was surprised but not offended. "A helicopter flight, is it? Well, then, that will be a change. I thank you for the opportunity."

"Alan," Tyro said, laughing, "if I asked you to jump naked into the ocean, you'd see the positive side to it."

"Actually, I'd just say no," Alan replied, keeping a straight face. "But the chance to have a helicopter flight, and land on Fortune, is something I've hardly dared ask for. Won't I just be in the way?"

"I have an important task for you, so you will have a right to be there," Tyro replied, thinking quickly. "I've told Lothar to carry out a detailed inspection of a five-hundred-metre square of the ice surface, ready for the helicopter landings to take the machinery away. I want you to record his observations."

"Gladly," Alan answered.

It seemed to him a contrived task, but if his friend didn't want him on the airship, that was his right, and this was a kind way of sugaring the pill. It was an exciting opportunity: a very acceptable consolation. When morning came, he met Jeffrey in the aircrew room, putting on flying overalls, and knew who had taken his place in the airship.

"G'morning, Alan," Jeffrey greeted him. "Are you coming on the flight too?"

"With Tyro, is it, in the airship? No, it's just you, I think."

Jeffrey was surprised. "What about Roly?" he asked.

Alan shrugged. "I think you'll find it's just you," he said, adding mischievously, "I have no doubt that Tyro has an important task for you."

"Oh yes, he's already told me. We're flying to the far end of the iceberg to take photographs and make notes. It's been cleared with Gary."

"Well, fancy that, now," Alan replied with a smile.

The task was just as contrived as his. Inwardly, he felt ill at ease. He had never forgotten Tyro's level of hatred when first they met, for Jeffrey as the murderer of Arthur and thief of his work. Jeffrey, alone with Tyro, would be beyond help, and now would be an ideal time for an accident to happen, with most of the hard work done and the journey home about to begin. Tyro had engineered this opportunity, and Alan asked himself the question, had Tyro created a sense of trust between himself and Jeffrey, in order to set him up for just such a moment?

He watched Jeffrey hurry over to where Tyro was waiting to walk him to the gondola and then muttered to himself, "I've done my best." He could not protect either man anymore. It was time for them to sort it out for themselves. "Anyway, if Tyro's landings don't improve, they'll both be in heaven tonight," he told himself, and smiling at the thought of Tyro and the resurrection, he prepared for the flight with Lothar.

Once the airship had been released and was gathering height, Jeffrey took several minutes to overcome his sense of exhilaration, and as they flew over the mighty iceberg, it was the fulfilment of his dream. When he was confined to his cabin after the take-off incident, he had felt as if his dream was being snatched away from him, but he had followed Anna's advice, took his humiliation, and gradually resurfaced to his rightful place, until he had been cleared for this flight, and his freedom was restored. This sense of release accentuated the impact of the sights and motion flooding his senses now.

Tyro flew high to enhance the panorama and took them way beyond the farther edge of Fortune, while Jeffrey alternated, unhurriedly, between the wide-angle and telephoto camera work. There was water enough here for a city – or a desert. His ambitions could become a reality. He felt elated. They joked, they discussed best angles, and occasionally, they lapsed into silence, each with their own thoughts. As they made their way back, they could see the small speck of the *Moringa* on the far side of Fortune. Tyro commenced a steep dive until the speck was hidden from view and Fortune was between them and the ship, hard, glistening, and treacherous. The sensation was wilder than a fairground ride; the vista changed from far to near. Jeffrey's fear response surged, then he laughed as the sense of control returned.

In the moments after the dive, Tyro urged him to slide back the door and lean out so that he could experience the true exhilaration of the air on his face. Tyro slowed the airship to hover, at the height of the cliff tops; it was the perfect chance. Jeffrey leaned out into the piercingly cold, breath-taking air. He raised his camera to take a self-portrait and record this ultimate moment of excitement. He looked into the flip-around viewer, and his pupils dilated at the sight; behind him, Tyro had a gun pointed at the back of his head. He twisted to try to pull himself in, but he knew he was too late. He became caught up in his camera strap, and his coordination had gone. He stopped his struggling, half-out of the gondola, and clutching with one hand at the frame of the gondola, he dropped the camera and raised his free hand in supplication.

"Tyro! In God's name, don't shoot. Please! Please!"

"Pull yourself in, Jeff, but stay in the door," Tyro ordered, keeping the old, heavy service revolver pointed steadily at him.

Jeffrey complied, and as his mind started working again, anger at Tyro's ambush took over from fear. "What the fuck are you playing at?" he demanded loudly, both his arms holding onto the frame either side of him.

"Careful, Jeff," Tyro warned. "I've wanted to shoot you for a long time. Nobody can see us. I could do it now. I could say that you fell out while filming. They would never find your body, even if they bothered to look."

Jeffrey's fear returned as he realised his situation. "What do you want?" he asked, his voice subdued now and still utterly perplexed by what was happening.

"I want you to tell me the truth about how Arthur died. The truth."

"I did not kill Arthur."

"The truth."

Jeffrey wriggled uncomfortably but did not release his grip. He closed his eyes tightly, trying to recall past events. "I can't remember the details after all this time, but we had spent three days together in the part of the game reserve that was away from the tourist areas. There should have been nobody else there. We were camped in an old rondavel that we had found sometime before and made use of whenever we visited our moringa plot. It was totally secluded. We were free to be ourselves when we were there." Jeffrey hesitated, wondering whether Tyro was more likely to shoot him for telling or not telling the full story.

"More," Tyro said, so Jeffrey continued, still looking away from Tyro and away from the gun.

"We were lovers. We slept naked, lived naked much of the time, when in camp. On the last day, we had packed up. We were about to leave. I was dressed. Suddenly, Arthur ambushed me. He had stripped again; he wanted us to make love one more time. We were struggling with each other. He was trying to pull my clothes off, and I was trying to hold onto them and yet let him win at the same time. We were making fighting sounds as if we were deadly serious. Then five men walked out of the long grass into our clearing. They had crept up on us without us noticing."

Now that he had confessed, Jeffrey felt more resigned to the bullet that would blow him backwards, out of the open door. He looked up, and Tyro saw the desolation in his eyes.

"They identified him, Tyro," Jeffrey continued. "They identified him as your gay brother. I don't think they knew me, but they knew you and your family. Two of them guarded me."

"What do you mean, they knew me?" Tyro interrupted, his shocked mind taking a second to absorb what he had heard.

"Tyro's lady-brother: that's what one of them called Arthur, and the others joined in."

"Go on," Tyro said sombrely.

"Two of them guarded me. I couldn't do anything. The others tied a rope around one of Arthur's ankles so he was tethered like an animal and then beat him with their spears and rifle butts. He was still naked. He had no protection. Those were the injuries you saw on his body, Tyro. Those were the injuries I lied about."

"And that's when he died," Tyro surmised quietly.

"Those were the injuries he died from," Jeffrey corrected him gently. "At the time, he fell to the ground and lost consciousness. Then they stopped."

"And you? What did they do to you?"

"They didn't do anything. They left me with Arthur. I thought they'd come back and shoot me at any moment, but they just disappeared. Can I close the door now? I'm getting bloody cold."

Tyro nodded; Jeffrey slid the door closed and took a seat. He sat silently for a moment, not knowing whether to continue or not. The gun was still pointed at him but in a lazy, aimless way.

"And what about the elephant in the lake?" Tyro prompted, like a child prompting its parent to finish a bedtime story despite knowing it to the end.

"All true. Arthur's beating took place about a hundred yards from the lake. He was semi-conscious. I got him as far as the water's edge, and we found the boat undamaged. I swear it was only when we were halfway across the lake we hit the elephant. There was a bump. Water bubbled in at the bow. Arthur was lying in the bottom of the boat, not really aware of anything except water coming round him. I looked behind us, and it was then I saw the elephant. It seemed unharmed." Jeffrey shook his head in disbelief at the memory and then continued, "By the time we sank, I was in my depth and could wade ashore, pulling Arthur. I was so scared. I knew the crocodiles were there. I took an oar from the boat as a weapon. I thought we'd made it, and then this croc flew at us from the water and just latched onto Arthur's leg. He almost pulled it off. Arthur died on the way to hospital."

Tyro saw that the memories were starting to cause Jeffrey real distress. He intervened. "I know the rest; there's no need to tell me more," he said gently. "At last I know the truth. I believe you. The elephant was trying to escape the poachers, just as you were. That's who those men were, and Arthur may have died as much because of me as because of you. We were at war with the poachers. They were not like poachers these days: foreigners with helicopters and sat-navs. They were local people who would have known me and known Arthur. They beat him for being the senior ranger's brother, as well as for being a homosexual."

Jeffrey knew that Tyro had run his own poaching outfit and thought of gang warfare, but he said nothing. He, too, was seeing the events in a new light.

Then Tyro's voice hardened again. "Why didn't you report them at the time?"

"I was so scared that night," Jeffrey replied, events now flooding into his mind. "I was in such shock that it was all I could do just to drive home from the hospital and lock myself away. I feared arrest as Arthur's lover. I feared the gang coming to get me. I feared what you would do, and I fear you now, with that gun."

Tyro looked down at the gun with a wry smile. "You shouldn't worry so much, my friend. The safety catch was on the whole time. I have the gun for my protection, not to shoot you."

He laid it down beside him. Jeffrey let out a long sigh of relief and, for the first time since the incident began, noticed that he still had the camera, dangling from its neck strap. He, too, smiled in surprise and, releasing his neck from the strap, laid the camera down at his side. The two men caught each other's gaze and knew that mutual respect had returned. Tyro focused once more on the flight controls, and the airship returned to purposeful flight.

"Arthur was born to be as he was, Tyro. It wasn't a choice that he made," Jeffrey said as he gazed at Fortune's cliffs, now directly below them.

"Do you think I don't know that, Jeff?" Tyro replied without animosity. "I loved him as my brother and spent so much time protecting him. He loved life – I don't mean just living himself, but all living things." Tyro was taking the airship in long slow traverses of the iceberg's surface, while Jeffrey looked out at the landscape and listened attentively. "Before he could walk, he would spend hours watching lizards, insects, birds ... any moving life. When we went to Father Willis's school, he learnt about the balance between plants and animals and such things, while the rest of us played football. Then, when the time came, he refused circumcision. Refused circumcision." Tyro repeated the unbelievable choice as if still unable to comprehend it. "Nobody refused circumcision. It was your passage into manhood. He said nature had fashioned him with the skin, and it was unnatural to remove it."

"Perhaps he didn't feel he was truly a man," Jeffrey ventured, proffering the reason that Arthur himself had once given him. Manhood conveyed relentless aggression that was not in him.

"In my village, you were a man with the normal desires of a man. If not, then you were a woman. There was nothing in between," Tyro retorted, forgetting how much of Arthur Jeffrey would have seen and known.

"He was so sweet-natured, so gentle. How could anyone hate him?"

"Well, they did," Tyro replied. "He went to live with Father Willis. They were with each other all the time, teacher and pupil. When Father Willis left us and went to be a teacher in a big school in Nairobi, Arthur went with him. That is how Arthur became so clever that he could go to university."

"It's funny that he never mentioned Father Willis to me by name," Jeffrey mused. "He just said that a teacher at the village school had taken him to boarding school. Thank you for telling me."

"Now we both know the truth," Tyro said with satisfaction. "Tell me, Jeff, was I right to think that Arthur's work was truly important to this?" Words seemed to fail Tyro at this point. He let go of the controls to make a broad expansive gesture with both arms "To all this?"

"He was inspirational," Jeffrey affirmed. "He was so observant, scientifically and in the field. He was so delicate in his touch and could interpret what he was seeing. My original studies gave him the basis for his PhD research, and the plan was that, together, we would develop the enhanced properties of the moringa trees. When I came to my senses later that night, I rescued his work so nobody else would steal it. I took copies on disks and then erased everything on his hard drive."

"But you overlooked the paper I was sent. I knew the marks on my brother's body were deliberate, and so I saw you as the man who had killed my brother and stolen his work. You can see why I came to England, ready to destroy you, Jeff, even to shoot you when allowed to do so."

"Yet, in the end, it was probably your letter that saved me. Why did you write it?" Jeffrey asked.

"Because I had met you and realised that you were not the man I hated. That man existed only in my mind, but my hatred had nowhere else to go. I was deeply troubled. I turned to God. He sent me Alan, and Alan saved my soul from its anguish. He helped me to see reason – to forgive. But it's thanks to that letter that I now have to carry this gun. Their plan was for me to destroy you, Jeff, not to spare you."

"How utterly ruthless. They must see greater commercial potential in this project than I had imagined - so now we're both in danger."

"I don't think so," Tyro replied. "You were in their way, but they got what they wanted. I think they will leave you alone, but I disobeyed their instructions. They warned me about that."

"The rest of us will protect you, Tyro, I promise you," Jeffrey said, and Tyro warmed to his sincerity but shook his head in disbelief.

"They are like that crocodile you described. They let you think you are safe, and then they strike without warning. You haven't taken a photo for several minutes. Have you finished? Then let's go back." They went well out over the ocean, and then Tyro began a leisurely turn and descent over the white plateau. "Have there been other men in your life since Arthur, Jeff?" he asked as he judged his flight path.

"I loved Arthur, Tyro, not men. I've never loved another man. Can we leave it at that? I desire women. In fact, since meeting Anna, I've increasingly desired just one woman."

"Ah, your lioness," Tyro said approvingly.

"My lioness," Jeffrey repeated.

"Well then, Jeff," Tyro said triumphantly, "there you are. She is both man and woman enough for you. I predict a long and happy future." He laughed as Jeffrey tried to protest. Then he suddenly became serious. "Now for the landing."

Ernst had given himself the night to think things through. It would not be in his interest or Stefan's interest for the Clerkenwell Angels to sense incompetence. When he put the call through to Jean-Pierre, head of the secretariat, he picked his words like a bomb disposal expert defusing a bomb.

"There's been an unexpected development," he said. There was an ominous silence at the other end of the line. He knew Jean-Pierre was still listening, so he continued, "We've had a visit from the navy."

Further silence.

Cherry Bonner's voice came on line. "Which navy?" she asked tersely.

"The British navy," Ernst replied with equal brevity.

"What ship? Why?"

"HMS *Cornwall*. They said they had been on a goodwill visit to Fremantle and had been ordered to monitor our activities on their way home. We had shown up on a satellite scan." He omitted any mention of the International Maritime Organisation and of Stefan's breach of security. There was a further silence as Cherry contemplated whether Ernst was telling the truth. She decided that the reason seemed plausible.

"What did they find?" she asked.

"Nothing," Ernst replied. "Well, a few tufts of marijuana that the foolish Indians planted among the trees in the main chamber, for reasons I don't understand, but they didn't find the cargo."

"Is that safe?"

"All safe. They weren't even looking for it. They were wholly occupied by the foolish antics of my foolish passengers."

"What else? Did they ask about your destination?"

"Yes. They know it is Mombasa. I was obliged to give them all such information."

"I see." Cherry said, sounding thoughtful, and then she added, "What about the fate of Tyro Mukasa?"

"Mukasa suspects nothing. We need him only for a few more days. They have almost finished here, and then we shall find a suitable moment for something to happen to him."

"I will let Mr Dukakis know. I'm sure that he'll be as satisfied with you as I am," Cherry said soothingly. "Is that all, then, Mr Brage? I think it should be."

"Yes, of course," Ernst said, conceding Cherry's ability to manage him.

"Goodbye, Mr Brage." Cherry put down her phone with a smirk. Ernst Brage was so simple, the type of alpha male incapable of accepting that a woman could be head of a powerful organisation.

Ernst put down the phone, feeling the need to reassert himself. He went back onto the bridge, where he was in full command. Stefan looked at him nervously. Ernst approached him, leant over him menacingly, and whispered in his ear, "I've just saved your life."

"Thank you, sir," Stefan mumbled, staying very still in his fear and not daring to ask the meaning of Ernst's words.

"Don't think you are out of danger. You're not," Ernst continued. "However, I'm loyal to my crew members. I protect them. I decide their punishment, and nobody else. Do you value loyalty, Stefan?"

"Yes sir," the miserable Stefan mumbled.

Ernst straightened up but stayed very close. "Then go and find Anna Jensen, and tell her she is needed on the bridge. Nobody else is to know. I leave it to you how you do it."

"Yes, sir," Stefan said submissively, sliding out of his chair so as not to push against his captain.

"Nobody is to know, Stefan, not even Lucy," Ernst said quietly.

A look of alarm passed over Stefan's face at the sound of Lucy's name on his captain's lips, adding to his anguish of just how much Ernst knew. Ernst played with his fear: "Don't look surprised. Lucy is the one that you and your playmate, Silvio, go chasing, isn't she?" Stefan looked at him in confusion, not knowing what to say. "Perhaps she even persuaded you to disobey my instructions. Who knows? Anyway, even she is not to learn about my message to Miss Jensen. Understood?"

"Yes, sir."

"Now go, quickly."

Stefan went abruptly and returned, hot and flushed, ten minutes later, with a cool, fresh Anna, dressed for the ice.

They greeted each other formally, in English, in front of Stefan and Ramos, then Ernst led her to his cabin on the pretext of needing to discuss the conditions on Fortune. Once inside his cabin, Ernst spoke immediately in Norwegian.

"You're not here to discuss the iceberg," he said.

"I guessed that," she replied.

"I need you, Anna."

"You can't just expect me to … I'm the partner of another man."

"Anna, I'm like a pent-up spring. If you don't release that spring, I may do something crazy – maybe even kill a man. I have the power."

Anna could see that Ernst was fighting to control himself.

"Just take your clothes off," he commanded her.

"What?" she whispered. "Look, I'm due to fly in half an hour."

"Take them off now, or a man may die."

There was something shockingly exciting about the moment. Anna hesitated a second and then started to undress: "You know the rules. You can watch but you can't touch," she said as she did so.

To her surprise, he started to undress with her. "What are you doing?" she challenged him, without stopping her own disrobing.

"Undressing. You know the rules, you can look but not touch," He echoed her in a gruff voice, his eyes fixed on her face. They reached nudity together, and stood, awkwardly, looking at each other.

"Satisfied?" she challenged him. "Can I get dressed now?"

His response was to reach out nervously with his right hand and take her left hand. He was braced for a slap, but she just looked at their clasped hands.

"I thought I said no touching," she muttered.

He dared to move closer, and her free hand came up, but it rested on his hairy chest and did not ward him off. His body contrasted so strongly with Jeffrey's light, lithe features. Here was strength, a greater strength than hers. He let her hand move tentatively up, across his pectoral muscles, exploring this new sensation. He realised that some arousal was taking place in her that needed to be let alone and not forced. He represented all that she detested in men, and yet these same features were now strangely appealing in him.

"Give me some room," she commanded urgently, and he stepped back a little, enabling her to slide up onto the bed, reclining, with her legs straight and her back supported on her elbows.

She watched him with her piercing gaze as he climbed on top of her. He tried to push her back onto the bed, but her arms resisted. He tried to force her legs apart with his own, but her strong thighs kept her legs together. He took his gaze from her groin to her face, a perplexed, desperate, and angry look in his eyes that then met hers.

"You promise not to kill any man, Ernst? That is the deal," she said defiantly.

"I promise," he whispered back and, as he did so, felt her legs yield to his.

His face was close to hers, and before anything else, he pressed a kiss onto her lips, expecting a firm, tight-lipped response. He was surprised that her lips were soft and seductive, and when he drew back, the ferocity in her eyes had been replaced by gentleness. She lay herself back, relaxed, and let him guide himself inside her. He was skilful, and she was moist, and he thrust with a force that was urgent but controlled. As the emotions deepened and his face contorted, she reached up to stroke his cheek, not scratch his eyes, and in the last seconds of ultimate intensity, as he raised his torso to look down on her whole extended body, she urged him, "Come, Ernst. Come."

And she gasped with delight at the burst of his orgasm, the writhings of which went on for many seconds, amid repeated thanks to God and Anna for what he had received. When he slumped onto her, she did not beat him with her fists but clung to him as she felt him slip out of her, and she tipped him off gently, to where he lay like a rag doll at her side. She reached out for a towel that she placed between her thighs, and both she and Ernst lay still at last, side by side, and recovered their senses.

"You needed that," she mused at last.

"I needed you," he replied, and the words pleased her.

She took his hand in hers and kissed it.

"Well, now you've had me," she replied solemnly. "Don't forget your promise."

With that, she got off the bed and took her clothes into the shower room. Ernst heard her lock the door. Clearly, he could not expect after-play. He rose, dressed, and called in through the door, a low voice, "Don't tell anyone, and be careful on the ice." He left without waiting for a reply.

Anna hurried the length of the deck so that Maggie and Jimmy would not find anything strange about her flushed cheeks. She felt languid after her sex and had to make a conscious effort to seem animated. She was confused. She wanted to feel guilty, but she felt wonderful. She could not escape the inescapable: Jeffrey was no longer the only man to have overcome her repulsion of masculine traits, and her sexual activity with Ernst had not been the selfless act of humanity that she had imagined it would be.

Maggie loved her too much not to notice that something was unsettling her. "Are you all right, love? Are you worried?" she asked.

"I'm fine," Anna snapped dismissively, further confirming Maggie's opinion that something was definitely wrong, but she did not ask any more questions.

Jimmy, in his wisdom, also realised there was something strange in the way Anna was acting, so he kept up a gentle flow of distracting conversation until they were strapped in and the beat of the helicopter engines had become a distraction in its own right, a mighty prelude to the next visit to Fortune. After take-off, the pilot took the helicopter in the usual arc over the ocean to gain height and to assess the surface before sinking gracefully to the landing site about one hundred metres in from the lip of the plateau.

Gary arrived on the ice. He wanted to assess for himself the progress that was being made. Fortune was pristine, except where the team was at work. Here it was like a building site with the foundations being laid. He felt scared, not invigorated like he did on oil platforms. He knew he was standing on melting ice. It could just shear beneath him, and yet those who were now used to being on its surface were wandering around as if on solid granite. He saw the gouges in the ice where the hydra heads had been in action. He noticed that one of the hydras was being moved on its soft, broad tyres to a virgin site at the far end of the line, with its heads drawn in and its howitzer pointing to the sky. It was being pulled along by a radio-controlled diesel bulldozer, with Jimmy walking beside it, manipulating the handset, like a twelve-year-old controlling a model racing car. The noise that Gary had been immediately aware of as he stepped down from the helicopter was of Ferraris being gunned at maximum revolutions, coming from each of the three harvesters currently in action, the white arcs of ice-tracer disappearing over the rim of the iceberg. Anna in her all-white arctic battle-dress was overseeing the robotic activity of the hydra-heads of the active machines, while Maggie, identifiable by her vivid orange anorak

243

and black salopettes, was working with three crewmen to refuel another one with the propane canisters that powered the compressors. They were unloading the canisters from a pallet, though other empty pallets littered the site. He would need to organise a tidy-up.

Behind him, the two crewmen starting their shift with him had swapped places with the three crewmen coming off duty. Lothar increased power in the helicopter cockpit, and the chopper started to rise. Gary turned, frightened for a moment, and instantly looked up higher, to where he could just make out the airship, gliding securely above them. Then he looked round and spotted one of the monitoring drones on the ice, and pulling himself together, he gave a cheery wave to Jimmy and walked over to him. As he had told himself many times on oil rigs, if that guy can be here, then so can I.

"Yo, Jimmy," Gary called to him as he approached. "Can I have a go?"

"In a moment, Gary. You'll have to wait till I've repositioned this harvester, but I'd welcome your help with that," Jimmy replied.

"I'm your man."

Gary relished the chance to become involved; his anxiety disappeared, and he felt the welcome return of his self-confidence. He let Jimmy give the instructions. This was not the time to pull rank. Lives could be lost in this environment, and Jimmy was the man with the experience required. They worked well together. They had an American way of doing things, and an American way of talking as they worked, which seemed normal to them, and Jimmy could give his instructions in a way that didn't rile Gary.

The hydra was soon ready for action. Jimmy passed the controller to Gary, saying it was time to activate the heads. Gary avidly carried out the procedure under Jimmy's guidance.

"This is so cool," he said, laughing.

Only a matter of seconds later, a red light on the harvester went out, and a green light came on to indicate that the compressor had enough ice stacked ready to fire the first shells. Then Jimmy picked out a headset from a pouch in his anorak and handed them to Gary.

"Here," he said to Gary. "Now, you notify Roly. He's controlling events from the ship today. When you're ready, you press that button and step

244

back. He'll then aim the howitzer at the lagoon. We just watch to make sure the harvester is secure."

Gary followed the instructions again and was amused by Roland's surprise at hearing his voice. It was only a brief exchange, and then he pressed the button and stepped back on hearing the first stirrings of the compressor. The howitzer burst into life with a distinct explosion as the first shells fired, but the sound quickly became the guttural roar as was coming from the other harvesters.

"Shit, man! That's power," Gary shouted approvingly. "That's real power."

He now felt ready to stay on the ice all day. They watched the barrel shift a few degrees, causing a snake-like bend in the arc, as Roland made the necessary changes to the angulation of the barrel. When he radioed back that this was correct, Jimmy and Gary's final task was to place two stays under the barrel to keep it steady and take some of the weight.

"That's it," Jimmy shouted. "My shift ends with the next chopper. We'll take the tug back to the main base." He pointed to the little shed that Gary had completely discounted on his first scan of the surface.

"What's in there?" Gary asked.

"A kettle and a chemical can," Jimmy replied. "Don't get them muddled."

"Hell, you mean they're both in the same shack?"

"It's the only place you can get your dick out without it freezing off. I suggest you use it if you have to go," Jimmy shouted back cheerfully as they made their way over to it, walking beside the tug chugging across the ice.

"What about the ladies?" Gary asked.

"If one of them is in there, just ask her if she wants tea or coffee," Jimmy said and then winked. "Frankly, I don't think it bothers either of those two."

They stopped close to Maggie, but not so close that the tug's weight might significantly load the ice. Gary was already picking up the rules and found himself automatically checking weight distribution of everything he looked at.

They were helping Maggie, Hans, and Silvio load the empty propane cylinders onto one of the pallets when a cracking noise was distinctly audible above all the other sounds. They all stopped and looked at each other, shared shrugs and smiles, and carried on. Part of the perimeter had snapped off a few hundred metres away, but on the opposite side to the ship. They had all received the warning that it would happen sometime soon, so it was a reminder to them of their vulnerability rather than a shock.

"Roland was right about that one," Maggie commented.

"Ah, German efficiency," Hans joked, standing erect and puffing out his chest; he laughed good-naturedly at the insults and bits of ice that pelted him from the others, as their morale was restored. Hans was the bosun and took his responsibilities on board the *Moringa* seriously, yet here, on the ice, Gary noted, there was a sense of elation that transcended all earthly matters.

As they finished the task, Gary looked up and gazed excitedly across the length of Fortune, stretching into the distance. "Wouldn't it just be so cool to walk across that ice, right to the opposite side?" he mused to Jimmy.

"Sure," Jimmy replied, following his gaze. "I guess I'd have already done it by now, if some guy on the *Moringa* hadn't said it was strictly out of bounds," the guy concerned being Gary, of course, and he recalled giving those instructions.

"I don't really know that guy, Jimmy," Gary replied with a sigh. "I guess he had his reasons."

"I guess he did," Jimmy replied and added cryptically, "I don't recognise him half as well as I recognise you, but I reckon he knows something the rest of us don't, and he just won't say what it is." Gary turned to him, startled by his words, but Jimmy was looking innocently into the distance, and when he did turn to him, there was no animosity. "Come on," he said. "Let's get some coffee. I'm going back soon."

Oh, for a conscience as clear as this ice, Gary prayed silently, before following Jimmy and the rest of the team. Then, it struck him how treacherous even the ice could be.

Gary completed his full three-hour stint on Fortune, and then three hours more, to set a leader's example. After he had returned to the ship, changed, and relaxed for a few minutes in his cabin, he went in search of Jeffrey. He guessed that the laboratory would be a good place to start, as David and Lucy were so frequently there together, so he made his way there. Sure enough, David and Lucy, each with a mug of tea, were seated side-by-side, chatting away as any father and daughter might, while they sorted through a set of centrifuge tubes. The homeliness of the sight seemed unreal to Gary. When he entered, it was as if he were back in the university laboratory in Cambridge. Neither of them seemed surprised. They smiled in casual recognition of his presence, and Lucy asked him if he would like a mug of tea.

"If so, help yourself," she offered.

"Thanks," Gary said; he was tempted. "But I've got to find Jeffrey. Any ideas?"

"Yes," David replied. "Come and sit down and have a mug of tea, and he'll arrive. It's a well-tried British method of meeting people at teatime."

"What? Sitting down and having a mug of tea?" Gary queried.

"Yes," Lucy added. "Scientifically tested. The results are marginally improved by a chocky-bic, but we haven't got any."

"Well, if you say so," Gary muttered, yielding to the temptation of a hot drink and walking to where he saw the mugs and the tea-bags.

He felt a sense of tranquillity as the kettle boiled. It really was Cambridge in Antarctica. "This is just so British.' He laughed as he concentrated on pouring water over his teabag. "You guys fucking scare me. I'm not going to look out of that porthole, in case I see the River Cam instead of the ocean."

"Gary, what the hell are you on about? Have you been at Arnesh's grass?" Jeffrey's voice so startled Gary that he spun round, still holding the kettle, splashing hot water over himself and the floor. The three Brits laughed delightedly at Gary's mess. Jeffrey had just walked in.

Gary made the best of his ridiculous situation, raised the kettle, and asked, "Tea, anyone?"

"Yuh, I'll have a mug, please," Jeffrey said, making use of Gary's offer. "I'm glad to find you here. I need to speak to you."

"Well, I need to speak to you, too, Jeffrey, buddy. I was looking for you when I got lured into making tea. I'm told there are no chocky-bics, by the way."

Gary finished pouring the two cups of tea, put in the powdered milk, and handed Jeffrey his mug. Then he told them about the ice that had broken away from the rim of Fortune.

"We knew it was likely to happen, but when it did, the suddenness still surprised us. It was a reminder that however well you plan, there's always an element of luck. We've got enough water to prove our point. We've been lucky so far. We've not had any major incidents, and the weather's been good. If we get going now, the mission will have been 100 percent successful."

"You don't need me to give the orders," Jeffrey pointed out. "You're the boss. If that's what you want, you do it."

"We're friends, buddy. I want us to work together: you, David, and me. I don't want to go against you. If you two say we must stay a while longer, then we stay," Gary almost cooed goodwill.

"What does our beloved captain think?" David asked.

"That's not my concern right now. I want to know what you think," Gary said, showing he was clearly allied to their wishes.

Jeffrey looked across at David, who nodded his agreement. "I think we agree with you, Gary," Jeffrey said. "We've got what we need. Let's go. The sooner we finish all the hard work, the sooner we can all relax."

"I'm glad that's settled," Gary said, smiling. "Now, what did you want to see me for?"

Jeffrey looked at David and Lucy a moment, as if unsure about speaking in front of them. Then he said, "As God's my witness, Gary, something strange is going on aboard this ship. You're the appointed project leader. I want to know what the hell it is."

Gary stayed cool. "What makes you say that?"

"You might as well know, all of you, that Tyro is in fear of his life."

David and Lucy were troubled at this, but Gary showed no emotion. Inwardly, he was jubilant. This was the chance to isolate Ernst, to drive a wedge between Ernst and everyone else.

Jeffrey continued, "I flew with Tyro yesterday, as you know, and he's in no doubt that an attempt will be made on his life on the next leg of the journey." He decided not to say anything about the handgun.

"That fits what I know. Brage's got it in for him," Gary said calmly. "I had no idea it was this serious."

"Sounds to me like another visit from HMS *Cornwall* is required to put Commissar Brage back in his box," David remarked indignantly.

"David, you can't just order up a naval ship. Life isn't that simple," Jeffrey remarked tersely.

"Mum did," Lucy remarked, which irked both Jeffrey and Gary immensely.

"Why, Gary?" Jeffrey asked. "I've promised Tyro that we'll protect him, but what's he done, and who else is under threat?"

Gary looked as if he was about to reply, but he was stopped by the sudden appearance of a crewman in the doorway.

"Silvio!" Lucy exclaimed, flustered that her other secret lover and her father should be in the same room.

Silvio wasted no time on politeness. "Lucy," he said in an urgent, low voice, pointing at her to emphasise his words, "you don't know me. Stay away from me. Stay away from Stefan. I mean it. I mean it. Just stay away." Then he was gone.

Lucy jumped up as if to follow him, but Jeffrey barked out, "Stop," and David, more lovingly, stood up and placed his arms in gentle restraint around her waist, coaxing Lucy back onto her seat.

"Better stay here, my darling," he said.

Gary stayed where he was, just sipping his tea, interested to know which of Brage's crew might be against him. "I think that was a friendly warning," he said. "I don't think that came from Brage. How do you know that guy?"

"He's Stefan's best friend," Lucy explained, trying to be as detached as possible. Then, seeing by the look on the men's eyes that she hadn't explained anything, she opened up some more. "Silvio and Stefan signed up together as crew for this voyage. They have plans to open up a yacht charter business and are saving money. I like them. We hang out together when they're off-duty."

"Well, Brage has obviously put the fear of God into Silvio," David observed. "Lucy, love, sorry to seem harsh, but you must give me your word that you'll do as Silvio said, and not try to contact him or Stefan."

"If Stefan's in danger, I want to be with him," Lucy said defiantly.

David took her hand in his. "From what Silvio said, my darling, going to them would probably put them in grave danger. Until we know what's going on, you've got to stay away. Will you promise?"

"Oh, very well," she said in a resigned voice. Then she pulled out her mobile phone and started to fiddle with it. "Bloody hell," she said. "I can't get a signal."

"Oh Lord, we're not back to that, surely?" David muttered glumly.

"What's going on, Gary?" Jeffrey asked again.

"No idea, buddy," Gary lied. "But between us, we can lick Brage." He even managed a friendly smile.

When Cherry first contacted Jean-Pierre and suggested that they meet to walk their dogs, he went out and bought a muzzle for Boris. Boris was his Rottweiler, who had never bitten another dog in anger in his life, but he was boisterous, and if he had forgotten himself, in a moment of exuberance, and given Cherry's little Mitsy a shake, the day would have ended badly for Boris, and Jean-Pierre was taking no chances.

Jean-Pierre lived in an apartment overlooking Lake Leman, in Lausanne. Cherry lived in an apartment overlooking Lake Geneva, in Vevey. It was the same lake, and almost the same view, but they both held on, tenaciously, to their cultural differences. It would have been easy to meet in either town, but everywhere round the lake is beautiful, so Cherry chose Montreux. Wisely, Jean-Pierre had taken Boris for a long walk already, to burn off his energy and sort out his ablutions, so that when they met up, at the statue of Freddy Mercury, and began to saunter along the flower-lined promenade, Boris was very well behaved. Mitsy was pulled along at the end of her lead, her invisible legs propelling her smoothly like a battery operated toy.

It was a sparkling February day, and they were almost alone. In the heat of July, tourists throng the promenade, and the casino and restaurants along it, representing all cultures and creeds, milling together and enjoying themselves despite the awful crowding.

"It's not really Switzerland, here, in summer," Cherry commented, looking at the mountains across the lake. "I prefer it at this time of year, when we have it to ourselves, and the mountains are covered in snow." Cherry was wrapped in her luxurious mink coat, so the cold air was welcome.

"Cherry, with respect, it is always Switzerland here, whatever the time of year, and I'm proud of it," Jean-Pierre replied with hurt dignity.

He was so easy to tease. "Have I hurt your feelings?" she asked in amusement. "Then let's talk about some other continent, shall we? How about Antarctica?"

Jean-Pierre must have guessed that this was the reason for the walk. He shrugged. "I've no news to give you," he said. They walked a little way in silence, while he waited to discover what she had in mind.

"I need your advice about the *Moringa* and HMS *Cornwall*," She spoke while still looking across the lake to the alpine peaks on the other side. "I've been thinking about it, and my view is that the authorities had received a tip-off, and the arrival of the *Cornwall* was not coincidental. What do you think?"

"I think you could be right. Yes. Very probable. In which case, they will return with a bigger search party," Jean-Pierre said, nodding in thoughtful agreement.

"So I want to move the cargo in the middle of the ocean. Do you think that's possible? The *Clarissa* is sailing to Mauritius. I suggest we rendezvous with the *Moringa*, as scheduled, and transfer the cargo at that time. Could you organise that, Jean-Pierre?" she asked, anxious that, even for him, it might be too much, at such short notice. "You're so clever at these things."

She saw him grimace at the prospect of all the extra work.

"I know it'll be hard," she explained. "And we run the risk of detection, but we could slip easily into Dar-es-Salaam harbour which the *Moringa* can't, and that would be such an advantage. They won't be lying in wait for us there."

Jean-Pierre could see that the rewards justified the risk. After a moment to assess the situation, he agreed. "Yes," he said. "But you realise it will be messy."

Cherry recognised his euphemism for bloodshed. She had to be pragmatic. "There must be forty people on the *Moringa*, if you include the crew. Do you think they all have to go?"

"Not all, perhaps. We shall bring them together below deck and machine-gun them. It will take less than a minute. What do you wish to do about the captain?'

"He's expendable," Cherry said. "Duke Dukakis will want the first officer and Gary Murdoch to be saved. We better humour him."

"Do you think the Angels will wish to be on board the *Clarissa* in the circumstances?"

"We can offer each of them the option of staying on Mauritius, while the rest of us sail off with all the heroin. How many do you think will stay behind?" she taunted him gently.

He shrugged apologetically. "They don't need to see anything that happens on the *Moringa*, I suppose. They can relax in the lounge while the sacks are loaded, then he paused before adding: "It might not be an occasion for Abi to join us, however."

"No. Quite right," Cherry agreed. It was settled, and it was time to reward Jean-Pierre. Cherry knew very well where she was aiming for, but she feigned surprise. "Oh look, Jean-Pierre, a place to buy crepes. Let me treat you to a crepe," she announced.

"But what about our walk, Cherry?" Jean-Pierre said.

"We've walked all the way down here, and after we've had our crepes, we'll walk all the way back again," she replied firmly. The three-hundred-metre stroll had been quite long enough for Mitsy's little legs.

Jean-Pierre bowed graciously. "Of course, I was forgetting the walk back. A crepe would be excellent." Oh, he was so polite, that dear man.

Boris and Mitsy each had one too.

Chapter 14

THE JOURNEY NORTH

After returning from another stint on Fortune, Anna decided to avoid both Jeffrey and Ernst, and sought out Maggie, who was relaxing in her cabin with Leena.

There was very little about each other's bodies and emotions that Anna, Maggie, and Leena did not know intimately. There was no need for secrecy. Anna stripped, nonchalantly, in front of her friends and took a shower. Seeing her enjoying her shower so much encouraged Maggie to strip off and step into the shower as Anna stepped out, and Leena followed Maggie. Now Anna lay on the lower bunk, while Leena rewarded her with a facial massage, and Maggie did likewise with a foot massage, their towels draped casually over their torsos. It was sensual bliss for them all. Leena's hands moved in caressing strokes down Anna's throat and neck, onto the breastbone, smoothly across her chest, and up to the shoulders, and back to the neck to repeat the rhythmic cycle.

"If you're wondering whether I want my tits done, yes I do," Anna murmured.

The other two laughed as Leena complied.

"With Maggie, I would have known, but with you I wasn't sure," Leena confessed.

"She's just as much of a hedonist as I am," Maggie said, underlying her point by squeezing the base of Anna's middle toe between her index finger and thumb, and gliding the pressure over her toe-tip.

Anna winced pleasurably. "Toes are like the clitoris really, aren't they?" she mused.

"I beg your pardon? Speak for yourself," Maggie said indignantly, working on another toe, while Leena giggled.

"Because you don't really think about them until they get stroked, but having them stroked is exquisite," Anna continued.

Maggie thought of her riposte, and she started to say, "But toes drop off from frostbite while your clit—"

But she couldn't finish because Leena gave a little shriek and put her hands over her ears.

Anna sat up in frustration. "I was enjoying myself until you said that."

Maggie smiled and kissed Anna's foot. "So were we all, probably too much. Jeffrey will want his share."

"Jeffrey has his good points, but massage isn't one of them," Anna said, pouting.

"He's got a gentle side, though," Leena said artlessly. "Unlike Gary, who's all energy. It's so exhausting, and he grunts all the time." There was an embarrassing hush.

"You're the only one who can draw that comparison, love." Maggie commented drily.

"Sorry, I ..." Leena apologised hastily, glancing at Anna, but Anna was not in the mood to be cross.

"Don't worry about it," Anna said kindly. "You've paid a high price for that bit of knowledge." She gave an understanding smile and swung her legs round, saying, "I should find Jeffrey." She stood up, looking for her clothes in the pile of garments in the cabin. Maggie and Leena looked on in amused silence. The socks were easy to identify – knee length and bright orange – so she put those on then stood perplexed, her socks accentuating the nakedness of her beautiful thighs and torso.

Maggie turned away, trying to brush the sight from her eyes. "Bloody hell, girl, put your knickers on," she pleaded.

"I would if I could find them," Anna retorted.

"I think I can see them," Leena said and rolled onto her tummy so as to reach down to the floor. As she got them, she suddenly rolled back onto the bed, wincing and muttering, "Ow! Ow!"

Maggie was at her side like a shot, her eyes focused on Leena's face as she brushed past Anna. "Are you all right?" she asked in concern.

Leena lay on her back, gently rubbing her tummy. "I think so," she said. "I'm just at that stage where I go to do something and forget that I'm not the shape I was. My body's changing, inside and out, and it doesn't like certain movements."

"Well, I'm here to look after you," Maggie told her, laying a soothing hand on Leena's tummy and tossing Anna's knickers to her with the other. She took Leena's hand in hers. "You're going to be fine, really you are. You're through the dangerous time. These are the good weeks."

Anna, having put her knickers on, was about to tell Maggie to stop fussing, but she stopped herself. There was something about their shared body-language that told her to mind her own business. It was clear that Maggie still felt deeply responsible for Leena's condition and needed to share the experience. Just as she was ready to go, she caught Leena's eye.

"Are you feeling better now?" she asked.

"Yes, I'm fine," Leena replied. "I'll get to bed early tonight."

"Tomorrow is probably our last day here," Anna continued. "Gary was saying in the helicopter on the way back that he thought we ought to leave. We'll probably turn off the cannons at midday and let the pumps drain the reservoir."

"And then it's all over?" Leena asked.

"Well, we may need another day or so to bring the hydras back and dismantle the reservoirs, so my guess is that we shall leave the day after tomorrow. You know, you haven't had the chance to stand on Fortune yet, so why not come with us tomorrow?"

Maggie intervened on Leena's behalf. "She'll see how she feels tomorrow, won't you, my love?"

Leena spoke back as if seeking her permission. "But I can if I'm well enough, can't I? I think I'd really love it."

Anna went back to her cabin, realising that Maggie and Leena's commitment to each other went much deeper than either was admitting.

Gary and Jeffrey went together to see Ernst and found him looking over some satellite weather printouts. There was the risk of a storm building over the ocean, and if it came their direction, the dangers of being close to Fortune when it struck were obvious. The three men had all reached the same conclusion: Their good luck was coming to an end, and it was time to halt all operations and return the harvesters to the ship.

It was foolish to take too many people onto Fortune at one time, but given the imminence of the storm and the need for haste, Gary encouraged everyone daring enough to do so, to fly to Fortune and help pack up the site. Even Leena made it, accompanying Maggie on her shift. Her excitement seemed to transmit itself to her baby, whose movements became very apparent to her and added to her sense of exhilaration. She felt like running across the ice, arms extended to the sky, but accepted the task of making tea for the others and stood outside the hut, taking photographs of the action.

After dropping them, the helicopter left and returned about ten minutes later with a load of pallets on which to pack the apparatus. Maggie radioed Gary to say that all was well and he could switch off the last of the harvesters when he was ready to do so. He had managed the project to its conclusion without any major incident occurring, throughout the continuous activity of the helicopter, airship, and boats, and the deployment of crews on the ice and the ocean. They had Gary to thank for that, despite his bullishness, which David had still not forgiven.

Gary arrived shortly after Maggie had made her call, and walked with her to the remaining active hydra, which he switched off with a flourish. After that, he conducted his own assessment of what had been successful and what could be improved, in preparation for any further expeditions and commercial exploitation of Antarctic ice. He became absorbed in his note-taking and left everyone to get on with their work.

He had been on Fortune about forty minutes when Jimmy came over to him. "Gary, Ramos has just been on the shortwave radio. I'm sorry, man, but we're being called back to the ship."

He passed the receiver to Gary, who immediately called the bridge. Ramos came on line, strangely formal and distant.

"Hi Ramos? How're you doing? We need more pallets up here. What's the delay? Any ideas?"

"There are no more pallets available, Mr Murdoch, sir."

"What do you mean? There's a stack of them. I saw them myself."

"Captain Brage has impounded them. He said it was too dangerous to wait longer. The storm is building, and he will move the ship tonight."

Gary's pretence at friendship gave way to instant unbridled anger. "Ramos, I don't give a damn what Brage has told you. Those are our pallets, and I want them now."

"Mr Murdoch, do you want the helicopter now or not?" Ramos asked firmly, ignoring Gary's outburst. "If not, I will give the airship clearance to land."

Jimmy, standing right next to Gary, gripped his arm, just as he was about to launch a verbal onslaught on Ramos. Gary glanced angrily at Jimmy, saw him put a finger over his lips as a warning, and wisely followed his advice. "Yes, send the helicopter, Ramos. We'll do without the pallets for the moment," was all he said. Then he turned to Jimmy. "What the hell's going on, Jimmy? What do you know about this?"

"I know to stay cool in times of uncertainty," Jimmy replied steadily. "It looks like we'll have to leave some kit behind."

"I'm sorry," Gary apologised, regaining his sense of balance.

Anna was watching the two men from a distance. "What do you want us to do, Gary?" she called.

"Just dismantle the hydras one at a time and put them in their containers," he called back. "That's all we can do."

"I think you should get back to the *Moringa* as soon as possible," Jimmy advised him.

It was good advice. Gary was in a dilemma. If the storm really had built up and was heading in their direction, then Ernst had a duty to call an emergency end to operations.

"I guess you're right. There isn't enough time for rescuing all the equipment. The best we can do is salvage the tools. If the storm doesn't come, we'll be back for the last two hydras. Sort it out, can you?"

Gary flew back to the *Moringa* with a dismantled hydra and then made his way to the bridge. When he arrived, both Ernst and Ramos were waiting for him, absorbed in Tyro's latest attempt to land the airship.

"Ah, Gary," Ernst greeted him. "You are just in time to see how not to dock an airship."

"Good. One day, I'll teach you how not to fuck about with things that don't concern you," Gary replied. He knew his words would sting Ernst. Then he turned to Ramos. "Ramos, you piece of shit, I control operations. We've had two weeks without deaths, injuries, or accidents thanks to my

logistics. Got it? I've checked those pallets again, and they're good to go."
Then, without a break, he turned back to Ernst. "Ernst, I want to see those
weather charts. If the storm is as far away as I think it is, you can back off,
man, and let us finish the job."

Gary became aware of two crewmen in the room and quickly reckoned
he would lose any punch-up, so he made no aggressive moves.

Ernst turned with disdainful slowness to face Gary. "It seems Tyro has
survived," he commented. Then, he added calmly, "You are out of line. I
am captain of this ship, Ramos is my first officer. I withdraw your right
to be on the bridge without an invitation. Leave or be arrested."

"I'm in charge of operations," Gary retorted.

"Which are now over, as from this minute, under my orders, for the
safety of this ship," Ernst said emphatically. "I suggest you return all
personnel to the ship as soon as possible and salvage your swimming pools
if you so wish."

Gary saw, with shock, that he was powerless. He remembered Jimmy's
remark, "I know to stay cool at times of uncertainty," so he just nodded his
head and said quietly, "Yes, I'll get on with that right away," and walked
off the bridge.

"That was easier than I thought," Ramos said, with a smirk of derision.

"Don't be a fool," Ernst chided him. Ernst had just made a mistake,
and he knew it. He had acted in anger at Gary's taunt. In return for
total command of the ship, he now had an outright enemy on board. He
cursed his impatience. No more mistakes from now on. "Keep printouts
of those weather charts," he instructed Ramos. They did, at least, show a
developing weather front. If he were to be called upon to explain himself,
his actions would be seen as over-cautious, but he would have some excuse
for his behaviour.

"Do you think he'll tell the others?"

"Of course. By the end of the day, they'll be like a troupe of angry
meerkats, all looking this way and that to find something to criticise and
complain about. We shall have to be very careful. I will speak to our lads
myself once we are under way. In the meantime, let them help clear the
iceberg. Keep Stefan out of the way, so that he doesn't make any more
mistakes. He gets a beating later, but only to frighten him. I expect him
to make a full recovery, Ramos. Nobody dies."

"Except Mukasa," Ramos commented quietly, as if he and the captain shared a mutual secret.

Ernst hesitated a moment and then added, "Not even Mukasa."

"We've had out instructions," Ramos reminded him, in surprise. To him, they were like divine commands.

"And I've given you your orders. Leave me to sort out the details," Ernst snapped back at him. He then left the bridge to go to his cabin while Ramos made arrangements with the crew members.

Gary contacted Maggie and told her to send any equipment they had packed. He gave Arnesh the go-ahead for his team to bring in the reservoirs and pressured Tyro and Roland to go up one last time. There then followed a frenzied two hours on the ice to load what they could into the Hind, piloted by Lothar, who flew shuttle missions returning personnel and bits of equipment to be sorted out later. Ernst did not interfere. Ship's crew and Warlocks were working together. When two hours had passed, he ordered a blast on the ship's foghorn. It was a bluff. It had no meaning, but it worked. After it, six people returned on the next helicopter. The helicopter next flew back, overloaded, with a hydra swinging dangerously beneath it, on some improvised rig, which was released as it reached the flight deck, then the Hind flew off to the plateau yet again. The frenzy was an accident waiting to happen.

Ernst sounded two blasts on the foghorn, giving the effect of a countdown. Those on board seemed to take it as the signal to make ready for departure. The boat teams slashed the last inflatable sections to empty them of air and hauled them in. Arnesh was determined not to leave any debris on this beautiful ocean. Tyro lined up the airship and, at last, made a dream approach so Council, Jomo, Henry, and Alan had only to reach for the landing lines as they dropped and not struggle for dear life. Jeffrey went up to the stern deck to look across to Fortune one last time, to think over all that he and Arthur had believed possible, and wished Arthur could be there beside him.

The tender, RHIBs, and zodiacs were the last objects to be pulled aboard. The gantries were pulled in, and the cargo doors were closed. The airship was secured in its shed. The *Moringa* gave three blasts on her foghorn. The light was fading; the storm was actually building and heading their direction, so it was not unreasonable to leave Fortune behind.

The Hind returned with its cabin stacked dangerously with a maximum payload of equipment; Lothar was a brave man. He flew back to Fortune one final time, with Gary, to collect the other team leaders, who were the last to remain on the ice.

Jimmy was standing on Fortune with Maggie and Anna as Gary joined them. He was looking into the distance, where the ice merged with the darkening clouds. "This is my last big adventure, you know, Maggie," Jimmy said sadly. "It's the one I've waited for all this time, and now it's done. I can't believe it. That's it. Karen gets her full-time husband."

Maggie turned to the others. "Jimmy needs a hug," she said. Jimmy laughed in embarrassment, but Maggie persisted. "Come on, Anna," she said. "He represents the original Warlocks, and he's leaving the iceberg they all dreamed about."

Anna stepped forward willingly and gave Jimmy his hug. "I admire and love you, Jimmy," she said.

Jimmy was helpless with confusion, laughing and demurring about his place in the scheme of things.

Then Maggie said, "Your turn, Gary. Come on. You weren't one of the first. You give him a hug too."

"Oh, come on, Maggs," Gary protested. He felt his anger dissolving. It was supposed to be an occasion of spiritual intensity, but instead, there was laughter.

"Come on, yourself. Come on. Man-hug; you owe it to him."

The two men, amused and hugely embarrassed, bumped chests and bear-hugged as ordered, then she gave him a hug too. Jimmy balanced his pocket camera on a cairn for a group photo, and each one of them, just before clambering aboard, turned for one final glance at the plateau of ice, marvelling at what they had experienced. So with a great sense of achievement, and with much good humour, they left Fortune behind.

Later that night, they started the long journey north. Jeffrey felt the powerful thrust of the engines and the changing motion of the *Moringa* as she started to force her way through the ocean swell. He was tempted to go on deck to take a farewell look at Fortune, but Anna's warm body tempted him more, and he stayed beside her as she slept. The iceberg had served its purpose. It was done. One day, it would break up and melt away. Several hundred million tonnes of fresh water, enough for the needs of a whole population, would sink some distant atolls by a few millimetres more. The sample they had harvested would be enough to prove a point. Twenty years of dreams had condensed into two weeks. The image of David, Raja, and Jimmy sitting with him round the table, with bridge cards in their hands and port gasses on the table, seemed as fresh to him as the thoughts of Raja and Jacqueline waving from the helicopter as it swooped round the bows. Both events were as yesterday, and somewhere, there was Arthur too.

The *Moringa* gave everyone on board a sense of dominance over all the elements, as she pushed her way out of Antarctica and back to the Indian Ocean. There was much work to be done, and everyone settled into a new routine for the final stage of the voyage. The equipment they had been forced to leave behind so hastily amounted to tens of thousands of pounds, but the equipment saved was worth several times more, so there was much to be thankful for and congratulate each other about. For two days, they were menaced by the storm front but seemed to be avoiding it, though the ocean was rough, and nobody ventured outside willingly.

The third day after leaving Fortune, amid all the cleaning and stowage of apparatus, and the checking of inventories to see what remained and what was missing, a meeting of the Warlocks was held by general consent, ostensibly to discuss arrangements for returning home once they reached East Africa. When the meeting took place in the laboratory, the weather was deteriorating by the hour; the sky was unnaturally dark, and even the mighty *Moringa* had an irregular rhythm to its sway among the peaks and troughs of the waves.

Within minutes, it became apparent that beneath all the cheerfulness and cooperation, most of them were feeling very suspicious of Ernst Brage and Ramos Hernandez. Jeffrey told them he had invited Tyro to attend, but Tyro had declined, saying that he felt safer in his hangar, protected by his own team. That summed up the angst of the meeting.

"This meeting isn't just about getting back home from Mombasa, is it?" Leena said. She was comfortably dressed in a tracksuit borrowed from Anna, the folds concealing her changing shape. "It's about how worried we feel aboard this ship. I think Arnesh should be here to represent his team. They could be feeling worried too."

"Leena's made a good point," Gary intervened.

261

Jeffrey broke in. "Leena, I suggest that you and Maggie work on preventing any sense of 'us' and 'them' developing with Arnesh and his team. Would you go and see them and make sure they feel welcome to join us at any time?"

"Good idea," Gary said. "If we do that, it'll be Brage and his crew against the rest of us in any showdown he tries to have."

"Showdown?" David scoffed. "What are you thinking of, Gary, a sort of 'Gunfight at the OK Corral'?"

To his surprise, nobody laughed; on the contrary, Jimmy answered him with unusual criticism. "David, you need to realise you're the one out of step here. Haven't you noticed how strangely the crew is behaving?" Everyone save David nodded in agreement. "They're going out of their way to avoid talking to us now. Not all of them, but most. I've seen Hans turn down a corridor and Ewan back into a doorway just to avoid speaking to me."

David shrugged and shut up. He disliked Gary intensely but never seemed able to get the upper hand over him. He wished he could find an ally, but nobody else seemed to share his mistrust.

"It's as if they've been given an order. We need to find out what's going on, that's for sure," Gary came back loudly into the discussion, trying to reassert control over the meeting.

Anna ran her hands through her long, auburn hair in an eye-catching way. She had been silent since the start of the meeting and seemed in a world of her own. Now, she spoke up in a bored tone of voice. "Leave it to me. I'll find out what Ernst is doing."

"I don't think that's a good idea," Gary intervened with a voice of authority, looking round the room, seeking approval for his intervention. Instead, he was savaged by the lioness.

"Fuck you," Anna retorted with shocking indifference, concentrating on putting a band round her hair and not even bothering to look at him.

There was a startled silence in the room, then Gary tried to wipe away the smear.

"Cut the attitude," he began, but Anna wasn't the least bit interested in his views.

"Oh, piss off, Gary," she said, utterly dismissive of his arrogance. "As Ernst said, you've not got any authority now." She saw Jeffrey looking at her with disbelief, and she grimaced at him. "You know what I'm talking about," she muttered.

"Anna, whose side are you on?" Maggie asked gently, voicing what everyone else was feeling.

"Why do I have to be on anyone's side?" Anna retorted, getting up to leave. "Ever since the start of the meeting, I haven't heard anyone saying anything good about Ernst. He protected us all the time we were on the ice. The ship was always in reach, always where it was needed. Have you thought how hard it was to hold the ship in position day and night for all that time? No, of course you haven't. You just took it for granted." Then she turned to Lucy. "And Lucy, is it any wonder that he's told his crew to stay away from you? You've been fucking two of them ever since the start of the voyage."

"Enough's enough!" David shouted at her, outraged.

But Anna disregarded him just as she had done with Gary. "And you probably got one of them to send a message to Mummy, totally against the captain's orders, which then had the navy breathing down our necks. So is it any wonder that he's told his crew to stay away from the lot of us?" Anna finished her assault on Lucy against a background of silent hostility, as everyone saw the harsh truth of her words.

"I don't know what's got into you recently, Anna," David began with the anger of a father.

"I'll handle this, thank you," Lucy cut in, her face and neck flushed with emotion. David shut up and sat down. "You might as well all know that she's right, in her own vulgar way," Lucy continued. "My private life is my own affair, but yes, Stefan, Silvio, and I are still trying to work things out. It's not so unusual these days," she added, defensively.

"My darling, I had no idea, but you have my full support," David mumbled, shocked by this revelation from his perfect daughter.

"Thank you, Dad," Lucy replied. "Stefan risked his job, and more, poor love, to send a message on our behalf, against his captain's orders, and aren't we all glad that he did?"

Everyone in the room except Anna replied, "Yes." Anna's isolation was complete.

"So what have you to say for yourself now, Anna?" Jeffrey challenged her gently. "How about an apology to Lucy for a start?"

"Forget it," Anna replied and walked out of the room.

"Anna! Come back, Anna," Jeffrey called out, distress evident in his voice.

He lingered a moment, as if it was his duty to stay, then followed her with eyes downcast, while the rest looked at each other, embarrassed by what they had all witnessed.

"She's not been herself for days," Maggie commented quietly.

"I'll second that," Gary replied.

"If you don't mind, I'm going as well," Lucy mumbled and left without looking up.

"I'll come with you, my love," David said gently. He turned to Alan and Roland, who had sat together, wide-eyed and speechless. "You better go to the bows and brief Tyro. We'll have to talk about him some other time," then he left with his attention focused entirely on Lucy.

Roland and Alan, still without saying a word, pushed each other out with apologetic nods to Gary and Jimmy, Maggie, and Leena.

"I guess that brings this meeting to a close," Gary announced with a bemused look. "Unless you think I'm exceeding my non-existent authority by saying so."

"It was pretty pointless anyway," Maggie said, giving Leena's hand an affectionate squeeze. "I'm afraid we're sheep penned in with wolves."

"There's safety in numbers," Leena replied confidently. "Let's go and see Arnesh and Anwar right now and hear what they have to say. Come on." Maggie reflected a moment and then nodded in agreement and picked up her anorak.

As the two women rose, unhurriedly, together, Gary turned to Jimmy. "Why don't you go with them?" he suggested. "You three make a good team."

Jimmy looked admiringly at Maggie. She epitomized the perfect woman in his eyes – courage, wisdom, and looks. He had to remember Karen. He had to be careful. "Those two make a good team on their own," he replied and was rewarded with appreciative looks from both of them. "I think I'll go for a stroll, in a while," he added. He was curious that Gary had seemed to want him out of the way.

Gary was alarmed by the thought of Jimmy nosing round the ship but concealed this with a pretence of concern for a friend. "Hell, Jimmy, the storm's building. This is no time to go wandering round where you don't know the landmarks. You may get lost or something."

Maggie, now standing arm-in-arm with Leena, laughed at Gary's words. "Oh, Gary, be serious," she exclaimed, which surprised Gary, who thought he was being serious. Maggie saw his confusion and explained, "You've just told one of the greatest adventurers of our times not to get lost on a ship."

Gary still didn't see the humour. "Oh, never mind," Maggie said, giving up on him, and she and Leena went off happily, laughing at Gary's remark, and their own unsteadiness, as the *Moringa* lurched.

"What are *you* going to do?" Jimmy asked Gary, who was clearly seething at Maggie's light-hearted ridicule.

"I guess I'll stay this end of the ship and try to patch things up with Jeffrey," Gary replied, trying to suppress his emotions.

Jimmy noted Gary's body language. "Good idea," he said and then added, "Maggie's all right. Don't worry about it. Well, see you later." Jimmy rose as he spoke, gave Gary a friendly pat on the shoulder, and followed Maggie and Leena out of the door, leaving Gary alone, listening to the growing storm.

"Now or never," Gary muttered to himself. He could not evade the matter forever. His survival depended on Tyro's death. It wasn't personal. It was part of the deal, to do as ordered. As he sat looking round and thinking where to begin, he noticed something lying on the bench near where Alan and Roland had been sitting. It was a monkey wrench, made of heavy metal. It belonged in the hangar and needed to be returned to Tyro. "Well, there's a sign if ever I saw one," he said with satisfaction.

The least anxious group in the whole ship was in the meditation room, where they had gathered to see out the storm. Arnesh's team had arranged a roster that had to be adhered to, but those off duty could think of nowhere better to be together. Quiet conversations in Punjabi and Hindi were taking place in the tranquil surroundings.

"I could live on the *Moringa* forever if only we had women," Anwar muttered as he exhaled smoke from a delicately rolled reefer of the purest marijuana, which rendered him oblivious to the rolling of the ship.

"You want your wife here?" Arnesh queried in mild surprise.

"My wife? Good God, man, are you mad?" Anwar retorted. "Have you ever known such freedom? There are no bosses, no wives, all the weed we can smoke, and all the food we can eat. This is heaven, I tell you, except we need women."

"We have different views of heaven, clearly," Arnesh responded, then sighed. "I would like my wife to be here," he said.

"Our views of heaven are the same. It's our wives who are different," Anwar replied. "I have seen your wife. She is still a peach ripe for picking, after all the years of marriage to you." He paused to suck in some smoke. "My wife was once a peach," he continued sadly. "Now the fruit is gone, and I am left with the stone."

"That is because your wife is married to you, and my wife is married to me," Arnesh explained simply.

"There is only one Indian woman on the ship," Anwar mused. "But she is a peach. She is truly a peach."

"You mean the boss's niece?" Arnesh snorted derisively. "Even in your present state, your thoughts should not be drifting there."

"Ah, but what a peach," Anwar continued dreamily. "So tender, so rounded, so free; what does she care for customs? She would unpeel herself for me if I asked her right."

Arnesh giggled. "You should be careful, my friend," he said.

Anwar shrugged. "Why? She cannot hear me, more's the pity."

"Can I come in?" Leena had poked her head round the door and spoke to them in Punjabi.

Anwar looked at his joint. "This is good weed," he commented. "I can hear her voice; would you believe?"

He felt a nudge in the ribs and looked at Arnesh, and then followed his gaze to where Leena's smiling face was looking down at them.

"Is that really you?" he asked benignly.

"Yes, it's really me," Leena replied, entering the room.

"Then life has improved for both of us, my peach. Come in, take off your clothes, and relax. Your Anwar will look after you."

Arnesh, meanwhile, had struggled to his feet. He was a devout man, able to sample temptation in restricted quantities, so he was more clear-headed than Anwar. "Leena, this is indeed a surprise," he welcomed her.

266

"We were not expecting your visit. Please excuse Anwar his manners. He is off-duty and missing his wife and—"

"And wondering what I look like without my clothes, you naughty man," Leena said light-heartedly, looking at Anwar. She had realised instantly that she had been wrong to enter the room. Maggie and she had used it frequently, but always on their own, at agreed times, so no man would see them in their yoga postures. This visit was a personal error on her part. If she remained joking with the men in Punjabi, she felt she could rescue the situation, despite being with five men in the room, as the vulgarity would be forgotten by morning, but if Maggie came in and English had to be spoken, it would be a cultural embarrassment that might have the reverse effect of the goodwill intended.

Maggie was already entering the door hesitantly, when Leena pushed her back and whispered, "Go! Arnesh will see me back. Go!" and closed the door.

Maggie walked back to the main corridor and wondered what to do. She decided to hang round the area for a while to see if she could help Leena back to the cabin, but after five long minutes, this struck her as a complete waste of time. She started to feel cold and put on her anorak. It would be exhilarating to go up to the main deck for a while, if she dared. *Do I dare?* she asked herself, and after the heady excitement of Fortune, there seemed nothing she couldn't face. She walked along to the mid-deck stairs and, as she did so, heard footsteps behind her. She spun round, pressing herself against the wall.

"Surprise," Jimmy said. "Didn't mean to frighten you, Maggs."

"Then don't creep up on me, you bastard," Maggie said with a laugh.

"I'm just nosing around in and out the corridors. There are one or two mysterious paths in this ship worthy of a great adventurer," he said, smiling as he echoed Maggie's words from the meeting and sidled past her. "Where's Leena gone?"

"She doesn't want me around. She thinks she can do the goodwill job better on her own. I'm just going up on deck for a few minutes."

"You're mad," he said.

"What about you?" she retorted as he ambled away.

"I'll only be a few more minutes myself," he called back without turning round. "It's a good time to be exploring, as there's nobody moving about the ship."

"Well, don't get lost," she said fondly. "See you in an hour."

"Sure thing," he replied and continued along the corridor, while Maggie climbed the stairway, opened the heavy iron door, and stepped onto the deck.

Night was descending. The last glow of light was being quashed by tumultuous clouds carried on powerful south-easterly winds. Ten-metre-high waves were rolling the ocean top, crashing into each other, forming peaks, plateaus, and troughs in perpetually shifting patterns of disruption, until a mighty wave came rolling through again. It was bitterly cold as waves broke against the hull, and the wind sent spray sweeping along the deck, yet the sheer magnitude of all that surrounded Maggie was breath-taking and irresistible. She walked into the centre of the deck to feel even more diminutive and experience the full impact of this vast release of energy on her senses.

The mightiness of the ocean and the isolation of the ship were even more awesome as she spread her arms and looked to the clouds while the spray and drizzle stung her face and eyes; noise like ever-rolling thunder blocked out all other sounds. In barely a minute, she was soaked through and frozen, but she stayed mesmerized, fighting her discomfort until one wave, majestic as it struck the hull, sent water cascading along the deck. The impact shocked Maggie into reality, and she was no longer in awe of the power around her but fearful of it. It was no longer drizzle, but driving rain and spray that was whipping into her eyes. If she did not walk back to the stairway now, she risked being washed away in an instant, yet she stayed where she was, overwhelmed by the cold, staring at the waves coming head-on to the bows, any of which could break along the deck and wash her feet away from under her.

The only visible sign of life was the light on the bridge and from a few windows of the tower a hundred metres away, half-hidden by the airship's shed, buffeted in the gale. Maggie began staggering towards its doors, cursing her stupidity in not heeding the rapidity with which the storm had struck. The deck was now perilous to move on. She slipped again and again as she stayed as close to the centre of the deck as she could. She held on desperately to anything she could grab, panicked by her loneliness, and the lurching of the *Moringa*. She realised that even if she cried out, nobody would hear her. The *Moringa* was strong enough to face the storm and the waves, but she was not; not tiny Maggie. Then, a spotlight beam shone along the deck from the base of the tower. Someone was approaching her like a spectre in the mist of spray and rain. It took almost a minute, as she clung to the hangar doors, for the figure to reach her, and she could make out, at last, the form of Ramos, the first officer.

"You are in great danger," he shouted. "You must come inside at once."

"Yes, yes, please," she shouted back and, steadied by Ramos, who was properly equipped for the conditions, struggled thankfully past the hangar, past the roof of the Grand Chamber, to the doorway at the base of the tower, and stepped inside.

"I saw you from the bridge," he explained. "What were you doing out there? Are you mad?"

"I think I must be," Maggie replied through chattering teeth as she stood meekly in front of her saviour, accepting the ticking-off.

She was so obviously cold and contrite that he found it impossible to stay as angry, as he intended. She humbly thanked Ramos for rescuing her and went straight to her cabin, stripped off her clothes and showered, then climbed into her bunk to let her body warm up; she drifted into sleep and out again. She lay on her back in the darkness and imagined the towering waves with each movement of the ship. The imagery was so vivid, she shook her head and sat up, clutching at her quilt to remind herself that she was safe – then lay back, thinking of Ramos's bravery in rescuing her. The suave Ramos had been caring and attentive as he helped her to safety. He was a good-looking man about her age, and his attempt to be angry with her had been completely undermined by the affectionate smile he had given her when she impishly raised her eyes to his.

You're still a bloody good flirt, Maggie told herself admiringly, distracting herself from the storm, and tried to imagine rewarding Ramos, but her thoughts turned automatically to Anna, with all her playful ways of exciting her. She curled herself into a ball, and a wish swept over her that she had never introduced Anna to Jeffrey. If she hadn't done so, she and Anna would still be a couple, living their life in Cambridge, taking holidays, kayaking, mountaineering, and stretching out together beneath the sun.

They would still be kissing each other good night and lying embraced in each other's arms. *None of this would have happened,* she complained bitterly to herself, and then the thought took another dimension. None of this would have happened, not Antarctica, not India, not Africa, not Leena. At this, she snapped abruptly out of her self-pity. She was back. "You wouldn't miss this for the world, and you know it," she muttered with a smile, hoping Leena would be back soon.

When another half-hour had passed and Leena had not returned, it unsettled her. The *Moringa* was feeling the full effects of the storm, and Leena might lose her balance in the uncertain movements. Maggie realised this was silly rubbish if she were honest with herself, as Arnesh and Anwar would see Leena safely back, but Maggie couldn't just lie in the cabin any longer.

She dressed, tidied away her damp clothes, and then went in search of company. The restaurant was empty, which probably indicated that most of the team were in their cabins. Maggie made her way to Anna and Jeffrey's cabin, hoping they were not still angry with each other, and knocked.

"Who's there?" Anna's voice demanded.

"It's me. Maggie."

The *Moringa* gave another lurch. Maggie heard Anna stumble against something and swear. Then the door opened; Anna grabbed Maggie and pulled her into the cabin. While Maggie tried to regain her balance, Anna swung the door shut and then turned and wrapped her arms round Maggie's body in a loving hug. "Maggs! How did you know that I needed to see you so much?" she cooed.

"Actually, I was looking for Leena," was not an appropriate reply in the circumstances, so Maggie stayed silent, hugging Anna back by way of response. "Where's Jeffrey?" she asked.

"Don't know, don't care," Anna mumbled, resting her chin on Maggie's shoulder.

"Had a tiff, have you?" Maggie prompted, feeling very close to finding out the reason for Anna's erratic behaviour.

"You could say that," Anna replied, her voice barely audible, indicating that something substantially worse had occurred.

"What about?" Maggie asked, nudging Anna closer to the truth.

"Fucking Ernst," Anna replied flatly.

"Now what's he done?" Maggie cooed sympathetically.

Anna pulled back, breaking the mutual hug. She looked Maggie in the eye, as if trying to deduce something. "I mean what I said, Maggie," she said. "I fucked Ernst, or he fucked me, or we got fucked – I never understand how to use the word – but we were naked, I opened my legs—"

"All right, all right, love; I've got the message," Maggie interjected, after a second of stunned bemusement. "No need to go on about it." She sank down on the bunk, rubbing her forehead. Then she looked up at Anna again, amazement in her eyes. "Bloody hell, that's going some," she said accusingly. "I thought it was Lucy who was screwing the crew, but you're streets ahead of her."

"There's no need to be rude, Maggs," Anna said, pouting. "It's not helping."

"What about Ramos?" Maggie asked.

"Who?" Anna said, perplexed.

"Ramos, the first officer."

"What about him?"

"Well, he's good looking. Is he on the list?"

"I thought you'd come to help me," Anna retorted in a huff.

"Don't get angry with me," Maggie replied with equal feeling. "It's you who's sleeping with the enemy. I'm just—"

"I'm not sleeping with the enemy," Anna protested, sitting down beside her. "I sleep with Jeffrey. I love him. I do whatever I have to, to protect him. I look after him. If you love someone, you'll do anything for them, even if they don't realise it."

Maggie smiled in astonishment and thought of all that she had done for the spiritually lost woman Anna had been on the day they first met, at the Territorial Army recruiting event; all of it for love. "I didn't know that," Maggie teased her, gently, but the irony was lost on Anna.

"Yes," Anna said. "It's true, but there is a price. Things happen." Anna was trying to convey something she could not bring herself to say.

"Always," Maggie said, beginning to understand the situation. "Let's see if I've got this right. You're telling me that you've had sex with Ernst as a means of protecting Jeffrey."

271

"Yes," Anna said, avoiding Maggie's gaze, while her fingers fiddled aimlessly with each other.

Maggie paused so that all was calm before she asked her next question. "Is that the only reason, Anna? To protect Jeffrey? Is that the only reason you've been to bed with Ernst? Seriously?"

"It was," Anna said quietly, adding, "Not just Jeffrey. I think I was protecting somebody else too."

"Who?"

"I don't know, but there was someone," Anna said, sounding totally sincere.

Maggie accepted this.

"And what sort of feelings are you getting now?" Maggie continued. "Who do you feel protective towards now? You mustn't mind me asking, love, because you seemed quite protective of Ernst at the meeting, and if I'm to help you, I need to know. You don't fancy Ernst, do you?" The way Anna now raised her hands to her forehead as if to stop it from bursting told Maggie that she had arrived at the truth. "Oh, Anna," she said in disbelief.

"He's not a bad man. He's not," Anna said plaintively.

"Yes, he is," Maggie insisted. "There's something bad going on in this ship, and he's right in the centre of it. Stay away from him. Stop seeing him before it's too late."

"If I do, we won't find out anything," Anna replied.

Maggie felt a rising sense of despair. "Anna, if my love for you means anything, you won't do this. Think of Jeffrey. You've just said how much you love him. Once we're off this ship, you'll forget Brage. You'll wonder what came over you."

The *Moringa* juddered, as if reminding them of her power and presence.

"I think he loves me just as much as Jeffrey. He's more attentive."

"Oh, Anna, don't be ridiculous," Maggie protested. "He's lusting for you. When he's finished with you, he may even kill you."

"I think you better go," Anna said quietly.

Maggie hesitated and then remembered why she had come. "You're right," she conceded. "Where's Leena? Any ideas?"

"How should I know? I left the meeting before you did," Anna replied, and again, the *Moringa* juddered. "I'm glad we didn't have this weather two weeks ago."

"The storm's getting worse. I'm not going to try to wander around in this. I think I'll just go to my cabin." Maggie stood up, and as she leant over to kiss Anna, the ship lurched so that she fell forwards onto the bunk, pinning Anna beneath her, her lips hovering above Anna's. "Oh, quite like old times," she said with a smile, and they looked lovingly into each other's eyes. "Don't die trying to protect the rest of us," she pleaded gently. "I'll forgive you anything but that." Then she kissed Anna on the forehead and made a second, more successful attempt to reach her own cabin.

Chapter 15

FEAR AND LOATHING

Gary Murdoch had never murdered a man, but he had killed one. During his time in London, a pedestrian, hurrying along a pavement with his back to Gary's car, had momentarily slipped into the road. It happened near Hampton Court. It was one minute past seven in the evening, a bus lane had just become open to all traffic, and Gary was speeding up the inside of the line of traffic before other drivers swung in and blocked the lane. There was insufficient evidence of Gary's speed for him to be charged with dangerous driving. The verdict was accidental death, and Gary had walked away from the coroner's court without a prosecution, but he knew, full well, that his actions had killed the man. Likewise, he knew he could kill Tyro now. Tyro had already stepped into the road, so to speak, by antagonising the Angels; on this occasion, Gary would use a monkey wrench in place of his car. If there were no witnesses, he might be able to make the death look like an accident. If there were a witness, he might have to claim self-defence or maybe kill the witness as well. It would prove his reliability to the Angels, and the reward would be worth it.

He made his way to the bows, on watch all the time for Maggie, Jimmy, or anyone else moving around on the corridor deck, and reached the aircrew quarters undetected. However, the storm which had kept everyone else in their cabins was too strong for Tyro's stomach, and he was locked away in his cabin too. There was nobody else around to notice Gary skulking among the contents of the helicopter hangar for an hour before giving up, and he decided the strategy, itself, was a good one. He returned to the tower, still with the monkey wrench, to try his luck when the storm lessened.

As he made his way back along the long corridor, he listened to the noise of the storm and countered the wallowing movements of the ship with his shift of weight; he felt that he was an integral part of the malevolence of the storm, able to harness its fury to carry out what had to be done. He wanted to kill while the storm raged, sometime in the next two days. Walking along the corridor now, still an innocent man, there was no sight or sound of Maggie or Jimmy or anyone else, until he heard giggling down one of the small corridors towards the middle of the ship. He looked along it and to his surprise found Leena walking towards him, alone. She was barelegged, carrying her shoes and tracksuit bottoms.

"Oh, hello Gary, baby," Leena greeted him in the way she used to do before calling off their relationship. In his adrenalin-fuelled state, it filled him with excitement, as did the sight of her semi-naked body.

"Hi, babe," he said, greeting her in a way he hadn't used throughout the voyage. "Where's Maggie? Why aren't you dressed?"

"I am dressed, honey; don't be silly." She giggled. "Anwar was missing women, so I took these off to show him my peach-like skin, as he called it. But then he got a bit too excited, so I came away. It's all right, nothing else was removed; no harm done." She seemed free of care. "Do you still like my peach-like skin?" she asked, eying him provocatively.

"Where's Maggie?" he persisted.

"I don't know, baby," she replied, unconcerned. "Maggie's gone, Arnesh has gone; there's just Anwar and a couple of others left, having their party." She pointed, vaguely, over her shoulder. "You still haven't said you like my skin," she said accusingly.

"Don't play games with me, Leena," Gary said with frustration in his voice, all the while aware of the sounds of the storm and the shudder of the *Moringa*. "You're the one who called things off between us, so don't flirt with me now. Come on, come here; let me help you put your things back on."

"Don't be so serious, Gary," she said, reeking of marijuana, coming close and kissing his cheek. "You used to be better at taking my clothes off than putting them on. Remember?" She giggled again.

He took her slacks from her and bent down to lift up one of her legs while she balanced herself against him. Her kiss was like food to a starving man. "You're the one who's going to live in India for the rest of your life with a man you've not even met," he said, irritated by her provocative behaviour. "I've honoured your wishes and stayed away from you."

Her proximity, after all these weeks, was tantalising. Her skin was beautiful. He looked for something critical to say to stop the urge that was growing inside him. "You're growing fat," he said, noticing her waistline as he raised her sweater.

"I'm not fat," she said, giggling. "I'm pregnant, stupid."

Gary stopped. He stayed motionless a moment, set aside her pants, and then stood up slowly. "Since when?" he asked, looking down on her.

She looked surprised. "Since six months ago," she replied. She reached out for her slacks, but he pulled them from her grasp. She giggled, thinking he was playing.

"You've been pregnant for six months without telling me?" he repeated, with a tone of such utter contempt that it became clear to Leena that she urgently needed to get dressed and manage the situation.

"Gary, baby, please, give me back my things, and we'll talk all you want," she coaxed him gently, but the roar of the storm and the hum of the engines were against her, and she struggled to keep her balance.

It was over swiftly. The back of his hand caught her like the strike of a whiplash, twisting her head and sending it crashing into the wall. She collapsed at his feet. Picking her up by her collar and scooping up her shoes, he carried her limp form to the narrow iron staircase that spiralled its way round the lift-shaft, not caring what she struck as he did so, her feet thumping off each step, until he reached the storage deck below. Here, there was a door to the lift. He pressed the button; the door opened, and the lights flickered on. He stepped in, dropped her body on the floor, and threw her slacks and shoes into the corner. The door closed of its own accord. He pulled off her knickers, tossed them onto the pile, and bared her body to her breasts; stripping naked except for his socks, he parted her legs and raped her.

She groaned just once, indicating some awareness of what was happening, so he snapped her head forward and back to the floor without disturbing his rhythm, and she lay, silent, as he took his grubby revenge. When it was over, he stayed lying on top of her, panting with satisfaction, and then, realising he had given himself a problem, he put his clothes back on and sat down beside the slender, still body, stroking her hair.

"This was your fault," he told the motionless body. "Are you still alive?" he asked her, poking at her head with his finger, but her head just lolled to the pressure of the finger, and he cursed softly to himself.

The lift had three stops: the main deck, above; the storage deck, its present location; the maintenance deck, way below. The maintenance deck was out of bounds, unless you had a key, and Gary still had one of the two keys; the other was on the bridge. So he took the lift down to the maintenance deck, a claustrophobic space beneath the water tanks, which seemed the safest possible place for him to be at that moment. The door slid back, revealing a narrow, poorly lit passage where the engine noise reverberated, and at the end of it – Jimmy.

He found himself staring straight at Jimmy, who was standing about ten metres away. He had clearly been trying to prise open some double doors along the passage when he heard the lift arrive and looked horrified, as surely as Gary, at this sudden encounter, but he stood his ground, and two seconds later, a slight smile came to his lips. He had feared it was Ernst. Ernst would have meant trouble; Gary was all right. Gary he felt he could handle.

Gary moved swiftly towards Jimmy, distracting him from looking into the lift. "Jimmy," he said in a friendly tone. "How the hell did you get down here?"

"I just kept walking down the stairs," Jimmy replied in his slow, amiable manner. "I came to a chain across them with a notice saying 'No Admittance,' so, being a great explorer, I disregarded it."

"A chain," Gary echoed, smirking. "They have a special key made for the lift but just put a chain across the stairs. Ernst is his own worst enemy, thank God."

"What has Ernst got to do with it? And what's that in the lift?" At that moment, the lift door closed.

"The war has started, buddy," Gary said, putting a friendly arm on Jimmy's shoulder. "It's us against them, whether we like it or not. That's a body in the lift, and I'll show you right now what Ernst has got to do with it."

"Whose body?" Jimmy asked, dismayed, turning to look at Gary, who had moved to the double doors and was inserting a key to activate the coded lock.

"The person who was trying to warn me," Gary lied. "If you want to understand, Jimmy, just look in here first."

"I guess I want to see that body first," Jimmy said guardedly.

Gary, in desperation, put all his cards on the table to distract him. He threw open the doors, and the lights flickered on from the room behind.

"Heroin, Jimmy, such as you've never seen heroin before," he said, disappearing into the chamber behind.

Jimmy came and stood in the doorway; he gasped. "You're kidding me," he said, amazed by the sight of row upon row of sacks.

"No, pal, I'm not," Gary replied, standing inside the door and looking into the room.

Jimmy came to join him. "How much are we looking at?"

"My source tells me that these sacks have a street value of about $200 million. The Angels, as they call themselves, are making their big push on the heroin market. The *Moringa* has given them their route to get it undetected to Africa."

Jimmy was aghast. He walked a little way down the aisle between the sacks, which stretched three sacks deep and two sacks high for several metres along both walls of the low chamber.

"Don't go too far, Jimmy," Gary warned. "If any of the crew come down now, we're trapped."

Jimmy remembered the body and came back to Gary. "So who is it in the lift?" he asked, fearing the reply.

"It's Leena. They must have known I was on to them. They left her in the lift as a warning to me, Jimmy. They guessed I was on my way here."

"The bastards," Jimmy growled, loading the word with loathing. "But why Leena? Show me, Gary."

He turned to leave, hesitating at the doorway as if there might be someone on the other side, waiting to attack. The monkey wrench caught him at the back of his head, where spine and skull connect. He never uttered a sound as he fell to the floor. Gary swiftly bent down and looked at the angle of the head and the wide-open, unfocused eyes. Jimmy was already well and truly dead, but Gary gave him another sharp blow to the back of the head for good measure, and the eyes just stared, unconcerned.

"It was your fault," Gary told the corpse. "No admittance means no admittance, buddy. You're a lawyer. You're meant to obey the law. Now look what I've had to do." Gary stared down at his victim. "Now I've got two bodies to get rid of instead of one." He gave Jimmy's body a kick of resentment at this additional work and also for the guilt that he was having to suppress. He feared the guilt.

Gary decided he would dispose of Leena's body first. He took a fire blanket from its container on the wall and returned to the lift. He threw it over Leena and pressed the button for the main deck. His plan was to throw Leena overboard, return for Jimmy, and throw him overboard too. Once again, as the lift doors opened, he was struck by the unexpected. On the main deck, the darkness was pierced by a light too close to the lift for comfort. The ship's motion was violent; it could easily tip him overboard. He realised that others, perhaps on deck or on the bridge, might see him if he ventured out. The ship was pitching unevenly, and icy spray came at him as he stood back from the door of the lift, holding Leena in his arms. Thankfully the door closed and shielded him.

He needed time to think, so he took the lift back down as far as the storage deck and sat there in its protection, thinking things out. He needed support. The only person he could turn to was Ramos. It might take thirty minutes to get to the bridge, speak to Ramos, and return with him, but nobody else was likely to use the lift in that time, and Leena's body was well hidden, should anyone else pass by. He came out of the lift and stumbled his way up the stairs to the main corridor, leaving Leena out of sight in the lift, still covered by the fire blanket. The movement of the *Moringa* had caused him to lose his footing at one point and to be buffeted against the sides of the staircase, so he paused to catch his breath and then started back towards the tower, along the long, empty corridor, and was just passing the door of the Grand Chamber when he saw Frank, head down, coming the other way, unaware of his presence.

"Frank, what are you doing here?" he called, agitated that anything should delay him.

"Hello there, Gary. You're just the man I need," Frank called back, approaching him. "I've just come to carry out a safety check of my trees. The boss doesn't want anyone else to go into the chamber during the storm, but he's agreed that I should keep an eye on things. What about you?"

"I'm just checking things out like you, Frank," Gary said cheerfully. "I didn't know you were coming, so I just had a quick glance in the Grand Chamber. It seems fine."

"Well, I'm here now. Best have a quick look myself to say I've done it," Frank said hastily. "I'll only be two minutes, if that. If you could stand by the door, perhaps you'd be ready to come and help if I call out."

He looked so hopeful that Gary felt unable to refuse. "Sure thing, Frank," he agreed, hoping that nothing else would delay him.

Frank did not venture far along any of the walkways. He had switched off the rotary mechanism as the storm approached and could see, using the chamber's lights and his spotlight, that all was well. The occasional severe judder of the *Moringa* was enough to make any loose attachment vibrate. One such moment made him grasp a handrail for support, and as he did so, he noticed two bolts had loosened. It was not anything major, but he decided to ask the maintenance crew to check the bolts. Other than that, he was satisfied and returned to where Gary was standing.

"Thanks for your help, Gary. Nothing major. We can go," Frank said above the clatter of hail now beating on the roof.

"Good. Let's get out of here," Gary replied and walked away from the door, taking several paces towards the stern of the ship, before turning to speak to Frank again. He was startled to see Frank heading off towards the bows.

"We should head back, Frank," Gary called out.

"I'm going to see if anyone's in the workshops," Frank answered. "I've got my sea legs on; I'll be all right."

Gary cursed this turn of events but hid his anger. "I guess I better come with you," he replied.

"Suit yourself," Frank muttered under his breath.

He had seen how agitated Gary was and assumed he was scared of the storm. He resumed his walk up the corridor, leaving Gary to catch him up. The spotlight he had used in the Grand Chamber wasn't necessary, but he amused himself sending its beams up the corridor and flicking it around.

"You can turn that thing off now," Gary said, in a manner that expressed his irritation, but Frank kept it on.

Gary felt his self-control slipping again, and then what he wanted not to happen, did happen.

Frank suddenly ran forward, calling out, "Gary! Quickly!" He stopped beside the stairs, where something had caught in the beam of his spotlight: a woman's hand peeking from under a blanket, her body sprawled on the upper steps.

Frank picked up the edge of the blanket and gasped in horror at the sight of Leena, her face bruised and swollen, bruises and grazes on her arms, her tracksuit top and torn bra just covering her body. Frank dropped to his knees beside her, not sure what to do. He wanted to feel for a heartbeat but hesitated to touch her.

"Is she alive?" Gary demanded, staggered that Leena could have made her way up the stairs. "Feel for her pulse."

"I don't know how," Frank replied, then he thought to shine the light in one of her eyes. He detected a constriction of the pupil as he held a puffy eyelid open.

"I think she's still alive. I'm not sure, but I think so," he said nervously. To his relief, Gary seemed eager to take over, and he willingly got up as Gary pushed him aside.

Gary, at that moment, still saw half a chance to smother Leena in the dim light.

"Why has she covered herself with this?" Gary asked, knowing her clothes were still in the lift.

"It's a blanket of some sort. It's wet too. You don't think she tried to go outside, do you?" Frank replied, genuinely perplexed.

"It'll do. I'll wrap it tightly round her." Gary pulled Leena up the last steps. "I'll carry her. Why don't you go ahead – and turn your fucking light off."

"All right," Frank said, objecting to Gary's language and defiantly turning it on Leena one last time as Gary bent to lift her up. Leena groaned as the light hit her eyes. "She *is* alive," he exclaimed excitedly.

"Damnation," Gary muttered, his frustration at the turn of events reaching the bursting point.

"Something wrong?" Frank asked, surprised.

"Yes, that fucking light of yours. I nearly dropped her because of it. Turn it off, now."

"All right, all right," Frank said, doing so at last, but too late for Gary's purpose.

Gary, aided all the time by Frank, carried Leena to the medical room. Emily Ross's cabin was adjacent to the medical centre. She came hurrying in at the sound of the commotion, saw Leena, and on being told by Frank that he and Gary had found her unconscious, ordered the men out of the room. She then phoned Maggie in her cabin. Maggie was with her barely a minute later. She passed Gary waiting anxiously outside and gave him an encouraging smile. When she entered, she saw Leena lying on the examination couch, a bed blanket over her body, and Emily struggling to set up an intravenous line in Leena's left arm.

"I can't find a vein. She's in shock and very cold," Emily said and then added nervously, "I could try to put a central line up."

"Stay within your level of competence," Maggie replied firmly. "With the ship moving around as it is, you'd probably do more harm than good."

They removed her upper garments, attached a heart monitor, and took an initial blood pressure reading. Leena was unresponsive except to pain as she was moved. Maggie drew a diagram of the human body and had started to record the visible bruises and grazes on Leena's head when Anna joined them. Leena was lying naked, her body covered by the blanket, her heart monitor beeping rhythmically.

"How is she?" Anna asked immediately.

Emily did not look pleased at this intrusion into her sick bay and told Anna to stand to one side. "We better start cleaning her up," she said to Maggie, folding back the blanket to expose Leena's breasts and shoulders.

Maggie gave the diagram and pen to Anna. "She's shocked and barely conscious. As we clean her, record every bruise, mark, cut, whatever. All right?"

"Has she been raped?" Anna asked simply, as she made ready to do as Maggie had described.

"Probably," Emily said, as the three of them diligently worked at their respective tasks. "Her trousers and knickers are missing. Look at this cut in her scalp. Can you see it?"

Anna recorded its position. Leena's face was bruised but not cut, her teeth intact; there were no bruise marks on her throat. There were bruises on her forearms and wrists, and grazes on her hands. Then Emily lowered the blanket farther to expose Leena's tummy.

She looked pointedly at Maggie and Anna. "Judging by your reaction, you both already know that she's pregnant. If we were going to have a pregnant woman on the ship, I should have been informed."

"She wasn't supposed to be on the ship. She flew in as a sort of stowaway after we'd left," Maggie explained.

Emily was unimpressed. "I remember. But that was weeks ago, and she's had no antenatal care in the meantime." Then she shrugged. "It's immaterial now. There's no bruising or injury to the abdomen that I can detect, so baby may be all right." Emily ran her hand delicately over Leena's abdomen. "When the weather settles down, I'll do a scan, but there's too much movement at present. Now, ladies, it's time for the lower end. Do you want to stay?" Maggie and Anna both nodded sombrely. "Very well, then."

Emily shifted the blanket so all the body was covered above Leena's waist, and all was exposed below it.

Anna set to work recording all the bruises and abrasions while Maggie and Emily pointed them out.

They turned Leena on her left side, inadvertently causing enough pain that she roused briefly, moaning in agony, then clearly said, "I'm pregnant. I told you, I'm pregnant."

They stopped, and Emily quickly checked her eyes and called her by name, but Leena, having come round enough to notice where she was, just lay her head back on the pillow and drifted into sleep. Emily gave up trying to rouse her. They continued to clean her body gently, revealing yet more signs of violence. Emily gave Leena an intramuscular injection of hydrocortisone into her thigh, then, turning her half onto her back, opened her legs. The rape had been brutal. The three women went silent as they saw the aftermath of the heartless penetration, the swollen labia, the torn mucosa, and the reddened contused tissues.

"It's vile," Anna muttered. "Whoever did this is vile."

"It's bad, but I've seen worse," Emily said quietly, trying to keep the proceedings objective rather than emotive. "Have you finished recording the injuries?"

Anna took the hint that Emily wanted her to go. "Yes, here's the piece of paper. I'll go now." She put her mouth to Leena's ear and whispered something the others could not hear, except for the words at the end: "I promise you." She gave Leena's arm a loving squeeze and left.

283

"Thanks for your help," Emily remembered to say, by way of polite dismissal. She watched Anna leave the sickbay and then caught Maggie's eye. "She frightens me, that one. There's something about her that gives me the goose pimples. Is she a friend of yours?"

"Yes, a very dear friend, actually," Maggie replied. "But she doesn't like men very much at the best of times. Given half a chance, I think she would actually put a bullet into the man who did this."

"This must be very upsetting for you too," Emily acknowledged. "I could do with your help, but not if it's too much for you."

"Thank you," Maggie replied. "But I'm clinically trained. I wouldn't want anyone else to take my place. Also, nobody else knows about the pregnancy yet, and it's important they don't."

Emily finished cleaning Leena's feet and pulled the blanket gently down to cover her. "The rapist knows," she pointed out. "If some man shows up knowing about the pregnancy when he shouldn't, well, I think you should get your friend Anna to have a word with him."

At that moment, Gary put his head round the door. Emily pointed out that Leena was asleep. He wanted to stay, but Emily sent him away.

The ocean seemed so solid and the force of the waves so strong that as each one crashed against the hull, it was like a blow to the solar plexus of the *Moringa*, and the heaviest ones made passengers and crew suck in their breath as if the mighty ship had felt pain, while it leant with the punches and wallowed slowly forward with relentless determination. Eventually, after three days, the bad weather passed. The margin where the clouds ended was clearly defined, and it took about an hour from the time a thin gleam of sunlight appeared on the horizon until the blanket had rolled away, and the *Moringa* was bathed in sun. The ocean was quiet at last.

News of the attack on Leena had spread throughout the ship, and in the absence of facts, suspicion was rife as to who might be the rapist. Leena's critical condition when she was found had been due to a combination of concussion, hypothermia, and terror, which had sent her body into shock. If Gary and Frank had not found her, she would have died on the staircase. They were the heroes whose courage in carrying out their duties during the storm had led to Leena's discovery, just in time to save her, so they were above suspicion. This was Gary's one-time partner, poor man; so went the

284

reasoning. Leena, herself, could not help in the search for her attacker. She started to regain consciousness after a few hours of nursing care and proper sleep, and Gary went immediately to see her. Emily caught him at the bedside where he had slunk without her noticing, and he left immediately.

Following his visit, Leena was visibly agitated; Emily could not tell whether Gary was responsible or not. Leena told Emily she could not bring herself to leave the sickbay or even look at a man, any man, again, so the men were all told to stay away. When Emily questioned her, she could remember something about the meditation room and coming round briefly as Gary carried her to the medical room, but all facts in between were gone from her mind, she said.

Arnesh was greatly distressed. He had left the meditation room to take over his shift, and it had never occurred to him that Leena was in any danger. He realised, now, that the marijuana had affected his judgement, and he should never have left her without an escort. Anwar could remember very well Leena's sensuous legs. If he lived to be a hundred, the memory of Leena taking off her trousers to show him her legs would be the one he died with. He lived in an agony of uncertainty for many hours, wondering whether to tell Arnesh about the moment, but his courage failed him, and he decided to wait until Leena spoke about it. He even asked himself whether he could be the rapist and be suffering amnesia, but he knew that he could never have physically performed such a dreadful act, even in his most lecherous state. Gurpreet and Manik, who had been with him in the meditation room, were his alibis, as he was theirs; they had diplomatically forgotten the striptease. They all knew that Raja would sack them without hesitation, if they leaked news of his niece's behaviour.

Ernst Brage was struggling to control events. There was an uneasy three-man stand-off between him, Ramos, and Gary, none of them seeming to trust what the other two were doing, each of them trying to guess what the other two knew. Ernst was sure that Gary and Ramos would betray him to the Angels if Tyro were still alive by landfall, and yet his promise to Anna was paramount. She was not someone to play with. He much preferred that Tyro should live than risk losing her. Now to add to his problems, a man was missing, and a woman had been raped – and not just any man or any woman. They were a highly respected Harvard lawyer and the niece of an industrial magnate. Passengers are always trouble (How often he had told himself this?) and he cursed himself for the thousandth time for accepting the bribe that had first ensnared him and led him to this voyage. He could not keep a communication blackout for much longer; there could only be a matter of a day or two remaining to him, and he had to have some answers when the enquiries began.

"We'll let the search continue for two more hours, and then we'll support the rumour that he went overboard in the storm," Ernst instructed Ramos, as they stood together on the bridge.

He was looking towards the ocean and felt he was where he belonged. He was meant for ships and the ocean, not for handling people. It gave him hope that Jimmy had, indeed, gone overboard, whether accidentally or pushed, and so his death was just unfortunate. After all, Ramos had rescued the psychologist from the deck, so maybe the lawyer had followed her but been unlucky.

"Very well, Captain," Ramos replied.

Ernst noticed that he seemed agitated and wondered what he knew.

"Still keep the crew from away from everyone else. I don't want any other rumours starting," Ernst added.

"Captain, I was just thinking that I should just check the cargo," Ramos answered respectfully. "Neither of us has been down there since the storm, and we will need to be sure that all is in order for when it's unloaded."

Ernst was grateful for the reminder and said, "You already know the code, and you can take the key from my desk."

"Thank you," Ramos replied, not mentioning the key that Gary had passed to him only the previous evening, along with the news that Jimmy was inside the storeroom.

"Good. Well, go then," Ernst said. "Don't tell anyone; just go alone," he advised.

I had no intention of telling anyone, you poor fool. There's a dead body down there, was Ramos's mutinous thought, but he said nothing.

A short while later, Ernst granted a request from Gary for a meeting. Now that the storm had passed, and the *Moringa* was entering warmer oceans, Gary realised that any hope of murdering and disposing of Tyro was going to need more than one man, however determined. If Ernst were to change his mind, and join with him and Ramos, it would make everything possible, but without Ernst's support, he and Ramos could not succeed. Gary did not want to have to kill Ernst as well; that was a very dangerous step to contemplate. It would be hard to contrive and, even if successful, could well lead to a fight breaking out in the ship, with disastrous consequences for the shipment of the heroin. It was much better that Ernst should overcome his passion for Anna and return to the original plan.

They met in Ernst's cabin, and neither had time for small talk, though Gary tried an understanding approach. They were both in this together, he said. Neither of them liked it, but they had no options, and if they did as they were told, they would be well rewarded. Their instructions were to see the heroin safely delivered to Mombasa without arousing the suspicions of the expedition team, and to execute Tyro for disobedience and betrayal. They were well on their way, literally, in delivering the first task; they really needed to concentrate on the second. Ernst said very little through all this.

"Ernst, you know as well as I do that by the time we next speak to the Angels, Tyro has to be dead."

"That's my business," Ernst said quietly. "You needn't worry yourself about it."

"My life and my money are on the line, just as much as yours," Gary replied, still trying to seek common ground. "Ramos told me that you had countermanded the order. Why?"

"That is also my business," Ernst responded, interested that Ramos had seen fit to talk the matter over with Gary.

"It's our business, Ernst. You don't disobey instructions with this bunch," Gary pointed out uneasily. "You're doing this because of Anna, aren't you?"

At the mention of Anna's name, Ernst sat back, glowering at Gary.

"Gary, I don't care what you and Ramos think; Ramos is my first officer and will do as I command, and as long as you are on this ship, so will you. Now get out, and mind your own business."

Gary got up, all pretence at compromise over. "I warn you, Ernst, she's not worth it," he said, scathingly, as he left.

He consoled himself as he went down the steps that he had tried to make Ernst see sense. If he wouldn't talk about it, then anything that happened to Ernst now was his own fault. Gary wondered where Ramos was, as they had things to discuss.

In the bows of the *Moringa*, there was more consternation when Tyro appeared from his cabin, carrying his revolver in a military holster. He called his team together and included Alan and Roland in the summons, as they were in the hangar.

Tyro seemed in a friendly mood to begin with, as he arranged the meeting with Lothar, Solomon, Council, Henry, Jomo, and the two white men, Alan and Roland. Roland made an unfortunate remark about this being like apartheid, but Tyro seemed to let it pass. He told them all to sit down in a row in front of him, on some crates of empty gas cylinders.

"Now, my friends," Tyro began in a slow, melodious voice, "I knew the missing man, Jimmy Moule. He was a truly good man. He was brave. He was wise, and he was to be trusted. He was not the rapist, but he cannot be found, so he is dead, either in the ocean or on the ship." He looked down at his feet, hesitating a moment, and then he looked up.

For the first time, Alan saw Tyro as he had so often described himself in his confessions. His eyes were wide, satanic, and now his voice conveyed a threat.

"I am a bad man," he continued; this time, the words were spoken not with remorse but as a warning, a boast. "I am a bad man," he repeated slowly, and Alan felt a shock of fear as he realised that he was confronting a man more violent than anyone he had ever met.

Nobody dared to meet Tyro's gaze. He was dominant. As Alan desperately tried to remember his training in managing violent confrontation, Tyro took out his revolver and pointed it at Lothar.

"Tyro, please," Alan said, daring to speak, though he could only manage a hoarse whisper.

The barrel of the revolver swung his direction. Tyro put his finger to his lips to signal silence, and Alan bowed his head and put up his hands as if to catch the bullet. The barrel swung back to Lothar, who was sitting as still as stone.

Tyro clicked back the hammer on the revolver. His finger was firmly on the trigger. "Did you rape the Indian woman, Lothar?"

"No. I swear," Lothar said, hardly moving his lips.

"Did you kill the missing man?"

"No. Tyro, I swear."

"Do you mean to kill me?" Tyro demanded. He could see that Lothar was hiding something. "Tell me, or I shoot you now."

"No. No. My instructions were only to be ready to take command of the team if you died. It might be at any time. I was not to tell anyone or I would be next." Lothar fell to his knees, horrified that he had been surprised into giving so much away, but this attack had come without warning.

"Ah," Tyro said with satisfaction. "Now we get somewhere. Who gave you your instructions?"

"Ramos. But he was getting them from someone else," Lothar stammered.

"Who is your boss, Lothar, Ramos or me?"

"You are my boss, Tyro," Lothar said hoarsely.

"Louder, Lothar! Louder!"

Tyro bellowed his staccato instruction with such force that Lothar fell to his side, lying with his knees drawn up. He started to cry, unable to control his terror. He felt the gun barrel pressed to his temple. "You are my boss," he whimpered, sobbing piteously.

The gun barrel swung to Solomon, the senior mechanic. "Did you mess with the Indian woman?" Tyro asked calmly.

"No, boss, I was not well that night," Solomon replied. "I was in my bunk."

"Who gives you your instructions?" There was no sense of recognition in Tyro's voice.

"You do, boss, you do. I—"

"Quiet," Tyro ordered. Solomon stopped in mid-sentence. The gun barrel moved along the line to the three mechanics. "My brothers," Tyro said, his tone friendly again, but they watched him submissively, their eyes focused on the gun. "Are your dicks getting itchy?" Tyro teased them. "Could you not wait a few more weeks?"

They looked from one to another, then Council dared say, "It was not us, boss; we were all together."

"And what about the Sudanese woman you took in the War of Separation?" Tyro reminded him.

"That was war. She evened out the score. It was less than they were doing to our women," Council replied sullenly.

"I will shoot one of you," Tyro replied flatly.

"We didn't do it. None of us did it," Council pleaded, while Tyro eyed them.

"Peace, my brothers. I will not shoot you now, but if I find you did it"—his eyes opened wide again—"I will shoot one of you. Who is your boss, my brothers?"

"You are the boss, brother," they all replied, while Lothar picked himself up off the floor, realising that no bullet had not gone through him. Still shaking, he dared to sit back on the crate in a cringing pose.

Now Tyro's eyes turned to Roland. "You think apartheid is a joke?" he asked.

"No, Tyro," Roland said through dry lips.

Tyro swung the gun on Roland and took aim along the barrel. Roland felt the blood drain from his face.

"Nor do I," Tyro replied, unmoving. Then he smirked derisively and lowered the revolver.

Satisfied that his supremacy was absolute, Tyro put away his gun and waved Alan and Roland away with a flick of his hand. They no longer belonged. As they slipped away, they heard him start to interact with his team as if nothing had happened. Someone even laughed.

"Are they really his brothers?" Roland asked Alan in a low voice as they hurried away.

"Same father, different mothers," Alan muttered back. "But blood relatives all the same. Dear Lord, anybody wanting to kill Tyro now will need an army to get to him after that show of strength. We need to find David and Jeffrey."

While these things were going on, Lucy was singing to herself to counteract her anxiety at being alone, as she carried out the research that was one of the main objectives of the trip. Jeffrey appeared in the open door of the laboratory.

"Come in, boss," she said fondly. "What can I do for you?"

Jeffrey went in and sat beside her. "Look, you know I have the greatest respect for your father," he said, clearly trying to be diplomatic. "But Jimmy may be dead, and we may have to meet force with force, if you understand me, and, well—"

"My father's a bit of a softie, a pacifist, and you want me to keep him out of the way. Is that it?" Lucy said, finishing his sentence for him.

"I couldn't have put it better myself," Jeffrey acknowledged.

"Don't worry. I'll look after it," Lucy replied happily. "Coffee?"

"Yes, please, but later," he replied. "I've got a meeting with Arnesh in a few minutes. Anna and Maggie are working like sleuths to identify the rapist, and they want to go over the plans of the ship. I'm joining them. We're keeping it secret, so don't mention it if anyone asks where I am."

"See you later, then. Good luck," Lucy said, picking up her own mug of coffee and sipping from it temptingly, while looking at him over the rim.

"How are Stefan and Silvio these days?" he asked, not moving, and saw a bashful smile cross her lips.

She shrugged. "Where there's a will, there's a way," she replied coyly. He was still staring at her mug. She gave in with a sigh. "Oh, very well, but only one sip."

He avidly took the mug from her hands, took a big gulp, and then handed it back to her with a self-satisfied smile. "Pure telepathy," he said.

"Time for your meeting, Professor Harvey," Lucy replied, hating herself for finding him adorable.

When Jeffrey reached Arnesh's small office, Anna and Maggie were already there and the scale drawings of the *Moringa* were on the screen, as well as on A3 pages strewn on the table. The meeting quickly settled down again after his arrival, but Jeffrey could not absorb, initially, all that the plans revealed.

"How did you construct such a vessel?" he asked Arnesh in admiration.

"There were moments when we needed divine intervention," Arnesh replied as the others laughed. "There are so many parts of this magnificent ship that unless you had been involved in her building, you would not know them all, and even then, you might forget one or two." He gave an apologetic nod of his head at his last remark.

"Does that mean you've thought of something?" Anna asked, sensing an exciting possibility.

"This lift shaft, you see, here," he said, using the cursor to highlight the cargo lift.

"That goes from the main deck to the storage deck, doesn't it?" Jeffrey asked, seeking confirmation of his knowledge. "I've never used it."

"Why should you? It's a cargo lift. It has little use except when we are loading and unloading the ship," Arnesh replied.

"So?" Anna asked.

Arnesh continued, "Well, you see, it goes beyond the storage deck, right down to the lowest level of the ship, where we added some additional storage space that I did not mention earlier. The lift can only access that level with a key."

"What's down there?"

"There are passages for maintenance work and further storage. It's where the sacks of fertiliser have been placed for the duration of the voyage. To be honest, I had forgotten about it. Only my team have access to that level. I doubt that it's important, but it's a part of the ship we have not examined."

Maggie raised a quizzical eyebrow, and Jeffrey said, "Let's check it out. Can we use your key, Arnesh?"

"I did have one, but Mr Murdoch took it as head of operations. I was to ask for it, if needed." Arnesh shrugged. "It is easier to just use the stairs." He guided the cursor to point out the steps on the screen.

This was enough for Maggie. "That's just the sort of place Jimmy would have gone. I told you he was exploring that night. Where better to go exploring?"

"Then I'll use the stairs and go take a look," Jeffrey said, acknowledging the logic in Maggie's thoughts.

"I'm not letting you go down there on your own," Anna scoffed. "You'd get lost in those dark passages."

"And I'm coming too. Jimmy's down there, alive or dead, I'm sure of it," Maggie insisted.

"Once you are past the storage deck, there is no way out," Arnesh warned them. "You must carry on to the bottom or come back up. Actually, I will come with you. I know this ship. After all, I built her."

"As you keep reminding us," Jeffrey said with good humour. "Come on. Let's go."

Their walk to the staircase took them along the main corridor. "This is the last place I saw Jimmy," Maggie said wistfully. "It's the last place anyone saw him."

"It's also where Frank and Gary found Leena," Anna pointed out, and as they started to relive that night, the conviction grew that they would find Jimmy.

Jeffrey pointed out a darkened streak of blood on the steps as they descended. "Could be Leena's, could be Jimmy's," he muttered.

They came out on the storage deck, open plan, with wire cages where various items were stored. Behind them was the steel wall of the Grand Chamber, with its closed double doors in the middle. In front of them, the storage deck stretched all the way to the bows, a hundred and fifty metres away, though the far end was cordoned off as hangar space with wire mesh. They could see the helicopter.

Arnesh had opened a small doorway beside the lift shaft. "We walk through here and then find ourselves at the top of the stairs. After this, we must continue to the bottom. It is not well lit."

"Not the best place to come in a storm," Jeffrey muttered.

"Jimmy saw it as the perfect time to explore, when nobody else was around," Maggie said.

"Enough talk," Anna snapped, pushing to the front. "I will go first. If Jimmy did come this way, he didn't come back, so be careful. I suggest we go quietly and keep our eyes wide open. If I signal to go back, you go back at once, no argument." This was Anna the soldier speaking, and the others just nodded agreement.

They made their way quietly down the steps, the next three levels taking them past the giant water tanks, and then Anna came to a chain across the stairs from which dangled a sign stating 'No Admittance.' She undid one side of the chain and continued down, all of them being careful not to slip or miss their footing on the metal steps, lit only by dim wall lamps. At last, they reached a narrow corridor, and when they were all in it, Anna walked forward and cautiously opened the door at the end.

She spun round immediately and signalled silence, although nobody had begun to talk. One by one, they emerged into the wide, dark passage, reverberating to the engines of the ship, and saw what Anna had seen. A door was open, and there was light coming from within.

Anna ran silently forward to the edge of the doorway, looked in briefly, then dived into the entrance, gone from view. There was a man's shout of alarm and then his cry of pain. Jeffrey and Maggie burst in behind Anna, in time to see Ramos, trying to rise from a kneeling position, take the full force of a second kick in the ribs from Anna.

"Anna, stop before you kill him!" Jeffrey shouted.

Ramos was lying in agony, curled up and clutching his damaged left side, but for a few seconds, nobody gave him a second glance. Jimmy's body was lying sprawled on the floor, where Gary had left him.

Arnesh came and stood in the doorway. "This is what I feared," he said. Then he bent down and picked something up near the door frame. "What's this?" he asked. "It's not one of mine."

He held up a monkey wrench, and Maggie reached over and took it from his grasp. Then he disappeared, too shocked by the sight of the dead man to be able to enter the room.

Jeffrey, Maggie, and Anna turned their attention on Ramos. "Please; I had nothing to do with this," he pleaded. "I have only been here about two or three minutes. I haven't moved him."

"How did you get down here?" Jeffrey demanded.

"I took the lift. Captain gave me the key so I could come and check the cargo. I had no idea that I would find the missing man," Ramos lied softly, with painful, laboured intakes of breath.

"What was this wrench for?" Maggie asked.

"I don't know. I didn't even notice it. It's not mine," Ramos replied.

"Let's face it. That's probably the murder weapon." Anna took it, feeling its weight and tapping the head of it on her outstretched palm. "He's got a wound on the base of his skull." She gave a nonchalant nod towards the corpse. Once again, it became the centre of attention.

"Poor Jimmy," Jeffrey moaned as he turned and looked down at the corpse. "What am I going to tell Karen?" His question was to himself, and neither woman tried to answer it. "How could this happen? Why?"

"It's something to do with these sacks," Anna replied. "I'm sure of it." She still held the wrench as she walked farther into the storeroom, looking to either side.

"Why does fertiliser need a temperature-controlled environment?" Maggie asked, as she had done earlier. "It's cold in here."

"What fucking fertiliser is this, anyway?" Jeffrey queried angrily.

Anna bent down by the corpse and stood up again. "I think Jimmy was killed the night he disappeared. The cold has stopped him decomposing," she observed, unaware that her pragmatism over such a delicate issue made Jeffrey shiver more than the cold. Maggie noticed and gave Jeffrey a reassuring smile.

Just then, Arnesh reappeared in the doorway, clearly very agitated. "Please come," he begged. "I have just looked inside the lift. There's a pile of clothes, a woman's clothes."

Maggie was her professional self in an instant, reaching out and taking hold of Arnesh's hand. "It's all right to be upset, Arnesh, love; don't be frightened. Just sit down a moment, and I'll go and take a look."

"Anna, if you go with her, I'll look after Jimmy and our friend here," Jeffrey said, nodding towards Ramos. Anna was already on her way.

The two women approached the closed doors of the lift together. Maggie pressed the button, and the doors slid back. There was a small pile of clothes in one corner, with a shoe lying on its own on the floor, where Arnesh had picked it up and then dropped it in horror at what he had found.

Anna and Maggie stood looking into the lift without entering it, as if it were hallowed ground.

"This is where it happened, Maggs," Anna said quietly. "This is where she was raped."

They walked in. The doors closed as they stood looking round. There was blood on the floor from Leena's scalp wound and marks where she and the rapist had lain. Each woman squatted down to stroke over them, like a blind person seeing through her hands. Anna walked to the corner and picked up the clothes. She passed each of them to Maggie: tracksuit bottoms, knickers, socks and a shoe.

Maggie had already picked up the other shoe. "I honestly believe Ramos," she said gently. "He didn't do this. He was on duty on the bridge that night. He saw me in trouble on the deck and came to help me."

"Which doesn't leave a very long list to choose from, does it?" Anna reflected. "In fact, I can only think of one. We better collect Jeffrey." Anna had the faraway look in her eyes again.

Alarm bells started to ring in Maggie's brain. Anna was frightening her. She was clearly fighting mad; Maggie reached out to stop her opening the door.

Anna turned to her. "The person who killed Jimmy had access to this lift key and used it. The person who raped Leena felt safe in this lift. It's stupid to think that it was not the same person, on the same night."

"All right. I admit that," Maggie replied. "But let's do a bit more detective work before making any accusations. Let's see what we learn over the next few days. Don't let's kill anybody else just yet, hey?"

Anna gently broke free from Maggie's grasp. "Perhaps I agree with you," she said and pressed the button. Then she gave Maggie a kiss on the cheek. "You always look after me."

As the door slid back and they stepped out, they saw that Jeffrey was standing just outside the storeroom with both Arnesh and Ramos sitting beside him. The storeroom door was closed.

"Too cold in there," he explained. "I suppose they were Leena's clothes you found?"

"Yes, they were," Anna replied, saying nothing about the marks on the floor.

"Where's a policeman when you need one?" Jeffrey complained.

"A policeman would just get in the way," Anna replied in a brutally frank way. "On the *Moringa*, we can police ourselves." She looked down at Ramos. "You: What is in those sacks?"

"You don't want to know, believe me," Ramos answered. "For your own sakes, don't ask."

Anna looked ready to strike him, but Maggie said quickly, "No, Anna, he's hurt enough," and Anna relented. Maggie caught Ramos's eye. "One good turn deserves another," she said kindly, but he did not smile.

"This is one hell of a situation," Jeffrey muttered, knowing he needed to start directing events. "Anna, please, I know better than to order you to do anything, but I beg you not to go near Ernst or to contact him, just at the moment."

"If you will agree not to go near Leena without consulting with me," she retorted sharply.

He looked abashed, and she added, with less venom, "There are feminine issues men do not understand, and if a man blundered in, the results could be dreadful."

Jeffrey sighed. "Fair enough," he agreed, not wanting to add feminine issues to his list of problems. Then he sat down beside Ramos. "What's in those sacks, Ramos? Somebody killed my friend to stop him finding out, but they can't kill us all. Tell us."

Ramos leaned his head back against the wall in resignation. "It's heroin. You were never supposed to find out. You would have ended your journey and gone home, and the heroin would have been unloaded, and you would all have been safe." He looked up at Maggie. "I'm sorry," he said with a sad smile. "You're all dead, and the more people you tell, the more will die."

"We've got to get help," Maggie said. "We've got to. Who else knows about this heroin?"

"The captain, and a small number of the crew," Ramos replied, deliberately leaving Gary's name off the list. "To send a message for help, you'll need to get to the bridge and send the message from there."

"I thought there was an agreement that nobody would die," Jeffrey said with disdain to Anna.

It was a remark that Arnesh and Ramos did not understand, but Maggie did, and she wished Jeffrey had kept it to himself. Goading Anna in her present mood was not going to help. However, Anna did not show any anger at his remark.

"I came on this voyage to see your project succeed and to protect *you*, Jeffrey," she replied. "I'm doing my best every way I know how. I'm sorry that's not been good enough for you."

Ramos now intervened to say that if he did not contact the bridge soon, the captain would become suspicious and send some of the crew to look for him. Jeffrey was in a quandary as to who to trust. Anna pointed out that Tyro could be trusted and suggested that she should go to inform him that Jimmy had been found dead. Jeffrey agreed. She would just say that Jimmy had been found at the bottom of the steps, without mentioning the heroin or Ramos.

Maggie volunteered to go with her, "just to make sure," and she and Anna were taken up to the storage deck in the lift by Arnesh, who then brought it back down to pick up Ramos and Jeffrey.

Jeffrey was still confused about what to do with Ramos. He wished, on second thought, that he had kept the group together. He and Arnesh were alone with Ramos, who could turn nasty at any moment, and nobody would hear their shouts for help.

"You must see I can't let you go back to the bridge," he said to Ramos. "The captain must be in this up to his neck. Obviously, you are too. There's nothing to stop you and the crew from killing us, just like Jimmy. You've said as much yourself."

Ramos was feeling much better than a few minutes previously. He raised himself to his feet, still clutching his side, and said that as he was the first officer, he would give the orders. "You must trust me. I'm in as much danger as you. I believe the captain killed your friend, and therefore, he must have been the rapist too. If he finds out that I let you know all this, he will kill me when he kills you. This cargo is worth hundreds of millions of dollars. There's no room for mistakes."

"The *Moringa* is *my* ship," Jeffrey answered Ramos sharply. "It is a ship with a humanitarian aim; it is not a drug smugglers' cruise ship. It is my ship; this is my project, and you are my employee. That heroin is going over the side just as soon as I can arrange it."

This bluff made no impression on Ramos.

"You're not even supposed to be on board," Ramos retorted. "You have no power at all. Now, you have already assaulted me; are you going to abduct me as well?"

"No," Jeffrey said wisely. It was a very tangled situation, but he could see that kidnapping the first officer would certainly make matters worse. The person he most wanted to consult was lying dead in the next room. "Something about your story doesn't add up, Ramos. If Ernst knew that Jimmy was here, why were you surprised to find him? If Ernst didn't know, and you didn't know, then somebody else did. I have to trust to your common sense. I want a meeting with the captain at noon today. Arnesh, will you join us?"

Arnesh shook his head and put up his hands. "No. I'm a man of peace. I must do everything to protect my men. The less I'm involved, the safer it will be for everyone."

Jeffrey shrugged. "Well, I'll bring David Emmerson, Gary Murdoch, and Tyro Mukasa."

"Not Tyro," Ramos said. "It's too dangerous for him."

"Very well," Jeffrey conceded. "I'll ask Anna to stay away as well, but I may include Maggie. Do we have an agreement?"

"Yes," Ramos said, extending his hand to shake. "I'll say I met you in the corridor, and you asked for the meeting. None of us will mention what's happened here today."

Jeffrey accepted the handshake but wondered what it was worth.

The anger and confusion in Anna's mind as she went up in the lift made her shake and twitch restlessly, and she started walking towards the hangar the moment the lift door opened, with Maggie calling out after her to wait a moment. Anna stopped a second, impatient that Maggie was delaying her. She then continued on, expecting Maggie to keep up.

"Remember the story. Don't say anything else," Maggie managed to hiss, as their approach was noticed by Tyro and his team, who were going about their tasks. They were immediately on the alert.

"Tyro! Tyro!" Anna called out. "We've found something important."

By this time, she was at the hangar, and Tyro came through the door in the mesh to meet her, with Maggie following on, wondering what Anna was about to reveal. Tyro immediately led them to some crates to sit down, and the team gathered round, eager for news.

"We've just been doing a search of the ship and found this monkey wrench at the foot of the stairs by the lift. Do you know who it belongs to?" Anna produced the object from under her sweater. "Arnesh says it isn't his."

"Nobody's allowed to go down there. Absolutely not," Maggie intervened, as she realised that the bored team of young men were more than ready to charge down the steps that they had not known about before. She turned to Tyro for support.

"Nobody goes down those steps," Tyro said simply, and the team immediately quietened down. "Does anyone recognise this wrench?"

He looked round at his men, who were only just recovering from his previous bout of anger. Solomon remembered Roland being the last to use it, and it had been missing for a few days. Anna and Maggie stayed calm at this news and quickly established that Roland and Alan had returned to the hangar after the meeting, having forgotten the wrench. They had not gone back for it immediately, because the meeting had shocked them. Then the storm had come, and the wrench had been left where it was. This was the final piece of information needed for Anna to be sure that Gary was the prime suspect. Maggie and Jimmy had left Gary, alone, with the wrench in the room. The question remained whether he was acting alone or there had been a conspiracy.

She turned to Maggie, disregarding their onlookers, and said, "I think we need to speak to Gary."

To which Maggie replied, "So do I."

"Tyro, there's something else I must tell you in private," Anna said.

She took Tyro aside, and Maggie saw her whisper something that made Tyro nod his head. She had passed him the news of Jimmy. Then she returned to within hearing.

"Jeffrey, Ernst, and Gary are meeting in a couple of hours," Anna said. "Jeffrey doesn't think it's safe for you to be there, but I promise I'll keep you fully informed of anything I learn."

Tyro smiled at her. "I'm sure you will, Anna, when it seems right to do so."

"Look, I'll give you more details later," Anna promised him. "But I think Maggie and I had better go and join the others now. There are some things which have to be discussed before the meeting."

Maggie had noticed how much calmer Anna had become in his presence. Tyro and Anna understood each other. They were both hunters and, as such, made decisions and judgements instantly. The two women rose, took their leave, and walked briskly up the steps to join the long corridor towards the stern.

They had gone about a hundred metres when Anna clasped Maggie's arm and stopped.

"I've just remembered something," she said. "Maggs, you go on. I'll catch you up."

"Don't fuck with me unless we're in bed," Maggie retorted sharply. "You're up to something. Perhaps you wouldn't mind telling me, your best friend, what it is."

Realising Maggie loved her too much to be deceived, Anna shrugged, ready for Maggie to blast her. "I saw Tyro was wearing a revolver. I'm going to ask him if I can borrow it for this meeting."

Maggie looked at her with fondness. "Well, why didn't you say so back there?"

Anna grimaced. "I think it may take some flattery to make him agree. I am more likely to succeed if he and I are alone. Don't you mind that I want it? I thought you would tell me I was mad."

"Not on this occasion. I think, to be honest, that it's a great idea. If we need to make a hasty exit, we'll be glad to have you covering our backs. Good luck. You'll find me with Leena. I think I'll jog. It's good exercise." With that, she started to run along the corridor, and Anna returned to Tyro and asked to speak to him alone.

Tyro laughed out loud at her courage in asking him for his revolver; nobody else would have dared. However, he declined her request. "My need is greater than yours," he told her firmly, as if that was the end of the matter.

Anna laid her cards on the table. "Jimmy is dead. I know who killed him, and he also raped Leena. Don't ask me how I know, but I do. I need to protect myself when we meet, and I may need to protect others too."

"Ah, but you won't tell me who it is, so that I can kill him for you? No. I suppose not," Tyro mused. "What about Jeffrey or Maggie? Can't they protect you?"

"They aren't warriors, Tyro," Anna explained simply, and Tyro understood very well what she meant. "They would always try to reason."

Tyro nodded his head and gave a sigh, then he walked over to a steel chest and unlocked it. "I can fight a lion, but not a lioness, not when she looks like you. Come here."

Perplexed, Anna obeyed. Tyro raised the lid, reached into the chest, and picked out a box; then he closed the lid. "Soon, you will have made me reveal all my secrets," he said, in a way that showed her how much she was trusted. He handed her the box. "Here is a Beretta and a full clip. Don't ask how I got it; I, too, have secrets, lioness. Do you think you can use it if you have to?"

Anna carried the box over to the table, took out the pistol, tested the mechanism, loaded it, and put it in her pocket. "That's better," she said. "I'm not anxious anymore. Now I'm happy."

Tyro saw how steady her gaze was. "Use it well, lioness. Good hunting," he said and then added, "Such men are ruthless. Don't hesitate when the time comes."

She bowed to him in acknowledgement of his understanding and then left.

When Ramos returned to the bridge, he was thinking desperately hard. He explained his sore chest by telling Ernst that he had collided with the edge of the door of the storeroom, but otherwise, all was well. The cargo was in good shape, and there had been no storm damage. That was all. He wanted to talk to Gary urgently but could not think of a reasonable excuse to leave the bridge again.

Gary heard that Jimmy had been found from Jeffrey, who came to the laboratory and told him and David. Gary kept cool and reasoned silently and quickly. Jeffrey had seen the body. The door of the storeroom must have been open. Ramos must have been down and left it open. Jeffrey had not made any mention of heroin – he would have seen the sacks, but not known what they contained – or of Leena's clothes, either. Ramos would have already taken them, of course. This was how Gary reasoned it to himself. Now, there was to be a meeting with Ernst. Far from being the disaster it had seemed a moment ago, the chance discovery of Jimmy's body had played right into his hands. He and Ramos could implicate Ernst, make him the main suspect, then, if he could kill Ernst, Ernst would die as the culprit, and he would be in the clear; at least, nothing could be proved against him. Furthermore, he and Ramos would have control of the ship. He made his excuses and went to his cabin, saying he would meet Jeffrey and David on the bridge.

About twenty minutes before the meeting was due to begin, Anna appeared at the door of the bridge. Ernst was glad of this brief diversion from his problems and opened the door personally to talk to her.

"Can we go to your cabin quickly? I really want to talk to you," she murmured so only he could hear.

"Anna, I have an important meeting soon; come back later," Ernst said in a normal voice, though the hot sun, and the warm breeze, and the sight and sound of his lover made him desperate to strip her.

Anna could read him well. "You're tense, my love; I can tell. Give me twenty minutes, and I will calm you. You will feel so much better," she cajoled him quietly.

"I have so many problems," he whispered back, and she shrugged and smiled as if to say, "That's why I'm here." He lost his will to resist and, without attracting the attention of the crew on the bridge, nodded towards the door of his cabin. A few seconds later, he followed her. The moment she heard him lock the door, she spun round, whipped out the Beretta, and pointed it straight at his chest.

"You promised there'd be no killing. You promised," she hissed, slipping into their native tongue, in which the words poured out more easily.

Ernst cursed his own lack of guile to be caught by such an old trick. "I trusted you," he said. "I thought I had one person on the boat I could trust. How stupid of me."

Her eyes were now hard, and he knew he was in real danger.

"I trusted *you!*" she flung back at him. "You promised there would be no killing. You betrayed me."

Ernst stayed calm. "I have kept my promise to you," he said. "There hasn't been any killing. Your friend, Jimmy Moule, is missing. If he has died, he must have met with an accident."

"Jimmy is dead, you liar," Anna said coldly. "Who did you tell to do it?"

Anna noticed that Ernst was clearly taken aback by the news. He was not an actor and could not have feigned such surprise. "I know nothing of this. I am truly saddened. I'm sorry," he said. "Where did you find him?"

Anna hesitated a moment and then challenged him. "Don't you know? He was at the base of the stairs, by the lift. Actually, he was in a storeroom, and Ramos was there, bent over his body."

At this, Ernst held his head in his hands, overwhelmed by the threats and crisis that were coming out of nowhere and sweeping over him.

Anna took all this in but was unrelenting. "You forced me to have sex with you to save a man's life. Wasn't I enough? Did Leena have to be sacrificed as well? Is that how your crew functions? Wasn't she enough, either?"

There was such anger in Anna's voice that Ernst believed that she was working herself into a state where she might really pull the trigger. He bowed his head, defenceless. "Anna, you are more than enough for me. I never deceived you. Truly, I love you," he pleaded, standing before her, rough-shaven, strong, yet full of childlike sincerity.

"What do you mean, you love me? You had sex with me."

She made it sound as if the two things were incompatible, and she saw him try to suppress a small smile. In that instant, she knew he had not betrayed her. She knew exactly what had just passed through his mind, and the memory made her want to smile too, and she realised how distorted her thinking had become; subconsciously, sex was only manipulation and extortion. She clicked the safety catch off and then back on again as a token of frustration that he should find the moment funny.

"In my world, people who love each other do have sex," he said, daring to look up.

Anna was looking at him unsmiling, but the ferocity was gone. "Next time, don't smile when I'm about to shoot you. I might do it," she warned, putting away the gun.

"Then don't remind me about what you're like in bed," he replied with equal gravity.

His arms shot out, and he grabbed her arms, and though she could have broken his grip and his neck, she allowed herself to be pulled towards him and hugged against his chest.

"Huh," he said, triumphantly. "You see, you have made the mistake I made. You have trusted me, and now I will crush you." He growled with all the savagery of a St Bernard puppy having a tug-of-war.

At that moment, there was the sound of voices; a heated exchange was going on at the door of the bridge. "Crush me later, dearest; you must go," Anna whispered hurriedly.

"Stay here," he ordered. "I don't want Jeffrey knowing you've been here."

There was a knock on the door, and Otto's urgent voice called in English, "Captain, you must come to the bridge at once. There's been an invasion."

Just before leaving, Ernst turned to Anna and said gently, in English: "Anna, the death, the rape: I had nothing to do with them."

"I know that now; beware of Gary," she replied hastily, then he was gone, and seconds later, she heard his angry voice barking out commands: "Silence! At once! Step back!"

Ernst was back on the bridge and had in front of him Ramos, Danny, and Otto, plus Gary, Jeffrey, David, and Maggie. "Except for my crew, none of you has any right to be on the bridge. We shall hold the meeting downstairs. Get out at once."

"We've already held a meeting, Ernst," Gary answered back with menace. "You've got some questions to answer, and Ramos may be in charge when you've answered them."

Ramos realised this was the turn of the final card. Gary had staked their bets; now for the play. He stayed still, but his shifty eyes told Ernst a tale of conspiracy. Ernst quickly made a move towards a wall cabinet.

"Stop! Turn around," Gary shouted at him, and once again, Ernst heard the click of a safety catch on a gun. He did as he was told and saw the big American pointing a pistol at him. "I know you've got a gun in that cabinet, so you just stay right there, Ernst."

"I didn't know you had a gun, Gary,'" David said angrily. "I don't think you're helping the situation. It's tense enough as it is."

"Shut up, David," Gary retorted, not taking his eyes off Ernst. "I know how to handle men like Ernst Brage here."

"So do I," David came back at him. "And it's not behaving like a gunslinger in a cowboy western."

Gary disregarded him. "A man's been killed on your ship, Ernst, and a woman raped – a woman pregnant with my child. Do you think you can get away with that? Do you?" The shock of this revelation shut everyone else up. Gary made use of the moment. "It all points to you, Ernst. You had the key, you had the access, and none of us knew where you were the night of the storm. You knew about the heroin. You killed to keep your greedy secret, and you raped my lovely Leena along the way."

Jeffrey and David were standing like a pair of garden gnomes with fixed expressions of astonishment on their faces. Maggie, standing at the back, looked round desperately and found to her profound relief that Anna was standing in the doorway, unnoticed by anyone else. She was motionless, her eyes focused on Gary.

"You've disobeyed orders, Ernst," he growled.

Ernst recognised the Clerkenwell Angels' death sentence. Only Ramos would recognise it as well. To everyone else, they were further ambiguity, but to Ernst, they spoke of his failure to kill Tyro. His head flicked instinctively to seek help from Ramos, but Ramos turned his head away. Danny and Otto were too far away and easy targets themselves. Ernst's frightened gaze returned to Gary.

Anna broke cover. She called out from the doorway in a firm voice, "Gary, how would you know there's heroin on the ship?"

Her voice transformed Gary in an instant from predator to prey, as he realised he had made a mistake. He glanced quickly over at her and turned back to Ernst. There was still time to shoot.

Her voice struck him again: "And how did you know Leena was pregnant?"

Gary thought of Leena telling him in the corridor and moaning it out in the lift.

"She hasn't told any man except the man who raped her." Gary felt every eye in the room piercing into his soul. "Put down your gun, Gary."

He lowered his arm and then realised if he hesitated any longer, the moment was lost. He had to shoot now and find answers later. He raised his gun again, almost at once, and even Ernst thought he had fired. But it was Anna who held a smoking gun. She had positioned herself well, and the bullet passed, obliquely, into Gary's spleen. Now Gary fired, as he twisted in shock and agony, but unsteady and off-balance; his gun kicked up, and the unaimed bullet passed over Ernst's head. Gary stood, his knees starting to buckle, his left arm clutching his side, as everyone around him crouched in fear, and he swung his gun, searching for Anna. But she had moved, and her second shot passed into his heart, threw him to the ground, and removed him as a threat forever.

It took a few seconds of stunned silence for the survivors to realise that the shooting was over. Then life returned to the bridge.

"Anna, what have you done?" Jeffrey's muted words were full of distress. "That's Gary. That's Gary. That was murder."

"That's what happens with guns," David said in a shaking voice. "Somebody uses one, and somebody else gets hurt."

"He's dead, David," Jeffrey retorted. "He's not hurt; he's dead."

Maggie, meanwhile, had shown presence of mind by picking up the dead man's gun, lying loose on the floor.

David just bumbled on, "I assume it was an accident. Anna, you—"

"She shot him twice, David. This was murder," Jeffrey said; he and David were both in a state of shock, burbling at each other, rather than knowing what they were doing.

"Anna shot in self-defence," Ernst spoke firmly, as if the matter were settled. "She put herself between me and him. She saved us both." Then

306

he spoke to the two crewmen: "Otto, Danny, you will need to clear up the mess. Clear the bridge now."

"Please, not yet," Jeffrey pleaded. "We need the Reverend Alan."

Ernst refined his instructions. "Very well; one of you, phone the hangar and find the priest. Get him here. Otto, get a mop and disinfectant. Say nothing to anyone except that the captain is safe and master of his bridge. Let nobody doubt that."

It was Maggie who phoned the hangar and then the service centre to notify Arnesh. Anna walked over to Jeffrey, who was kneeling beside Gary, and placed a comforting hand on his shoulder, but he shook her away, saying, "No, don't touch me. I don't know you at the moment."

She shrugged as if his rebuttal were of no consequence and went away to stand as a lonely figure, looking out on the deck below.

Ernst had time to think over Gary's last words: "You've disobeyed orders." He realised that Gary, under the pretext of a crime of passion, was about to carry out a gang-related execution, and Ramos was going to let it happen. He and Gary would have had control of the ship, but with Gary dead and Ernst alive, Ramos's position was now precarious.

Ernst chose his moment, came up to him, and took him to the far end of the balcony for a private conversation. "That didn't go according to plan, did it, Ramos?" he said quietly to his first officer.

"I don't know what you mean, sir," Ramos said nervously.

"Oh, I think you do," Ernst replied. "You and Gary, together – kill me, take over the ship, kill Tyro, blame all errors on me, and wait for instructions from your masters. Very neat, but it has gone wrong, Ramos. You backed the wrong side."

Ramos drew himself to attention. He felt very close to death and sensibly decided on total subservience as his best hope of survival. "Sir, nothing could be further from the truth. I have full confidence in you as my captain. I will obey only your orders. You can have full confidence in me, sir. I swear," he said. *Please don't shoot me* were the words he left unsaid, but they echoed in his mind.

Ernst stayed silent, letting Ramos fry in his own oil of sizzling anxiety, so that the moment would be seared in his mind.

"I don't doubt you, Ramos," he said at last. "Because if you make one bad move from now on, you will follow Gary. Are you clear on that? Ah, it seems Jeffrey has recovered enough to seek my attention."

Ernst walked dismissively away from Ramos, who sent a fervent prayer of contrition to Almighty God and recovered his composure before resuming his duties.

Jeffrey was looking ashen and haunted, and his voice was quivering. "You won't get away with this, Ernst, I warn you," he said. "There'll be a full enquiry, I'll see to that, and you'll be held fully responsible. You're the captain. Now I require to see you in private."

"Let's wait for the priest, Jeffrey. I don't think anyone is in an emotional state to think clearly at the moment," Ernst replied patiently. "Ah, here he is."

Anna stayed where she was, as she watched Alan kneel beside Gary, and Jeffrey stand by Alan. Maggie moved sombrely over to greet Arnesh and then took Jeffrey's arm to comfort him and to feel comforted in turn, as they bowed their heads, listened to Alan, and intoned the Lord's Prayer with him.

Arnesh stood with them, his own prayers winging silently out with theirs, and he joined in the final "Amen."

Only a few seconds later, the telephone rang. Ernst picked it up. "Bridge," he said curtly.

"This is Tyro. I need to know who has been shot. I was only told Alan has been summoned to the bridge because someone has been shot dead. I want to know who has been shot."

"It was Gary," Ernst replied quietly. "Anna shot him to defend me. She fired just before he did. It was enough. His shot missed us both. That is all you need to know for now."

"Thank you, Captain, thank you," Tyro said, his voice full of pleasure. "The lioness protected you. The rapist is dead, and you are alive. I congratulate you."

"She saved you, as well. If you want it spelt out for you, then ask me later," Ernst muttered into the receiver. He replaced it and then turned to Jeffrey. "What?" he asked.

Jeffrey said he wanted Jimmy Moule's body brought up from the storeroom. Ernst sent Ramos and Danny with strict instructions to bring the body up to the main deck and not to let anyone else down to the maintenance deck. There was no point in secrecy over Jimmy's death now, but there was plenty of reason for security regarding the heroin. The body, covered in a blanket, was taken on a cargo trolley to the sickbay.

It was not like being next to Gary. Jimmy had been dead for several days, and even in the chill temperature of the storeroom, changes had occurred, and there was a smell coming from his body. It was unpleasant, like the body odour of a living person is unpleasant. It was not repellent, but it was the smell of death, not of anything living. It helped his friends to realise that Jimmy was gone and that what they were looking at needed quick and reverent disposal. They had shuffled into the sickbay, but they remained standing round the entrance. Inside. Alan, alone, said a prayer beside the body, to which they said a hasty "Amen," and they all filed out again, quietly relieved to be away from the odour.

The subsequent meeting between Ernst, Ramos, Jeffrey, Arnesh, Maggie, and Anna went on for three hours, at the end of which pragmatism took precedence over justice. There was little doubt that an enquiry would condemn Gary as a rapist and murderer, which was not how they wished him to be remembered. It would bring publicity to Leena, who would be disgraced and disowned by her family. It would receive sensational worldwide publicity. It could easily bring academic condemnation and financial ruin to Jeffrey and David, for their unauthorised genetic modification and growth of the moringas. Everyone on board would be implicated as a smuggler of heroin and marijuana, and there was more.

So it was decided that the heroin should remain on board, the authorities should not be notified, and the remains of Jimmy and Gary should be consigned to the ocean, no photographs or records kept of their injuries. Jimmy had died of a fall, Gary of a heart attack. The communication blackout would remain. It was not the outcome anticipated at the start of the meeting, when a shocked David had been ready to notify Buckingham Palace, the White House, and the Royal Navy.

The bodies of Jimmy and Gary were committed to the deep just before sunset. Tyro went to the trouble of making the airship ready, with both bodies inside, while a funeral service was held beside it, attended by all on board who could be spared. Tyro was the pilot. As soon as the service ended, he started the engines, and Alan went with him, with Solomon and Gurpreet to assist.

It was the funeral of two men who had shared a common dream for over a decade and lived to bring that dream to reality. That was how it would be remembered. Jeffrey took photographs to send to Karen when he notified her of Jimmy's accidental death. She would find accidental death easy to accept. She had expected it over many expeditions. Tyro took the airship in a flypast over the *Moringa* and then brought it to hover just ahead of the ship, off its starboard side, and cut the engines, floating silently in the air. As the ship drew level to it, all on board could see first one and then the other weighted white sheet, released from the trapdoor in the floor of the gondola, and lost to view beneath the gentle ocean swell.

Chapter 16

BOMBSHELL

During the following week, as they sailed across the Indian Ocean, the climate became more tropical, and there was anxiety throughout the *Moringa* as everyone went over what had happened and what was likely to come. Leena still refused to come out of her cabin, and the rift between the Warlocks and the ship's crew grew more hostile. Those who knew about the heroin kept their secret, out of fear for what would happen if the news spread, but they could not trust any of the crew. They met frequently, every day, to bolster each other's morale and to confirm that they were all still alive. Ernst had the entrance to the staircase padlocked and guarded; he allowed Jeffrey to contact Karen to give her the tragic news that Jimmy had lost his footing in a storm and fallen to his death down a stairway. Anna suggested a pre-emptive strike against the crew, but the chance of success was small, and many innocent lives, even among the crew, might be lost.

The Grand Chamber was a haven from all the violence and distress of the past few days, and Frank became accustomed to visitors sitting silently or strolling down the aisles while he was tending the troughs. Sitting quietly beside the small trees, Frank recognised, in himself, how deeply traumatised he had been; he felt relief at the resurgence of his normal ebullience, as the numbing horror receded. Lucy was sitting with him. She had been very worried about him and, with David's assistance, had persuaded Frank to spend a few hours each day absorbed in the small tasks that she and David had found for him to do, while his mind went through the process of healing. It could not be hurried. However often he told himself to man-up and get a grip, he could not shake off the sense of despair that made him want to hide in a dark place. It scared him that this depression that he despised was not under his control. He sensed its passing with great relief. It had lasted eight days. It could have, as easily, lasted eighty. Today, at last, Lucy felt that her father's long-standing worker and friend was back to his old self, as she suggested that it was time for lunch.

"Lunch? It's a bit early for that, isn't it?" he asked in surprise.

"It's one thirty, Frank."

"Is it really? I just hadn't noticed," he replied contentedly.

"Well, I'm cheating a bit," Lucy replied with a giggle. "Still, it's almost one thirty, and that's our three hours for the morning."

Frank looked around at the terraced trees, slowly moving on their conveyors, so each had its share of the sun. "This is what our voyage is all about," he said. "It's not about guns. It's about pure water, the moringas, saving lives in Africa." He paused between each of these assertions, as his visions expanded. "I'm not giving up. I'll not put up with any more nonsense, either. What do you say, Lucy, eh?"

To be honest, Lucy was uneasy to hear Frank talking with such zeal. However, she hid her misgivings and gave him a hug, saying, "Oh, Frank, it's such a relief to have you safe and well. Do you think we should try to encourage Leena to come in here with us?"

"Why not?" Frank replied with enthusiasm. "But I'm told she's off all men at the moment."

"You don't count, Frank," Lucy said. "She wouldn't mind being with you. You saved her life. Gary had left her to die, then you came along."

Frank felt a glow of pride. "I did play a part, didn't I?" he reflected. "I know it's a bit improper to say this, but wouldn't you think she'd have recognised Gary as her attacker?"

"Not if he knocked her out."

Frank was not entirely convinced. "I think she may have known and tried to protect him. I'm not sure I believe all that amnesia business. I think folks generally know a lot more than they let on, but I don't suppose we'll ever find out, and nor should we. That's for her to live with."

Maggie and Anna were on the upper stern deck, partially shielded from the sun's direct light by the shadow of the funnel, and enjoying the warm breeze as they lounged against the rail, looking down on the wake of the *Moringa*.

"I can't help thinking," Maggie muttered lazily, "that three of us set off that night after the meeting: Leena, Jimmy, and me. Leena and Jimmy stayed below deck, and I actually went up on deck, putting myself in the greatest danger of all of us, yet it was probably the safest thing I could have done. I wonder what my fate would have been if I'd stayed below deck that night. What do you think, love? Isn't it funny how fate works?"

When she got no response, she turned to look at Anna and saw that she was in a world of her own, staring into space, her bottom accentuated by the angle at which she was leaning on the rail. So Maggie gently massaged Anna's bottom.

After several seconds, Anna said quietly, "That's my arse."

"I know," Maggie said, continuing her massage.

"Why are you stroking it?"

"You were away with the fairies, sweet, so I thought I'd please myself," Maggie said, without a hint of contrition.

"Well, I'm back," Anna replied emphatically. She straightened her posture and turned a critical gaze on her ex-lover.

Maggie removed her hand with a sigh. "I was just saying—" she began again.

Anna interrupted her: "I know. I heard you. I have no idea what might have happened to you. I'm sorry that I wasn't there to protect you."

"I was there to protect Leena. Fat lot of good that was. How do you think I feel?" Maggie said with a shrug at the vagaries of life. "Anyway, I survived, and by a miracle, so did she, and the baby."

Anna nodded, as Maggie's remark focused her mind on the baby. "It's time Jeffrey knew about Leena being pregnant," she muttered.

"He does know. So does everyone else by now, I should think," Maggie retorted.

"You know what I mean, Maggs. It's time he knew that he's the father."

"It opens up a whole new can of worms for you, sweetheart," Maggie said, placing her arm sympathetically round Anna's shoulder. "Are you sure you're ready for that?"

In response, Anna freed herself from Maggie's arm and sympathy. Instead, she clasped Maggie's hand. "I think I've lost him, Maggs," she said, sounding resigned but strong. "I think I've lost him, but I really don't care. I did what had to be done. Ernst understands it. Tyro understands it. If Jeffrey doesn't understand it after all that I have done for him, then I really don't care. I know Leena still says she isn't ready to tell Jeffrey, but he needs to man up."

Pleased with herself for using an English idiom, she tossed her head, released Maggie's hand, and started to adopt some karate poses while Maggie watched, hardly able to keep up with her antics.

Maggie gave a little laugh. "This time last year, he was your hero," she said. "Poor old Jeffrey."

"Well, perhaps if he starts behaving like one, he'll get me back again," Anna replied without stopping her exercises.

"He's just lost two friends, love. Remember? You shot one of them in from of him."

"I shot a murderer who was about to kill the captain. Jeffrey would have let it happen. He did nothing. I have no respect for that." Anna stopped her antics to catch her breath, hands on hips.

Maggie could see that she would make no headway pleading Jeffrey's case for him and then thought that she didn't want to, anyway. Just maybe, she could persuade Anna to come back to her. She needed Anna to lighten up, though, and not be quite so unforgiving.

"Come on, then," she said brightly. "First we'll go and see Leena, then we'll find Jeffrey and make him man-up, as you put it, and by this evening, with luck, you'll be tucked up, back in my arms."

Anna laughed at Maggie's loving optimism and tolerated the arm that had snaked around her.

Jeffrey was about as far away as he could be. He was visiting Tyro in his kingdom, as the hangar had become. Tyro had not left this part of the ship since the shooting, but in it, he was all powerful. Jeffrey had ceased to be amazed at the size of the *Moringa* and just how many parts of the ship there were. Here, in the hangar, which looked so huge with the flight deck raised as a roof above them, was the Hind and Roland's three drones, and off it, the workshop and storerooms. During the storm some damage had occurred where the gas canisters were stored, and this was what Tyro had been examining when Jeffrey had arrived. They greeted each other warmly, though Tyro looked daunting, wearing battle fatigues over his big frame, with the heavy revolver, in its holster, at his left hip. Jeffrey sauntered round, in a distracted way, while Tyro completed his inspection.

"Are those gas tanks for the airship?" Jeffrey asked, pointing to two large metal cylinders. Tyro looked round, stared at him a moment for making such an obvious enquiry, and then said, yes, they were. This was a gas retrieval system, so they did not have to waste the gas they removed from the airship. Jeffrey still seemed interested in gas cylinders, so Tyro pointed out that most of the smaller gas canisters visible were reserve cylinders to top up the main cylinders. Then Jeffrey asked about the cost of helium, at which point Tyro decided that they had wasted time enough.

"Jeffrey, my friend," Tyro remarked, "I'm sure you didn't come here to talk to me about gas tanks. What do you need from me?"

Jeffrey darted his glance here and there to check that they were alone. "Tyro, mate," he replied, "I'm so bloody frightened. I'm trying to tell myself I'm coping, but last night I could hardly sleep for fear, and when I did sleep, it was to have nightmares. I was in this small room, sitting with Jimmy and Gary, and we were laughing about something, and I looked round and there was Arthur sitting in the corner, grey and silent. Then Anna started coming in and going out of the room, and the laughter stopped. I looked at them, and Jimmy and Gary were sitting grey and silent, and Anna said it was time to go. I got up and went to the door, and when I looked round, she was sitting in my chair, also grey and silent. The door was starting to close, and I was trying to keep it open and to get back into the room to rescue them, but I wasn't succeeding. I was panicking. Then I woke up, and my heart was pumping, and I was sweating, and I looked for Anna, but she wasn't there. The woman I fell in love with has gone, and the woman I'm left with, I don't care whether she's with Ernst or not. For a few seconds, I felt trapped between dreams and reality, and I just have to face it, that I'm fucking scared."

"Why tell me?" Tyro asked indifferently. "You should tell this to your English friends."

"I can't," Jeffrey moaned. "They belong to a life I don't feel part of anymore."

"But you are part of it," Tyro replied dispassionately. "That is where you belong. The life in Britain is very good. It gives you security, wealth, and freedom from fear and hunger, yes, indeed. It protects you from the hardships that most of the world endures. Do you think you are alone in seeing a friend shot in front of you? Do you think anyone would stop to listen to you if you were in the Congo, or the north of my country, or Sudan, or Iraq? For most of humanity, Jeffrey, each day is a fight for survival against armies, or gangs, or nature." Tyro left no room for compromise.

Jeffrey sat a moment in silence and then asked, "Did you give Anna the gun?"

"Yes."

"Knowing she was going to kill Gary?"

"She said she was going to protect the man she loved. I thought she meant you, but now I wonder about who she loves, your lioness. In any case, I told her not to hesitate when the time came."

Jeffrey shook his head in disbelief. "The two of you have some sort of understanding, don't you?" he asked pointedly. "Right from the night you first met, some sort of animal instinct has seemed to bind you. You can read each other's minds, and killing doesn't offend you."

"You are not in Cambridge now, Jeffrey," Tyro reminded him, with patronizing disdain. "You thought you'd bring your world with you on this ship; well, you didn't. This is Africa. This ship is tribes. This ship is civil war. This ship is not law and order and democracy. This ship is where power takes all. Anna did right. She hunted; she killed. She didn't let sentiment cloud her mind, like you do. Gary was a threat to us all. He didn't let sentiment stop him when he raped Leena and killed Jimmy. He wanted power. Didn't you see: When he needed your support, he was your friend, and when you were in his way, he was your enemy? He had you arrested for stopping him crashing the airship; it took Anna to free you. She told me, when she shot him, he had his gun pointed at the captain's chest, and only by luck – and no hesitation – she shot first. David tried to say something, but you did nothing. Even when he stood with his gun at the captain's chest, you still saw a friend. He could play with you. He couldn't play with Anna. You know what I think? You are not man enough for her. That is what I think." This final opinion was delivered like a judge's verdict.

Jeffrey stayed where he was sitting, staring at the ground with a perplexed look on his face, and scratched the nape of his neck. "You know, Tyro, mate," he confessed, "as I was walking up here, well, almost running actually, I was wondering who I needed to talk to: you or Alan."

"You should have chosen Alan," Tyro muttered, his vehemence gone. He, too, sat down on a nearby crate, remorseful about his last words to his enemy-turned-friend.

"No, I chose right. You are just who I needed to speak to. How could I forget Africa?" Jeffrey looked Tyro in the eye. "I'm back, Tyro. I'm Jeff. I'm the man who saw Arthur die in his arms and stole Arthur's work to keep power. Are you still going to shoot me for that?"

"You are laughing at me, Jeff," Tyro said grimly, then his face broke into a smile. "That is good. That is very good. We are friends again." They chuckled together, as men often do in place of speaking, to indicate a common bond. Then Tyro added, "It is good, because I think you will have to kill someone or be dead yourself, before this voyage is over."

Jeffrey saw this as a joke and continued to smirk. "With what weapon? A fire extinguisher?"

"Would you like a hydrogen bomb?" Tyro replied and was gratified to see a look of surprise flash across Jeffrey's face.

"Where am I going to find a hydrogen bomb?" It was preposterous, but Jeffrey couldn't help asking, as with Tyro, anything seemed possible.

Tyro pointed to the crate that Jeffrey was sitting on: "There," he said.

Jeffrey glanced down, urgently seeking some means of identifying the bomb-like cylinders he was sitting on. "Tyro, you bastard," he laughed. "They're just helium canisters. I'll get you back for that."

He was perplexed that Tyro did not seem to be sharing the joke. "Helium, hydrogen, what's the difference, Jeff?" he asked amicably, but with a straight face.

"Hydrogen blows up, helium doesn't," Jeffrey replied. "That's an important one, to start with."

"Yes, which is why we fill airships with helium instead of hydrogen," Tyro said as if talking to a schoolchild. "But as you said, helium is expensive, and the world supply of helium is running out. So if person X buys me helium for my airship, and I sell it to person Y, I get rich."

"But your airship doesn't fly, because you haven't any gas," Jeffrey added, perplexed by Tyro yet again.

"So I buy hydrogen from person A, because it is cheaper than helium, and I still have a profit, and my airship flies. Such things happen all the time in Africa, Jeff. Among the poor, there are brilliant engineers and chemists and doctors, and they work with what they have got, to do some amazing things. With the right connections, I found that the same things happen in India too."

The full implication of Tyro's words took a few seconds for Jeffrey to appreciate, and then he gasped; this whole end of the *Moringa* was, in effect, a massive, hydrogen-filled bomb. "Am I sitting here surrounded by hydrogen? Is that it?" he asked, astounded.

"You see those three cylinders?" Tyro said, indicating them by a nod of his head. "They have helium in them, so that if anyone wishes to test the gases, they can have those to test. The rest is hydrogen, except those, which are empty," Here, he pointed to a pile of loose cylinders that had become free during the storm. "I have been wondering what to do with them, and this idea came to my mind. They looked like bombs to me. We should make bombs."

"Why would we ever need a bomb?" Jeffrey asked, as if the idea were unreal.

"Because there is heroin on this ship," Tyro answered, unperturbed by Jeffrey's scorn. "Men kill each other for small packets of heroin, Jeff, my friend. What do you think they are going to do for large sacks of it? We will need to protect ourselves by every means we can."

"We're not involved, Tyro. Whatever they want to do with that heroin, we just let them do it. The Clerkenwell Angels have invested heavily in our project. My concern is not losing their backing. I'm a pragmatist, which means I accept things as they are. I can't change the world. Whoever is behind the heroin doesn't matter to us, as long as they get it off the ship without harming us or implicating us."

"Too late," Tyro said. "You are already implicated. We all are."

Jeffrey sprang up angrily but kept his voice low so as not to attract the attention of Tyro's team. "No, we are not. This is a research vessel, on a humanitarian mission. The heroin is nothing to do with us, and we are powerless to interfere with it, anyway. We just pretend we know nothing about it and let whoever's responsible take it when we get to Mombasa. We safeguard our mission; that's what we're funded to do."

Tyro shook his head sadly and replied, "Jeff, delivering the heroin – that *is your mission*, as far as the Angels are concerned. You just haven't known it. The voyage of the *Moringa* has been the cover for moving their hoard from India to Africa, and from there, it will disappear across the world. We've been used, Jeff, just like they use everyone. Gary knew about it. The captain and the first officer know about it. Lothar was told to be ready to take over the flight team, so maybe he knew. It makes you wonder who else knows without us knowing, does it not?"

Jeffrey stared, speechless, as Tyro continued, in sympathetic tones, "I spoke to Arnesh, and he told me what he had seen when you found Jimmy. Don't blame him. I had guessed. He will still keep the secret from his men, for their sake. He thinks there were a hundred sacks of heroin, or even more. That must be at least one hundred million dollars of heroin. It was then that I understood why you have had so much support from the Angels. The *Moringa* isn't a ship, Jeff; it's a stable, and we are the mules."

"Good ones at that," Jeffrey muttered. "We even fooled the Royal Navy." He reflected on what Tyro had said. "Do you think Arnesh knew about the shipment? After all, he managed the reconstruction of the ship. He must have known about the hidden storeroom."

Tyro nonchalantly tapped his fist against one of the empty cylinders as he replied, "I asked Arnesh, who told him to build the storeroom. Such things cost money, like an airship costs money. He said it was all ordered and controlled by the financial director, specially appointed for the project. He did wonder why it was there, but he did not ask questions. The financial director authorised the marijuana room at the same time, as a bribe. They both remained secret. It's how the Angels work. But it was always planned that the *Moringa* would be used to smuggle heroin."

Jeffrey realised the truth in Tyro's words. "I see it now. The Angels intended to get rid of me and put Gary in my place. You were their means of doing it. Then, you messed up their plans, so they wanted rid of both of us. It all adds up now. I don't see why Gary wanted to kill Ernst, though, unless he and Ramos had hatched a plan to cut him out of the deal and take control themselves."

Lothar appeared and cautiously approached the two men. "I'm sorry to disturb you, boss, but the lioness and the giraffe are here and would like to see the professor when he is free."

"Tell them to join us," Tyro commanded.

Lothar respectfully withdrew and disappeared round the corner.

Jeffrey raised his eyebrows. "Giraffe?" he murmured to Tyro.

"That is what they call Maggie," Tyro replied solemnly. "You are the professor."

Jeffrey was so delighted that he lost the thread of the conversation. "What do they call David?" he asked eagerly, but Tyro seemed not to hear, possibly because Anna and Maggie came into view.

"We've been looking all over the ship for you," Maggie called cheerfully, as they approached.

"Just a moment, Maggie," Jeffrey replied, as a late thought crossed his mind. "Tyro, are you telling me that they've got at Raja, as well?"

"I do not think that. He is too rich and too honourable. The project was in the hands of the new financial director."

"So Raja wouldn't have known?" Jeffrey then answered his own question. "No, of course not. All that our consortium was interested in was the Grand Chamber, the laboratory, and the water tanks. We went into great detail about those, but we just gave general specifications about the rest. We left it to Raja, and he delegated it to Arnesh, and Arnesh negotiated with the financial director. With his influence, the Angels could get all the specifications they needed. Hell, I've been so naïve." He became aware of Anna shifting impatiently, looking directly at him, arms folded. "Anna, what is it now?" he asked irritably.

"Jeffrey, you're about to become a father," Anna replied in a stern voice.

She heard Maggie's sharp intake of breath, followed by her whispering, "That was brutal."

"We needed his attention," Anna replied, not caring that they could all hear her.

Jeffrey clutched a hand to his head and said, "Anna, please, Tyro and I are discussing a matter of life and death. You and I both know you can't be having a baby, so whatever you're on about, it'll just have to wait."

"I'm not the mother," Anna replied grimly.

Jeffrey looked up, trying to fathom what he was being told. "Maggie?" he queried in disbelief.

"I beg your pardon?" Maggie retorted fiercely.

Jeffrey waved his arms at her as if trying to rub out his mistake. "No, no, Maggie, please forgive me. I'm not thinking clearly. I'm struggling here. I'm going into overload with bombs and babies."

"Jeffrey, you're babbling," Anna said mercilessly. "Who is the pregnant woman on board this ship?"

"Leena. Leena? Leena!" Jeffrey exclaimed. "But she's having Gary's baby."

"That was Gary's mistake—" Anna started harshly, but she was stopped mid-sentence by Maggie clamping her hand over Anna's mouth and saying, soothingly, "Jeffrey, love, Leena's been pregnant since the August bank holiday, when you went round to nurse her while Anna and I were away."

Tyro sat back, his arms crossed, and a broad smile spread across his face. Jeffrey and Maggie shared a look, as the full effect of her message penetrated Jeffrey's thoughts, and Anna struggled free of Maggie's grasp.

Anna started again, in gentler tones, eyes downcast, rubbing her neck in a way that showed the stress that she was feeling: "Leena was frightened Gary would kill you if he found out, so she swore us to secrecy. She never told any man she was pregnant, except her rapist, in the hope that he'd stop."

"That was how you knew it was Gary," Jeffrey mused. "Anna, sweet, I'm so sorry I doubted you. I'm still frightened by what you did, but I'm starting to understand."

Anna shrugged dismissively, still not looking at him.

Maggie explained, "Leena's still resistant to telling you, but Anna and I decided that now that Gary's dead, you really ought to know. I'm sorry to drop this bombshell on you like this."

Jeffrey noticed how skilful Maggie was in pitching her words. He could think with her. His brain clarified the stunning effect of Anna's first impact. Anna came uppermost to his thoughts: "Anna, I'm so sorry. I thought this was all behind us," he said, his sincerity evident in his voice.

"Don't worry," Anna replied forgivingly. "I've known about it since our ladies-only safari in Africa." She smiled with affection. "If I was going to shoot you, I'd have done it long ago."

Maggie added, "A hippo took your bullet, right between the eyes." This remark was too much for Tyro, who roared with laughter at the news, annoying Maggie, who had been trying to add drama to the occasion.

Not even Anna could remain impassive, with Tyro holding his sides with laughter. She shook her head in amused exasperation, went over to where Jeffrey sat, and rubbed his shoulder. She suggested that he should go and see Leena. He asked her to come with him, but she declined. As she said, she did not feel like watching her fiancé discussing pregnancy with his lover.

The words were not spoken unkindly, but they stung like a whiplash, and Tyro, recovering from his mirth, rallied to Jeffrey's support:

"Maggie, you should go with Jeffrey to see Leena, but Jeffrey, you must be quick and come back. Anna, you stay with me."

Jeffrey shook his head. "Leena has to wait," he said. "Anna, you've tossed me a bombshell, so here's one back for you. We've got about one hundred million dollars' worth of heroin on board, and Tyro thinks that we are in imminent danger from Ernst and his crew now that we know. It's decision time for you, honey. Whose side are you on?"

Anna sat down beside him and leaned forward, her forearms resting on her thighs. "Tyro's right," she said. "There's a fortune in heroin on the ship. The traffickers will want it, but Ernst is not the threat."

"Why do you say that?" Tyro asked.

"Ernst had orders to kill you but didn't carry them out. Now he feels in as much danger as the rest of us."

"Why? What stopped him?" Tyro asked, unaware of the debt he owed Anna for his survival.

But Jeffrey and Maggie both knew and felt sympathy for Anna as she avoided the question.

"He's not the bad man you take him to be," Anna replied simply.

Jeffrey butted in: "Tyro, you owe Anna a lot, but we won't go into details, now or ever. I'm not so sure I share her views about Ernst, though.'

"Well, I always listen to Anna, unlike you, Jeffrey," Tyro said, and Jeffrey felt sandwiched between the two of them, in mind and body. "If Anna's right, then that explains why Ramos and Gary tried to take control. Ernst told me, just after the shooting, that I should hide from Ramos."

"Oh, I think you're being terribly unfair to Ramos," Maggie objected, still finding it hard to believe anything bad about her saviour on the night of the storm.

So with Jeffrey and Tyro suspicious of both Ernst and Ramos, Anna defending Ernst, and Maggie defending Ramos, they had a futile discussion about likely friends and foes among the crew. Judging by events since the shooting, Ernst and Ramos were acting as a team again, but Anna was adamant about Ernst.

After everyone had given their opinions, there was silence.

Jeffrey shrugged and said, "I've run out of ideas. But we all agree that with that much money at stake, something's going to happen."

Tyro stood up and brushed his hands on his fatigues: "Forget the crew," he said. "For the sake of a hundred million dollars, I would wait until the *Moringa* was a hundred miles from shore, and I would send in a helicopter, with six men, armed with AK-47s. They shoot everyone. I then send another boat. It takes the heroin. Blow a hole in the *Moringa* and sink it. That is what I would do."

"I agree," Anna said immediately, also rising to her feet. "Their plan was total secrecy. It worked well until the shooting. Now all of us know. Ernst still believes he can control the situation. I don't think he can. I agree that a surprise attack is the most likely route the traffickers will take. Those crew members siding with Ramos will wait until it starts. They won't do anything on their own. Ernst is too strong."

Maggie commented morosely, "Well then, we've had it. We can't very well fight them off with that old revolver of Tyro's and Anna's pistol."

"What happened to the pistol Gary used? I saw you pick it up," Jeffrey reminded her.

"She gave it to Ernst," Anna interjected, giving Maggie a dig in the ribs. Maggie shrugged apologetically.

"Enough," Jeffrey said, suddenly revitalised. "I'm not giving in to anybody. This voyage has been twenty years in the making. It's been my dream for twenty years, as it has for David and all the other members of the consortium. It's Arthur's legacy, Tyro. It cost Jimmy's life, and Gary's life, and what we achieved on Fortune has never been done before. Tyro's worst-case scenario is that we all die and the *Moringa* ends up at the bottom of the ocean. My best-case scenario is that we sail into Mombasa, fit and well, and complete the project. If we can't fight, then we have to negotiate, pure and simple. We need a negotiating position."

"What have we got that they'd want?" Maggie asked.

"Their heroin, Maggs, their heroin. If we concentrate on getting control of the lift, then we have their heroin. If they want it back, they have to negotiate." Jeffrey's excitement was growing as he realised he had hit on a way out.

"Supposing it's not worth the bother to them," Maggie said, acting as devil's advocate, testing Jeffrey's idea. "Supposing they just blow us up, and the heroin."

"Not this amount of heroin," Jeffrey said, on reflection. "It may actually be worth much more than a hundred million. This is their big move. They've been planning this just as surely as we've been planning the project. In fact, Maggs, you've just identified our negotiating position: Armageddon. If anyone tries to gain access to the heroin without our permission, we blow up the ship."

This complete turnaround in tactics took a few seconds for the others to comprehend, but at least it offered some hope.

Anna was intrigued at the idea. Gaining control of the lift was an achievable objective, but what about the threat to blow up the ship?

"Have we the means to do that?" she asked.

Jeffrey turned to Tyro and asked, "Well, have we?"

"I think so," he said, nodding encouragingly. "I will ask Roland for his advice. A bomb. That is good."

"Well, it's a start," Jeffrey replied. "It's not exactly ideal, but if we get that set up, we're not totally defenceless. We'll get Arnesh and Anwar involved. They're bound to have ideas."

Maggie was not so optimistic: "Personally, I'd like to know what to expect," she commented. "As things stand, I'm facing death from my enemies or death from my friends. With a bit more information, I might be able to advise on a rather better negotiating strategy. Has anyone any ideas about getting information?"

Everyone went silent. Maggie felt appalled that she had accidentally pointed to the elephant in the room: Their best source of information from Ernst would be via Anna at the cost of further stress to her relationship with Jeffrey. Anna cast a look of resignation at Maggie and then addressed

Tyro: "In case you haven't guessed, Ernst has been giving me things – concessions – in return for personal favours."

Tyro smiled kindly at her. "I understand," he said. "I had already guessed, lioness." Then he added enigmatically, "Perhaps I understand the reality of what is taking place even better than you do."

"Anna, darling, I didn't mean what I just said," Maggie interjected. "Ernst is just using you, love. If you can't trust yourself to see that, then you shouldn't have anything to do with him."

"Maggie's right," Jeffrey added. "I don't want you seeing him again. We'll find some other way." But his words sounded hollow.

Anna was looking at Tyro. She hardly registered what Jeffrey had said. Tyro was holding her gaze. Then he gave her the nod she was looking for.

She turned to Jeffrey: "Time for action," she said. "Jeffrey, I'm so sorry I've lost you. I'm so sorry. That's what I really came to say. Good luck with Leena." Then she left.

"Time for action," Tyro said, echoing her words. "I'm going to find Roland. Somewhere." He, too, walked out, leaving Maggie and Jeffrey alone.

"Time for you to see Leena, I guess," Maggie said, sliding her arm under his. "It needn't take long. I'll be with you. Everyone else can wait."

They walked back along the main deck, in the warmth of the sun, feeling the breeze and sharing the impression that they could just fly away from their troubles. They peered down through the open roof of the Grand Chamber, and the sight fortified Jeffrey's resolve: "I'm ready to fight for this, Maggie, I really am, and to protect you," he said.

"That's very sweet of you, Jeffrey," Maggie replied, nudging him playfully, "but I think, for both of us, the best chance of survival lies in stopping a fight before it begins."

The door to the midships stairway opened, and Arnesh and Anwar appeared, followed by five of their colleagues. They were laughing and talking loudly among themselves. The sight was cheering in itself, and Jeffrey called across to them: "Arnesh, what's going on?"

"We are about to practice our slip-catching. Why don't you join us, Jeffrey?

Jeffrey was very tempted by this burst of normality into his world of surrealist threat but declined: "No thanks, Arnesh. I've got something I must do."

"That's why India always beats England at cricket," Arnesh called back. "We practice, you don't."

Batting off this jibe with a friendly wave, Jeffrey returned to his task and made his way to the stern with Maggie, while the group behind him started to throw their ball to each other, shouting loudly. He did not see Anwar walk up to Arnesh. "What did he say?" Anwar asked in their shared Punjabi.

"He said he had something to do," Arnesh replied.

"What could be so important that he hasn't got time to throw a ball with us?"

"I'll have to find out and let you know. People keep passing us by, Anwar, without stopping to talk. There's something big going on. We must increase our defences."

"Later," Anwar said. "Now, let's get back to the important things in life – like slip-catching."

With that, he made a sudden dash and leapt to intercept the ball to a cheer from the others, and then, in one smooth movement, directed it straight and fast to Arnesh, who had intercepted the move and caught the ball neatly, to another cheer. It was a satisfying catch. Arnesh felt he had his life under control, smiled, and tossed the ball high in the air, to catch it again.

Leena had moved into Jimmy's cabin, which was only a door away from Maggie but allowed her the seclusion and privacy she badly needed after her assault.

Maggie knocked on the door, calling out at the same time, "Leena, it's me: Maggie. Open the door. I've brought someone to see you."

She and Jeffrey heard signs of life, and, eventually, Leena opened the door slowly, peeping from behind it. "Oh, it's you," she said to Jeffrey.

She seemed sleepy but not upset to see him. They all stood, looking at each other for a moment, as if none of them really knew why they were there.

Maggie broke the silence: "Leena, love, I've told Jeffrey that he's the father. Anna and I did so together. If you're going to be angry, be angry with me, not him."

"I'm not angry. Why should I be angry?" Leena looked shyly at Jeffrey and held out her hand to him. "We need to talk," she said.

Jeffrey sidled into the room, and Maggie drew back, graciously, knowing that she was not required. "You look after her, Jeffrey Harvey," she muttered sternly.

Leena closed the door. She was wearing a tee-shirt and shorts, in which she had been sleeping until a few moments ago. Jeffrey felt awkward and uncomfortable in her presence, in contrast to her natural charm. He could see that she was more relaxed than he was.

"When did you find out?" she asked, going to the mirror and starting to comb her hair.

"About half an hour ago."

"And how do you feel, now that you know?" She moved to the basin and sprinkled some water on her face.

"I need to hear the news from you," he replied, still standing beside the door. "If you tell it to me, then I'll believe it."

She walked up to him, dabbing her face with a towel. "Dearest Jeffrey, you are the father of the baby inside me. There is absolutely no doubt about it." She had come within hugging distance. "And if this news makes you joyful enough to put your arms around me and give me a kiss, I would be so happy."

"I didn't think you'd want any man to touch you," he replied.

"You are not any man. You are the father of my child. I have only ever loved two men in my life, and the other one is dead. Who else is there to caress me?"

Jeffrey stayed where he was. He did not reach out. "Leena, you have an effect on me I can't control," he said. "If I kiss you on the lips and caress you through that tee-shirt, the next thing is I'll be kissing you on the neck and lifting off the shirt. I'll be no better than Gary."

"Perhaps I don't want you to control yourself. You are so gentle, Jeffrey. Don't compare yourself to Gary. He was always rough. He didn't know any other way. It was exciting, but it was always rough. The rape was just an extension of who he was."

"Be honest: Have you known it was he who raped you all along?"

"Don't ask me to recall what I've mercifully forgotten," she replied, sidestepping his question. "Right now, I want you to take me in your arms.

I don't mind what happens. I know you'll be gentle. I want to feel your love for me and baby." Her hair was brushing against his chin as she spoke; she was standing, ready for his embrace.

"I can't," Jeffrey said, this time with firmness in his voice. "I want you to have our baby more than anything, and I'll do all that I can to support you, but I can't give up on Anna. Don't ask me to."

Leena did not fall to pieces, as he had feared she might. She shrugged and turned away, out of reach. And when she turned again to face him, she was unemotional; her arms were crossed: "I'm going to have the baby in England. It's my right as a British citizen. She – or he – will grow up British, with all the advantages of the British links with India and with Europe."

"Yes, we can see to that between us," Jeffrey said encouragingly.

"The baby will be adopted at birth. It will not know you or me," Leena continued, softly and defiantly.

Jeffrey took a moment to register what he had just heard. "You can't mean that. We've got to think this through," he protested, light-heartedly, thinking that she was cross with him for not hugging her.

Her reply changed all that: "I've had six months to think this through. If I'm not your wife, then I shall return to India, as planned, without the child. Nobody – not even dear Uncle Raja – will ever know that I have had a baby. Nobody in India is to know. I will accept whichever husband my parents have chosen for me, and we shall be happy."

"But I'll still be in Britain," he said, perplexed that she seemed to have overlooked the fact.

"My baby is to grow up in a secure, loving family home. You cannot offer that, Jeffrey. You can't offer security or a family home. You are an adventurer. You are beautiful, but you live dangerously. You are not a suitable parent."

"I'm not going to argue with you, Leena," Jeffrey said gently. "You have been through a horrible time; you're still going through it in a way, and life must seem full of harsh reality. Do you think you are having a girl or a boy?"

Leena warmed to his question. She smiled, uncrossed her arms, and placed her hands on her bump: "Give me your hand, Jeffrey. Come on, I'm not going to seduce you."

He cautiously extended a hand, which she took and placed on her abdomen.

"There! Did you feel that movement? And there! There was another one. Did you feel how smooth they are? I've not had any hard kicks. I'm sure it's a little girl. I've already named her: Ariona."

Jeffrey could not take his hand away, knowing that this was the closest he might ever get to feel the movements of his child. Anna would never bear him a child, a fact which had been of no consequence to him until this moment. Now, as he felt Ariona beneath his hand, her life became more important to him than his own. He moved the hand gently, without any awareness that he was stroking Leena's skin. Leena did not draw back or hurry him.

"Thank you," he said at last, taking his hand away and kissing Leena on the cheek.

She noticed how close to tears he was and stored the memory away. She gave a sigh of satisfaction and would have continued the conversation, but he started speaking before she could do so.

"There's a possibility that we're in grave danger, all of us." He hesitated but then told her. "There's a heroin shipment on board. Some drug traffickers hid it on the ship without us knowing. We only found it when we were looking for Jimmy – me, Arnesh, Maggie, and Anna. Its discovery puts us all in danger. We've told Tyro, and we're putting together a plan of action, but I don't know how much time we have."

Instead of scaring her, this news excited Leena: "Is there anything I can do?" she asked. "I'm slow on my feet, but I haven't lost my mind."

Even as she spoke, she felt her spirits start to break free from a dark, turgid sludge. She was going to get better now.

"I'd like you to save yourself: you and Ariona," Jeffrey replied. "We need to get you off the ship. It'll take courage," he added, to remove any insinuation of cowardice.

"How?" she asked.

"We're not in range of land by helicopter yet, but we could be by airship. I'm going to ask Tyro to take you up at the first sign of trouble and stay out of range of gunfire. If, God forbid, any shooting starts, he can make landfall somewhere. If the traffickers just take the drugs and leave, then he can fly you back to the ship."

"Do you think he'll agree?" Leena asked with obvious doubt.

"For anyone else, no, he wouldn't. But for you, with an unborn child, I think he will, especially if I get Alan's help. Look, Leena, I've got to go. There's much to do. You stay here, and I'll be back — or one of the others will let you know what's happening."

In response, Leena stretched her right hand to lay it gently on his chest, feeling his heartbeat. "I've been on my own long enough," she told him. "It's time I was back. You go ahead. I'll follow you." She gave him a playful kiss on the cheek, and he lingered a second. "Go on, off with you," she said with a flirtatious smile. "That's all you're getting."

Anna acquiesced to her own desires and Ernst's entreaties, in the window of opportunity that chance afforded her, and now struggled to find a satisfying position, semi-naked and ungainly as she and Ernst were. He, naked to his ankles, entrapped by his trousers and pants; she, her trousers and knickers discarded, with one sock on and one sock off, her shirt undone, and her bra uncomfortably turned up above her breasts, would have done much better to take an extra minute to undress properly, but ludicrous haste was part of the magic of the moment, and they stifled laughs and shuffled against each other until they felt they were ready, in a position they could never have consciously contrived.

Her elbows were propped up by pillows and the edge of the bed, her knees almost fully flexed. His hands gripped her buttocks, raised them and slotted her onto him. Her shoulders aching, she wrapped her legs round him for support, and they shared his thrusting and lunging between them, looking into each other's eyes until the last, uncontrollable moments. Having floated with desire, they sank with leaden relief, their joints stabbing them with pain as they struggled messily to adopt some semblance of dignity. He passed her a small towel from a shelf, and she dabbed away the moisture round her groin.

"Love-juice," he said as he watched her.

She gave a short, derisive smirk. "Love? I don't think you really love me," she said, still breathing heavily, finishing with the towel and pulling straight the legs of her discarded trousers so she could put them on. "You think I'm a tart to be fucked and killed, don't you?"

330

"Why do you say such things? Why do you hate yourself so much?" he asked, sitting beside her and pulling up his pants.

"I'm engaged to Jeffrey. In five years, I haven't had any other man. Now, I can't stop myself wanting you. What does that make me?"

"A free woman. It's better that you find out now than later."

"Find out what, that we're good in bed together? But when the time comes, Ernst, aren't you going to shoot me? Or will it be one of your crew members who does it for you?"

He stayed silent, caught off guard by the question. She noticed his confusion and chose to twist it her way.

"I am going to be killed, aren't I? It's true, isn't it? That has to happen now that I know about the heroin."

"Stop this nonsense," Ernst protested, clearly troubled by the direction of the conversation, after which he said nothing more until he had finished dressing. Then, it was if he had made up his mind about something. He took her hand and kissed it. "Anna, I love you. If you stay with me, nobody will harm you, I promise."

"I started giving you my body on the promise that *nobody* would die," Anna replied sadly. "Now you can only promise my safety alone, and tomorrow, probably not that, either. I'll just be a tart all over again, waiting to be disposed of."

Ernst could not understand this reference to her sexuality. "Making love to me doesn't make you a tart, Anna," he said, perplexed. "I loved you before you saved my life. I love you a thousand times more, now. You're free to give your love wherever you wish."

Anna stopped dressing and thought of those critical moments when Gary's gun was aimed at Ernst's chest. "I suppose I did save your life," she mused. "But I almost shot you myself about two minutes beforehand."

"I never felt in real danger from you," he lied. She looked at him and raised her eyebrows. He backed down. "All right, maybe a little. I felt a little frightened," he admitted grudgingly, and they both laughed as she rested her head on his beefy shoulder.

"I don't want to die, Ernst. Please don't kill me," she entreated him, feeling his arm wrap around her shoulder.

"I won't kill you, and nor will any of my crew," he declared defiantly, but his tone hinted that he had left something unsaid.

331

"Who, then? Who is coming to do it?" she coaxed him.

He stayed silent for several seconds, during which she held her breath, wondering whether she had picked her moment well or not.

"The cartel behind this drug racket is ruthless," Ernst said at last. "They are making their move into the international heroin market, and their gangs have already killed to make space for them." Anna kissed the hand on her shoulder but stayed silent, encouraging him to continue. "They had this ship designed to smuggle heroin on a massive scale, without any of you knowing, or me. I was given my instructions when I took command. They didn't like it when their instructions to block communications were disobeyed and the navy turned up. That young fool Stefan put us all at risk."

"Nothing was found – nothing of importance." Anna said, perplexed that the brief naval inspection had been seen as a problem.

"No, but disobedience is the biggest sin possible to the cartel. It undermined their confidence in me and in the whole deception. It made them fear that the *Moringa* was a marked ship. After that, I received orders to rendezvous with another ship and transfer all the heroin before we reach territorial waters. That's a bad sign. Gary said just before you shot him that I had disobeyed orders. He didn't say whose orders. He didn't need to. It means I've lost the confidence of the cartel."

"So what happens to us?"

"That's what I don't know. Ramos and Gary were planning to take over the ship. With Gary gone, Ramos has not the guts or the support to try on his own. I hand-picked the crew, except Ramos. He sees my love for you as a risk to the whole operation." Then Ernst hesitated and added gently, "Too bad."

He turned her face to his and gave her lips a very exciting kiss, which aroused her in spite of herself. He detected it and smiled at his achievement.

"Ernst, you gorilla," she chided him good-naturedly. "We're talking life and death here, but all you are thinking about is sex."

"I'm thinking about protecting the woman I love. When that other ship arrives, we all need to be on guard," he replied gruffly. "I need to regain the cartel's confidence, and I think I can do it." He stopped abruptly. "Uh, how foolish of me," he joked. "I'm forgetting our circumstances. No doubt, you will now rush off to the arms of that foolish professor of yours and tell him all the things I have said."

"He needs my protection as much as you do," she affirmed strongly, without any pretence of denial. "You've just confirmed what they'd guessed. Why don't you side with us, and we can summon help?"

He shook his head. "Myself and some of the crew have been promised a fortune if we deliver. I'm not giving up yet, nor are they."

Anna deftly released herself from his grasp, gave his face a light slap, and moved to the door, while he stared at her in surprise.

"Don't give up on me either," she said. "Whatever is about to happen, if you do protect me, you're welcome to come calling when it's over – assuming you're still alive, of course." She gave him a tantalising pout of the lips and was gone.

David did not accept that anything was really wrong aboard the *Moringa*. He was always in the Grand Chamber, from early morning to late in the evening, with occasional short breaks to the cafeteria or to the main deck, but he was never prepared to talk to anyone except Lucy and Frank. Visitors to the Grand Chamber had to speak in low voices, if at all, and they were not allowed to mention anything negative, which might upset the trees.

Jeffrey was exasperated that David would not accept the situation. He needed David's involvement and found it hard to accept Maggie's professional advice that David was a pacifist and had to be respected for it. Despite Maggie's reservations, he had come to reason with David but found he was making no progress.

"But David, you've got to appreciate that our project is not the driving force for this voyage. It is just a brilliant cover. I should have asked myself why the Clerkenwell Angels would invest in us if nobody else would."

"I remember we asked ourselves that at the time, and we put it down to the string-pulling by the family of that Swiss doctor friend of yours," David replied, feeling cornered and uncomfortable. Jeffrey had seemed so reasonable five minutes previously, but now David wished he would go.

"How naïve can I be?" Jeffrey moaned.

"Well, as long as you blame yourself, not me," David retorted. "I kept asking for details of our financing, and you just kept saying it was fine – whatever we needed. There was just one occasion, quite late on, when you admitted to me that we were in the hands of some shady characters, but you still expected me to trust you. 'Everything's fine,' you said."

"It was," Jeffrey said, sounding aggrieved as he tried to justify himself. "They just kept financing whatever we needed. They handled everything except for the pocket money, which Gary was in charge of and promptly squandered."

"He trebled it, according to him," David replied unhelpfully. He was clearly in no mood to be sympathetic.

"Once – one night. How much did he lose on other occasions? Even if he didn't squander it, he stole it all right. He embezzled it. He was a crook in league with crooks and corrupted by crooks. They don't give a damn about the project or the trees. They want their heroin delivered, and they don't want us. We're no longer a disguise; we're a threat."

"I disagree entirely," David objected. "The case for investing in us was damn good. They may be crooks, but they are brilliant with it. This one shipload of cargo has given them a short-term return, namely the heroin, and a long-term return, namely, the moringas. I think they saw us as a good investment, and they were right to do so. The commercial return on the trees could be massive once their potential is realised. They're not going to destroy us just because they have the heroin. There may be some tough negotiating ahead, but they want both."

Jeffrey let his frustration cloud his judgement. "David, you've been talking to the trees too long. You just don't realise what's going on behind these walls," he said, then cursed himself for mocking David's pacifist doctrine; it was too late to recant.

David erupted, "Is that right? Well, do you know what I think? I think you've lost the plot. That's what I think. You should have stuck with what you know, instead of flailing around in a world of drugs and murder, where you don't belong. Come back to our world, the world of science and sanity. If we deliver our dream, nobody's going to harm us."

Jeffrey nodded and took a few moments to think about what to say next. "You're right, David," he admitted. "This place represents all that's good about what we've done. It would be great if we could just wall ourselves off from the bad guys and let them massacre each other. What's it to us? Why should we care about Arnesh and his team? We can leave them outside the wall."

"I didn't say that," David muttered, wincing at the implications of his outburst.

"Not in so many words, no, but that's what it amounts to. Let's not worry about anyone else. The really nuisance thing is that good and bad exist side by side. If we let the bad guys blow up the bad bit of the ship, the good bit of the ship is going to sink with it. It's not going to carry on sailing to Mombasa. And that's why I'm mixing it with all those nasty guys, so that, with luck, you can get home to your comfortable country estate."

Lucy had been watching from a gantry below and came running up the stairs as she heard Jeffrey's voice rise in annoyance. Jeffrey turned at her approach; when he saw the anger and concern in her face, he realised he was making matters worse for himself.

Lucy brushed past him, her eyes focused on David. "Are you all right, Daddy?" she asked.

David had his face turned away, looking at the trees. "It doesn't matter," he said as she put his arms around him.

Lucy, clearly distressed, looked at Jeffrey and mouthed very clearly, "Please, just go." He shrugged and walked out, not sure whether he was more annoyed with himself or David. He realised that he should have had Lucy there to start with. He had to stop seeing her as a girl and start treating her as a woman.

Lucy's familiar touch restored David in barely a minute, and once reassured, he felt profound thanks for her presence and remorse over Jeffrey. He declined her offer to go to the laboratory; instead, they stayed on the gantry, holding hands, while David unburdened himself about his concerns for his great friend.

"He's getting all caught up in this heroin business, when he ought to leave it alone. We should just let the traffickers take it. We can't stop them. Once they're gone, it'll be as if the ship was never involved – except for the loss of Gary and Jimmy, of course."

"It's not quite that simple," Lucy replied gently, trying to sound as nonchalant as possible. "Stefan's a bit worried too."

David's interest was aroused: "Stefan? I thought that Silvio told you to stay away from both of them," he said.

"Oh, I don't see Silvio any more, the wimp, but Stefan and I weren't going to be kept apart. Ramos and two other crewmen beat him up for sending my message. They watched him like hawks for a couple of days, but we've found a way since."

"Do take care, my sweet," David said, secretly relieved that he would not have to explain to Jacqueline that Lucy had two lovers. At the same time, he felt a surge of admiration for Stefan.

"Stefan has found out that Ernst Brage was in command of a tanker that sank in suspicious circumstances. Four of the present crew were with him on the previous voyage. The rest of the crew are now worried that these men are on board to sabotage the *Moringa*. Most of the crew were as much in the dark as we were about the heroin."

"That is intriguing, isn't it?" David said, and even as he spoke, he realised that he was feeling better. Lucy's example of resilience had stirred his cerebral pathways. It was as simple as that. "You're beautiful, my sweet, in more ways than you know."

"I don't quite see your logic, Dad, but thank you, anyway," Lucy replied, pleasantly baffled.

"You've got me thinking again; that's the logic, my darling. If what you say is true, and I'm sure it is, then I may have been rather unfair to Jeffrey. I still think he's being overdramatic, but a few precautions may be wise. Lucy, dear, I'd like you and Frank to prepare a few necessities, so that if necessary, you can lock yourselves in here and look after the trees until any crisis has passed."

"For how long?" Lucy asked.

David shrugged. "I don't know. I suppose a day and a night."

"A day and a night," Lucy echoed, aghast. "With Frank? What if I need the loo?"

"You can rig up something in one of the trenches," David said, as if there was no problem. "Dig a hole and put a tin in it; something like that."

"Oh, Dad. Really?" Lucy protested. "What do you expect me to do – wee in it when it comes round? Or maybe you expect me to sit on it and go round with it. 'Hello Frank, don't mind me. I'm just having a wee.' I can tell you one thing: I'm not bloody sharing my tin can with Frank."

"Well, rig up one for each of you. I don't know," David retorted with embarrassment and spluttered at the thought of Lucy slowly gyrating on her tin can. "It's just a precaution, anyway. It's not as if you'll need them. Look, sort it out. I'm going to have a word with Roly."

Roland and Alan were busily working together on the task that Tyro had asked them to consider. They were in the maintenance workshop in the hangars, drawing, designing, and talking over possible approaches to the challenge. Every so often, they would stop to sort through available bits of equipment. They saw it as an engaging intellectual exercise, rather than a project with real practical intent. Tyro wanted them to design a bomb. It was an intellectual and engineering puzzle, obviously. As Roland said, Tyro was not exactly Herr Krupp: the industrialist whose factories armed the Germans in two world wars. Nearby, Tyro's brothers and Arnesh's team worked here and there to strengthen the mesh fence as a defensive wall.

"Don't you have any moral qualms, as a priest, working to design a bomb?" Roland teased Alan light-heartedly, focusing on his priesthood, rather than his previous life as a structural engineer.

"Don't you, as a pacifist, have any moral qualms about designing a bomb?" Alan countered. "If I really thought that the bomb we designed would be used, I might be upset, but I don't really believe it. I think this is just to bolster our morale. Anyway, even priests have a right to protect themselves. That's what the bishop's mace is all about."

"The bishop's mace?" Roland queried. "What is that?"

"You mean you don't know about the bishop's mace?" Alan asked, his Welsh voice intoning the question with a lyrical cadence. "A mace is a weapon: a thick rod with a heavy lump of metal at the end." He gesticulated with his arms to simulate the wielding of a mace. "At the Battle of Bouvines in 1215, the bishop of Beauvais used his mace to slay the Earl of Salisbury, rally the French army, and defeat an Anglo-German army that was attacking them." Alan's arms and his musical voice emphasised each stirring moment of this anecdote. He sighed with satisfaction and then continued calmly, "As a direct result of which King John had to flee to England, was confronted by his barons, and was forced to sign the Magna Carta: the first step towards freedom for the common people. So, you see, Roly, the Lord works in mysterious ways, even making use of belligerent priests."

Roland, realising that Alan had at last finished, started to laugh: "Alan, I agree with Tyro," he said. "If you are on our side, then God is on our side."

"I am on God's side," Alan corrected him meekly. "But yes, he lets me defend my friends."

"Ah, but is a bomb a weapon of defence?" Roland asked, thinking he had found a gap in Alan's reasoning.

"My uncle fought in the Second World War," Alan replied thoughtfully. "He said that when the bullets started flying, any weapon was defensive if he was behind it and offensive if he was in front of it. Probably your uncle was thinking just the same thing, at the same time, but on the opposite side."

Roland nodded and sighed. "If your God exists, Alan, I can only hope that this bomb is never made."

"I pray to God the same thing," Alan replied. "If Tyro starts mucking around with bomb-making, he's far more likely to blow all of us up instead of anyone else. I don't think Jeffrey will let him." At that moment, Alan caught sight of David coming down the steps. "Hello," he muttered. "Adam has left the Garden of Eden." Roly looked at him, perplexed. "I mean that your boss is coming."

"Dressed only in a fig-leaf?" Roland asked, without turning round.

"Now, that would certainly scare our enemies," Alan replied, so that David came upon the curious site of a pacifist and a priest laughing as they designed a bomb together.

When David found out what they were doing, he surprised them both by not only showing an interest in the idea but actually taking command.

"My first degree was in chemistry," David said, rubbing his hands together with enthusiasm. "With what we've got on board, I expect we can come up with something quite explosive. Time to combine our skills, gentlemen."

He sat down with them, and they all set to the task with great concentration.

Chapter 17

COMPANY

Jeffrey procrastinated over putting his request to Tyro to take Leena to safety. He was far less confident about persuading Tyro to go than he had shown to Leena. Knowing Tyro's character, Jeffrey felt he would want to stay and fight, so he was very surprised when Tyro told him that he would be escaping before the rendezvous. They were talking quietly in the hangar together. He told Jeffrey that he had been using GPS throughout the voyage and knew well enough where they were; he could now reach land, taking off at night and flying at low speeds. He felt that if he stayed, he would be a risk to himself and everyone else on board. Jeffrey immediately asked if Leena could accompany him, and he agreed after a brief discussion. He said that he needed two hours to prepare the airship and asked Jeffrey for his help.

"Jeffrey, it is most important that Lothar doesn't see what I'm doing. He could sabotage the airship. You must divert his attention. Occupy him until we are ready to leave. I don't trust him."

"Leave it to me," Jeffrey said decisively. "I'll ask him to come with me to support Arnesh's team. We'll get him rolling up bandages if we have to, but we'll find something."

Tyro smiled. "You're too nice, Jeff. I will ask Lothar for you," he said. Then he shouted, "Lothar!" and Lothar jogged up from nowhere like a trained hound. "Lothar, the Prof needs you. You go with him. You do what he says. He'll tell you when you are not needed anymore."

"Yes, boss," Lothar said without a sign of dissent.

"There, Jeff: all the help you need. Now go. I would like to discuss something with Anna when you see her."

Jeffrey realised he was being ordered about, just as surely as Lothar, but he was delighted at this turn of events; in return for getting Leena away safely, he would have rolled on his back, if necessary, and allowed Tyro to scratch his tummy. Knowing that Lothar was not a threat at the moment, he extended friendship towards him: "Lothar, I'm glad of your help. Let's get along to the workshops."

None of the Warlocks went to the stern of the ship that day. They had all agreed to have their meals in the central canteen. This part of the ship belonged to the engineers by common consent, but there was no ill feeling, despite the cramped conditions. They saw it as a temporary arrangement that would be back to normal in a few days. The change meant that it was much easier to know the whereabouts of everybody, and so Jeffrey was able to pass on Tyro's message to Anna in a few minutes, and she went off to see what he wanted.

When she arrived, Tyro immediately led her to his cabin and asked to see the Beretta that she was still carrying. She gave it to him, suspecting that he was going to take it away, and wondered what she might have to do to purchase it off him. He already had its case on his desk, but instead of putting the pistol away, he brought out cleaning materials and started to clean it himself.

"You have looked after it well," he said as she watched him, "but all guns need to be cleaned to stay in good condition."

"Is that all you wanted?" she asked suspiciously, for his behaviour now told her that he had something far more important to discuss.

Tyro looked up from where he was sitting: "When you came to ask me for this pistol, Lioness, I said that I was tempted to tell you all my secrets, but things were too uncertain, and the time was not right, but now it is right." Anna stayed silent and did not show any reaction to what he had said, so he continued, "You will have to look after the safety of your friends when the traffickers come, and they will come, you can be sure of that."

"If you take that Beretta away with you, I'm not sure I can do anything," she replied pragmatically. "But I don't think you will do that."

By way of reply, he handed the clean pistol to her, saying, "You will need more than this pistol. Open that chest." He indicated the metal box from which he had taken the Beretta when he had first given it to her. She did so and saw a layer of overalls, which she brushed aside. "Now you know all my secrets," he added, as she looked excitedly at the contents. "Three AK-47s, serviced and ready for action, with a thousand rounds of ammunition for each. You will also find two hundred rounds for your pistol and a hundred rounds for this one." Saying that, he undid his gun belt and passed it and the heavy revolver over to Anna.

She looked perplexed and protested, "You'll need this yourself."

"No, I'm leaving, Anna," he replied. He noticed her stifle an angry response; he could sense how deserted she felt. "If I leave now, I can reach Mauritius in the airship. I am taking Leena to safety, and if I am not here, there is much less risk of violence. I am sorry, Lioness, but I must go."

She took the gun belt and laid it in the chest, while she thought before she spoke. Then, with resignation, she accepted the necessity of his departure.

"It makes sense," she conceded. "I'm going to miss you, though. Where did you get these guns?"

"The same place as I got my helicopter. There were so many weapons then. You could buy them almost as cheaply as you could steal them. All the militias were supposed to hand in their weapons, but my brothers surrendered theirs to me, and I have been slow to do anything about them. I thought the Beretta would be a good present for my wife, but she never wanted it, and then the fighting stopped."

"Will Council be going with you?" she asked, searching for a gleam of hope.

Tyro smiled, guessing her thoughts. "No, Council will be with you, so will Jomo and Henry. They are good warriors; they shoot well and obey orders. You, your friend Giraffe, and my three brothers should be able to warn off any gang that boards to take away the heroin. They will realise you are not to be messed with. If you leave them alone, they will leave you alone."

"Who else is going with you?" Anna asked, picking one of the AK-47s out of the chest and then reaching down for two of the ammunition magazines.

"I'm taking Leena, Solomon, and Roland."

Anna shrugged. "Leena and Solomon I can understand, but why Roland?" She clipped a magazine into her rifle as she spoke.

"He's not needed here," Tyro explained, looking as if he now wanted to do other things. "He will get in your way if there is any shooting. There is something else in there too, but you can look at it later."

Tyro tossed Anna the key to the chest. She locked it, slid the key into her pocket, and then kissed Tyro on the cheek; as she left, she felt that there was now some point in the defensive work that had been done. She found Maggie, whispered the news to her, and the two of them went to look over the plans of the ship on Arnesh's computer. They were surprised to see Lothar sitting in a corner of the workshop, looking very cross as he cut a bedsheet into strips to make bandages, under the watchful eye of Anwar.

Jeffrey had left Lothar in order to seek out Leena, and he took her aside for a last entreaty about the pregnancy. He told her that she should make contact with Jacqueline and Tom Emmerson, David's wife and son, the moment she reached England. She could stay on the estate, and the family would look after her. For all their sakes, she was not to say anything about the heroin and was to say that Jimmy and Gary had been lost during the storm. Then he raised the subject of the adoption.

"Why not stay in Britain yourself? Why go back to an arranged marriage in India, when you have the freedom to be yourself and to make your own choices in Britain?"

"Freedom? Freedom? It's always the same with you, Jeffrey: You put freedom above everything else."

"Freedom is so fragile, Leena. If you give it away, you may never get it back."

"Jeffrey, listen: You don't have to lecture me about freedom. I love freedom. I've made more use of my freedom in this past year than most women do in a lifetime. Think of all the experiences I've enjoyed. I've been kidnapped, imprisoned, extradited, poisoned, had sex with another woman's boyfriend, been raped, and I've still got all the pleasure of an illegitimate birth to come. I mean, just how much freedom can a woman take? How many more experiences can freedom give me?"

Jeffrey looked at her, stuck for a reply. "Travel?" he blurted out.

"Travel! Oh, let me not forget travel," she jeered. "Who wouldn't prefer to fly across the ocean at night, in a bloody balloon, to escape being shot, rather than first class in a beautiful jet with a husband who cares for you? Oh Jeffrey, the joy of freedom."

Leena barely came up to Jeffrey's shoulder, but she had floored him with her vehemence. So much so that she relented a little so that they could at least say a civil goodbye to each other.

"Jeffrey, you're a wonderful man in many ways," she said contritely. "Yes, you've taught me the value of freedom, and I have had some truly fabulous times that I'd never have had without your influence, and I've learnt so much, but *you* need to learn about the joy of commitment." She put a hand on his arm while he looked down, avoiding her gaze. "I want what my life in India holds for me before that is lost forever too. I want to be a good daughter. I want to be a good wife. I want the respect that comes with that, and I know that I will love the husband my parents choose for me, and I will commit myself to him. I will be a good mother to Ariona by finding her a secure home with parents committed to her happiness, more than I can offer her as a single parent or that you can offer her. That's how it is, Jeffrey. I'm sorry. You need to learn about commitment to people, not just to life." She intended to walk away from him, but he held onto her.

He replied without anger, but with a voice as strong as his grip, "You think I don't know about commitment? I've spent twenty years committed to this project. I've put heart and soul into getting where we are today. Maybe I have to die if it's to go any further. Maybe the whole ship sinks, and all I've worked for, and with, go to the bottom with it. Given that possibility, is it so strange that I would like Ariona to know who her father was and what he died trying to do? Freedom isn't easy – you have to keep making choices – but it gives us the chance to do what we believe in, and I'd like her to know that too."

She shrugged him away. "I'm sorry," she said and left to find Maggie to say goodbye.

He stayed alone, trying to think of something that was going right for him. He closed his eyes and thought of a road, but he could not see it, as it led into darkness.

It was just after six in the morning. The darkness was fading into light; that was how Ernst saw it. Daylight was coming, and with it, an ominous darkness. He and his crew would live to see dusk, but almost certainly nobody else, unless he could think a way past the critical fact that they all knew that the heroin was on board. If he could disguise that fact, they might stand a chance. It would require the whole crew to be with him, and that was the issue. They were hardy men who would all have stood up for themselves at one time or another, but he doubted that any of them had experienced a gun battle. They were sailors, not gunmen. The exception was Ramos. This could be a good time to put his loyalty to the test. They were together on the bridge. They had been discussing the imminent arrival of the *Clarissa* and working out their tactics, neither of them being sure what was on the other's mind.

"Ramos, from what I know, the passengers don't want a fight. They want the heroin removed. They'll only fight if their lives are at risk. If we organise a swift transfer of the cargo, then we can make it in everyone's interest to avoid bloodshed.

"I want you to take a group of men and secure the heroin. Take the key and the pistol. Give Gary's gun to Hans. I don't expect either weapon to be used. I don't think you'll have any trouble. Leave two men to guard the lift and clear the area around the lift doors on the main deck and the storage deck, then report back."

Ramos left the bridge with the gun and the keys, but he was back much sooner than Ernst had anticipated, bringing with him the news that, unless he was allowed to use the guns, they could not get near the heroin: "The passengers have barricaded the corridor."

Ernst brought his fist down on the console, in sheer frustration at not having acted sooner.

"The fools," he said angrily. "If only they'd let me handle the command of my ship, I could sort this out. The more they interfere, the worse it becomes for all of us." He became aware of Otto at the helm listening intently, so he signalled Ramos to one side, where they could talk discreetly.

Ramos gave him a more detailed picture: "They've taken over the bow section. They've strengthened the fence, and the engineers have made a barricade along the main corridor, so they can seal themselves off from the stern section. The ship is essentially divided between us and them, with the lift in the middle."

"We can't ask the men to fight, not in these circumstances," Ernst said, as he realised the likelihood of further bloodshed. "It's too cold-blooded.

They've worked together. They've helped each other on the ice. They've been together for weeks on this ship."

He paused, seeking support. Ramos looked implacable. Ernst agonised over what was facing him.

And you're in love with Anna, Ramos thought, but he knew better than to say it. He chose a different line to overcome his captain's scruples: "Sometimes death is necessary. A man died when the *Ocean Cantabria* went down."

"That was an accident," Ernst snapped back, seared by the memory of the insurance scam that had brought him into the clutches of the Clerkenwell Angels.

"He still died," Ramos replied coldly. Then, with a smirk, he added, "For the money I stand to make, I'll shoot two or three of them. That's all it will take. They won't fight after that." Anna and Tyro were the two he had in mind. Ernst would be the third, unless he pulled himself together.

"Not yet," Ernst said, trying to deny the inevitable. "Maybe later, but not yet."

"We cannot wait. We need to be careful of our own skins, Captain." Ramos sounded concerned. "We are in the contact zone already. Some of us may be more at risk of being shot than the passengers."

Ernst knew he was right. They had failed to kill Tyro; they had failed to keep the heroin secret. They could not afford to lose control of the heroin, as well. That would be unacceptable incompetence. Only by keeping command of the ship could he hope to protect Anna.

As Ernst turned away in frustration, he noticed that Otto looked angry. He had overheard enough to know that his prize money was at stake and maybe his life. It gave Ernst an idea. One lie was all that it would take.

He turned to Silvio, standing watch at the radar console. "Call the men together. I want Hans, Ewan, Danny, and you, and anyone else you can rouse in the next few minutes. Get someone to bring some glasses. You are going to have to fight; I'll give you something to make you invincible."

A few minutes later, they all crammed in, haggard and bleary-eyed, so that Otto had to demand space enough to do his job, and Ernst greeted them with rough good humour. He disappeared to his cabin and returned with three bottles of Jägermeister. The existence of the Jägermeister on the ship had been a more closely guarded secret than the heroin.

"Attention everyone," Ernst called out. "Everyone to have a Jägermeister now, Captain's orders." There was an immediate scramble for the glasses, but nobody dared drink until the captain had filled his glass. Someone cheekily called out if they could have some of the heroin too.

Ernst let this be the last joke; he stood on a chair, with his glass of Jägermeister raised above his head, demanding silence by his gaze. "Men, I give you the *Moringa*!" he bellowed, dropping his glass to his lips and knocking back the contents. The wildness entered his belly, as all around the crew followed his lead. "The *Moringa* is our ship," he went on. "Some of the passengers want the heroin for themselves. They have barricaded themselves in. They are endangering us all by denying us access. I need you to take it back, now, so we can give it to its owners, who are arriving at any moment. If not, we won't get paid."

That was the lie. He paused. He could see that they were with him.

"Ramos and Hans will lead you. Ramos is armed. Hans, you can have my hunting rifle; Danny, you take the other handgun. The guns are just for effect. They won't want to fight. Once we have control of the lift, we have what we need. If the passengers resist you, as you clear the barricade, then you can fight them, and good luck to you. Now, go!" He passed his rifle to Hans and murmured, "If you get a shot at Tyro, take it. Good luck."

The crew divided into two groups under Ramos and Hans. Ramos first led his team to try and take hostages, but he was too late. The cabins were all empty, as were the cafeteria and the laboratory. Hans attacked along the main deck, while Ramos's team made their way to the barricade along the corridor deck below. They were in fighting spirit and started to haul away the metalwork, while the defenders poked metal poles at them. Hans and his men found the lift doors sabotaged on the main deck, but the door to the stairs was unlocked. They descended and came onto the corridor deck behind the barricade. The defenders were now surrounded, trapped against their own barricade.

If Hans had been in charge of the whole crew, they could have overwhelmed Anwar and his men, but Ramos and his team were on the wrong side of the barricade. Hans, waving his rifle, managed to drive some of the defenders down the next flight of stairs to the storage deck, where their cries of alarm alerted those guarding the hangar. Hans and three of his men followed them, and he was triumphant as he secured the lift entrance on the storage deck, but once again, as on the main deck, he found that the doors had been sabotaged by the engineers and would not open. He and his men were in full view, and all sorts of insults were hurled at them from the hangar and from the small group of engineers who had stopped a short way along the storage deck. Hans's frustration boiled over; he raised his rifle and fired a shot towards the bows. He had deliberately aimed high, and the shot ricocheted off the metalwork of the walls and sent everyone diving for cover.

The psychological effect of the shot was greater than any physical damage it caused. Until that moment, a sense of common purpose had existed between the two sides, but the shot instantly dispelled it and opened hostilities. On the storage deck, the engineers who had retreated from the barricade realised they were looking at an armed enemy only thirty metres from them. They turned and ran towards the hangar. Hans, liberated by having fired the shot, ran into the centre of the lane, laughing with exhilaration, his attention focused on the retreating group.

Ramos squeezed through a gap in the barricade and almost fell down the stairs in his haste, exuberant at finding the crew now had possession of the lift entrance.

He shouted, "Shoot, Hans! Shoot one of them."

Hans raised his rifle but hesitated. Ramos stood watching with Ewan and Danny, and the three of them were perplexed by the sound of a thud from Hans's body. A solo staccato drum beat snapped above the orchestral hum of the *Moringa's* hull. Hans crumpled like a rag doll, his rifle clattering onto the centre of the deck. Ramos thought the rifle had misfired and moved to pick it up, but then he saw the hole in Hans's chest, the widening blood stain, and they threw themselves back so that he and the other two were sheltered by the steps.

"Hans has been shot!" There was disbelief in Ramos's voice as he confirmed the obvious. "It was a rifle shot," he continued, voicing his thoughts as they came to his shocked mind. "I thought they only had a handgun at most."

Ewan was sweating and breathless with the combined effects of exertion and adrenalin. "It was a good shot too," he said urgently. "Who could have fired it?"

"The captain's Norwegian bitch," Ramos retorted. "Who else? I'm going to try to get our rifle back." Then he shifted position slightly. "Don't shoot!" he shouted. "I need to help Hans." He edged to where he felt he could dart out for the rifle and then dive for cover.

"Stay where you are!" Anna's voice came back. "Hans is dead. He doesn't need your help."

"You're going to die, bitch," Ramos called.

"So are you if you try to get that rifle," came Anna's reply.

Ramos was still crouched, weighing up his chances, when his handset buzzed. "Yes, Captain?" he responded immediately.

"We have radar contact. A ship is heading straight for us." Ernst's voice came back.

"Get away from the lift." Anna's voice came clearly down the deck.

The three men could see her. She had come twenty metres down the deck and was pointing an AK-47 at them. Ramos fired his gun, but at that range, he had no real chance of a hit. Anna didn't even flinch.

"We're still armed. Don't get too careless, bitch," Ramos shouted as he backed towards the stairs. He needed space to think. He spoke into the intercom: "I'm coming, Captain. There are things we must discuss."

"Quickly," Ernst snapped and switched off.

The three men retreated to the protection of the first few steps. "Chief, the engines are slowing. Listen," Ewan whispered.

"The captain's buying us some time. You two stay here. Don't let them take the rifle or the lift."

He gave Ewan his gun so that both he and Danny were armed and then darted back up the stairs to the corridor deck. He was ready to fight his way through, but the barricade had been largely dismantled, and a close quarter fight was going on where both sides were throwing missiles from hiding places, neither side able to gain an advantage. The deck was littered with metal bits. A pole was hurled at him as he emerged from the stairway, so he sprinted along the deck back to the tower and went up the stairs to the bridge.

Ernst asked Ramos for an update as he entered.

"Hans is dead," Ramos said. "He was shot by Anna." Before Ernst could reply, Ramos went on, "We could have secured the entrance to the lift if it hadn't been for her. She's got a rifle from somewhere and was shooting at us from the hangar."

"Where's my rifle?" Ernst asked with a concerned look.

"Lying in the middle of the deck," Ramos replied. "Hans was using it when he was shot. Anna has his body and the rifle covered from her position."

"Where did she get a rifle?"

Ramos gave a derisive smirk. "I guess from Tyro, the pilot you were supposed to kill, remember?" There was no sign of respect in his voice or his behaviour. "We need backup. How soon before it gets here?"

"Look for yourself," Ernst said with contempt, indicating the radar screen.

A solitary craft was making straight for them. Ramos gauged that the ship would be with them in fifteen minutes at most. Within thirty minutes, he would have the fully armed support that he needed. He lingered over the screen, watching the rate of movement. It was coming fast. Whatever was coming was a powerful craft. He looked up, satisfied by what he had seen, and was about to comment on it to Ernst, but he noticed that Ernst's attention was fixed on something happening on deck. Alarmed, he immediately joined Ernst, scanning the deck. The first light of dawn had come over the horizon, and the deck had a russet glow and could be seen for its full length, beyond the glare of the deck lights. It took him two seconds to take in the scene and then focus on the airship slipway a hundred metres away. The airship was out.

"What are they doing? What's happening?" he demanded of Ernst.

"They're launching the airship," Ernst replied calmly.

"I can see that. Why? How many of them?" Ramos said excitedly.

"Watch and you'll find out," Ernst replied disdainfully.

Ramos turned on him: "Do something!" he shouted.

"What do you suggest?" Ernst's logic angered Ramos even more.

"Turn the ship. Fire a flare at it. Do something to stop the take-off," Ramos said, grabbing at desperate thoughts, not even worthy of a reply. As they watched, the ground crew released their hold on the cables, and the airship seemed to be catapulted into the air, so swift was its ascent.

"That was quick. Trying to get out of range, I think," Ernst commented, adding, "Just in time, Tyro," as if speaking to the airship. He pointed to where a shape had appeared on the skyline. He passed the binoculars to Ramos. "Here," he said. "Tell me what you see."

"I see a dead man," Ramos said, looking Ernst directly in the eyes for a second. "They'll not forgive you this debacle, Captain."

He smirked, looked out of the window, and had just focused on the sleek motor yacht when Ernst brought the butt of a snub-nosed revolver down hard onto the back of his head. Ramos collapsed against the bridge window with a yell of pain and slumped, semi-conscious, to the floor, where he lay, helpless and groaning.

Otto, standing at the helm, looked aghast. In the second that it took him to overcome his surprise, Ernst had turned the revolver round and was pointing it at him. Otto looked defiantly at Ernst.

"You didn't really think I'd leave myself defenceless, did you?" Ernst taunted him drily. "Come with me, Otto," he commanded.

Otto stayed his ground. "No," he said decisively.

Ernst clicked back the hammer so the gun was cocked: "Then stay where you are," he said. "Don't try to stop me."

Ramos stirred.

Ernst uncocked the hammer and ran from the bridge. He sped down the stairway, almost colliding with the two cooks, wandering uncertainly about the ship. "Quickly," he shouted. "Get ready. The other ship is almost with us." Then he was gone, leaving the two men muttering as to what they should actually do.

Once he was on the corridor deck, Ernst steadied his pace and reset his cap, so that he had the bearing of a captain as he approached the group of men standing back from the remnants of the barricade.

"Why are you here?" he demanded.

"We can't get beyond them," one of the group replied. "We're waiting for orders."

"Who's downstairs?"

"Ewan and Danny. They've got the pistols. They're covering the lift."

Ernst went to the stairway and called down, "Danny! This is your captain. I need you up here. Ewan stays."

Ewan and Danny, together and armed, were too powerful for him. This way, he had split them up. Danny stomped his way up the stairs and was pleased to be ordered to go and meet the boarding party from the other ship.

"You two go with Danny; Silvio comes with me." Ernst had noticed the slight figure of Silvio, and by choosing him, unarmed, he greatly improved his chances of survival if he had to fight his way through.

"What about the barricade?" Danny asked, uncertainly.

"The boarding party will have machine guns. That'll sort out the barricade. But we need them quickly. Go."

Ernst felt despair at the thought of the guns soon coming aboard but hid it with bravado that satisfied Danny's suspicions. The three men ran up the stairway to the main deck. Ernst started to go down to the storage deck. He needed a few seconds to decide whether to shoot Ewan or just disarm him. He had never shot a man before, but if he did so now, he would have a clear run to Anna. He reached the bottom step still undecided, saw Ewan, and just launched himself at him. Ewan was caught off guard but had the presence of mind to clutch the gun tightly and start yelling for help.

Silvio saw Ernst's clumsy attack and stood at the foot of the steps, trying to work out his own next move. Ernst punched Ewan in the face. Ewan's head snapped back and hit the metalwork. He fell to the floor, knocked out. Ernst looked to the bows. He needed twenty seconds to reach Anna and be in the safe zone. Ewan would be out for double that time, at least. This was his chance. He started running to the bows, shouting, "Anna, don't shoot. It's me, don't shoot."

Silvio heard voices above him, the sound of footsteps on the stairs, and stepped aside just in time as Danny rushed past him and ran to the fallen Ewan, fumbling for the pistol in his belt.

Even before he had a firm grip on it, he shouted at Ernst, "Stop, you bastard, or I'll fire."

Ernst kept running in desperation, but he could see that Anna was struggling to get a bead on Danny. He shouted for her, again, "Anna! Anna!"

Silvio at last took sides. He hurled himself bodily against Danny to disrupt the shot. Danny was completely unbalanced, and his shot went into nowhere as he staggered three or four steps, trying to remain on his feet. For a brief second, Anna had a clear shot and fired. Danny cried out, clutching his stomach and dropping his pistol. Elated that he, too, might escape, Silvio started his run towards the bows. He could see that Ernst was now safe. Ten seconds more and he would be safe too, but Ramos had arrived. The fallen handgun was in his reach. He snatched it up and fired at Silvio, and cursed himself for firing too high. Time for one more shot. He aimed low and fired, his hand was steady and his aim calm and accurate. He had meant to hit Silvio between the shoulder blades, but the shot stayed as low as he had aimed. He saw Silvio's right side burst open at waist height, and he fell, screaming in fear and pain.

"Captain! Captain! Help me!" Silvio cried as other shouts started to echo around the deck. Ernst turned and saw Silvio stretched out, left hand extended as if to be grasped and pulled to safety.

Ernst started back towards him, though voices from the bows begged him to stay where he was. Ramos, desperate for a kill, risked a third shot to finish Silvio off. He darted from cover, fired, and darted back. The shot was a hard one. It went long. It hit the floor, ricocheted, and struck Ernst in the chest.

Ernst felt a piercing agony; his breath seemed to leave his body, and his legs became like lead. He sank forward, increasingly distanced from reality that pulled away from him as his only light in a dark tunnel, and as he fell to his knees, he heard Anna shriek his name, as if from far away. She had leapt up as Ernst was hit, shouting "Ernst, darling, no. No!"

Ramos, sensing a triumph, dared to glance from his hiding place. What he saw thrilled and terrified him. The captain was on his knees, Silvio was lifeless, but Anna was coming straight for him, her AK-47 in her hands, and in that second, she let loose a spray of bullets that ricocheted around him and killed the luckless Ewan outright. Ramos leapt for the stairs and raced away, surrendering the lift and leaving Danny to bleed out his life alone.

When Anna rushed towards Ernst, she unconsciously led a small charge. Tyro's armoury had been a godsend. Anna had given Council and Henry the two other AK 47s. Jomo had accepted Tyro's revolver; Maggie had the Beretta. Anna only had thoughts for Ernst and rushed to his side, but Maggie used her Territorial Army skills to form a unit with the three brothers. She was impressed at how disciplined they were. She deployed Council and Henry to cover the staircase and then went forward with Jomo to gather the hunting rifle and handgun from the deck and to check on the fallen crewmen. Both were dead. Jomo found some more bullets in

Hans's pockets, so she let him have the rifle, which pleased him greatly. When a white flag on a long broom handle appeared round the corner of the staircase, Maggie held her ground but signalled the brothers to drop back to good defensive positions. After a few seconds, the holder of the white flag dared to poke his head around the corner. The scared crewman froze as he saw Maggie only a few steps away, her gun raised. It was Emilio, one of the cooks.

"Please, don't shoot, don't shoot," he begged. "We want to stay with the captain." His friend, Alfredo, nervously appeared.

"How many of you?" Maggie demanded.

"Just the two of us."

"Emilio, you're a nice man," Maggie replied, "but I'll blow your head off if you try any tricks. The same goes for you, Freddy."

The two men just held up their hands in complete submission.

"He's lying up there. You better get to him. See if you can help," Maggie said.

The two men immediately ran to where Anna, Alan, and two of the engineers were tending to Ernst and Silvio.

Maggie did a quick headcount and realised they had left themselves unguarded at the rear. "Council, Jomo, get to the flight deck quickly."

The two young men ran like trained athletes, shouting advice to each other as they went. She saw Jeffrey and David standing together, urging on two more of Arnesh's men, who drove one of the tugs out of the hangar and over to the wounded men. They were both loaded onto it. Maggie went over to Jeffrey and said, "We're too widely spread if gunmen arrive from the other ship. We have to all move forward to the bows. We can defend ourselves there."

Jeffrey shook his head and replied, "If we fall back, they retake the lift; they get the heroin, and then we're finished. We've got to stop that."

"We've got no choice. Council and Henry can't hold their positions against a mass attack of machine guns. Anna and I will be dead seconds after that, and you and the rest will be defenceless."

"Then we have no option. We'll have to deploy the bomb," Jeffrey said, turning to David. "Is your bomb finished?"

David gave a slight dismissive laugh and said, "Well, of course it is, but—"

"Sorry, David, there's no time for moral scruples," Jeffrey said brusquely. "We need it if we're to survive. Load it onto that trolley and get it into the lift quickly. It's our only chance. I'm going to have to negotiate, and this is the doomsday option."

"All right, Jeffrey." He called sharply to Alan, looking at him with a firm, unyielding gaze. "The bomb is ready. Let's get it into the lift."

Alan read the look in David's eye, took in a deep breath, and said, "Yes. I'm ready. Let's load up the bomb. We'll need Arnesh to open the lift for us." He and David then walked quickly over to the tug to arrange everything.

"David, you know we haven't put anything into that cylinder," Alan whispered, perplexed.

"Jeffrey thinks we have. Keep it that way," David replied tersely.

"Arnesh," Jeffrey called. "Can you come over here? I need you to open the lift door when we're ready."

Arnesh gave a wave of acknowledgement and started to feel frantically in his overall pockets, in a way which was absurdly funny in this moment of crisis. Jeffrey heard a splutter of laughter from Maggie and turned back to her, seeking support.

"Truthfully, how are we doing?" he asked her.

"Holding our own," Maggie replied, giving him a smile. Then she sighed and said, "I haven't dared to go over to see how Ernst is doing."

"Nor me," Jeffrey replied. "Anna will call me if she needs me." He paused and then asked, "Did you hear what she called him as she charged off?"

Maggie grimaced. "Yes, I did. But don't let it upset you now. Stay focused. We need you. You're doing really well." She gave him a sympathetic squeeze of his arm, as Arnesh found the remote he thought he had lost and came over to them. As he approached, she became business-like again. "Now, Henry and I will stand guard while David and Alan place the bomb. It'll be a vulnerable time if we're attacked before it's in place."

With that, she ran to the lift to join Henry, while Arnesh and Jeffrey waited for the bomb.

David drove the tug to the lift with painstaking slowness, and Arnesh, in his anxiety, pressed the remote button too early, so the lift doors were open for what seemed an age before the bomb was trundled up to them. A concerted ambush would have wiped them out, but they were all having to get their individual roles right first time, and nobody chided anyone else. At last, the bomb was in the lift, on its trolley; the four men walked away, and Arnesh closed the doors.

"How do we activate it if we have to?" Jeffrey asked.

David handed a mobile telephone to him, saying, "Whatever you do, don't switch on this phone. If you do, you'll activate the timer to the bomb, and it will detonate ten seconds later. They won't have time to do anything about it. Nor will we."

Jeffrey looked solemnly at the mobile phone in the palm of his hand. "Arnesh, David, Alan, I can't thank you enough for what you've done. I know you're all pacifists at heart, and yet you've produced the weapon that could save the ship. The chances are that we won't have to use it, and nobody else gets harmed. Thank you."

"Our nuclear deterrent; we've done what we can, Jeffrey," Arnesh replied for them. "The barricade has been rebuilt too. We've moved it up the corridor, this way. My lads learnt from their experience. This one is stronger and has some nasty things in it as well."

"Thanks, Arnesh, mate," Jeffrey replied. "But gunmen are expected from the other ship at any time. I suggest your guys leave their quarters now and make their way up to the bows."

"That gives them most of the ship," Arnesh protested, hurt at the thought of retreat. "But we'll do it. The barricade will hold the bastards back for a few minutes."

"Yes. Good," Jeffrey replied dismissively. His attention was on the double gates that connected the storage deck to the Grand Chamber. "David, I'm mad," he said. "I've just realised that if the gunmen enter the Grand Chamber, they can throw back these gates and enter the storage deck."

"That's all right, Jeffrey," David replied. "It's taken care of. Lucy and Frank are in there. They've locked themselves in, and it'd take dynamite to blow open the door."

Jeffrey was about to voice his concern for Lucy, but events were taken out of his hands by Council running halfway down the deck, shouting to Maggie, "Miss, miss. They're coming. Twelve men in two boats. They have machine guns, miss." He turned and ran back to his station.

"Get back to the bows now, all of you," Maggie shouted at the group of men around the tug. "Leave the defence to me. Henry and I will fall back when you do. Anna, we need you. Jeffrey, fall back. We can't go till you do."

Jeffrey shook himself out of his startled state, angry at his momentary hesitation. "Sorry, damn it," he called back. "David, get us back to the bows now. We're just endangering more lives. Let's go, damn it."

David engaged the gears and gave the tug maximum throttle, Alan and Jeffrey hanging on as best they could.

Lucy and Frank, alone in the Grand Chamber, realised something was happening from the commotion they heard through the gates to the cargo deck. Lucy went up to check that the door from the corridor deck was properly locked and bolted, and while there, she was overjoyed to hear the coded knock she had worked out with Stefan. She quickly unlocked the door, completely forgetting David's strict instructions not to open the door in any circumstances. As she threw it open, Stefan darted in and gave her a rib-cracking hug and a suffocating kiss, all in the name of love.

"I hoped you wouldn't be here," he said, gasping with desire.

"Then you're hiding your disappointment very well," Lucy commented. "Stay with us."

"No. I must go. I'll be missed," he whispered into her hair. "There's been shooting. Men are joining us from the other boat. You must hide and do not open the door at all. Remember, they may look in from above."

Hearts in mouths, they opened the door between them, and he slipped away, after which she locked the door and set about making hides for Frank and herself. Realising that they might be needed for several hours, she put them well apart, with a neat little pit in the earth for hers.

The flight deck was already raised so that it formed a roof above the hangar. Anna and Maggie went up on deck together to check the situation; they realised that Council and Jomo were too vulnerable to an attack if they stayed in the open, so they would just have to relinquish control of the flight deck. Maggie sent them below to guard the forward spiral staircase. Then the two women followed, locking the stairway door.

"If they break the door down and start lobbing grenades, we'll know all about it," Maggie commented. "I'll ask Arnesh if he can do some quick welding of the door."

"This door might be our only way out," Anna warned her.

"If they get in, we won't need a way out," Maggie replied. "Anyway, if they start throwing grenades near the hydrogen tanks, it'll probably blast the bows off. We can go out through the hole."

Anna smirked, looking to left and right to see what more could be done. Then she shrugged. "We're going to die, aren't we, you and me?"

"Probably," Maggie replied, looking down at her rifle. "Two worn out AK-47s can't offer much resistance to twelve machine guns. At least we'll die together; that's a promise. I won't let you die alone."

Anna smiled at her friend's gesture of unremitting love in all circumstances. "Love you," she murmured.

"Love you too," Maggie murmured back, knowing her love was the greater. "Now, I must talk to Arnesh quickly. You get to the fence, and shout for me if needed. Good luck."

When Jeffrey arrived, David and Alan were manhandling crates of empty gas cylinders into a defensive wall inside the hangar fence. "Have either of you seen Roly?" he asked. "I've been doing a head-count, and I can't find him anywhere."

"He went with Tyro," David replied, grunting with the effort of his task. "I let him go. We attached one of his drones to the underside of the gondola to aid take-off. I think it helped a bit."

"Why?" Jeffrey asked, puzzled.

"In case someone started shooting. Nobody did, but we couldn't be sure. The airship made a nice target for a few seconds."

Jeffrey shrugged and said, "Oh well, he's safe at least. I can't blame him for taking his chance."

He looked at the defensive wall of cylinders and was just about to compliment them when Anna shouted, "Take cover! Take cover!"

Jeffrey turned just in time to see Lothar run towards the staircase from a hiding place halfway down the deck. Anna followed up her warning cry by sending a spray of bullets that hit the deck just ahead of Lothar and spat in all directions. Lothar spun round and ran back to where he had been.

"You missed him, Anna," Jeffrey called over to her.

"I meant to. He's our only pilot," came back her reply. "Lothar!" she shouted. "Come back here with your hands up. Come now, and I won't shoot."

Lothar came swiftly back and was greeted by Henry with a friendly tap on the shoulder from the heavy wooden butt of an AK-47, which almost dislocated the joint. Lothar grimaced and rubbed his arm, saying grumpily, "We'll all be killed if we stay with the Prof."

"Then you die with the rest of us, like my brother wanted," Henry replied firmly.

Maggie knew the sound of Anna's gunfire would have carried around the ship. It would alert the gunmen and hasten their attack. The AK-47s seemed to have given everyone a false sense of security, but she and Anna were facing death in the next minute or so, unless she could get negotiations under way.

She called Jeffrey to her. "Jeffrey, you've got to negotiate," she whispered urgently. "Why not call the bridge on Tyro's phone? If Ramos knows about the bomb, he'll delay any attack. He has to."

"Bless you, Maggs, I never thought of that," Jeffrey said, cursing himself for his own oversight.

Tyro's phone was in the office on the floor above, still defended by Arnesh's barricade. It had direct access to the bridge, to facilitate take-offs and landings. Jeffrey ran fast, praying not to have a heart attack; he reached the office, steadied himself for a few precious seconds to catch his breath, and then picked up the phone. "Hello, bridge? Hello, bridge? Are you there, Ramos?" he demanded urgently, but nobody spoke, although he could hear voices in the background. "Hello, bridge!" he shouted again. Again there was silence.

Then came the reply.

"Good afternoon, Professor Harvey," said Cherry Bonner.

Chapter 18

EYE TO EYE

Stefan had gone briefly on deck to watch the gunmen approach from the yacht. The sight of their weapons had terrified him, and he had gone to hide in the Grand Chamber. He had struggled in panic for a few seconds when the door wouldn't open, until it dawned on him that it might be locked, so he tried the coded knock he had worked out with Lucy, not expecting her to be there or hear it. The combined rush of adrenalin and testosterone at the sight and feel of Lucy had swept away his panic, and he found that he could think clearly and positively about action he could take. He knew that Silvio was wounded, and he needed to protect Lucy, and he was going to help both of them. Instead of seeking a new hiding place, he sped straight to the sickbay through empty corridors; he rushed in, expecting it to be empty, startling Emily Ross in the process.

She was standing by the operating table. "Oh, Stefan, you frightened me," she said with a little laugh.

He desperately signalled to her to lower her voice. "Doctor, armed men have come aboard. Get to the bridge, or hide, or something."

He could see the anxiety in her eyes, but she stayed immovable. "I'm the ship's doctor," she said firmly. "It's my duty to be at my station. It's not for me to hide at times like this. I don't understand what's going on, but there's some sort of crisis, and I'm needed. But what about you? Why are you down here?"

"I want to help Silvio. He's been wounded."

Emily thought for a moment. "You'll find some intravenous packs in the storeroom. If someone can get a line into one of his veins, it could save his life. Come on, we'll find them in the store-cupboard."

She led the way into a small room stacked with boxes and lined by shelves. She went to the back of the cupboard and put useful things into an empty box. She had just finished and was handing it to Stefan when they heard unfamiliar voices approaching. Stefan's eyes widened with fear.

"Hide yourself in here," Emily whispered. "I'll tell you when they've gone."

Stefan moved quickly and silently to the back of the room and lay behind some boxes.

Three men entered the sickbay. Emily could tell they were from somewhere around the Horn of Africa, but whether Sudanese, Ethiopian, or Somali was beyond her knowledge. They wore a guerrilla-style uniform of berets and battle fatigues, each armed with the same style of machine gun, which had no stock and was held loosely at his side. They looked around, identifying the purpose of the room before turning their attention to Emily, standing as she had been when Stefan entered.

"Who are you?" one of them asked.

"My name is Dr Emily Ross. I'm the medical officer for the *Moringa*." Emily avoided looking them in the eyes, like she had been trained to do when managing violent patients. She felt nervous but in control.

The men looked at each other uncertainly. "How many medical officers are there?" the first one asked.

"Just me. They're a healthy crew. They don't—"

"Do you know about the heroin?"

"Yes, I've—"

"Are you really a woman? Show me your breasts. I want to see for myself."

So she was to be raped. If she shouted for help, Stefan might emerge from hiding, and that could be the death of both of them. She accepted rape as the lesser evil. It might just be, after all, that they needed to be sure of her gender before leaving her alone, so she complied. She calmly undid the buttons of the jacket of the white safari suit she wore as her uniform, slipped it off, and undid and threw aside her bra. Then she stood, unashamed, eyes still averted, her fists tightly clenched out of sight behind her, so they should not detect her fear. The men looked at her.

360

A short burst of machine-gun fire shattered the quiet; the bullets passed through her chest and split the flimsy storeroom door that swung back under the force. Emily's body thumped to the floor against it. The men could now see into the storeroom but not easily enter it. From where they were, it seemed unoccupied. They left, talking among themselves about where to go next. Their orders were to clear the ship from the stern forwards, but it was tedious. The cabins had been empty, as were the cafeteria, kitchens, and, now, the sickbay. They shot away the lock of the laboratory and found that it was empty too. They made their way along the corridor deck, coming to the door of the Grand Chamber. It was made of steel, and the bullets would ricochet everywhere if they shot at it. One of them suggested they should go on deck, where they had seen the glass roof, so that they could look into it. This seemed sufficient.

The roof still had a small gap which had been left for ventilation. They each of them fired a random burst into the chamber for good measure; laughing at the joke, they went back down to the corridor deck. There they met up with three more of the squad, hovering around the steps to the storage deck.

"If you go down those steps, you get shot," they were told, so all six decided to approach the barricade farther up the corridor to see if they could get round it. They held their guns pointed at the barricade as they made their way past the debris of the previous fight, but like the rest of the ship, there was nobody to defend it.

This second barricade was a mass of convoluted bits of iron, more carefully put together than the previous one, though they did not know that. The engineers had learnt some lessons and had realised their lives were at risk. Among the grey, black, and chrome scraps, there was a brass bar that shone out and seemed as good a place as any to start pulling the bits apart. One of the gunman leaned forward and pulled it; he never had time to cry out. A two-centimetre-wide sharpened bolt, spring-loaded, smashed into his forehead and pinned his skull to the barricade, his body slumped against the barrier. The others jumped back, all realising how attracted they had been by the same brass bar.

"Now I'm angry," their leader said. "Very angry."

He led them to the stairs, produced a grenade from a pouch on his belt, and removed the pin. "They're all down there," he said, pointing down. "Kill them as you see them."

He went to the last corner of the stairs, threw the grenade, and then sprang back. The gunmen heard the warning shouts from Maggie and then the stunning explosion that blasted shrapnel all over the deck. In the seconds after the explosion, while the noise still echoed off the walls and smoke lingered in the air, they attacked down the steps, forming a line across the deck and firing blindly up to the hangars.

They had expected to find token resistance from a group of panicked amateurs but started to take wounds from disciplined shooting that was accurate and sustained, so that the random rapid fire from their Uzis was nullified by the semi-rapid fire of the heavier bullets of the AK-47s. They didn't know where to aim because the hits were coming from direct fire and ricochets; within seconds, they were back as a frightened group, pinned down and boxed in near the steps, trying to nurse their wounds.

The leader called urgently for support on his radio, and his appeal was passed hurriedly to the bridge, where Ramos and six gunmen stood waiting for orders. Cherry Bonner saw amusing irony in the fact that both sides were attempting to communicate with the bridge at once, for this was the moment that she had been passed the telephone by Ramos to speak to Jeffrey Harvey. She had Ramos on one side of her and Duke Dukakis on the other, and felt in supreme control.

To Ramos, she whispered, "Wait for my orders," and then, she said to Jeffrey, "Mr Dukakis is here and is willing to speak to you."

"Duke Dukakis?" Jeffrey asked excitedly, sensing the presence of a possible ally amid the chaos.

Cherry mouthed to Duke, "He's yours, Duke; we've got him."

Duke slipped some gum into his mouth. He allowed himself to speak with arrogant superiority: "You're trapped and outgunned, Harvey. Just give yourselves up, and you won't be harmed."

Jeffrey was amazed that Duke Dukakis, himself, was on the *Moringa*, but he did not waste time over it. "Mr Dukakis," he shouted angrily, "if you want your heroin, shut up and listen. We have a bomb set to blow up the heroin and any means of getting to it. So you tell your men to retreat right now, and then you and I can start talking."

Duke whispered over the receiver to Cherry, "They've put a bomb in the hold. He wants a ceasefire and a meeting." Cherry signalled her agreement.

"Where?" Duke asked.

"The storage deck," Jeffrey replied.

"The storage deck," Duke repeated, looking at Ramos. Ramos nodded. "I'll be there in ten. Tell your guys to stop shooting."

"Tell your guys to get off the storage deck," Jeffrey insisted. He couldn't know, from where he spoke, that the gun battle had gone very much in favour of the defenders. He imagined that there was carnage in the hangar. "They must stop shooting now and get out – all of them."

"Harvey," Duke said in a pained voice. "My guys have stopped shooting. It's your guys who are pinning them down. You stop shooting, and they'll leave."

So it was. After a nervous minute of silence, the five gunmen stood up and retreated up the stairs – without their guns or bullets. Maggie saw to that. Ten minutes later, Ramos and his gunmen appeared, as escorts to Duke and Cherry.

Jeffrey had used those minutes to see how everyone was coping. Anna was self-composed in her dual role as soldier and nurse. Ernst was breathless but stable. There was much to talk about, but not at that moment. Emilio and Freddy were doing what they could to look after Silvio, who was semi-conscious and in agony, moaning continuously. Alan gave Jeffrey a thumbs-up to indicate that he and David were all right, so Jeffrey carried on to Arnesh. He passed Maggie, doing her check of her soldiers, and they caught each other's eye.

Arnesh and his team were in good spirits, many of them armed for hand-to-hand combat, though Arnesh, true to his beliefs, was not among them. Jeffrey asked Arnesh to go forward with him to the meeting. Arnesh did not show fear but queried whether he was the appropriate choice for the circumstances.

"Of course," Jeffrey replied. "After all, you built the ship."

Arnesh smiled at this remark. "Very well," he retorted. "I will join you, on condition that the next time we have cricket practice, you join in."

"Agreed," Jeffrey replied. He started to walk down the deck to where Duke would appear and saw that Alan stopped Arnesh to have a quick word with him. *Two devout men, supporting each other's faith*, Jeffrey thought to himself and felt strengthened by the sight.

The two parties stopped about five metres apart.

"Professor Harvey, you are a nuisance to me," Cherry began.

"Shouldn't I be addressing the chairman?" Jeffrey retorted with disdain, imagining he'd put the arrogant woman in battle fatigues in her place.

"You are," Cherry replied. "I am the chairman of the Clerkenwell Angels, who made your venture possible."

"At what price?" Jeffrey asked. He made no attempt to hide his bitterness.

"I'm beginning to ask myself the same question," Cherry replied. "I was advised that you'd be trouble. We had to get rid of you. We'd almost succeeded in that, until that fool Mukasa let you off the hook. Anyway, here we are, and here's my offer: You defuse the bomb, you let us transfer the heroin, and you continue on your way to Mombasa. We continue to back your project so long as you continue to meet our needs. You ask no questions. Your ship just carries some extra cargo from time to time that only the captain will know about. Do you wish to lose your funding?"

"No, of course not," Jeffrey muttered sullenly.

"No, I didn't think so. If you agree to these terms, we'll give all your team their airfares to their respective homelands. Does that seem reasonable?"

"Once you've got the heroin, what's to stop your gunmen shooting us all?"

Cherry was lost for words at Jeffrey's question, as there was nothing to stop the gunmen, beyond a few moral scruples. She tried to think of some convincing line of response.

Duke came to her aid: "You've got my word that you'll be safe," he said, sounding sincere. Cherry looked at him with disdain, but he kept his eyes on Jeffrey. "Professor Harvey, I've got great respect for you. I don't understand you, but I respect you. You've devoted your life to this project. It's a fucking eccentric way of improving the world, but you're almost there. I'm ready to offer my guarantee, in return for a guarantee of silence on your part."

Cherry smirked and said, "You're a fool, Dukakis," but Duke disregarded her. "If word of this gets out, you'll be implicated up to your necks. We've got lawyers who'll protect us, but you'll be fed to the sharks. So do we have a deal?"

Cherry butted in: "We get the heroin. You have free transport home, and we don't mention to anyone that you wanted to plant illegal trees in Africa." She paused. "You're just as big a criminal as the rest of us," she added, to taunt him.

Jeffrey turned to Arnesh. Arnesh shrugged hopelessly and gave the nod of assent, adding, "Perhaps Mr Dukakis stays with us while they load the heroin. Once the two ships are well apart, we can take Mr Dukakis back to his ship. It is just my suggestion."

Both Cherry and Duke looked taken aback. "I hardly think you're in a position to set conditions," she protested.

Jeffrey swept her remark aside: "Stop bluffing," he retorted. "Agree now, or we'll blow up the heroin and take our chances. If you want the heroin, you agree to our terms, just as we have to agree to yours."

Cherry and Duke muttered between themselves for a few moments and then agreed to the deal. "Just be clear," Cherry warned Jeffrey. "If anyone breaks the code of silence, they're dead, I promise you that, and the rest of you will be ruined for life."

"Agreed," Jeffrey acknowledged.

Cherry turned to Duke: "Call Ramos. He's to put out a call on the speakers – no more shooting. There's been a deal. Now let's go and check the goods. If there's been any damage, the deal is off."

"And any of your men seen carrying a gun from now on will be shot by us. Ramos better say that as well," Jeffrey added.

Cherry looked unimpressed but Duke conveyed the message to Ramos.

"Well, open the lift doors," she said petulantly.

Jeffrey felt that there was nothing more that he could do. "I guess we better bring the lift up," he said to Arnesh, who pressed the controller in his pocket, and a few seconds later, the lift arrived, and the doors slid back.

"So that's the bomb, is it?" Cherry asked, showing no sign of fear and strolling over to where it lay on its trolley on the floor of the lift. "Looks like a gas cylinder to me – a helium cylinder, at that."

"That's what it was. Now, it's a bomb."

Cherry laughed. "You accused me of bluffing, now I'm tempted to accuse you of the same thing, but"—she gave Jeffrey a penetrating stare—"I don't think you are. So it stays here while our men go up and down with the cargo, is that it?"

"Just as we're about to do," Jeffrey replied, and all together, they went down to the maintenance deck so that Cherry and Duke could see the sight of their heroin; she brought out a camera and took some pictures.

"That's the sight of $200 million," Duke muttered.

"We estimated £100 million," Jeffrey replied with satisfaction.

"Maybe you're better at this business than you think, Jeff."

"Professor Harvey to you, Mr Dukakis," Jeffrey corrected him.

Cherry laughed in malicious satisfaction at this put-down of her overfriendly colleague, then she turned to Jeffrey. "Get me up to the surface," she ordered. "I've seen enough. I want to get back to the *Clarissa*. I'll give the good news to the other board members in person."

"Are more of the partners here?" Jeffrey asked, surprised by the thought.

"The whole bang shoot," Duke replied affably. "We're all aboard the yacht to keep an eye on each other. This is our first venture into the heroin business, Professor. It's the most excitement we've ever had. Money can get so fucking boring, believe me."

"Have you finished? You talk too much," Cherry commented, tempering her criticism with a slight smile. "Now, get me back to the *Clarissa*. I want to go back on the helicopter. I don't want to have to climb down that rope ladder. Where's Tyro?"

"He'll be in Mauritius by now," Jeffrey replied, stretching the truth.

"I might have known it, flying that blimp of his, I suppose. But you've still got a helicopter here, because I saw it upstairs. Presumably you have a pilot to fly it."

"Lothar, yes, but he was wounded earlier," Jeffrey lied, "so he won't be able to take you." Jeffrey was not going to let Lothar and the helicopter out of his sight, least of all with Cherry Bonner on board.

Cherry rolled her eyes in exasperation and shook her head. "Don't push me too far, Professor," she warned.

The bullet that had hit Ernst Brage had ricocheted off the floor, coming up as it hit his chest. The force had shattered a rib, but the bullet was deflected further upwards, grazing another rib and tearing open his left pectoral muscle, but not penetrating the chest wall. The pain, shortness of breath, and bleeding were real enough, but he would survive. When Anna, having cut off his shirt, discovered this, she surprised herself by bursting into tears, making Ernst fearful. "Is it that bad?" he asked, speaking in their native Norwegian and expecting to be told the worst.

"No, it's good, very good," she replied, likewise disregarding the fact that he had lost a lot of blood and the full use of his left arm.

"It doesn't feel good," he complained. "If it's so good, why are you crying?" he asked, convinced that she was hiding the truth.

"It's good because the bullet hasn't gone into your chest, and I'm crying because I thought I had lost you, and now I haven't, so I'm happy, very happy, so I'm crying, and I never cry, and I know I'm not making much sense, but you'll just have to get used to it." The Norwegian words poured out of her in a fluency she could never find in English.

Suddenly, through his pain, Ernst's fear melted away. "I have to get used to it?" he asked.

Anna sniffed and smeared the tears away with her hands. "I didn't mean that," she said hurriedly. "Now lie still. Your wound needs dressing. And take that silly look off your face." She gave him a playful cuff on the arm, which did nothing to remove the goofy adulation that had come into his eyes. "Lie still," she told him. "I'll be back later."

Stefan emerged from hiding when he heard the announcement of the truce. Praying that Ramos's announcement was not a trick, he crossed himself beside Emily's corpse, grabbed his box of medical stores, and made his way to the storage deck. "Miss," he pleaded with her, "please use these to help Silvio. Can I see him?"

"Later, Stefan, there's no time to lose on sympathy. I must work quickly, and you're needed too. Where is Emily? We need her here for Ernst and Silvio."

Stefan dropped his eyes and made the sign of the cross. "She's dead, miss. She said it was her duty to be in the sickbay. She was shot in front of me by three soldiers. She hid me so they did not find me, or I would be dead too."

He saw an almost satanic look come into Anna's eyes at his news. "Go to work," she said firmly. "Right now, it is the best thing you can do for yourself and for Silvio. I will avenge Emily later. Go, now."

Anna's battlefield training enabled her to put up an intravenous line into Silvio, who had lost a lot of blood, and a morphine injection stopped his restless groaning, but that was all she could do without Emily's expertise.

Some of the gunmen escorted Cherry back to the *Clarissa*, taking their remaining Uzis with them. They were then responsible for crewing their RHIBs to ferry the heroin sacks the two hundred metres between the two ships. It would soon be dawn; the light was getting ever brighter, behind the *Clarissa*, to starboard of the *Moringa*. The ocean was calm, and the lights of the mighty *Moringa* and the elegant *Clarissa* were there to guide them. Both ships were keeping at a slow speed just to maintain steerage, so the whole scene had an eerie romanticism for those on the water, but not for those who were busy moving the sacks, lowering them from the open storage deck doors on the port side of the *Moringa's* hull, and loading the RHIBs. They had the sinister threat of the bomb as a continual reminder of the slender truce protecting them.

The *Moringa* defenders had a quick conference and decided to join in the task, to speed up the operation. The sooner it was over, the better. So the *Moringa's* RHIBs were launched, and the rate of clearance of the sacks was doubled, crewmen and passengers working together as they had done on Fortune, but the divide from the *Clarissa* forces was absolute and coldly hostile.

Ernst fell asleep, and no amount of disturbance roused him. Anna remained patient and understanding for two hours and then decided that he had rested enough, waking him as she applied a new dressing over his torn flesh. She soothed him with a discreet stroke of his face, but she realised the time for happiness had come and gone. Ernst had to be told.

She spoke softly in their mother tongue: "Dr Ross should be doing this, but she can't. They shot her while she was working in the medical room." Then she continued in English, all familiarity gone from her voice, "I will give you more morphine if you like, but I consider you fit enough to resume command of your ship."

Ernst reacted at once to Anna's words, in the way she had hoped. "So do I," he said in English. "I must get back to the bridge. I don't need morphine." She could see that he was in pain, but neither of them referred to it again. She loved him for it.

"You'll need a bodyguard." She caught Maggie's attention as he struggled alone to his feet, and Maggie sent Henry over to them. Ernst was trying to walk, hunched over with pain. Anna acted as if she hadn't noticed. "Ready when you are," she said to him simply. Her abundance of strength sufficed them both.

"Let's go," he said.

Jeffrey saw them start their walk along the storage deck and came over to them. Ernst carried on walking, Anna beside him, Henry following.

"Ernst, we must set our differences aside," Jeffrey said, glancing briefly at Anna who did not look at him. "You can't leave the storage deck now. It's all we control. There could be armed men anywhere else on the ship."

"No, Professor," Ernst gasped, "I control this ship. All of it. I am the captain. My place is on the bridge, and I'm going there."

"Ramos could be there – armed."

"Ramos is under my command. He will do as I say," Ernst replied angrily, though shortness of breath made him stop and gather himself.

"The captain's place is on the bridge," Anna interjected. "I will shoot anyone who gets in his way."

"Including me?" Jeffrey asked, without any show of humour or affection.

Anna stayed silent, glaring at him.

"Ernst," Jeffrey persisted, "the situation is critical. We need you alive and in command. If Maggie uses her negotiating skills, maybe we can arrange for Ramos to be taken off the *Moringa* and transferred to the yacht. That won't be possible if you're not here to retake command."

"Get out of my way, Professor, and I will retake command. That's an order from the captain."

Maggie had watched the confrontation develop and saw that Jeffrey had, once again, got himself in the worst of situations for the best of intentions, just as he had done with Gary and the airship. She quickly sent Emilio over to him to say that she needed him urgently. Emilio had such a mild, likeable character that he could safely intervene without riling anybody. When Emilio delivered his message, the three protagonists looked across to Maggie and saw her beckon to Jeffrey.

"You better go, Professor," Ernst goaded him.

Jeffrey gave him an exasperated look and then walked quickly over to Maggie. "Yes, Maggie, what is it?" he asked, unable to conceal his irritation.

Maggie was ready for his mood and smoothed his ruffled feathers: "We're running out of time," she said in a gentle voice. "There are only about two or three more loads left in the storeroom. I need your guidance as to what we should do."

"Yes, of course," he replied. "We should get our RHIBs back on board. Make them use their RHIB for the final load. They don't need eight of their crew on the *Moringa* now. Get four of them back to their own ship."

"Good thinking; so shouldn't you be giving those orders right now?"

Jeffrey felt abashed. "I was just trying to stop Ernst going back on the bridge. I'm worried for him."

"Priorities, Jeffrey, priorities." She walked with him over to where Arnesh and Anwar were directing the loading operations. Arnesh quickly took in the situation and put the requirements into effect.

"Thanks for the kick up the backside, Maggs," Jeffrey muttered.

"The pleasure was all mine," she assured him. "Will you come with me to the hangar? I think it's time to re-establish our fortress."

"So do I. Even with Dukakis as our guest, they may well try to sink us, now that they have the heroin. It's unlikely, but not impossible. We need to be ready for them. You'll need Anna, won't you?"

Maggie smiled. "Good try, Jeffrey," she teased him. "It's not for me to give Anna commands. It was good thinking on her part to get Ernst to the bridge. Don't look at me like that. I'm not being unsupportive of you. But I think she was right. I'll look after this deck and the hangar. We're up five Uzis – and what's left of the crew are with us, poor blighters. We're in a much stronger position if those bastards come for us now. You better keep an eye on that American. He'll do a runner if he gets the chance. I'm sure of it."

Jeffrey cast an involuntary glance towards Dukakis, sitting on one of the cylinders used for defensive cover, his corpulent body leaning back comfortably against one of the crates. He seemed very content to be watching what was going on.

"I think Dukakis doing a runner is one of our smaller problems," he mused.

Maggie looked for herself. "Maybe I am being a bit obsessive," she admitted, "but don't blame me if you're caught out." As they looked at each other, their eyes met for a second time and lingered more than friendship, alone, merited.

"We're still alive," he said to her.

"We're just going to have to hold on for another half-hour or so," she replied.

"I better go and have a word with David. I think he's getting frantic about Lucy. I don't want her opening the doors of the Grand Chamber until all the gunmen have left."

"Ask him what we should do about the bomb. That might be a good distraction," Maggie suggested helpfully.

"Thanks," Jeffrey said and with that made his way over to where David was pacing up and down, looking at his watch, and not quite sure what to do with himself. "Are you comfortable, Mr Dukakis?" Jeffrey asked as he passed.

"Very comfortable, thank you, Professor," came the contented reply.

"David, it's almost over, this whole nightmare. They'll be gone in twenty minutes," Jeffrey said as he approached his dear friend.

"Jeffrey, I'm not sure I can wait twenty minutes. I really need to find out about Lucy and Frank."

"They're hidden away behind thick metal; they'll be fine. The moment the other crew have left, they can come out. Just leave them a few more minutes. Now, what can we do about defusing the bomb in the lift?"

"It's not a bomb, it's just a helium cylinder," David replied tetchily, as if it were the most obvious fact in the world.

"What? But I—" Jeffrey thought of his confrontation with Cherry.

"Yes, because you were convinced that it was a bomb, you persuaded that damnable woman as well, and saved all our lives in the process. It was a bluff, a bloody good one. You convinced her, even against the evidence of her own eyes. That's how wars are won."

"This isn't exactly war, David," Jeffrey retorted, angry that he had not been told the facts in advance.

"Yes, it bloody well is," David replied emphatically. "My grandfather fought in the Great War, my father fought in the Second World War, and now it's my turn. It's kill or be killed, in defence of those you love – and that is war. If we come up with a way of tricking them instead of killing them, then they're lucky, because I'd kill them if I had to."

"I think you're exaggerating things a bit," Jeffrey mocked him, and he received a bitter reply from David:

"That's because you don't love anyone, Jeffrey. Not really. You don't have any close family member who means the world to you like I have Lucy. You couldn't even stay faithful to Anna for two minutes, even though you'd told me you were wild about her. You don't know what love is. Lucy and I are being kept apart by invaders threatening to destroy us both, and I will fight them every way I know."

Jeffrey grimaced and said, "You've changed your tune a bit since the start of this voyage."

"Yes, I have," David replied. "Sow a wind, reap a whirlwind."

"I'm very displeased."

Cherry Bonner's anger had been evident from the moment she returned to the *Clarissa*. She was now voicing her irritation to the other Clerkenwell Angels, seated comfortably in the lounge of the yacht, with a panoramic view of the ocean around them. "Our plans to remove Professor Harvey failed because of Mukasa's disloyalty. Today, I learnt that our instructions to punish Mukasa failed because of Brage's disloyalty. Our plans to put Murdoch and Hernandez in control failed because Murdoch was shot by Harvey's girlfriend before he could shoot Brage. The level of incompetence is farcical." She looked round the room, expecting her words to have aroused the anger of her colleagues, but they were all sitting back, relaxed, complacent, mostly with an air of amusement at the list of mishaps. "Added to which," she continued, trying to change their mood, "added to which, our plan to eradicate anyone who knew about the heroin has failed, because they are armed to the teeth, with guns almost certainly provided by Mukasa."

"Don't forget to mention the bomb," Jean-Pierre prompted her. She looked at him, saw that he was teasing her, and threw a cushion at him.

Her change of mood caused them all to laugh. "I admit it. I'm certain it was just a helium canister. I can't believe that I let Professor Harvey make me doubt it. He must be a poker champion. I won't let him bluff me a second time."

"Madame President," Jean-Pierre addressed her with courteous formality, "may I, on behalf of everyone here, congratulate you. Under your guidance we have, aboard this yacht, $200 million worth of cargo, safely delivered from Afghanistan, without anyone knowing where it has gone. Untraceable. We thank you."

As he finished talking, all her partners applauded her in admiration, and she visibly blossomed in response to the flattery.

Cherry interrupted the applause before it had a chance to die down. "Please, we can congratulate ourselves later," she said, "but now, we must decide the fate of the *Moringa* and those on board her. Do we just leave, and trust them to stay silent under the terms of our agreement? Do we attack them now and try to remove the threat they pose, or do we finance an Al Shabab-style attack, with better weapons, in a few days?"

Jean-Pierre spoke up again: "Ramos is still on the bridge. If Brage gets there, he can call for outside assistance. I don't trust him or the rest of them. I regret they cannot share our good fortune, but I recommend that we shoot them all, now." It was immediately obvious that his view was favoured by everyone in the room.

"I'll arrange it," Jean-Pierre continued. "I'll need to act now while we still have men aboard the *Moringa*. Ramos needs to hold the bridge. Excuse me." He went out and contacted Ramos.

Dukakis had slipped a walkie-talkie phone to Ramos when he and Cherry first went aboard the *Moringa* so that the bridge of the *Moringa* and bridge of the *Clarissa* were in shortwave contact. Jean-Pierre used the link now to contact Ramos. "Ramos, is that you? This is Jean-Pierre aboard the *Clarissa*. I appointed you. Do you recognise my voice?"

"Yes," Ramos answered nervously.

"Ramos, you've done good work," Jean-Pierre said encouragingly. "You've earned a big bonus and that has already been agreed. But to get it, there's one more task for you to do."

"Yes. Tell me."

"You must hold the bridge until we are back with you. It should not be too long. We intend to liquidise unwanted assets. You understand? But you must prevent external contact. If you cannot hold the bridge, destroy the communications system. Your bonus, even your life, depend on it."

Ramos's morale was lifted by this message. He had been feeling isolated ever since the gun battle. The crass brutality of the guerrilla attack had wiped out his key supporters, except for Otto, who was still with him as helmsman; the remainder of the crew had sided with his foes. He was desperate to join the *Clarissa* before it sailed away, but it seemed the tables were about to be turned again, and he could yet be on the winning side. All he had to do was lock the door of the bridge. The captain was wounded, perhaps dead. It was unlikely anyone else would try to take command. Ramos said nothing to Otto but inwardly felt full of hope, until he received a phone call from Duke about a minute later.

Jeffrey and David were so engrossed in their discussion on the nature of conflict that Jeffrey had forgotten the corpulent and docile Duke, who had ambled away from his seat, casually asked Jomo where the internal phone was, and phoned the bridge.

"Ramos, is that you? This is Duke Dukakis. I got you your job. Do you remember me?"

With a sense of déjà vu, Ramos replied, "Yes, Mr Dukakis."

"I want to tell you Captain Brage is on his way to the bridge. He's got Anna and another man with him. They're both armed, and they're sure looking mean. I'd get the hell out if I were you, but it's your choice."

With that, Duke put down the phone and returned downstairs, emerging from the gas canisters as Jeffrey challenged him: "What do you think you're doing?"

"Nothing harmful, Professor. I'm unarmed, and not exactly cut out for heroics, as you can see. No, I was just interested in how many more bombs you had like the one in the lift." He looked at Jeffrey with a disarming smile. "That was a good bluff, Professor. I congratulate you."

Jeffrey was full of confidence. He didn't question Duke further but told him to sit down, again, until the cargo doors were closed. "Then, Mr Dukakis, you can wander round and talk to who you please."

While plans for a second attack were being put together on the *Clarissa*, there was much activity on board the *Moringa*. Arnesh and Anwar were overseeing the safety of their men engaged in the transfer of sacks, Maggie was watching the four gunmen still on board, as well as trying to master the actions of an Uzi machine gun – she was delighted when she discovered the folding shoulder-butt – and Jomo and Council were reloading magazines for the AK-47s.

Meanwhile, Ramos had made up his mind. He could probably hold off Brage and the other man with him, but not Anna too. Anna meant death; Ramos had no doubt about it. "Otto," he said, "I've been ordered to find the captain. Lock the bridge door after I leave, and don't let anyone in until I come back."

Then he left Otto to battle out the last five minutes of his life trying to hold the bridge and started quietly down the stairs. He heard the approaching sounds as Brage struggled up the steps, with Henry in the lead and Anna in support. He moved swiftly into an empty cabin as the small group continued up to the bridge. He waited for a few moments and then continued his silent descent, emerging on deck through the doorway, where Maggie had seen him silhouetted on the night of the storm. The sun was just above the horizon behind the *Clarissa*, casting a dazzling light across the starboard side of the *Moringa*. He stopped to decide his next move. The light was too bright as he glanced towards the *Clarissa*. As he looked away, towards the opposite side, he noticed the top of a rope still attached to the port rail. Two dead men were beside it. He moved quickly over to it and saw that a zodiac was at the bottom, attached to the end of the rope, being pulled slowly along by the *Moringa*. The gunmen who had used it had killed the crewmen sent to greet them, and were either dead or otherwise engaged themselves. Ramos let himself quickly down, dropped into the speedboat, and cast off. A shout told him that he had been spotted. He revved the engine and escaped towards the stern.

Most sounds were masked by the engines and the wash of the *Moringa's* propeller turning slowly to maintain way, but a sudden noise reached him over the din. It was a crash and a crump that stood out from the familiar sounds of the voyage. It was a noise like a huge tree being felled and hitting earth. He knew he had not imagined it and spun round to squint towards the *Clarissa*.

On board the Clarissa, everyone in the lounge sat up or stood up, in shocked silence, looking at each other with concern. Then came the cries of alarm from further forward.

"Jean-Pierre!" Cherry shouted. "Nobody leaves this room! Stay here all of you till I know what's happened." She ran out of the door.

Jean-Pierre stood like a faithful hound, blocking the doorway, while the Angels variously wondered whether to pull rank and push past him or to stay huddled. It was their last doomed minute. The roof gave way. A huge gas cylinder crashed through the room, gouged the floor away from under Jean-Pierre, and continued its downward arc towards the bows. Jean-Pierre disappeared with a scream; the other Angels were flung to the deck. From where he lay, Jean-Pierre could see, through the choking cloud of dust and glinting high above them in the morning light, the airship floating like a heavenly body, beautiful and silvery white. He knew with dreadful certainty that this was, truly, a bomb.

"Cherry! They fooled us both," he yelled.

The *Clarissa* disintegrated in a stupendous bang, a roar of flames, and several lesser explosions, burning from bow to stern with coils of grey billowing smoke, before a final blast cracked open its stern, and its fractured remnants listed and sank, leaving only flotsam where the ocean-going yacht had been. It was a once-in-a-lifetime sight, a horribly magnificent event, dissociated from the loss of life it represented. The heroin stored in every crevice and along every corridor had acted like a fuse wire, igniting the whole ship in seconds from the initial detonation that had fatally cracked the hull. Ignition of the fuel tanks had provided the terminal blast.

Tyro looked down with sombre satisfaction through the gap in the floor of the gondola. It had been a patient wait, floating above the two ships in the hours of darkness, using the engines as little as possible, and then in the dawn, using the poacher's trick he had done several times before, of letting the craft drift silently over his prey unseen in the dazzling light. They had used the time putting together the primitive guidance device that Roland had devised. The hydrogen cylinder they released first had been unguided, a tester of the wind that had made a lucky hit, but the bomb that followed had been guided from its launch, with the deliberate intention of maximising its chances of destruction.

"We did that," Roland muttered nervously as he joined Tyro to look down through the gap in the floor, and the last scraps of flaming debris disappeared below them.

Tyro gave him a smile of reassurance. "Don't be frightened," he said. "It's what Moses would have done. I don't claim to be better than Moses."

If you speak to Roland today, he still remembers those words. They were so unexpected, but so full of comfort. Together, he and Tyro re-secured the floor, and Tyro returned to the controls which Leena had kept steady for the attack.

Ernst, Anna, Henry, and Otto watched with disbelief from the bridge of the *Moringa* as the *Clarissa* seemed to self-destruct. Otto had surrendered to Anna as soon as she appeared with an AK-47, and Ernst had accepted his submission. To them, the explosion on the *Clarissa* was an inexplicable miracle that they hailed with shouts of triumph and retribution, as they watched the remnants sink. Ramos was hit by flying shrapnel as he sat in the zodiac between the *Clarissa* and the *Moringa*, and collapsed unconscious and invisible, while the craft wallowed in the turbulent waves.

"A miracle," Ernst muttered. "We don't need to look for any other explanation. That's enough."

"Wait a moment," Anna replied and pointed ahead, to where the airship was now visible and descending towards them. "What are they doing back?" she muttered. "They must have been waiting up there all night. They'll have seen the explosion."

"We must get away from here as fast as possible," Ernst said. "Henry, find your brothers and bring the airship down. I'm not waiting very long." He was already focused on getting the ship under way as fast as possible. He contacted the chief engineer, who had stayed at his post throughout the night. "Chief, we shall need full speed."

The giant tanker was slow to increase its speed, but its efforts could be felt by all on board.

Ernst turned to Anna. "Do you think I am wrong not to look for more survivors?" he asked her.

"No, you are absolutely right," she assured him, turning her attention to his needs. "Nobody could survive that, and if they have done, then it's better that they die quickly."

Ernst nodded. They understood each other well. Then he returned inside and switched on the loudspeaker system. "This is the captain. Close the cargo doors now. Arrest any prisoners. All ship's crew to resume normal duties. Inform me of any gaps in crew numbers."

Much of what he had said was already in progress. The crane crew had swung in the crane, and six of the project team had hauled in the rope to which was attached the last of the *Clarissa's* boats that had been loading up sacks when the explosion occurred. To their surprise, one of the gunmen had been in the boat as it started to go vertical and had clung desperately to the rope, surrendering willingly as he reached the safety of the storage deck. Maggie had already made the four gunmen on board sit in the lift, doors closed, out of reach of rescue. Like many on board, she had heard the noise but had not seen anything and had little idea of what to expect next. They all felt the increasing vibrations pulsing through the *Moringa* as the engines went to full power. Duke, sitting on his pile of gas cylinders, looked nervously around him, unsettled by the change in events and desperate to know the extent of the damage. He tried to move to the phone to contact the bridge, but several people at once told him to remain seated. Everyone was still nervous.

Instead, Jeffrey reached the phone and called the bridge. "Ernst, what's happening? We need to know."

"We've won, Professor," Ernst replied.

"What about the other ship?" Jeffrey persisted.

"It exploded, Professor. It's gone," was all Ernst said on the matter. "What is the situation where you are? Are the prisoners secure, and are the hull doors secure?"

"Yes, on both counts. The storage deck is secure."

"Then I need you to organise volunteers to take all bodies to the sick bay. Anyone with nothing to do is free to go where they wish. It is over. The airship is landing, by the way. It seems that it stayed with us all night."

The moment Jeffrey gave this news, there was a flow of survivors to the stairs. Stefan didn't join them. He sat and kept Silvio company, rocking unawares, tears streaming down his cheeks, stroking Silvio's lifeless body as if soothing an aching muscle. Alan had not been neglectful. He had been with Silvio and Stefan in prayer, as Silvio passed unconsciously from life to death just moments before the explosion, and now Stefan just needed time alone. Alan was making his way on deck when David accosted him.

"Alan, I'm just about to go to the Grand Chamber, and frankly I'm rather scared what I'm going to find. I told Lucy and Frank to hide in there, and, well—"

But Alan was unmoved. "I need some fresh air, David. You know where to find me if I'm required."

"Aircrew to the flight deck! Aircrew to the flight deck! The airship is landing." Ernst's voice on the loudspeaker system made Alan turn back to David.

"That detonator that we set about making – you didn't finish it did you? It wasn't actually put into any device, was it? I mean, we couldn't have been responsible for that explosion, could we?"

David looked impassively at Alan. "No," he remarked in a quiet rebuff. "Now, if you'll excuse me." David did not feel a moment's remorse as he said this, and realised that he no longer valued total honesty. He and Roland had completed it after Alan went back to his cabin for a rest. It was a timed device set by Roland seconds before Tyro tipped the bomb out.

He found Lucy and Frank physically unharmed and already back at work, tending the trees. The bullets fired from the skylight had not touched either of them, though they had severed the branches within a few metres of their hiding places. They sat through the ordeal fearing discovery or, worse still, not being discovered while a massacre went on outside. David was ready to give Lucy an effusive hug, but she seemed incredibly calm and detached, and shook him off with a little giggle and went on with her work.

"Let's not make a fuss, Daddy," she said quietly. "We can talk about things later, not now. Come and inspect the moringas with me."

"Yes, of course," David replied, hiding his anxiety. "Frank, you're all right, are you?"

"I'm all right, boss," Frank replied with a slight smile and nod of his head. "Nothing that a mug of hot tea and a plate of sausage, egg, and chips won't fix – and some hot buttered toast to go with 'em."

"Excellent idea," David agreed, glad of the excuse to sound jolly again. "Emilio should be back in the kitchen soon. See what he can do. I'll stay here. We're back to normal, thank God." With that, he turned back to Lucy and started talking about the trees.

To everyone's surprise, Tyro brought the airship down in a perfect docking procedure. There were a few relieved cheers, some clapping, and friendly waves to the occupants in the gondola.

Arnesh's team, despite their excitement, saw the airship safely anchored under the guidance of Henry, Council, and Jomo, and after everyone was out, they shepherded it back into its hangar, in a boisterous exchange of friendly vulgarity that nobody else could understand.

While the airship was disappearing into the hangar behind them, Tyro, Leena, Roland, and Solomon stood alone on the main deck. They had expected a heroes' welcome and were bemused by the lack of congratulations or any real emotion. Nobody came rushing up to them. Instead, they all seemed involved with each other. Curiously, to Tyro, even Alan did nothing but give him a wave and then turned away and went down to the corridor deck. Arnesh approached them and asked, politely, why they had returned, as he thought they had escaped to safety before the yacht's arrival.

"My friend," Tyro said to him, "did you really think we were leaving you?"

"Yes, of course, and when we saw you leave, most of us wished we were with you. We did not blame you for leaving. Your life was in danger, and you took others with you."

Arnesh glanced in Leena's direction. As they talked, he led them to the mid-ships staircase. Leena refused to do down it, so she continued alone to her cabin, while Arnesh led the other three down to the corridor deck. As they came in sight of the debris strewn across the corridor, and the blood-covered barricade a few metres away, the three aviators realised what those they had left behind had been through. The body of the gunman caught by the booby-trap still lay at the base of the barricade; Alan was kneeling beside him, in prayer.

Arnesh whispered hurriedly, "In here." He led them into the workshop, currently empty. Then he continued, "Our fight was all below deck. Before you say anything else, I suggest you think most carefully of your friend, Alan, and say all talk of bombs, and the making of devices, was simply to fool those who wished to harm us. It was a deception that worked most successfully. We placed the pretend bomb in the lift, and with it, Jeffrey negotiated our lives. I suggest, most earnestly, that you say nothing, and ask nothing else, to do with bombs. We have endured much gunfire. Many people have died. Their ship blew up due to their wickedness. We do not know the reason. We were not involved. It is gone. Our friends and colleagues aboard the *Moringa* can recover."

Arnesh's meaning was very clear. There were some badly traumatised minds on the *Moringa*, and hope of permanent recovery might depend on feeling guiltless about the sinking of the *Clarissa*. Maybe the coolness of their welcome back to the ship was an indication of how little any individual wanted to know about what they had done on their flight.

Tyro pondered the situation and then shrugged, as if it was of no consequence. "It is not the first time I have had to forget what I was doing on a particular night. Roly, it seems we did nothing last night but look after Leena. We are blameless of any wrongdoing. Isn't that a good place to be?"

"If there is an enquiry into the sinking?" Roly asked.

"Jomo, Henry, and Council are my brothers. They loaded two empty helium cylinders into the airship, as ballast. We never returned till we noticed the other ship had sunk," Tyro explained. "We are beyond reproach." He noticed Arnesh nodding approvingly. "Solomon, here, is also my brother. We have forgotten many things that we did together, have we not?"

"I don't remember any, boss," Solomon said, innocently.

"How will I be able to look at myself in the mirror from now on?" Roland challenged them, as if desperate for an answer.

Arnesh seemed not to hear the question. "I have to tell you that you will not see your friend, the doctor, again. They shot her when they first came on board the *Moringa*. She saved a crewman's life in exchange for her own."

Roland took off his glasses and rubbed his eyes. "They didn't have to do that," he said quietly.

"And they took all the heroin and put it on their ship. The ship sunk with all the heroin. Some lives were lost, but many have been saved," Arnesh added.

Roland held up his hand to stop Arnesh saying anything more. He seemed to have lost all his energy.

"I need a shower," he announced and started walking towards his cabin.

"If there is a mirror over the basin, look at yourself in it," Arnesh called, as Roland went out. "You will see a hero – an unsung hero."

"Do you think it was a bomb that caused that explosion?" Anna asked. She was speaking in Norwegian. It helped ease her tension to speak in her mother tongue. Only Ernst and Otto were on the bridge with her.

"Who knows?" Ernst replied, moving round the bridge, tending the ship as David was tending his trees. "I must get Stefan up here to reconnect us with the world. We shall put out a distress signal on behalf of the *Clarissa*. We shall say that we found her on fire but that she exploded before we could offer assistance."

"What about the American downstairs? What about the gunmen still here? They can spoil your story."

"The gunmen are just hired militia. We can pay them to be on our side. The dead are more of a problem than the living. We will find it hard to explain so many dead bodies."

"They could all have been on the other ship. They went down with it as they were trying to help."

Ernst looked at her admiringly: "Now that is a good idea, very good," he said, gasping and then clutching onto the control console for support, grimacing with pain. "We need more crew for the ship. I will ask Arnesh for help. We are running low on fuel for the ship's engines. We shall have to conserve its use as best we can."

Anna could not bear to see him literally trying to retain his hold on the ship while so near to collapse. "Right now, we need help here," she said firmly. "You are going to rest, like it or not. Otto, please call Stefan to the bridge, and Professor Harvey and Reverend Mills."

"Why do you want Alan?" Ernst queried, though offering no resistance to Anna's other directions. She took his weight on her right shoulder and started moving him to his cabin.

"We shall need to organise a burial service at once if we are to alert other ships to where the *Clarissa* went down; otherwise, we cannot stick to our story. Alan can help with that. Now," she said, reaching the cabin, "you go in there and rest."

"I will," he said gratefully, "but please, Anna, send Jeffrey in for two minutes. After that, I will rest properly. I promise."

Jeffrey and Alan met on their way to the bridge. "It's time chains of command were re-established," Alan muttered. "I don't approve of being summoned to the bridge by any old member of the ship's crew. I'm here to support Tyro, and Brage is still a threat as far as I can see."

"Let's hear him out, anyway." Jeffrey replied. When they reached the bridge and saw the state of it, they understood why they were needed.

Anna could not look Jeffrey in the eyes but said softly, "I'm glad you're safe. I'm so glad."

"Likewise," he replied, but that was all.

"Ernst wants to see you in his cabin," she said. "Don't stay long. He needs badly to rest."

He had no room to doubt now who came first in her life; he walked through to Ernst's cabin, free of the emotional turmoil he had felt as he fought to retain her love. It was gone. He was free, and alive, and that felt good.

Ernst opened the door to him and then collapsed back onto his bed, clearly exhausted and in great pain. "Jeffrey, thank you for coming. I realise you must hate me, but—"

"I don't hate you, Ernst. I don't like you very much, but I don't hate you. I'm sorry to see you injured like this. What can I do to help?"

"For all our sakes, I need you to take command of the whole ship, your people, and the crew, what is left of them."

Jeffrey was stunned that Ernst should make such a request. "I can't do that," he retorted nervously. "I have no idea about command of a ship."

"Please, Jeffrey, I need to sleep for about three hours, then I will be all right. Otto will advise you on ocean matters. You are the only person that everyone trusts, and if you want your project to succeed, you must do this. There is no time to waste. You must remove anything from the *Moringa* that could link us to the sinking of the *Clarissa*. We shall need to report having seen the *Clarissa* on fire and seeing it blow up. If we are linked to the *Clarissa* in any way, we shall be linked to heroin smuggling. At the moment, there is no such connection. We have a naval inspection to rely on."

Jeffrey thought quickly and saw that the ruse might work. "Do you know how the *Clarissa* blew up?"

"No," Ernst said. "I don't want to know, and if anyone else thinks they know, they are to keep quiet. Anna suggests that we hold an immediate funeral service for the dead. It's a good idea. I know it seems harsh, but then we can link their deaths to trying to help the stricken vessel." Then he lay back. "I must rest. When I wake up, I will find out if you have saved us or been an honest man. I leave it to you."

Jeffrey patted Ernst's shoulder in a gesture of sympathy. The man was trying to save both of them. Freedom felt good. "That wound needs stitches, Ernst. I'll send Maggie as soon as I can. I'll call you if you're really needed, but otherwise, you rest now. I'll follow your advice; don't worry. Oh, and good luck with Anna." With that, he walked back to the bridge.

He had just reappeared when Alan called him excitedly. Anna and Alan were standing on the starboard platform of the bridge, scanning the ocean. "A flare has just gone up, a distress flare. There are survivors there, Jeffrey."

Jeffrey was just in time to see the last moments of the distant glow. Anna was tight-lipped and tense.

"We have to turn back," Alan said.

"We can't turn back," Anna countered. "We don't have enough fuel, and the chances of finding them are too low to justify the attempt. The captain will agree with me if you ask him."

Jeffrey wavered between the two points of view. Alan took his chance: "Anna, the killing has to stop," he said, as if giving an ultimatum.

Anna put down her binoculars. "We cannot go back," she said.

"Then let me phone Tyro," Alan pleaded with Jeffrey. "If he'll launch the helicopter, I'll go and help search for the survivors. Please, just slow the ship while we find out what's possible."

Jeffrey nodded. "Slow the engines," he commanded, but Otto hesitated, looking to Anna to see if she agreed, which she clearly did not. "Slow the engines, Otto," he repeated firmly. "You know what to do. Do it. Alan, phone Tyro. See what he says."

When Alan phoned, he discovered that the distress flare had already been seen by others on deck. Tyro had ordered readiness of the Hind for launching, with Jomo and Council for crew.

"I wondered where you were," he said to Alan. "The helicopter is not equipped for air-sea rescue, but we have done everything else with it, so why not this?" Optimism was flowing from his voice. "I need you to come, Alan. Don't refuse me. With you, we shall be safe. We shall succeed."

"Put your faith in God, not me," Alan chided him with benign exasperation.

"He listens to you more than me, my friend," Tyro replied with a laugh. "Now, hurry."

They took off about ten minutes later, while Anna and Jeffrey watched from the bridge.

Anna was scornful about Jeffrey giving way on the issue. "This is stupid. What if they find that evil woman? Whoever they find is going to be horribly burned. We won't be able to do anything for them."

"Stop being so negative, Anna, for goodness sake," Jeffrey protested. "It doesn't suit you."

Anna guessed she was not wanted. "I think perhaps I should go now. I will find a crewman to help you. Would you prefer Emilio the cook or Alfredo the deckhand?"

She walked off the bridge but turned, at the last moment, and gave him a wink.

After flying thirty minutes, Alan's hopes of finding survivors had almost disappeared. Neither he nor Tyro had said a word about why the *Clarissa* had exploded. His whole attention had been focused on the ocean, from the navigator's pod in the nose of the helicopter, while Council and Jomo in the fuselage had looked out through the open door on the left side, and Henry from a small window on the right. Then, there it was, a half-sunken RHIB, appearing as a persistent dark shadow on the undulating surface. They dropped down and flew low over it; they could see Ramos, clearly conscious, sitting in it, waving to them.

They had already secured a rope to the safety harnesses of the seats and made a loop of the free end. The three strong brothers lowered Alan a short distance, so that he could drop a life jacket into Ramos's hands. Tyro then took the Hind in a small circle, Alan gasping with excitement and fear, as he was hauled back up. Ramos put his life jacket on, the loose end of the rope was tossed into the water, and Tyro straightened up to begin a slow, straight approach to the RHIB. The propeller stirred up the spray so Ramos was half-blinded and half-drowned as the Hind passed overhead, but he kept his eye on the lifeline and seized it as it was dragged by in the water. He just had time to slip the loop under his shoulders, then let it whip him out of the RHIB and dump him in the ocean.

"Pull up, Tyro! Pull up!" Alan shouted as the helicopter tilted and Tyro struggled with the controls. Jomo had the power of an ox, but it was all he could do to keep his footing and not disappear out the door. The helicopter pitched then swung away from the RHIB, while Council and Henry took the strain and Jomo heaved in the line, tug by tug. Tyro headed fast for the *Moringa* at a height of about forty metres, and Ramos was still dangling a metre beneath the helicopter as it came into view of the ship; the watchers could sense the struggle for survival going on in front of them. They watched as Ramos reached the door. There was moment of intense anxiety as his life jacket seemed to snag on the door rim, and then he was in, and the door was closed. Hugs and laughter went among everyone on the ship in response to the relief of tension. After so many lives lost, a life had been saved. Tyro took the Hind in a final circuit over the ocean so that all was set for its landing.

On the floor of the helicopter, Ramos clung to Alan, shivering and breathless, nestling his head against Alan's shoulder for comfort, his right hand grasping Alan's life jacket, as confirmation that this was reality – he was alive. "The lost lamb is found, my son," Alan bellowed the words to be heard above the roar of the engine. "You are safe, my child; you are among friends. The lost lamb is found."

Council sat back and spoke to Tyro through his helmet microphone: "Tyro, my brother, that was very close for all of us," he said.

Tyro looked out of the cockpit at the beautiful sight of the *Moringa* on the deep blue ocean. "Why doubt?" he replied, talking more to himself than Council. "Why doubt?"

Maggie sutured Ernst's injured pectoral muscle and skin, using her best medical-student skills. She had brought all she needed up from the sickbay to Ernst's cabin. It was quite a social gathering, as Anna was there to assist Maggie, while Ernst kept up a conversation with Jeffrey. The conditions were not ideal, but the sickbay was full of the dead, and with Emily's blood still spattered over the walls and floor, it was better to work on Ernst comfortably stretched out on his bed than under the operating theatre light. Ernst was just about the only person on the ship who had missed Ramos's deliverance drama, and he had wanted to hear about it while being stitched.

Maggie listened while she concentrated but had the final word as she tied the last suture: "I'm so thankful Ramos didn't die. He didn't deserve to; he just didn't," she said in terms that made clear to Jeffrey and Ernst that they were to leave Ramos alone. She slapped a dressing onto Ernst's chest, stripped off her gloves, and announced, "I'm off to see that Ramos is all right."

"I'm coming with you," Anna said. "The sickbay has to be cleared." She looked at the surprised faces of Ernst and Jeffrey. "You'll just have to clean up here, yourselves," she told them, and before there could be any protest, the two women left.

"I need Ramos on the bridge," Ernst called after them, and he started to get up, then a piercing pain in the side of his chest forced him to lie back and let it ease. "Oh, let them go," he said, resigned to his incapacity.

"Funny, isn't it?" Jeffrey remarked. "You're captain of the ship, I'm the head of the project, and neither of us feels in control of anything."

"And least of all, in control of Anna," Ernst muttered crossly.

Jeffrey laughed and said, "She's your problem now, mate. Good luck. You're tougher than I am. I think you'll succeed where I failed."

"That's it? No hard feelings?"

"A few regrets, maybe, but no grudges. She's fabulous, but Tyro doesn't call her 'Lioness' for nothing. Don't hurt her. Love her. Let her look after you in her own way." Jeffrey's voice subsided into silence.

Ernst nodded in acknowledgement and after a reasonable pause continued, "It's been a fuck awful day, hasn't it? But here we are alive, the *Moringa* is still afloat, and our enemies are slain. There's some brandy in that cupboard you are leaning against. Let's drink to our survival, you and me, hey? What do you say?"

During the night, a funeral service was held for the dead. The service took place in the sick bay, where each of the bodies had been laid, covered in a sheet hastily sewn into a shroud, and weighted with lumps of iron. If you had told Alan, before the voyage, that he would take part in such an action, he would have denied it vehemently. Now, he just wanted closure, like everyone else, and the chance to survive. He read the service for the dead, and one by one, the bodies were taken out on a trolley and dropped into the ocean. Stefan and Lucy were there for Silvio, Roland for Emily, Anna oversaw the practical issues, and Maggie and Frank, with the help of Council and Jomo, managed the disposal.

When morning came, the *Moringa* slowed, thirty miles off the coast of Mauritius. The last of the *Clarissa's* RHIBs was lowered into the water, along with four cans of fuel. The five surviving gunmen clambered down the rope ladder with their guns (but no ammunition) and two hundred dollars from Dukakis in their pockets. They had expected to be shot, so this deliverance was like a miracle, and they were full of smiles and respectful farewells.

"We don't want no more trouble," one said as he left.

"Go in peace," Alan replied. "Safe journey." He felt his duties were at last done, and he staggered to bed, feeling that the last twenty-four hours were all a dream, anyway.

Chapter 19

THE HOME STRETCH

With Mombasa now so close, the trauma of death eased. The dead had been unlucky; the living needed to live. Everyone, when free to do so, went to the main deck, to the heat and light of the sun, subdued by their experiences but resilient. The bows became assigned to sun-worship, and Anna was stretched out on a towel-covered yoga mat in her bikini, with Lucy beside her, wearing sunglasses and not much else. Maggie and Leena were close by, Leena absorbed in her yoga meditation, Maggie trying to be, but losing her concentration, until she pulled off her tee-shirt, revealing she had no need for a bra to support such delicate, gentle breasts. She lay on her exercise mat, wearing only her black shorts, and said the men could complain if they wanted to, but none of them did.

Leena stayed demurely clothed, but as she was wearing silk pyjamas, the effect was entrancing. The brothers were on the flight deck, sitting in the shade of the Hind, while farther down the deck, the unofficial Indian cricket team carried out its exercise of slip-catching, laughing and joking, and making outrageous remarks, in Punjabi, about David and Frank, who were sunning themselves on deckchairs beside the roof of the Grand Chamber, both in bright shirts and khaki shorts – Frank in a white baseball cap and David in a Panama. Those with duties to perform came, in their breaks, to rest their elbows on the rails, take in the ocean air, and share small talk with anyone close by. As at the end of any long journey, the bonds of shared experience intensified the regret of separation, animosity gave way to understanding, acquaintances became friends, and a euphoric wish that the trip could last a few more precious days was felt as widely as the heat of the sun.

Only Jeffrey, Ernst, and Duke, standing as a lonely group, out of the sun on the tower deck, realised that these feelings were closer to fulfilment than anyone else appreciated.

"Well, that's your choice," Duke concluded. "Either dump the water or take it to Walvis Bay, Namibia. You tell me which, and I'll get my office to make the arrangements."

"I can't tell David what you've told me," Jeffrey said pensively to Duke. "He would never understand such betrayal."

"It cuts me up to tell you these things," Duke answered him, without sounding too bothered. "You deserved better. You all did. I could see the value of what you were doing, but the other Angels didn't care. All that mattered to them was the heroin. You were just its means of transport."

"So there really isn't any water depot in Mombasa?"

"Nope. I've told you. Your Swiss doctor friend was just shown some new oil tanks. As soon as he had gone, they were filled with Cantabrian oil."

"So I endangered this ship in Antarctic seas for nothing." Ernst's bitterness was almost touchable. "We went through all that danger for nothing."

"Unless you go to Walvis Bay; there's an empty tank there you can use."

"I promised Dr Huber that I would bring him pure water to combat any new cholera outbreak when it occurs," Jeffrey muttered sullenly. "What use to him is water in Walvis Bay?"

"Don't they have droughts in Namibia?" Duke asked callously. "Hell, it's all desert from what I've heard."

"Yes, but it's the Namib Desert, not the Sahara. I don't know a thing about the Namib."

"Then dump the water."

"No, not after what's happened. We'll take Walvis Bay," Jeffrey mused.

"We haven't got the fuel to go anywhere after Walvis Bay," Ernst warned them.

"I'll arrange for the *Moringa* to be refuelled once you're there. I hold the purse strings now," Duke replied grandly, enjoying the full extent of his influence.

"Then that's what we should do," Ernst said, sounding enthusiastic. "It's crazy, this project, but it's magnificent too. I admit it, Jeffrey: I admire your madness. I will take the ship to Walvis Bay, if you are prepared to stay on board and see your mission to its completion."

"I'll do so, and so will Duke," Jeffrey replied firmly.

"No fucking way," Duke snapped. "I'm arranging a boat to take me into Dar-es-Salaam."

"No, Duke, that was part of the original negotiations," Jeffrey pointed out. "You agreed to stay on board until the ship reached land. On the ship, you're an asset; off it, you'd be a threat, so I'm not letting you out of that agreement. Don't try to organise an escape, either. Just sit back and enjoy the cruise."

Duke took one look at the two men and realised that he would be staying on board. He shook his head, recognising how much the Angels had underestimated this quirky bunch of friends. "We should never have messed with you guys," he muttered.

"No, you shouldn't," Jeffrey replied emphatically.

They made their way back to the bridge. Jeffrey acknowledged Ramos and Stefan as he came onto the bridge and was surprised at how easily they both greeted him in return. Jeffrey thought of Silvio's body stretched out on the bloodied cargo deck, gunned down by Ramos. Ernst had excused Ramos his own wound and was leaving it to Ramos as to how to make amends for Silvio. Like this, he had his crew back. If Ramos had any sense, he would never mention the killing of Silvio to anyone, least of all Stefan. Ernst gave instructions to Ramos that they would not be entering the territorial waters of Kenya, but when the time came, they would need a new course to take them through the Madagascar Channel, round the Cape of Good Hope, and north to Walvis Bay.

"I'll have to speak to David and Arnesh and tell them what's happening," Jeffrey commented. "I'm sure Raja Kumar will understand, but it means his team will be away from their families for another three weeks or so. I don't know how they'll take that."

"I'll call everyone to a meeting," Ernst said. "We'll tell them there."

Before Jeffrey could react, Ernst switched on the loudspeaker system and announced a meeting in the cafeteria at noon. His announcement was met by jeers and protests from all who heard it.

Looking down from the bridge, Jeffrey could see from the body language of those on deck that urgent action was needed to prevent old animosities resurfacing. He took the microphone from Ernst and started speaking cheerfully into it: "Arnesh, mate, I need to speak to you. Please meet me at the base of the tower in fifteen minutes. I think I've found a way to improve your catching."

He watched as Arnesh looked up to where he was standing and waved, too polite to make the sign that Baljeet was doing on his behalf, beside him.

Jeffrey laughed and then tried again: "Tyro – it would be really valuable if you could come. We'll need your advice."

Jeffrey put down the microphone.

Duke gave a dismissive laugh. "Tyro Mukasa. He wasn't even supposed to be going home. He was supposed to be eliminated. He hated your guts, and then he rescued you and messed up all our plans. You can't trust anyone these days." He paused and then added, "You're a sort of lucky mascot on this trip; a talisman, aren't you?" There was no hint of mockery. "You're not an alpha male like me or Ernst here, but everyone on this ship looks to you. Don't think I haven't noticed."

"Nobody has said anything to me."

"They wouldn't, would they?" Duke replied. "It might spoil the karma."

On the flight deck, Maggie was lying on her back, motionless, bathed in the full sunlight of approaching noon. "Maggs," Leena said, nudging her gently, "you've been lying in the sun for over an hour. Don't you think you ought to cover up?"

"I am covered up," Maggie replied sleepily. "I've got factor fifty all over me, except my tits – they've got sunscreen."

"That's not what I meant, and you know it," Leena said, giggling. "We've got to go in soon for the meeting."

Maggie sat up effortlessly, using just her abdominal muscles, and plonked her sun hat on her head. "Will that do?" she asked.

"Perfectly," Leena said, giving her friend a kiss on the cheek. "I dare you to go into the meeting just as you are."

"What? And have all the men compare my flat chest to your curves? You mean cow." Maggie pouted.

"Well then, put your top on, which is what I've been trying to make you do."

Instead, Maggie looked out over the ocean. "Isn't it just beautiful?" she mused. Then she turned to Leena: "Give my shoulders a rub, would you, love?"

"All right, just a quick one," Leena agreed reluctantly. "Otherwise, we'll be late for the meeting."

"I'm not going," Maggie said, as she felt Leena's hands start their expert rhythmic motion over the trapezius muscles at the base of her neck, releasing dopamine by the bucket-load in the pleasure centres of her brain. "Why should I go?" she reasoned dreamily. "It'll just be about the end of the voyage, and I don't want the voyage to end. I'm on a ship on the Indian Ocean. I've got two days left to last me the rest of my life. I'm not wasting them being lectured to by Ernst. That's divine," she added, referring to the massage. "But you better go."

But Leena continued her massage. "Hunch forward," she commanded and then proceeded to knead the muscles between Maggie's shoulder blades and spine; such power from such delicate hands.

"Oh, the agony," Maggie groaned blissfully. "Don't stop. We'll just have to be tried for mutiny, both of us."

They watched as Anna and Lucy stood up from the very end of the bows, picked up their mats and towels, and made their way back to the tower. "Aren't you coming?" Lucy asked softly, while Anna, sensing the erotic thoughts Maggie was harbouring, gave her an affectionate nudge with her toes.

"I've had it with being ordered around," Maggie replied, looking up from under the brim of her hat and giving Anna's big toe a palpable squeeze at the same time.

"And I'm with Maggs," Leena added. "I'm her moral support."

"Or, in Maggie's case, her immoral support," Anna retorted, and all the ladies looked suitably shocked before giggling. "Go on then. Enjoy the sun. I'll tell you later if there's anything you need to know."

With that, she and Lucy continued their way to the stern. Maggie watched their retreating forms, oblivious of the length of her stare. Her heart ached for Anna, and her mind wandered into fields of scenes of what was and might have been, before finding its path back to the present, the heat, the blueness, and the persistence of Leena's caress over every part of her back. Maggie snapped out of her wistful thoughts. There was something needful in Leena's behaviour, and she, Dr Maggie Robinson, was neglecting it.

"You're an expert," Maggie said. "You really are."

Leena laughed appreciatively. She was relieved that Maggie was back with her; the aimless contact ceased, and she gave an extra-long firm stroke, with her thumbs, up the margins of the shoulder blades and into the nape of Maggie's neck. Then she wrapped her arms round Maggie's chest and laid her chin on Maggie's shoulder so she could whisper in her ear, "I love you, Maggs. I'd love you any way you wanted me to love you, and you could love me any way you wanted to love me, but – my parents."

"That's a very sweet thought," Maggie said, enveloping Leena's arms in her own. "But we both know that however much I tried to make you feel complete, I'd always be missing a vital bit of male anatomy: a hairy chin. You know what I mean, and it would be Anna all over again, and you'd have lost your family forever."

Leena released her embrace with a little chuckle of embarrassed laughter, giving Maggie a kiss on the neck as she sat back on her knees. "I'll miss you, Maggie. You always make me feel better. I'll carry this voyage with me for the rest of my life."

"And all its secrets, you'll carry those too; that's what scares you, isn't it?"

"Secrets?" Leena echoed the word furtively.

"The pregnancy you won't be able to mention to anyone, the rape you won't be able to mention, and the bomb that none of us can mention. Secrets."

"Oh, thank God, Maggie." The words burst from Leena with obvious relief. "You're so right. You understand. How did you know?"

"About the bomb? I think most of us have worked that one out, but if nobody mentions it, we don't need to know. Do you want to tell *me* about it?"

"Oh, God! I was the pilot when we dropped it." Leena gasped out the words, as if they'd been bottled up in her mind. "I'm a woman, Maggs; what was I doing?"

"Saving our lives. Every woman in the world should be proud of you."

"But I killed people, Maggie. I killed people."

Maggie thought for a moment and became aware that the sunlight was intense. "Pass me my top, would you, love? I've had enough sun for the while." She thought some more as she put it on and ran her hands through her hair. "You know that sacred text you lent me to read?"

"The Bhagavad-Gita?" Leena prompted her, helpfully.

"Yeah, that's the one. Well, in that, there's this man, this prince—"

"Arjuna?" suggested Leena.

"Arjuna, yes. Well, there's about to be a big battle, and Arjuna is standing between the two armies, and he realises that many of his uncles and cousins are in the opposing army, and he wants to stop the battle for fear of killing them. And this god, Krishna—"

"The Lord Krishna," Leena corrected her devoutly.

"Sorry, love, sorry," Maggie apologised instantly. "The Lord Krishna comes up to Arjuna and tells him not to be such a wimp. He's got to fight. His cause is a good one, and if his cousins are on the other side, then he must kill them, if he has to, so that his cause is triumphant. Well, the Lord Krishna didn't have to tell you in person. You did your duty. Your cause was a good one too. You helped blow up the enemy, save your friends, and destroy the heroin. Thanks to you, we were triumphant. Do you see what I'm saying?"

Leena stayed silent, but Maggie did not mind. She knew it was a good silence, and the longer it continued, the more she felt Leena's distress disappear, until she muttered a long, blissful "Mmmm," and she and Maggie caught each other's eye and laughed.

"Thank you," Leena said. "That was very soothing. As religious instruction, it was appalling, but as therapy, it was excellent." Then she leant forward to get up. "I must go and wash these things," she said. "I'm running low of clothes that fit."

"I've got some clothes I can lend you," Maggie offered. "They may need some adjustment here and there, but they would do you until you're home." She paused and then added, "Would you let me look after you, after the baby is born?"

"David said he and Jacqueline – yes, please, I would like that very much." Leena followed her true feelings. "I'm going to arrange for the baby to be taken away at birth, so I won't see her, and you'll only have me in the flat while I recover. You won't have any baby clutter."

"I wouldn't see it as clutter, my sweet. I'd love to have a baby in the flat."

"I cannot return to India with a baby. I must do my duty, as you said, and my duty to my baby is to make sure that she grows up in a loving and supportive family."

"Are you sure Jeffrey couldn't fulfil that role? Once he's home, he'll marry Anna, and—"

"Maggie," Leena interrupted her firmly. "Jeffrey is a lovely man, but he'll never settle down, and neither will Anna. She's not a natural mother and homemaker. Even if they get married, I wouldn't pick them as suitable parents for my child."

"It'll break his heart, all our hearts, yours included, I suspect," Maggie sighed.

"We'll get over it in time," Leena replied, and Maggie held her peace.

The outcome of the meeting was that the Moringa would sail north, past the northern tip of Madagascar, following its original course towards Mombasa. However, it would stay at sea. Tyro and his team were too close to Uganda to think of continuing to Namibia. They were not essential. Their work was done, and Tyro needed to return as soon as possible to Jinja to re-establish his position as the CEO of his company – and to fire the financial director. They would fly to the Moi International Airport in Mombasa. David, Frank, and Roland would go with him in the airship. Lucy did not mind at all. She could oversee the trees on her own; without saying anything to anyone, she fancied having some time alone in the Grand Chamber with Stefan. So David would meet Jacqueline in Cape Town and holiday with her while the *Moringa* made its way round the Cape of Good Hope, and then he and Jacqueline would fly to Walvis Bay, to be there when the ship docked. Frank and Roland would fly back to Cambridge.

Leena was also to leave. She did not disagree with the decision taken on her behalf when she was told about it later. She could travel to England with Frank, and then, when all were home, live with Maggie until the time came to fly to India.

With the meeting almost over, Duke asked to say a few words. His message was a dire warning to everyone: "Every single one of us could go to prison for a long time, or be the target of gangland reprisals, if it becomes known that you had the heroin on board this ship. It wasn't here. There was no fight. You went to the assistance of the *Clarissa*, which was on fire and blew up while some of your crew were aboard."

"Mr Dukakis is right," Jeffrey intervened. "He transferred to our ship to speak to the captain, then the tragedy happened. That's all you need to know and all you must say if anyone ever asks you. We depend on each other. We're innocents caught up in a dirty game, but we go down with the guilty if anything gets out."

"You seem to have this very well-rehearsed, Jeffrey, if I may say so, but I'm not sure I can go along with this." David spoke up, secretly hurt that he had not been involved in the discussion at an earlier stage.

Jeffrey felt his heart sink, as yet again, Honest David's principles threatened to cause complications, but Lucy, bless her, put her father swiftly back in his box: "Daddy, love," she said briskly, "you're in this up to your neck. Don't forget you gave your word of honour to that Royal Marine that there were no drugs aboard this ship. If news gets out, you'll be the first one they lock up; then me as your accomplice." She was sitting slightly behind David, so managed to give Jeffrey a wink as she was speaking. David was no match for the two of them.

"Oh, very well," David said. "I agree."

David's high moral principles were recognised throughout the ship, so his assent to the pact was the deciding factor for everyone else. Like a Masonic lodge, each person gave their individual pledge of secrecy to the others, including the crew. Anna fetched Maggie and Leena to take part. "Is there anyone we've left out?" Jeffrey asked the assembled throng. Glances and shrugs were shared. "Well, that's it then," Jeffrey concluded. "We're in the clear."

But it was David who had the final word: "Before we all go our separate ways, I just want to say something for all of us to share. As one of the founders of this project, I can tell you that its aim is to show that it is feasible to have depots of Antarctic water in different locations around the world, not just East Africa. The amount of ice melting away from Antarctica each year is enough to sustain people and livestock, literally in their millions, through times of drought. It doesn't matter whether our first depot is in Mombasa or Walvis Bay, and it doesn't matter that the *Moringa* is only carrying a fraction of that water on this voyage. What does matter is that we have succeeded. All of you have put so much effort into the success of this mission that you can rightly be proud of your achievement. I respect what you have all done. I admire it. You've all faced dangers we never imagined, but you delivered. And I know I speak for all of us when I say to you, Jeffrey, that out of all the hardship, and anguish, and hostility, and war that we have been through, you have guided us, and today, at the very end, brought us unity and friendship." There was a catch in his voice as he stood up, before the assembly, clasped Jeffrey's hand, and looking him full in the face, ended, "All I can say, dear friend, with all my heart, is bloody well done."

As Jeffrey looked round, he saw admiration in everyone's eyes, including Anna. So his intention as the meeting broke up was to speak to her, but he saw her turn away, say something to Maggie, and then concentrate on Ernst. In that moment of hesitation, he became surrounded by others wanting to shake his hand and wish him well, and the chance was lost.

Maggie whispered in his ear, "She's going to be with Ernst now. She'll come to you at six."

Ernst and Anna left together, and Duke accompanied them.

Jeffrey devoted the early part of the afternoon to Arnesh and his team and was reassured to find that they were all full of enthusiasm to see the *Moringa* docked in Walvis Bay and unloaded.

"It means an extra three to four weeks away from their families. I feel bad about that," Jeffrey acknowledged to Arnesh as the two of them stood chatting in the workshop, but Arnesh just smiled.

"Look on it as extra weeks of freedom and marijuana, professor, and then you see why they are not unhappy. Who knows, it may even be time to teach you how to catch."

Arnesh's comment put a thought into Jeffrey's mind. "The captain is still getting a lot of pain from his chest wound. I'm told it's disturbing his sleep. Do you think some of your marijuana might be appropriate medication in the circumstances?"

"His pain will go, and he will sleep like a baby," Arnesh replied with a knowing smile, and he immediately sent Ashok, who could look innocent in the guiltiest circumstances, with a reefer to the captain's cabin, to offer medicinal relief.

At four o'clock, Jeffrey went to the laboratory, certain of finding David and Lucy and a mug of afternoon tea. They even had some biscuits Alfredo had cooked. While he was there, Stefan came in and stood, unsure of himself for a few seconds, until Lucy extended her hand to him and pulled him close to her to give him a kiss on the lips. It was a polite kiss, of course, but their first in public, and as it was in front of her father and her ex-boss, it sent a very important message to everyone, not least Stefan.

At about five thirty, Jeffrey made his way to his cabin, shaved, put on clean clothes, and spent several minutes working out what his best opening gambit would be when Anna arrived. He need not have bothered. The moment he opened the door to her knock, Anna pushed him back into the cabin and onto the bed, and presented her lips for a long soft kiss that made words unnecessary.

She was wearing a white tee-shirt, jeans, and open sandals which she kicked off and then sat astride him. She allowed him to run his hands up the inside of her tee-shirt to confirm that she had no bra underneath. As his hands cupped her breasts, she leaned against them so he was taking some of her weight on his arms.

"Oh, my sweet, sweet Anna," he murmured, "you're back, you're back."

She slipped off her tee-shirt and sat astride him. He moved his hands to the fastening of her jeans, flicking them open and fumbling with an inner button.

"No, Jeffrey," she said, gently but firmly, in a way that left no room for doubt.

He looked up, and realised he had totally misunderstood the situation. "Oh, God, Anna, I'm so sorry," he blurted out, immediately removing his hands and laying them palm down on the bed. He expected anger, but now he had stopped, her loving smile was back.

"Don't be," she said, as she looked down and reclosed her jeans. "Of course you can caress me," she cajoled him. "Everywhere above the waist. Let's just lie close, hey?"

He pulled off his tee-shirt and made room for her to lie on the bed. "Now can you explain?" he murmured. "I'm totally confused, as usual, where you are concerned."

She was lying on her side, facing him, her head resting on her inner arm, her free hand tracing invisible patterns on his chest. "Why we're both here together? Because I love you, and I will always love you, and I will never stop loving you, and I want happy memories of you – forever." The "forever" worried him; he now lay still but alert. "Why didn't we make love? Because I'm not back, my darling. I'm leaving in the morning."

A pang of deep regret passed quickly through him and was gone, as he accepted the inevitable facts. He lobbed his last grenade, knowing it was dud. "I was hoping that I could have a second chance when we reached land. Must you go now?"

"Duke Dukakis hates Ernst. He blames him for the whole disaster, as he sees it. He is passing control of the ship to Ramos until we reach port. Ernst must go at once and not come within Duke's sight again. In return, he will be given a good reference and severance pay. Duke has advised him to get lost and always look over his shoulder from now on. He will never be fully safe again. Ernst has asked me to go with him. He needs me more than you do, my love. He needs me to protect him."

"Do you love him?"

She thought about her answer. "He loves me very much, and he has a rough power about him that I find very appealing, and yet he is very gentle with me. And he is Norwegian, and I like that. He needs what I can offer, and that pleases me, and I don't feel guilty because I'm not denying him children. He has a son by his previous marriage, and he doesn't want more."

"That doesn't really answer my question."

"I am very fond of him. You and me, we understand each other, but we are not compatible, not really. That is what this voyage has taught me. Fate brought us together for a purpose. We have done what we had to do. Perhaps I do not love Ernst in the same way, but we are very compatible, and that is what I need. I need to be compatible with someone. This is where fate separates you and me."

"Weren't you compatible with Maggie once, until I came along?" he coaxed her.

"Dear Maggs, she has a heart of gold," Anna replied, once again avoiding the question. "I must go and see her tonight. I don't know how to tell her I'm leaving. It will be too sudden for her, and I don't want her in floods of tears. I have so much to do."

With that, Anna seemed to reconnect with the world, put on her tee-shirt, and kissed Jeffrey tenderly on the forehead.

"Have you looked in my drawer?" she asked.

"No, I've never done so. Anyway, you've emptied it, haven't you?"

"Don't get up, now," she said. "I want to remember you like that. But it's worth looking, later. You'll find our engagement ring – the one I never wore." Then, with a smile and a shrug, she was gone.

The following morning, they launched the airship first. The airship symbolised the mission, and it was taking with it David, Frank, Roland, Alan, and Leena. Tyro had already said his farewells and was in the pilot's seat. The last two places were taken by Council and Solomon. They each carried just a backpack. Maggie fussed over Leena like a mother, checking she had her passport and other necessities. Leena was fine and enveloped Maggie in a reassuring hug. Then she gave Lucy a big hug and kiss and finally came to Jeffrey, for whom she had a light kiss on the cheek and a knowing smile.

"See you in Cambridge," she said.

Jeffrey helped her up the three steps into the gondola and then stepped back. David and Frank gave him quick, manly handshakes and climbed aboard with minimal fuss.

Alan was more emotional but realised that there was no time for a lingering farewell. He clasped Jeffrey's hand in both of his. "This has been an experience beyond anything I could have imagined, Jeffrey. I thank you. It will last me the rest of my life. God bless you." He nodded graciously to Maggie. "We must have a reunion in Cambridge. Then, we can talk for hours, but not now," and with that, he went up the steps after Frank.

The take-off was perfect, and the airship slipped away over the ocean with its engines humming; it rose unhurriedly, passing over the *Moringa* to give everyone, above and below, a final view and a wave, before performing a graceful curve ahead of the bow and setting off for land.

The watchers on the deck began to drift away, but Jeffrey and Maggie stayed gazing skywards together, and they noticed Lucy, standing alone a respectable distance away, as if hesitant to disturb them.

"Now that Leena has gone, I'm going to have to mother you," Maggie called. "Or else I'll feel like a hen that has lost its chicks."

Lucy smiled and joined them. "I'm sorry," she said. "I'm being pathetic over Dad. I'll see him again in four weeks. It's silly to feel sad all of a sudden."

"I think it's fully understandable. I feel sad," Jeffrey confessed. "We won't see the airship again, and probably not Tyro either, and, as for your

Dad, I always feel sad not to have him around. By the way, he was very excited yesterday about some discovery you've made, but he wouldn't tell me what it was. He was full of secrecy. He said it could make a significant difference to the outcome of the project."

"It's nothing, really," Lucy said, diffidently.

"Come off it, Lucy, you're my scientific assistant, or you were. I think you might tell me."

She giggled at his aggrieved tones. "It really is nothing, scientifically speaking. It was just that Dad was threatening to disrupt all the good will on the ship by insisting that the marijuana should be destroyed before we dock.

"Well, he was, until two days ago, and then it all seemed to die down," Jeffrey said, reflecting on the change.

"That's because I showed him that, where the marijuana is growing in the Grand Chamber, the moringa trees are bigger and thicker, possibly increasing the yield of seeds by 10%."

Jeffrey was amazed. "That was an interesting observation," he commented. "So?"

"So instead of Daddy wanting to destroy the marijuana, he now wants me to make further observations and to encourage Arnesh to look after his crop." Lucy looked very pleased with herself. "Arnesh is happy, Daddy is happy, and I feel good about it too."

"So you should. We'll talk more about it later," Jeffrey said, then dashed off to see that all was as it should be below deck, with preparations for the launch of the Hind. He left it to Maggie to say the right things.

"What a wonderful discovery; can you tell me more?" Maggie asked.

Lucy grimaced and waited till she was sure Jeffrey was out of hearing range. "Not really," she confided, with a sheepish grin. "While I was trapped in the Grand Chamber, I spent ages looking at the trees to take my mind off what was happening, and I happened to notice a line of them that has done better than the rest. When Daddy started to get difficult, I had an idea and replanted the marijuana next to where they were growing. I knew he wouldn't notice; dear Daddy."

Maggie looked at her, wide-eyed. "So you mean you tricked him, your own father? He's gone off thinking that a great scientific discovery has been made, and it's all for nothing."

"It's not that bad," Lucy replied sweetly. "I'll tell him when we reach port, and by that time, he won't be bothered anymore."

Maggie shook her head in bemusement. "I don't think any of us are who we were when we set out," she remarked. Then she spotted the Hind rising up from the hangar on the flight deck, and the focus of her thoughts changed instantly. "This is another sad moment, but it's for the best."

Lucy was not sure what she was referring to, until she saw that Ernst and Anna were standing beside the helicopter with Jeffrey; Lothar was already in the pilot's seat. They saw the flight deck come to a stop.

"If you'll excuse me, love, I'm just going to stand with Jeffrey," Maggie said, moving towards the small group.

"I didn't know Anna was going," Lucy remarked in surprise.

She watched Maggie approach the helicopter, calling out to Anna, but she just turned and waved and entered the Hind. Maggie and Jeffrey were together again, and once again, it seemed best to Lucy to leave them alone.

Maggie slipped her hand under Jeffrey's arm. He turned and smiled encouragingly. "Anna was close to tears, Maggs. She didn't want you to see. She did hear you."

"I understand," Maggie replied. "We said our goodbyes last night. Bless her, she even got under the covers with me for a bit." That was all she said. She did not tell Jeffrey how she lay with Anna, holding her naked form against hers and pleading through her tears, "What will I do if you leave?"

Anna had not answered for a while, as she let Maggie's agony melt away and felt her tall, firm body soften against hers. "I'd do anything for you, Anna, love, you know that." Maggie breathed the words into Anna's ear, in resignation that Anna would be leaving.

"Then help me with Jeffrey," Anna had replied, still holding herself close to Maggs.

"How?" Maggie asked.

"He likes you, Maggs, and you understand him. He'll be so lonely when I go, and I'm worried that he'll fall back into old ways. Be his friend, please. Be his support – perhaps, even, his lover."

Maggie smiled sadly. Her loneliness and heartache seemed to have passed Anna by. "Yes, possibly we could be good friends," she said. "But lovers – somehow, I doubt that."

"Let me tell you some things about him that may help you think differently," Anna replied.

Then she had talked while Maggie had listened. It was so comforting to Maggie that she had drifted into sleep, and satisfied she had done enough, Anna had sneaked out of the cabin in the early hours of the morning to re-join Ernst, still sleeping peacefully under the effects of his reefer.

"We have to move back a bit," Jeffrey advised, and arm in arm, they reversed to a safe distance from the helicopter.

"How do you feel?" Maggie asked.

"Better than I thought I would," he replied. "She's made her choice, and now she can live with it. I think it was the right one. It will hurt for a while, but I'll get over it."

The helicopter's propeller started to turn, its engine noise increasing in its intensity.

"What did you say to Ernst?" Maggie shouted to him.

"I said 'Good luck, and don't leave towels on the bathroom floor,'" Jeffrey shouted back. "I don't think he understood, but he'll soon learn." They laughed together.

"We'll probably see them again in a few weeks. You can ask him then," Maggie responded cheerfully, giving another wave.

"No, we won't, Maggs. Dukakis has sent him away. He and Anna will go back to Norway to find work."

Maggie was horrified. "Anna didn't tell me."

"Don't be angry with her, Maggs. She just couldn't face telling you."

Maggie let go of Jeffrey, and both her hands flew to her mouth as she realised that the shadowy outline of Anna was the last one she might see of her for months or even years. This was the actual separation. The helicopter was already hovering just clear of the deck. Then bravery overcame her distress, and she raised both her arms, waving flamboyantly as she mouthed the words, "I love you," over and over, so that Anna might notice but Jeffrey not hear. Then the helicopter swung slowly, like a compass needle, pointing to the direction it had to go. Anna was lost to view, and it set out over the ocean, both Jeffrey and Maggie secretly wishing that the mighty Fortune was next to them again, and her flight was only to its plateau. But there was just the ocean, and the helicopter flew so unerringly straight that, in sight and sound, it was soon barely perceptible.

"No fly-past, then," Jeffrey commented on the dead straight path that it took.

"Jeffrey, love, if you put Anna and Ernst together the last thing you're going to get is sentiment. Sentiment is for softies like us." Maggie paused and then asked, "Why did Dukakis fire Ernst?"

"Betrayal. Ernst failed to carry out the syndicate's orders. Dukakis isn't our friend, Maggs. I'm not making that mistake. At the moment, there's mutual advantage in cooperation, but I'll have to outplay him while I have the upper hand, or he'll screw us over if it suits his plans. Let's go below. I think he and Ramos are watching us from the bridge."

They walked down into the empty hangar. It was neat and peaceful and calm, and because the Hind had gone, it seemed vast.

"Thinking about all the good times you spent here?" Maggie asked.

"No, not at all," Jeffrey replied. "I'm thinking about the next voyage."

"You're getting ahead of yourself," Maggie scolded him gently. "Before you think about the next voyage, why not concentrate – and I mean *concentrate* – on sorting out Duke Dukakis? You can run rings round him, intellectually, but are you a match for him in the world of business, especially dirty business? How people think is my field of expertise. If you want me to help you, I will. If not, I'll just sunbathe."

Jeffrey hesitated. "Let me mull it over," he said. "You may have a point."

"Good idea," Maggie agreed. "Now, I'm going to find Lucy. See you soon."

With that, she headed along the storage deck; she turned round halfway along, and her sadness lifted a bit, because he was still looking at her, and she gave a wave. With Jeffrey still in her life, Anna was not gone, and she was not alone.

Jeffrey phoned the bridge. Ramos answered. Jeffrey acknowledged him affably but asked to speak to Duke. "Duke, once the airship and helicopter hit land, we can expect a lot of media attention. We can involve others later, but you and I need to clear up a few points urgently. I suggest we meet in the laboratory in an hour."

"Sounds good to me," Duke replied. "By the time we hit Walvis Bay, we'll have done some good business. We might even be friends."

"You'll have to travel farther than Walvis Bay to become a friend of mine, Duke, I warn you." Jeffrey said with a cautious voice. Duke laughed.

It was reasonable for Jeffrey to anticipate media attention. The *Clarissa* was a very big yacht, and some very rich men and women had died on it, and in ordinary circumstances, in the dull days of early March, news editors would have been glad of the story. But she sank on Friday, 11 March 2011, and later that day, the fourth most powerful earthquake ever recorded occurred in the Pacific Ocean, about seventy kilometres off the coast of Honshu, Japan. The resulting tidal wave, up to forty metres high, swept ashore with the speed of a jet plane, killing thousands of inhabitants and causing a meltdown at the nuclear power plant in Fukushima. For day after day, graphic scenes of the waves bearing down, with inexorable force, on streets and houses and people swept round the world, with stories of horror and heroism, devastation, flooding, and homelessness. Columns of newsprint speculated on the fires at the nuclear plant and the dangers of radiation and nuclear explosion. It was universally enthralling and visible; from Oslo to Sydney and right round the world, humanity was glued to newsfeeds on television and the web. People cried and exclaimed at the sights and found ways to send humanitarian aid. The news that a bunch of fat-cat bankers had sunk with their yacht in the Indian Ocean, unloved and unphotographed, went largely unreported and was barely noticed.

The meeting that day was the first of a daily series. Maggie attended all the others, as did Arnesh, now in regular contact with Raja. To their surprise, they found themselves pushing at an open door. Duke in his comfort zone turned out to be a big-hearted, sharp-witted financier, generous to those he liked, and with a keen sense of humour. Tact and diplomacy were not essential to him, but he was a good listener and could take advice if he saw value in it. Maggie quickly realised that Duke respected Jeffrey, and that Jeffrey was being held back by his own reserve, not by any barrier that Duke had presented.

"For goodness sake, Jeffrey," she said after the second meeting. "Stop dithering. If you want a seat on the board of directors as head of water operations, or whatever you want to call it, tell him so. He'll give it to you. You have the knowledge, drive, and experience to develop a new division. He would love to have a professor on the board."

"Do you think so?"

"Yes, and he'd give you a proper income. You can finally get rid of that awful old Land Rover of yours."

"Never," Jeffrey said, sounding hurt at the idea.

"Seriously, though, he listened to you for almost an hour. He is fascinated. His questions showed it. He's clearly wondering if Cantabrian Oil could diversify into polar water resources. The syndicate saw you as an eccentric fraud. He now sees you in your true light."

"Is that any better?" Jeffrey asked ruefully.

Maggie felt like hitting him, but she stayed calm. "Yes, it is," she said patiently. You're a man of great intellect, great drive, who is not to be messed with. You're so aware of your own failings that it's time somebody made you aware of your achievements."

"I'll see how things go. Perhaps I'll suggest it in a day or two."

"Today, you have his attention. Tomorrow, he may have spoken to his office in Geneva or Houston. Others, less competent, more greedy, will get to him before you. They'll put forward their ideas, their people. Jeffrey, it's so blindingly obvious to me. Please, just do it."

Duke jumped at the idea. "Hell, yes," he said when Jeffrey put forward his request. "I was wondering what I could do to persuade you to join us. You'll never know the terms I was willing to offer," and he laughed. "Jeffrey, I'm taking over the whole kit and caboodle. With Cherry Bonner gone, I'm moving to take over the Clerkenwell enterprise, only I'm going to call it all Cantabria. I don't know what Cherry left to her daughter, Abi, but it doesn't matter. She won't know where to begin. She'll have to turn to me. I'll buy her out."

"You lost a lot of heroin, Duke," Jeffrey mused. "Are you in danger for doing that?"

"Nah," Duke said, dismissing the idea. "I was never in the heroin," he lied. "Shipping is my side. We'll take the loss. Leave the heroin market to the likes of Ramos. We're heading to new things, you and me, Jeffrey – new things."

The days passed quickly, while the *Moringa* sailed down the east coast of Africa, past Mozambique, and along the South African coast. The daily discussions became ever more interesting as messages flowed in and out, instructions were given, and plans took shape. Duke arranged with Lucy to visit the Grand Chamber and stood in awe at the beautiful sight of the lines of young trees. Jeffrey made a point of showing him the larger shrubs growing adjacent to the marijuana, with the enhanced opportunities for commercial success, and Duke congratulated Lucy and said Cantabria ("Clerkenwell" was erased) would gladly fund her research; she was not to worry about any of the legal stuff. Outwardly, she looked excited at the news, but inwardly, she was distraught that her simple attempt to keep the peace had now grown into a giant deceit.

Ramos warned them all as they approached Cape Agulhas, the southernmost tip of Africa, to make the most of their last day on the Indian Ocean, so they set all tasks aside for the afternoon and played deck games instead. Jeffrey came third in the slip-catching contest, and Duke won the improvised deck quoits, through sheer determination not to be outdone.

"Both egos satisfied," as Maggie commented to Lucy.

The change in weather after they entered the South Atlantic was quite abrupt. The winds strengthened, the waves increased, and the chill factor was enough to send them back into warm clothing, but nothing could depress their spirits. It made them all think, again, of the challenges of their expedition, facing them as a team, and each unit of that team performing its essential role. Instead of a gentle cruise up to Walvis Bay, they had gale-force winds, and they were glad, because an achievement such as theirs needed a dramatic end, a symphonic cord, not a fading note. The *Moringa* powered on through the enveloping spray, unstoppable and immense.

And so it was that on 25 March 2011, the voyage of the *Moringa* ended. David and Jacqueline flew out by helicopter to see the mighty vessel into port. The wind had settled, and the sun was hot as the ship glided over the last, peaceful stretch of ocean. They put down on the flight deck, and the helicopter returned to Walvis Bay without them. Lucy, who had been on the tower deck, came running up the main deck to greet them, and David felt hugely grateful that he was in his rightful place aboard the vessel as it finished its voyage. David had time, between landing on the ship and reaching port, in which to show Jacqueline the Grand Chamber and its rotating troughs of saplings. He hurried her out before she noticed the marijuana, back to the main deck, where they re-joined Jeffrey and Maggie. They attracted huge interest from the shore as they anchored just off the coast.

David had a chance to take Lucy aside. "Tell me quickly," he said. "Did your hunch about the marijuana prove correct?"

"Go back in and see for yourself," Lucy replied with an innocent smile. She watched her father disappear and re-emerge two minutes later.

"No doubt about it," he muttered to her. "The trees next to the marijuana are double the size."

"Stop exaggerating, Daddy," she replied. "They're bigger, that's all. They're bigger."

The first on board, after the *Moringa* docked, were the port authorities. David had already had a series of meetings with various members of their agricultural and scientific staff, supported by staff of Cantabrian Oil, who were part of the country and its people. Several hectares of land at the edge of the desert had been purchased for some of the trees to be planted. David hailed the deal as a triumph of common sense, and the basic plan intended for the agricultural plant outside Mombasa was quickly adapted to the environs of Walvis Bay. By the time the *Moringa* docked, the essential work had been done, and every possible means of conveyance was used to move the saplings.

Maggie was keen to return home. She needed to earn some money before she lost all her clients.

"Maggie," Jeffrey said as he saw her off at the airport, "when I saw Anna leaving with Ernst, it didn't hurt as much as I thought it would. We both knew it was time to move on. I want you to know that she and I weren't in love anymore."

"Is that right?" Maggie replied, more distant than she truly felt. "Well, I wish I could say the same. I've got a great emptiness inside me."

Jeffrey kissed her lightly on the cheek. "Look after yourself, Maggie. Maybe I'll be home for the birth, maybe not. As I'm not going to be allowed to bring her up – Ariona, that is – I'm not sure I want to be aware of it happening. I'll stay out here as long as needed to see the trees established. Then I'll probably be needed in Geneva for a while, so don't expect me back in the UK anytime soon."

Maggie heard the sadness in his voice and gave him another hug. "Come round and have dinner with me when you're back," she said. "Before Leena leaves, I'm determined to establish the friendship there is between us. If you can get back before she leaves, so much the better. I can't bear all this separation."

As well as parting, there was togetherness. Jacqueline likened David and Jeffrey to two school friends home for the holidays. She felt lucky to have David to herself at night, making up for his lost weeks without her, but he spent all day with Jeffrey. They had two fruitful meetings with Duke before his private jet arrived, and he left for the long trip back to Houston.

They talked over many things aboard the *Moringa*, spending much time with Arnesh and Anwar. At other times, they would disappear to the Arthur Mukasa Orchard, where they planned an irrigation system for the trees. Jacqueline did not mind too much, as it gave her lots of time with Lucy. She was introduced to Stefan and made a point of requesting them to take her on a tour of the ship. She watched them together, out of the corner of her eye, listened to them talking, and saw how emotional they became when mention of Silvio came up. Alone again, in a cabin, mother and daughter shared confidences. Lucy felt she had to admit to her mother her polyamorous relationship with Silvio and Stefan; she expected a sermon on decency. Instead, Jacqueline responded with a hug and then said she had a confession to make too. She showed Lucy her new ring from Raja, with a single, big stone on it.

Lucy gasped and said, "That's the biggest diamond I've ever seen."

Jacqueline looked appreciatively at the ring, placed on the ring finger of her right hand. "Yes, me too," she said. "I never expected it. I couldn't refuse it without offending Raja, but I've told your father that it's diamante. I thought it better to tell him that; otherwise, he might have jumped to conclusions, bless him. Raja and Sunita were dear friends of ours in university days, but even so—"

"What did you do to deserve that? Was it very bad?" Lucy asked quietly.

"No, that's just the point," Jacqueline replied. "You've jumped to the same conclusion your father might do. I helped Raja to see his way forward with Leena. After we returned from seeing the *Moringa* leave, he asked me to have dinner with him. That evening, he had a heart attack. That settled it. I wasn't going anywhere. He needed me to nurse him and to stop him killing himself with worry. I made him relax, in a way that nobody else around him seemed able to do. We escaped the cold. We travelled in his jet to some lovely places in southern India, then we added two weeks on

410

his estate. It made him so happy. He said he hadn't known such happiness since Sunita died, and he thanked me for setting his mind to rest and giving him a new lease of life. Then he gave me this, asking me to accept it as a token of his deep gratitude and respect."

"That sounds exciting," Lucy said quietly, as Jacqueline finished.

There was a moment's silence between them. Then Jacqueline muttered, "You do believe me, don't you?"

Lucy smiled lovingly at her mother. "I know you love Daddy."

"Yes, I do."

"I know you love him very much. Adventures don't happen very often in life, and when they do, they should be enjoyed."

Jacqueline hugged Lucy again. "Oh, thank you, darling; thank you for understanding. This was just a magical interlude, and it brought such happiness."

"Dad and I were having an adventure. Why not you? I'm glad for you. Really. It must be nice when a man buys you a ring like this as a mark of respect."

"He didn't buy it for me, exactly," Jacqueline corrected her. "He gave it to me out of affection. It was Sunita's. He bought it for her when he became a billionaire."

Lucy pulled away from her and looked at her, animated and aghast. Her eyes widened.

"Raja is a billionaire? Raja is a *childless* billionaire?"

"Oh dear," Jacqueline said regretfully. "You're about to demand something for your silence, aren't you? I feel a bribe coming on. I can see greed all over your face."

"*Moi?*" Lucy asked innocently.

Later on that day, David and Jeffrey were paying one of their last visits to the Arthur Mukasa Orchard, and Lucy went with them. David was obviously desperate to tell the other two some incredible news. He kept looking around to see if anyone else could overhear them speaking.

Finally, all seemed well, and he whispered delightedly, "You won't believe what I've done."

Jeffrey and Lucy looked suitably intrigued.

"Lucy, my sweet, that brilliant bit of observation you made about the moringas and the marijuana: Arnesh wasn't the least bit surprised when I told him. He said he and his team had known all along that there was a link between the two plants, which was bound to be beneficial. As a contribution to the project, he has sold me their entire stock of marijuana, for a price well below their street value, so that the moringas may grow bigger and stronger, as he put it."

Lucy seemed to get something caught in her throat and asked nervously how much he had paid.

"Never you mind that," David said, chuckling. "It was a good few thousand, I can tell you, but the commercial prospects of a 10 percent – even a 5 percent – increase in yield of moringa seeds are fabulous."

"What about the Namibians?"

"Don't worry, my darling," David said affably. "I've been totally open about it. I told the police that I will be planting hemp here, as an essential symbiotic agent to promote growth in the moringas. I'm not sure they understood, but they seemed delighted. They told me I could go right ahead, and they would appoint guardians who will look after the entire orchard."

Jeffrey asked David whether he was quite sure about his purchase, and David, with all the pomp of a proud father, showed him the trees which had already benefited from the proximity of the marijuana. Jeffrey looked at the trees and then looked very hard at his ex-scientific assistant, commenting that he might have waited for the results of a controlled trial before drawing conclusions. Lucy had the conscience to blush at this, but not enough to change her plans. After Jeffrey had gone, she softened her father up with a loaded question as they drove back to town:

"Daddy, what's it worth for me not to tell Mummy that you have just bought a shipload of marijuana?" Lucy's question was so gently put and so full of threat that even Cherry would have been proud of it.

"Yes, I thought you might get round to that. I suppose you deserve something, but I refuse to let you bankrupt me, " he responded defiantly.

"If you're very good, I promise not to," Lucy said. "I have another idea that might be worth some investment. See what you think this evening."

She arranged a family dinner that night. She persuaded Stefan to explain the business plan that he and Silvio had put together about owning a yacht, crewing it themselves, and making it available for hire. In front of her parents, she told Stefan that she wanted to take Silvio's place. They would call the yacht *Silvio*, and they would work on it and see where life took them. When Stefan said that it would be a dream come true, if only he had the money, Lucy answered, without looking at either parent, that she was confident of getting it.

"Of course you will, my darling," Jacqueline answered immediately. "It's just the sort of thing I can get Raja to support."

"If you think you can, Jackie, dear, that would be splendid," David said encouragingly. "But naturally I'll make a sizeable contribution on the part of your mother and me – family honour and all that."

Family honour: It was such a quaint notion for a fraudster, a drug baron, and a billionaire's consort. Well, that was how the tabloids would see them, if ever the news leaked out.

Jeffrey and David stayed on in Walvis Bay while everyone else returned home. They watched the *Moringa* cast off on its journey back to Bhavnagar with a new crew and waved to Arnesh and his cricket team. After a further week of late nights, they had a business plan to present to a meeting of the full board at the end of June, in Houston. Then David, too, flew home.

"We did it, David," Jeffrey said triumphantly, as he shook his old friend's hand. "The Warlocks did it."

David nodded his head, with a sad smile. "Yes, a few trees and a tank of water, safely delivered to the wrong desert. But we did it. It's a start. See you in Cambridge."

Two days later, Tyro flew down to Walvis Bay, by secret agreement with Jeffrey. They greeted one another with unreserved friendship. Tyro had a sign with him that had been carved and painted in Uganda, and with the help of some local labour, it was hung across the drive leading to the oasis of moringa saplings. The sign said simply, "Arthur Mukasa Orchard," and Jeffrey and Tyro stood looking up at it, admiringly, together.

Jeffrey returned to England on Thursday, the second of June, having received news of Leena's earlier-than-expected confinement.

"Phone me the moment you get home. Maggie xx" This was the text Jeffrey received on landing at Heathrow at six fifty in the morning. He did not waste a minute. As soon as he closed his front door – it was just after eleven o' clock in the morning – he called her.

413

"Hello, stranger," she said. "Does this mean you're back?"

She told him to go round to her flat at once and she would meet him there. She reminded him that it was the old flat that she used to share with Anna. "Do you still have the key?" she asked.

"Yes," he said.

"Well then, let yourself in," she replied. "See you soon."

He rang off, closed his eyes, and thought of a road. It was long, and straight, and bathed in sun, with only one cloud in the sky.

Ten minutes later, Jeffrey walked through the main doorway and then went up the stairs. He came to the door of the apartment, unlocked it, and let himself in. "Hello," he called. "Maggie?"

"In here," came the reply. He tossed his jacket onto the hallway chair and walked into the living room. She was standing in exactly the same place he had surprised her, almost two years ago. Her posture was the same too. She was holding a newspaper in her left hand, at her side, but this time, she was in a light summer dress that demurely showed her lovely silhouette. She looked stunning to him.

"Maggie, I ... wow." This was the best he could manage, and he stayed admiring her.

"Thank you, Jeffrey. Your eyes are saying more than your mouth at the moment." At this, he strode forward, delightedly, and she allowed herself to be hugged and kissed on both cheeks.

"Oh Maggie, I'm lost for words, I admit it," he exclaimed in delight.

She let the newspaper fall on the sofa. "I still read the *Independent*," she commented, her eyes sparkling with feigned innocence.

"I did notice, actually," he replied. His hands moved to clasp hers. They stood in silence, encased in their mutual affection.

"Tea?" she asked, which seemed a rather abrupt manner to break the spell.

"Thanks," Jeffrey said; his guilty hopes of a quickie evaporated, and his mind started functioning again. "Come to think of it, I thought I heard sounds in the kitchen when I first came in."

Something wasn't quite right, and Maggie seemed amused at his assertion.

"Just how you like it too, you lucky man," said a familiar voice behind him.

Jeffrey spun round. Anna was holding out a mug of tea, as if they were on the *Moringa*. "Careful, or you'll spill it," she said. "This one's for you, Maggs."

Jeffrey was staggered – and acutely embarrassed between the two women. He had made his intentions towards Maggie painfully obvious. Anna rescued him by a gentle kiss on the cheek.

"Gotcha," she whispered mischievously. "I came to be with Maggie during Leena's confinement. And no, I haven't run away from Ernst. He has a permanent position on a cruise liner, and he happens to be at sea at present."

"Cruise liner? But he hates passengers."

"He and I have been working on that," Anna replied, and Jeffrey realised that she had taken Ernst under her protection as once she had taken him. He felt as if he were talking to an old friend. He was experiencing no desire and no regrets, and nor, apparently, was she.

"Anna, love," Maggie intervened. "Sorry to barge in, but I haven't yet given him the news about Leena."

"Ooh, sorry," Anna broke off.

Jeffrey turned at once to speak to Maggie. "How is Leena?" he asked.

"She's tired and sore, but doing well. She'll be coming out tomorrow."

"Who'll look after her?"

"Jackie will pick her up." Maggie's reply showed that she and the Emmersons were getting on very well. "Leena will stay with her and David for the while."

Jeffrey hesitated, obviously finding it hard to ask the next question. "And the baby?"

Maggie smiled. "You and Leena have a beautiful daughter, two weeks early, but perfect. Ariona came out without any problems. I was there throughout the labour."

"Congratulations, Daddy," Anna added warmly, but stayed where she was.

Maggie came to him. "We'll see them both this afternoon," she said, putting a reassuring arm on his shoulder.

"Ariona too? Is that allowed?" Jeffrey asked. "Won't Leena be angry?"

"Yes, it's allowed, and Leena will not be angry. It's what she wants."

Anna started to move towards the door, but Maggie stopped her with a raised hand.

"Jeffrey, this is where your life changes forever," Maggie said; she took his mug out of his grasp, put it on the table, and put her two hands on his shoulders. "I have persuaded Leena not to sign the adoption papers—"

Jeffrey looked at her, open-mouthed. "Maggie," he interrupted her. "My God, you're a true angel." He clasped her waist.

"On the promise that she becomes your wife," Maggie ended.

Jeffrey jerked as if he had been hit by a Taser. "I don't understand. She'd never agree, and, anyway, I came back to you," he gabbled in his confusion.

"I know, and I'm touched. But I love Anna. I will always love Anna. I'm very fond of you, Jeffrey, really I am, but you've made love to Anna and you've made love to Leena, and frankly, being another notch on your bedstead doesn't appeal to me. Sorry."

"Oh God, what you must think of me to have said that." He glanced to where Anna was standing. "What you must all think of me. But Maggie, I promise you, I never thought of you like that. You're incredible. I truly admire you – and you, Anna."

He shrank onto the sofa, a picture of remorse and embarrassment.

Anna came over, sat on his lap, and caressed his face. "Jeffrey darling," she murmured, "I wish you hadn't slept with Leena, but you did. I could cope with that. It was part of loving you. But you made her pregnant, and you and I no longer belonged to each other. There was no escaping Leena in our lives. I gave up trying." He continued to sit in miserable silence. "She thinks you don't care about her. Prove her wrong." The silence continued, as her words sunk in. "I am going downstairs to see if Katie is still around," she added, finally, and glided out of the room as if to see her one-time neighbour.

Maggie came and slouched on the sofa beside him and gave him a playful nudge. "Just think about it," she said in a kindly voice. "Leena, every night, in your bed. And each morning, you can get up nice and gently, without having to jump out of the window without your trousers."

"She'll never agree," he mumbled, in dejection, but he gave her a nudge back.

"She has agreed. She thinks you won't agree. Of course, she wants you. Without you, she'll be a childless outcast exiled to her uncle's estate. With you, she's got it all: family, love, respect, wealth. Everything – including a husband she secretly worships."

"Worship? Forget worship. She gave me a hell of a ticking off on the *Moringa.*"

"Good for her – what about?"

"Freedom and commitment. She said I was all about freedom, but it was time I learnt to value commitment." Jeffrey reflected on the moment and realised how pertinent it was.

They walked back to the kitchen. Neither spoke as they sipped their tea. Jeffrey was unsettled. Something was clearly on his mind. Maggie realised she had to let him think about what sort of life he wanted for himself. Perhaps a lifelong commitment was a step too far.

"Go on. Say it, whatever it is," she coaxed him, playfully.

"Did you arrange all this with Leena, just so that I could bring up Ariona? Is it really what *you* want?" he asked.

She was surprised. It was not his feelings that he had been dwelling on. It was hers.

"I arranged it so that you and Leena could bring up Ariona together. That's what I want," Maggie declared. "And the answer to your second question is, I want it more than anything I've ever wanted before." She paused, suddenly worried. "Have I made a complete balls-up of everything yet again?" She could see that he still seemed agitated.

He put down his mug.

"It's the opposite. Quite the opposite," he reassured her, his emotions bubbling to the surface. "I'll try desperately to make this work."

Maggie laughed in relief and hugged him. "You don't have to try too hard, my love, believe me. There's rarely a dull moment with you. Sleepless nights or not, I suspect it won't be too long before Ariona's going to have a brother or a sister, or something in between, to play with, and you're going to have a family life and be as near normal as anyone else." She gave him a squeeze. "All right, I admit I'll always adore Anna. And whenever Ernst goes to sea … just don't ask too many questions."

She looked at him, no longer scared to be honest with him. They heard Anna re-enter the flat, but she discreetly went into the living room.

Jeffrey's eyes did not stray from Maggie's. "You'll manage," he said, kindly.

She closed with him, again, so as to feel his arms around her lightly clad body. "I think we're all going to manage very well," she agreed. They uncoupled and put their mugs into the dishwasher together.

Jeffrey drew back a little to look into her eyes. "Will you two ever get married?" he asked.

"I'd say that's for her and me to find out – one day," she said innocently.

"Well …" He found himself stuck for words again.

"Oh, go and get the car keys," she laughed. "They're by the front door. I'll be ready in a moment."

"I'll be in the car," Jeffrey replied. He seized his coat from the hall chair and called to Anna in the living room: "Cheerio, Anna! See you later." Then he disappeared down the stairs.

Left in her bedroom, Maggie quickly smoothed her clothes and brushed her hair. Then she walked into the living room, where Anna was sitting on the sofa, gazing out of the window. Anna turned to her as she entered, and Maggie saw a wistful look in her eyes. She went to sit beside her and smiled, lovingly.

"Don't worry, my sweet, he'll always need us," she said tenderly, running her fingers lightly over Anna's cheek.

"It was the only way, Maggs," Anna sighed. "Leena would have denied him his own child. Like this, he has a family."

"And we are part of it and always will be, my love," Maggie whispered back.

"Maggs, are you coming?" Jeffrey's voice was full of suppressed impatience from halfway down the stairs.

"I'm on my way," called. She kissed Anna and went quickly into the hall, with joy in her heart. And as she looked back, Anna was there, smiling too.

It was a shame for Jeffrey that Duke Dukakis died. Jeffrey wrote in an obituary that it was a shame for Africa, but that was giving too much importance to Duke, in my opinion, and that of my mother, Cherry. If you betray a member of the Bonner family you get what is coming to you.

It was October. Witnesses recalled that Duke was standing at a street corner by the lake, in Geneva. He was looking away from the lake, up the hill, towards the railway station. He unwrapped a chocolate, placed it in his mouth, and then choked and fell to the ground. A quick-thinking man ran up to him as he collapsed and tried to clear Duke's larynx with his finger, and it took at least a minute before anyone noticed that there was blood coming out of his overcoat, and that the chocolate had nothing to do with his collapse at all. I watched it all. Duke was taken to hospital, but he was dead on arrival.

All hell broke loose in Cantabrian Oil after the news of the shooting, as we meant it to. The share price crashed. Consolidation was essential, and all soft projects were cancelled, including the Moringa project. The police investigated but found nothing. What was there to find? There were no CCTV cameras in respectable Geneva – not then.

I, and I alone, had noticed the motorbike and the two riders in crash helmets that had pulled up behind Duke that October day. I was waiting for them, holding Duke's gaze, smiling at him, so he stayed still. The bike had barely stopped – just long enough for my mother to fire with a silenced handgun into the back of Duke's overcoat – then Ramos had opened up the throttle, and they had sped away. She wouldn't let anyone else do it. It was personal. Nobody noticed her, alone in the ocean, when they rescued Ramos. She managed to crawl into the empty dinghy, and a lone yachtsman happened to spot it and found her inside. Duke was dead from that moment. In her eyes, the project had been his to deliver, and he had cost her everything.

Nobody noticed me, either, as I turned and continued up the hill to the railway station. I had enjoyed my lunch, flirting with Duke. I gave him the chocolate as we left and told him he could eat it when I turned to wave goodbye. It was easy. He was so trusting; my mother said he would be. I was lost in my thoughts of new horizons as the train glided round the lake to Lausanne.

Lightning Source UK Ltd.
Milton Keynes UK
UKOW04f0845141017
310952UK00001B/108/P

9 781546 282358